GROWTH

GROWTH

JON PULLI

PROLOGUE
GRAVEYARD FOR GIANTS

Weightlessness—and then a jolt of whiplash as the Jeep's wheels bit back into the dusty road. It was more of a trail, really, littered with ruts and rocks, and Gwen hurtled along it entirely too fast, but she had been searching for so long that nothing would hold her back now.

The Jeep skidded to a stop, and she flung herself over the side and sprinted up the hill, her dry, cracked boots churning, lungs burning. Cresting the plateau, she paused. The valley, filled with dust and tumbleweeds, crawled with archeologists. She scanned the scene for Doug, wondering whether she wanted to kill him or kiss him. Probably both.

There. She threw herself forward, hurtling across the rocks. "Show me!" she yelped, half-hugging, half-slamming into him.

Doug, a ruggedly handsome man of average build and considerable height, wore a devious grin. "Calm down," he said, but catching her eye, his smile vanished. He didn't want to be skewered alive and roasted in the broiling Texas sun. "This way," he said, gesturing with his hand and turning away.

He led her through scattered huddles of archeologists carefully dusting and digging to the precipice of a deep pit the size of an old stadium. She remembered reading somewhere about the Olympics, a primitive ritual where countries all over the world sent their most physically gifted to compete for medals and prestige. *How barbaric,* she thought, *but thrilling, too, to exist in a body not the result of your own decisions but of a biological lottery.*

1

Without a word, she strode down into the pit. Doug hurried after her.

She felt like a child again, wandering into her parents' room, seeing clothes she should not see, things she could not yet comprehend. There had to be thousands of them, all piled atop one another, so many her mind was unable to process what she was seeing. She bent down and tilted up a bone as tall as her.

"A femur this size would make a human, what, sixteen feet?" she said, her eyes bulging out of her head.

"You'd be right if that were a femur. Better study up on your anatomy, Gwen. Look at the top of the bone here." Doug pointed. "A human femur has a neck section right above the lesser trochanter and before the head, whereas a humerus has no distinguishable neck section before the head, so that big bastard would have stood ..." he looked up at the sky with his hand over his chin, "about twenty-two feet tall."

Gwen froze in place. She imagined freshly turned-up dirt, her nose filling with a perfume of rotting flesh, excrement, and maggots. It was the sort of smell that caused you to breathe through your mouth, and then to hold your breath entirely. She imagined truck after truck parking overhead to dump yet more bodies on top of one another, a day's catch from a fisherman's net, and then bulldozers, deep in the pit, emotionlessly plowing through mounds of wrecked humans, all dreams, aspirations, and hopes not only muted but entirely absent. Swollen skin, broken bones, and putrid flesh were stacked wide and deep as far as she could see.

She felt acid burning in her stomach and her head swam. Short, choppy breaths filled her mouth with grime; nothing was getting into her lungs. She collapsed, and Doug rushed over to her.

A few minutes later, she was back in the tent, jerking her head hard into the canvas cot, and then blinking and rubbing her nose. She moaned loudly as Doug pulled the salts away from her flared nostrils.

"Take a second. Don't jump right up and go running back out there," he said, pressing her gently but firmly down. "What's your name?"

She was not pleased but could use a moment to get her bearings. "Gwen Lori," she said through pursed lips.

"Good. And what year is it?"

"2139."

"Good. Can you tell me where you are?"

"Listen, cocksucker, make yourself useful and give me a fuckin' bottle of water. Then you can stand your ass up and take me back out there."

"Hoo-ah! There's my Gwen." Grinning, he stood and threw her a bottle of water. "You comin' or what?"

She bolted upright, chugged the water, and caught up to him a few strides outside the tent.

"Can you believe the size of those bones?" she said. "Do you know how much we can learn from them? I never thought—"

"You never thought what?"

"I never thought we'd have evidence. It's been more than a hundred years. Half the public doesn't believe it happened, and the other half doesn't want to remember. It's been written out of history. It's as if the Nazis won and wrote their own version of the past."

"I don't know if Nazi Germany is a fair comparison, Gwen. They weren't committing genocide when this happened, well, at least not in this country. They were dealing with a crisis."

"Then why did they burn all the bodies?" she huffed, "and why is there so little primary source material?"

"I don't think they burned all the bodies. They started with burial sites like this one, but then poor souls began digging up the bodies for sustenance. It is impossible to understand starvation without experiencing it, Gwen. True starvation, the kind with no imaginable end, will drive a human mad."

"Give me a break from your gory theories, would you? I just went down, if you don't remember."

But Doug wasn't smiling. "You won't want to hear this, but this is the first intact grave we've ever found." Gwen looked at him, and he sighed. "Because, in the end, they stripped the bodies down completely and used every part to survive. That's history, Gwen. That's what happened."

CHAPTER 1

WHAT COULD HAPPEN

"Get up! Let's go!" Len yelled into Michael's ear, pulling out his friend's earbud.

"Can't," Michael replied, snatching the earbud back without turning away from his screens. In his periphery, Len was going on about something, but he had to focus on his work. Then a hand waved in front of his face, and he pulled an earbud back out.

"Come, let us get out of here," Len said in his thick Eastern European accent. "Look, if I don't get away from screens, I break them, and," he twitched, "if you don't get up now and come, I break your shit, too."

Michael—short, broad-shouldered, tanned—looked up. He did not like the look on Len's face. "Where do you want to go?" he said slowly.

"Come. Now. I buying. I need out!" Len paced behind him.

"That's easy for you to say, you're almost done with your assignment. I've got hours of coding left."

"No shit, you're slow!"

"Dude, really?" Michael said in a depressed tone as he eyed Len over his shoulder.

"Come with and I debug your code, okay?"

"You still haven't told me where we're going."

"We go for burgers. New craft brew on South Main."

"And that's it, right? Then we're back and you'll help me debug? I have to turn this assignment in tomorrow, so don't lie to me." Michael stared into his friend's impassive blue eyes, hunting for any glint of deception.

"Yes, burgers ... and, like, one detour," Len said, trailing off.

"What detour?"

"Do not worry."

"Len, what the fuck do you have to pick up? Do you want me to go with you or not?"

"No worries, we get Lifio. Is this good?"

Michael leaned back in his chair and sighed. He blinked and rubbed his eyes.

"What, is problem? You think gimmick? Who gives shit, we try it," Len said as Michael rolled his eyes and raked his fingers down his cheeks. "Eric tried. Says we must try. Igor try, Ivan try, Omar try, Vlad—"

"I have a project," interrupted Michael.

"I went on boring day-long walk in desert with stupid trees with you, now you come with me," Len said, nodding his chin.

"Joshua Tree was an awesome hike!" Michael said, his face twisting as if he'd bitten into a lemon. "But if you want to try this crap so bad, fine. I don't give a shit, as long as it's quick."

Michael followed the jabbering Len through their white-washed apartment block, itching day-old auburn stubble. The fluorescent lights seared into his hazel eyes as they entered the elevator—perhaps it was a good time for a break after all. Len, oblivious, wouldn't shut up about Lifio. Michael had seen it all over social media; it stuck out like a sore thumb in between his usual pictures of majestic wildlife and grandiose landscapes. *It'll be nice to see what the fuss is all about.*

It certainly felt like another fly-by-night snake oil. Fake sugar plus caffeine and a ton of advertising had tricked a lot of people, including Len. *What do I have to lose? I get a break, some food, and Len helps me debug my code.*

Len drove his Maxima like it was NASCAR. Michael knew

the drill, but it still pissed him off when he tried to race people at traffic lights.

"Slow the fuck down. This guy doesn't want to race you."

By the time they found a convenience store, Len was frothing at the mouth. Michael waited in the car and typed out a response to a text from his mom.

"All gone," Len said, throwing open the car door. "We try again." The car flew backward, then launched out of the parking lot, tires screeching.

Later, Michael demanded, "This is the last one, you hear me, Len? The last fucking place. Then we're done."

"Then we go to Eric's place. It five miles away."

It might have been only a few miles but, exasperatingly, thirty minutes passed in the intense lunch-hour traffic before they reached the small store that specialized in sake. Len jumped out of the car and yelped as it crept forward. Michael, feeling the motion, dropped his phone, and pulled the emergency brake handle just before the car hit the curb.

Len poked his head back into the car, eyes wide, and murmured, "Thank you." Minutes later, he was back with six warm cans.

"What the hell, Len?" Michael said after his first sip.

Len just shrugged. "Who knows," he said, smacking his lips with a quizzical look on his face. "Took too long; we must finish them."

Michael swallowed the last bit down, crushed the can, and tossed it in the backseat. "Now that we've wasted an hour, can we grab a burger?"

With the perverse pride that comes from corrupting a friend's work ethic, Len smiled and hit the gas, giving Michael another jolt of motion sickness.

Letting hunger get the best of him, burgers and fries went down the hatch in minutes. Before he knew it, Michael was back at his computer, coding.

Fortunately, he didn't have the bowling-ball-in-the-stomach feeling he normally had after fast food. Actually, he felt pretty good. The break had definitely helped him recharge his batteries. He just couldn't afford to let Len know that, or he'd never hear the end of it.

* * *

A week later, Michael strutted into his apartment after receiving an A on his coding project. Plus, he'd already knocked out all of his homework for the week. The extra hours at the computer science lab had really paid off. As he waded into the front room, he was greeted with a nod from Len, who squatted on the couch, clothed only in briefs, socks, and a black T-shirt with Ukrainian letters scrawled across the front.

"Sup?" Michael said, but Len's eyes stayed glued to the screen. "Hey?" he tried again.

Still nothing.

"I have a few lady friends coming over and I wanted to see if you'd like to join ... but if you're too busy, I understand." Michael smiled to himself as he sauntered through into the next room.

"Girls. Girls coming here. When? How much time?" Len said suddenly, jerking from the sofa as if waking from a dream.

Michael didn't answer, he just set down his backpack on the kitchen table and opened up the fridge.

"When, girls, when?" Len yelled with urgency from the bathroom. Michael could hear the water running. Finally, he emerged, toothbrush sticking out of the corner of his mouth. "There are no girls?"

"Nope," Michael said, smirking as he shut the fridge, "but at least I got your attention."

Len pulled the toothbrush out of his mouth so he could spit the words "You fuck," then headed back into the bathroom.

When he reappeared, Michael asked, "What were you watching when I came in?"

"I do not believe. No girls."

"Get over it. What were you watching?"

"Do not know. Why care? Some fools in streets in Clark County."

Michael started rooting through the cabinets, trying to find something to eat. He found a packet of ramen noodles, emptied it into a bowl, added water, and set it in the microwave.

"So, were there girls and you lost them? Or were there never girls?" Len asked from the couch, cold eyes fixed on Michael.

Michael just snorted.

Satiated, he dropped next to Len, who was already engrossed in his phone, and flipped on the TV.

The news was focused on the protests Len had mentioned. It didn't look bad. There wasn't any major damage; people looked fed up about something but they clearly weren't ready to get locked up for it. *Maybe a union strike or something.* The protests or riots, he wasn't really sure which, looked like they were in New York City, not Clark County.

"Depressing, depressing, depressing," Michael murmured, moving through the channels. He glanced at Len. "Dude, that shit was in NYC, not Clark County." After no response, Michael reached out and flicked Len.

"No, Vegas, I sure," he replied without looking up from his phone.

Michael rolled his eyes. *No use arguing with him.* He stood, then glanced down at Len. "Yo, you want me to leave this on? I'm going to bed."

"Leave it," Len said, not looking up.

The next morning, Michael found Len asleep on the couch with the TV blaring and his phone stuck to his face. With no room on the couch, Michael sat in the kitchen, a cold Pop-Tart in front of him, and peered through at the TV Len had left on. They were still covering protests: a few thousand people gathered in a city center. The chyron at the bottom of the screen read, *Los Angeles*.

Reports followed explaining that the FDA had frozen the sale of Lifio in the United States. Apparently, the product was being pulled from shelves immediately. Video clips played of store workers pulling cases of Lifio away as customers tried to grab them out of their arms. Riots and protests were breaking out in a few major cities, and people were desperately trying to buy the remaining stock before it was yanked from the shelves. Then there were the reports of price gouging as opportunistic store owners raised prices through the roof. Protestors on the screen looked far angrier than they had the night before.

Unable to help himself, he grabbed his phone and found Lifio going on auction sites for a few hundred dollars a can, with tons of bidders. *I wonder if Len drank all those cans,* he thought. Michael froze suddenly. *Why are they taking it off the market? Is it poisonous?* Thoughts tore through his mind as Len, frowning and red-eyed, strolled in and dropped into a chair.

"You do not look good," Len said, wiping the sleep from his eyes and scratching himself.

"The FDA just pulled that fuckin' drink you made me try."

"So?"

"So, there's got to be a reason."

"You baby, nothing they sell here will kill you. They do not let you use ephedrine even for diet here. It no problem, I promise." He stood and headed to the fridge.

He came back with something in his hand. "Coca Cola used to make with cocaine. Did you know? I think those exciting days are behind us." He winked and took a swig from the can in his hand. "Maybe they did not pay your government enough money."

"That, or it's poison, and you killed me," Michael quipped as he saw the Lifio in Len's hand.

"You worry too much, Michael. What could happen?"

CHAPTER 2

MEETING IN ROOM 209

Just north of Washington, DC, in suburban Maryland, Melanie Delaney, commissioner of the Federal Drug Administration, drove through the parking lot, tires screeching. After pulling into a spot that was bound to result in a dent, she slammed back into her seat. She wrapped her fingers tight around the steering wheel. "One, two, three, four. One, two, three, four." Slowly, she reached down and unclicked her seatbelt.

Outside, the all-too-familiar scent of damp concrete greeted her as she hurried toward the security queue. Her past three months had been a whirlwind. While she had anticipated public outcry when agreeing to pull Lifio from the market, she'd been caught off guard by the intensity of the outrage. She felt pressure from all directions, and didn't like it. What had she been thinking, she chided herself, trying to fend off consumer ire with scientific procedure?

After escaping security without a fondling, she caught sight of a fire exit diagram on the wall. Bypassing reception, Melanie took the stairs to the second floor and headed straight for the gray, muted conference room, a carbon copy of hundreds like it. For the next hour, she'd endure the long-winded explanations of the testing and analysis team responsible for approvals.

"Alright, Carrie," she said, marching into the boardroom, "start us off. What are we looking at?" She was on time—actually, three minutes early—but she swore they always set up half an hour before meetings were due to begin just to make her look bad.

"Yes, Madam Commissioner," a stern, dark-haired woman said, stepping forward. "This is meeting seven, being held in room 209 of FDA Building Sixty-Six. Current members in attendance are—"

"Carrie, cut to the chase. We know why we're here. Can we approve yet?" Melanie didn't want to be cruel, but she also couldn't afford to spend four hours in another musky conference room waiting for Carrie to get to the point.

After a pregnant silence, Carrie replied, "No, Madam Commissioner."

There was another interminable silence as Melanie's heart slowed. Why was it so hard for scientists to communicate with other humans?

"Okay, now, that's not enough information. Let's try this again. Tell me everything that we've recently learned that I do not already know."

"I'll do my best, Madam Commissioner ..." Pause. "As we already know, Lifio has been officially reported to the FDA by nearly all major beverage brands—"

"Carrie," Melanie said, stone-faced.

"Oh, yes, new information only. My apologies. Our team has finalized our initial research, and we have prepared a report." Carrie passed a dense stack of report briefs around the room as a wry smile crept across her face.

"Carrie, this is eighty-three pages. Can you please summarize?" *How excruciatingly painful communication in the public sector can be*, Melanie thought. *To think I could be a CEO, kicking my feet up. I guess no good deed goes unpunished.* Melanie could tell by the look on everyone's face that she was scowling. "I made a mistake, that's all."

"Excuse me?"

"In our job, you only get mentioned when you screw up."

No one spoke. Melanie cleared her throat. "Never mind the mistake. Carrie, if you will?"

"I would really prefer that you read the report in full, but if I must summarize …" Carrie paused.

Melanie could have sworn she was doing all of this for dramatic effect. "Yes, please summarize, Carrie," she said in her most monotonal voice.

"Very well. We believe Lifio triggers a kind of balancing effect in the human body. By balance, I am referring to the body's autonomous maintenance of the ideal fat-to-muscle ratio, combined with rapid, enhanced healing."

"It's similar to how LSD and other psychedelics have been found to rewire the brain," a junior colleague put in, as if Melanie needed color.

"Somehow, Lifio's rewiring the endocrine system to function in a manner that finds a natural balance," continued Carrie, "leaving no overage of calories to be turned into long-term storage."

Melanie broke in. "You mean fat when you say 'long-term storage.' You're saying the drink doesn't let you get fat?" If Carrie and her team were intent on treating her like a Neanderthal, acting like one just might make her feel a little better about it.

"Yes, I suppose you could say it like that. If I may continue, it does more than just that."

"Now hold on, how exactly is it accomplishing this?" Melanie asked.

"Well, if you go by their packaging, it's a proprietary balance of micronutrients and antioxidants," Carrie said, gritting her teeth.

Melanie walked into it: "And what do you think is going on, Carrie?"

"We believe the constant balancing effect is achieved by somatic gene mutation."

"Okay, now that's a leap. How did you come up with that exactly?"

"Process of elimination; until they divulge their 'proprietary formula,' we have to backward engineer what they are doing," Carrie retorted.

The other scientists gathered in the room looked back and forth between the two women as if watching a tennis match.

"What effects exactly?"

"The effect is a state similar to, but not absolutely like, the adolescent growth process. We are seeing the pituitary gland reactivate and produce an abundance of human growth hormone. In addition, the body's stem cells start to divide and multiply. The brain of a young adult typically exhibits more control over the body through hormones, allowing the body to better utilize caloric intake to balance weight, new growth, cell repair, and energy levels. The adult brain, on the other hand, typically focuses calorie overages on building long-term stores—or fat, as you would say—and calorie deficits by reducing energy levels. After the consumption of Lifio, we are witnessing a highly engaged endocrine system—the thyroid, thymus, and pituitary and adrenal glands all working in concert to burn excess calories through increased energy and rapid metabolic changes similar to those observed during adolescence. The growth of new stem cells leads to the body having the ability to create any new cell that is required, allowing for microregeneration of damaged tissue."

"Carrie, are you legitimately telling me Lifio will let people regrow body parts?"

"No, Melanie, of course not. I clearly said *micro*regeneration. It is not possible for full structural regrowth of limbs, but what we have found is the regrowth of damaged tissue happening at a far more rapid rate than is traditionally seen. Typically, adults have a dominant inflammatory reaction when confronted with cell damage, and young children have a more regenerative response. Somehow, the gene mutations that we believe are being triggered by Lifio in DNA return subjects to the youthful response, with regeneration becoming the more dominant reaction."

"So, subjects regenerate, just slowly. Is that what you're saying, Carrie?" Melanie then added, "Be clear so I can understand," knowing full well she risked pushing the dumbass routine too far. But she couldn't resist; she swore endorphins were released every time she made the scientists' noses turn up.

"No, I'm saying that the subject's body is simply better at self-repair. Bones strengthen over time instead of degrading. Ligaments and tendons heal faster. The best way I can describe it is to liken the subjects to toddlers. On average, toddlers fall thirty-eight times per day, and none of them wake up with any of the ailments associated with adults falling. Imagine a geriatric falling thirty-eight times a day—they wouldn't have an unbroken bone left in their body."

"Carrie, there is no way kids fall thirty-eight times a day. Get out of here."

"She's right," that same cheeky junior scientist put in. "My kids fall more than that, I'm sure of it."

Melanie glanced from face to face; nearly everyone was nodding their head at her, confirming that kids do indeed fall a lot. One thing Melanie didn't know a thing about was kids; she couldn't remember being one and had yet to make time for having any.

Carrie jumped in just as Melanie was losing herself in her own head again. "Yup, I just Googled it. Look, it's right here: the average two-year-old falls thirty-eight times a day." Carrie held up her phone for all to see.

As murmurs about toddler fall rates swept the room, Melanie began to realize she had a real problem here; Carrie's report thus far hadn't mentioned any of Lifio's *negative* effects. The way Carrie made it sound, Lifio was the fountain of youth, damn it—surely there was a catch that could be exploited publicly to buy the agency some time. "Sebastian," she said, turning toward a straight-faced middle-aged man, "you've been awfully quiet. What were your findings?"

Sebastian, the deputy commissioner for food policy and response, had covered Mel's back since their time together in the private sector. He was one of Mel's closest allies in the room—perhaps, she thought grimly, her only ally. With his large glasses, small frame, and reserved nature, Sebastian wasn't the force of nature Melanie was, but she gave him a direct task, he completed it on time every time.

Unfortunately, as soon as Sebastian started reporting his findings to the group, Melanie understood why he'd been mute: double-digit reductions in cases of heart disease, stroke, high blood pressure, diabetes, cancer, osteoarthritis, osteoporosis, dementia, and Alzheimer's in subjects taking Lifio daily over the three-month period. Not only was Lifio preventing disease, but it was actually reversing it in subjects.

Sebastian fell silent, and Melanie winced. Everyone in the room was clearly thinking the same thing: if this was true, life spans were going to go through the roof. It was like everyone in the world had hit the lottery at once, and somehow Melanie got stuck with the task of verifying the results. It all felt too good to be true, and suddenly she wished she'd held a private meeting with Carrie and Sebastian—there were far too many potential leaks present. Then, despite everything, she found herself wondering whether she might be able to have children after all; if Lifio did everything they said, maybe it could reverse menopause …

A quivering hand caught her attention: a woman sitting in a chair against the wall behind Carrie looked like she had to pee.

"Just ask your question. Don't raise your hand here; you're not in school any longer," Melanie barked. "How can I help you?"

"Yes, ma'am, I mean Madam Commissioner," the woman replied in a squeaky voice. "Well, why are we even doing all this? Lifio is just a soft drink. I mean, no other new soda or flavored water has needed FDA approval to be sold, so why does Lifio?"

"Carrie, who did you bring to this meeting?" Melanie asked, lips pressed together.

But before Carrie had a chance to answer, Sebastian—*Bless his soul*, Melanie thought—responded with the politically correct answer: "The Food and Drug Administration is responsible for protecting the public health and the safety of our nation's food supply—"

"So, this has nothing to do with the fact that every beverage manufacturing conglomerate sent the FDA letters and pressured Congress?" the mystery woman asked.

Melanie wondered who this woman was. A thought echoed in her head: *This is why staff assistants should not be involved in meetings like this.*

Carrie, while not openly scolding her subordinate, turned and gave the mystery woman a private explanation she had clearly heard before.

"I'm sorry, Melanie. I assure you, Cassandra understands this was something no one should be taking lightly, even if market competitors brought the issue to the FDA's attention," Carrie said.

Melanie gave Carrie a long, steady look. *At least we both know that the team has to get on the same page and stop dissenting.*

"So," she said slowly, "if what you are all telling me is correct, then there is a lot that needs to be understood before we can give the go-ahead to the public to drink Lifio again, no matter how positive the initial impact looks. Right, Carrie? Give me a road map to approval. What do we need to accomplish?"

Carrie flipped through her report. "Page sixty-eight."

And there it was in five long pages: everything they needed to accomplish while the whole country waited. Research and test long-term impact over five- and ten-year spans; test dosages, from three servings up to one hundred; test and document short- and long-term side effects; test and document drug interactions with the top one thousand commonly used medications; test and document effects on children, young adults, senior citizens, pregnant women in each trimester, etc.

What the fuck.

"Carrie, that list will take a dozen years to complete," said Melanie, her voice hard, blood and patience draining from her face. "You can't possibly expect me to hold FDA approval from a product for that period of time."

"Why not?" Carrie snorted. "This product causes a genetic mutation. Don't you understand what that means?"

At times like these, Melanie always tried to remind herself why she'd hired Carrie—she was, after all, a holy grail of brainpower with three PhDs to prove it. Some social smarts would've been too much to ask for.

"Not to mention," Carrie went on, oblivious, "I think we ought to understand how Lifio does what it does, not just the implications of its use."

Melanie knew she'd been pushing since she'd gotten on this case to convince Lifio's creator, a genius in his own right from Iceland, to divulge his secret. This was something no one in their right mind would bother attempting, yet Carrie kept relentlessly pushing.

"Look, Carrie, you have a theory," Melanie said slowly, jaw aching. "A theory you have yet to prove unequivocally. A theory we cannot take to the public because it will put a company out of business permanently and result in a monumental lawsuit *if you are wrong.* So, until you can deliver to me concrete proof of wrongdoing here, nothing will be released to the public. *You* told me this was a crisis and that we *had to* pull Lifio off the market *immediately* to protect the public. Comments like those are generally reserved for carcinogens or salmonella outbreaks, not unproven theories on possible genetic modification! *And* you don't get years—you might not even get months at the rate the public is going. Just come up with the bare minimum we need to approve it and get the list to me in forty-eight hours."

When no response came from the group, Melanie waded deeper: "Am I understood?"

Carrie glared at her, lip quivering. "Oh, I understand … I understand you're willing to risk our careers and reputations in the name of profits and greed. I won't be blamed for this, you understand?" She threw a hand in the air. "You can't expect us to just approve without proper scientific testing procedures. There are procedures in place *for a reason*—"

"It is my decision, not yours. Get me the list in forty-eight hours," Melanie said.

Sebastian caught Melanie's attention, and the two made small talk until the room emptied. "Mel," Sebastian said at last, "what if we just retract the cease and desist on Lifio and require them to add a disclaimer to the product packaging?" he said with a meek glimmer of hope.

"I wish it were that simple."

"And why can't it be? I mean, cigarettes literally kill people, and all they need is a warning label."

"What do you propose we put on this disclaimer?" Melanie said incredulously. She made air quotes with her fingers. "*Warning*: product causes gene mutations known to increase life expectancy and prevent disease."

She immediately hated herself for taking out her frustration on him. He'd always been in her corner, following her from company to company and then to the public sector like an orphan shown a mother's love. More importantly, he never counterattacked when she lapsed into mockery or indignation. Carrie, on the other hand, challenged her at every turn, and did so publicly. The gall of that woman—just thinking about it made her blood boil. Melanie remembered a terse hallway exchange last week, where Sebastian had tried to play peace-keeper and an innocent janitor had turned scarlet before completely melting into the carpet.

"I'm *sorry*," she blurted out, teeth clenched and fists balled. Then, after regaining her composure, she added, "I'm sorry, Sebastian. I just have a lot going on. Thank you for trying to help."

"Don't worry about it. As soon as I said it, I knew it was a bad idea anyway," he said with resignation. "I mean, the way a disclaimer would read, it would just look like advertising."

"Plus, the cat's out of the bag," Melanie said. "We can't just put our tails between our legs and release the product for public consumption without FDA approval now. Could you imagine if we had to pull it off the shelf a second time? The first time caused riots. They might storm the castle with pitchforks if we did it again."

"No, you're right. I don't know about pitchforks, but we'd certainly have plenty of lawsuits on our hands." Sebastian fell silent, and a pensive look settled on his face.

"What is it?"

He sighed. "Well, we could consider making it available for clinical trials."

"That would allow a segment of the population access, and it supports our testing," she admitted, "but clinical trials are limited. Until we know what we're dealing with, they would be nothing more than a sham."

"True, although it would certainly show progress."

"Yes, but would it be worth the political price later on?"

"Since when have you been worried about the political price of things? I thought we were doing all this for the greater good, to make the world a better place. That's what I told my wife when you pulled us out of the last company. Where, I will remind you, we made a lot more money."

She glared at him. "Who are you kidding? You wanted out just as much as I did, and we *are* doing the greater good here." Her frown split into a warm smile. "We're keeping a lifesaving elixir from the country because crazy Carrie told us to, didn't you hear?"

She knew clinical trials would relieve some of the pressure, but there would be consequences, chiefly those involving the pharmaceutical industry, who would invariably demand their pound of flesh. She'd already thought through that scenario, along with a million others, prior to Sebastian bringing it up. The last thing she wanted was to involve big pharma; that road would only be taken if it became absolutely necessary.

"You know, just a few years ago, I would have just ordered you to run a few models to calculate the cost of potential fines and lawsuits."

"Oh, you don't have to tell me. I already did those workups, and they weren't pretty, let me tell you. That's why I'm not pitching you on reapproving before Carrie's got more for us to go on."

"We're pretty boxed in here, aren't we?" Melanie said sadly, reminiscing about a time when they would have just rolled the dice. Life in the private sector was a cakewalk compared to the bureaucracy and public pressure they faced working for the federal government. But they had chosen this; at least, that's what they kept telling themselves.

"Yeah, we're boxed in, all right."

CHAPTER 3
CALL ON LINE TWO

Melanie spent her entire day oscillating between operational FDA meetings and check-ins with Carrie on the status of her team's Lifio testing. Over the past few weeks, each one of her days had looked the same. The public pressure in response to pulling Lifio off the market had initially surprised Melanie, but the fact that it was continuing to build really concerned her. Two weeks earlier, the president had asked her to submit weekly briefing reports to her chief of staff, and the CDC commissioner had recently asked her if the FDA had anything it wanted to share, agency to agency.

Her assistant, Tiffany, came to the door. "Madam Commissioner, you have a call on line two. It's—"

"I closed the door because I have to work up a status update report and submit it to POTUS," Melanie said with a scowl. "Take a message. I'll call them back."

"It's POTUS."

"Yes, the president of the United States. Please take a message."

After a brief silence, Tiffany began again. "Madam Commissioner, POTUS is on line two."

Realizing she had just kept the most powerful person in the world on hold, Melanie cursed under her breath. Then she straightened up, composed herself, and said, "Thank you, Tiff," before picking up the phone.

The president began immediately. "Melanie, you have got to be kidding me here. Is your agency trying to make me look bad?"

Melanie winced. "Madam President, we are doing everything in our power to bring a swift resolution to the situation."

"Swift? The FDA, my FDA, yanked the fastest-growing beverage in the world from American's shelves thirty-four days ago without a public explanation, and now every day my press secretary spends half his time trying to dodge questions about Lifio because the FDA is not giving anyone any damn answers! Melanie, if your agency were moving swiftly, you would not have pulled the product before documenting your reasoning and preparing public messaging."

Taking a deep breath, Melanie replied, "Madam President, I understand you are displeased. The Food and Drug Administration is responsible for protecting the public health and the safety of our nation's food supply—"

"Do not test my patience, Melanie. If I wanted to hear someone say nothing in a thousand words, I would talk to Congress. You can put all of that in your official report, but at this moment in time, you need to tell me why you pulled Lifio off the market and when it will be back on American shelves."

Melanie knew the president had every right to be frustrated. After three challenging but fruitful years as president of the United States, Elizabeth Williamson had pointed the country back in the right direction. A few short months ago, a second term had been all but guaranteed. That was, until Melanie had allowed Carrie to talk her into pulling Lifio off the market. That single move threatened to wipe out all of the goodwill President Williamson had amassed through years of sound policy decisions and strong leadership.

"I'd feel far more comfortable updating you on our reasoning for pulling Lifio off the market after we have completed our research, Madam President," said Melanie.

"That's an entirely understandable position. Unfortunately, it's not plausible. A statement has to be issued, and the public needs to understand the FDA's reason for pulling Lifio."

"That is not something I can do at this time."

"Melanie, that's just not good enough. Why did you pull the product? Is it a carcinogen?"

"No, Madam President, it is not a carcinogen."

"Is it hurting people?"

"That remains to be seen."

Melanie couldn't believe the position Carrie had put her in. The stubborn genius had demanded that Melanie pull Lifio because it was a potential "existential threat to humankind." That had been thirty-four days ago, and, while Carrie's concerns sounded legitimate, none of the testing would be concerning to the public at large. Quite the opposite, in fact: Carrie's team had found Lifio caused dramatic reductions in nearly every disease related to obesity and aging. Carrie's stance, while scientifically correct—test and verify all scenarios before allowing anything into the public domain—didn't translate well into 140 characters that the nation could digest. The country had tasted the fountain of youth, and the FDA had taken it away.

"Melanie, are you trying to be difficult?" asked the president. "You are a smart woman, which is why I appointed you, but if you do not give me your reasoning for pulling Lifio off the market immediately, I will appoint someone else to head the FDA."

And there it is, thought Melanie. After stalling for more than a month, she was going to have to let someone outside of her circle in. She took a deep breath. "We have a theory that Lifio utilizes CRISPR technology to manipulate or mutate DNA."

Silence. Then: "That is a pretty serious accusation. Whose theory is this, exactly?"

"Carrie Roberts, Madam President. I believe you have met her."

"Yes. Dr. Roberts, smartest person in the room but socially impotent, if I remember correctly."

Melanie suppressed a smile. "Yes, I believe you remember her correctly, Madam President."

"Something must have led the FDA to test this product," said the president, deftly switching from outrage to pragmatism. "You need to release the reasoning for the FDA's concerns to dilute public discord and gain time to finalize your testing."

"Madam President, that's going to be an issue. Our team began testing Lifio to quell incessant complaining from other actors in the beverage industry. We thought we could do some testing and disprove their bogus theories and then stop responding, but Carrie—I mean, Dr. Roberts—found something she didn't like. After a back-and-forth with Lifio's creator, an Icelandic chemist who refused to divulge his company's chemical compound ingredient list, Dr. Roberts committed herself to understanding what the product was and how it was providing such positive effects on subjects. She found that every Lifio can contains trace amounts of a specific bacteria, and she believes this bacteria uses CRISPR to cause gene mutations."

"You are correct; telling the public the FDA looked into Lifio at the behest of beverage industry leaders would not look appropriate. You've given me sufficient information to trust that you know what you are doing. However, without scientific proof that gene editing is taking place or of negative side effects, my patience will run out. I will explain to the public that the FDA must finalize testing before releasing Lifio back onto the market, but that will not give you much time. You must accelerate your research and testing immediately."

"Understood, Madam President. Thank you."

Melanie hung up the phone, unintentionally slamming it down. Tension coursed through her body, making every muscle tight. She sank back into her chair and did her best to use the meditation techniques she'd learned a couple of summers back to help her relax and release stress. President Williamson inspired women around the world, even Melanie, who committed to increasing her level of dogged determination. Dimly, she wondered whether the president's political opponents, after debating her, felt like she did right now.

With the circle of trust increasing in size to include the president, Melanie didn't know how long they could keep Carrie's theory a secret. She trusted that the president would give her time to prove the theory, but the president would surely brief her own team, and Melanie knew that in politics, secrets were never safe.

She ought to tell Carrie and, more importantly, Sebastian about her conversation with the president so they could help her play out potential scenarios. Carrie wouldn't be much help with public messaging strategy, but letting her in on the conversation could potentially pressure her to move faster. Melanie just didn't have the necessary energy left to make those calls. After a day like today, she needed a glass a wine and a warm bath. Speaking with Sebastian and Carrie could wait until tomorrow; right now, she needed to take care of herself.

CHAPTER 4

TALKING HEADS

Melanie rolled over in bed, back arched, and sighed. A lifetime of cycling kept her slim, but at the expense of her hips, which were crying more than usual after the long ride home the night before. Thankfully, coffee and the couch were her only agenda items on Sundays.

After a hardboiled egg and toast, Melanie settled into her window seat with a red knit blanket her mother had given her and her laptop. *Still nothing,* she thought, smirking. Almost a week had passed since she'd shared Carrie's theory with the president, and it hadn't come out in the press yet. *Impressive woman.* The president took the brunt of the public outrage, yet she remained staunch in her support of the FDA's decision to pull Lifio—at least publicly. *If I think she's so damn impressive, I should probably force Carrie's hand*—but Melanie knew she'd already been riding Carrie as hard as she could. The fact that nearly every mention of Lifio in the media was followed by angry condemnation of the president was, she supposed, to be expected. *That's not a job I ever want.*

Attempting to clear her head, Melanie flicked on the TV and immediately saw the "Williamson Lifio Watch" counter flash up onscreen. The brainchild of some smug anchor, the counter showed the number of days since Lifio had been pulled from the market. Disgusted, she changed the channel, only to immediately pause to watch a spray-tanned moderator kick off a panel discussion with a decrepit grin. "This news, coming right on the heels of the *European Journal of Health*'s recent report, causes real concern. I'd like to welcome to our show Douglas McArthur, MD, PhD, and former chief medical officer at the CDC. Douglas, thank you for joining our round table."

"It's a pleasure to be here; I just wish it were under different circumstances. President Williamson's lack of transparency and clarity after the FDA pulled Lifio off the market is highly irregular. When I was at the CDC, communication was our top priority, and I think the president needs to take a page out of our book."

"But surely there were times when the CDC did not share data with the public," the moderator replied.

The man nodded coolly, his hands clasped in front of him. "Only in very rare circumstances—for instance, terror-related chemical attacks—and never with a consumer product. Compound that with the journal's report of Lifio being shown to reduce heart attacks by fifty-three percent, strokes by fifty-seven percent, and obesity by ninety-nine percent. These results are nothing short of astounding, and for me, they put President Williamson's motives in serious question."

The host smiled sweetly. "Understandable. Why don't we have another member of our panel weigh in here? Patrick Noble is a political commentator and creator of *Right Think*, a conservative podcast. Patrick, what do you make of the president's statement today that the public needs to 'exert patience' as the FDA completes their official inquiry?"

A portly ginger-haired man—Melanie guessed he was in his forties or fifties—cleared his throat. "I've said it before and I'll say it again: the United States of America is in peril with this president in office. She clearly has an agenda to control and oppress Lifio for her own political gain. This president pulled a product off the shelves without warning and is now watching public pressure build to re-release it. When she allows the product to go back on the market right before the election, I guarantee she will try to take all the credit for correcting a problem that she herself created. It's political maneuvering 101. Unfortunately, a large majority of the voting public doesn't see her for what she really is."

"That's an interesting take on the situation. Lindsey Rowe, professor of economics at the University of Minnesota, do you believe President Williamson's motives are politically based?"

Dr. Rowe, an older woman with sharp eyes, leaned forward in her seat. "As Dr. McArthur suggested, all of the published studies on Lifio are immensely positive. That begs the question: why is President Williamson's administration and the FDA keeping this product off the market? With more than a dozen globally recognized journals testing Lifio and reporting only positive results and no negative side effects, it is becoming increasingly difficult to have faith that the president has wholesome motives. Of course, speculation as to *how* Lifio achieves its positive effects is rife in the academic community, but, as far as I'm aware, no rigorous studies have yet produced any conclusive findings. It's possible the president—and, for that matter, certain members of the scientific community—are simply erring on the side of caution. But, if that's the case, why the silence? Why the secrecy?"

"Dr. Rowe, is that to say you agree with Mr. Noble's suggestion of a political motivation?"

Dr. Rowe stifled a snort. "I want to be clear that I do not agree with Mr. Noble's hypothesis; I'm simply saying the president's position is getting harder to defend."

At this point, Lesslie Guiles, op-ed columnist for the *Times Daily*, chimed in: "I have concerns over political motivation, but they surround big beverage pressuring the president to pull Lifio so they have time to react to its release. Everyone saw how the stock prices of the big three beverage companies rebounded after Lifio was pulled from the market. Now the public is waiting for an undetermined amount of time for FDA testing to be complete. That doesn't sound right to me. I think we need to take a closer look at the president's donor list to see if big beverage is behind this."

"This is just another Democrat trying to push the country into socialism," said Patrick, his eyes wild. "The next thing we know, President Williamson will be taking control of the company producing Lifio and turning it into a government-owned institution! She is against capitalism and the American way of life, plain and simple."

Trying to wrestle back control from the panel, the moderator pivoted. "Well, those are some, er, *imaginative* explanations. Dr. McArthur, perhaps you can get us back on track here."

"While I do not agree with Mr. Noble or Ms. Guiles, if President Williamson does not have darker ulterior motives, that begs the question of what the president and the FDA are not telling us about Lifio? And, perhaps more importantly, *why* are they not telling us?"

Lesslie Guiles, seeming a little too excited by the opportunity for air time, interjected: "Perhaps the president is concerned with an unsustainable population due to dramatic reductions in disease and assumed improvements in life expectancy. Maybe there is nothing negative to report about Lifio, and that is the problem. If everyone lives twice as long, what happens to our population? China was facing the same dilemma when it introduced the one-child policy in 1979. Perhaps the president is trying to devise a policy to mitigate the long-term impact Lifio will have."

"I do not believe long-term implications are at the heart of this matter," said Lindsey Rowe. "If they were, the president would have communicated those concerns and avoided the political damage she is currently sustaining from all sides. Perhaps she sees a potential solution to the country's ever-growing debt crisis through high taxes on Lifio. If one were trying to fix the national debt, they could, in theory, pull Lifio off the market, increasing public demand on Congress and pressure on the manufacturer to regain access to the US market. Then, when the discord reached its apex, one could likely cut a deal with both Congress and the manufacturer to rerelease the product with a heavy tax rate on sales revenue. The potential to fix our national debt was squandered when marijuana was legalized federally without heavy taxation. Perhaps our president has learned from our recent past."

"Ha, Lindsey, you give President Williamson entirely too much credit," Patrick said with a smirk.

Melanie slammed down the remote control and left the room. Enough of this bullshit—she needed a shower. She tore off her clothes and shrieked a curse after jumping in too soon, a cold shock ripping her back into the present. It felt like she was losing it; she knew she had to relax and recharge, but she couldn't get out of her own head. *Who the hell would think pulling a drink off the market would affect an election?!*

After lunch, Melanie checked her email on her phone and found yet another Williamson staffer grilling her for answers she didn't have. After redirecting, she reminded herself not to fault others for doing their jobs; reporters were paid to poke, prod, and find sources to break stories. As for the cabinet staffers who harassed her daily—well, she didn't know why they did half the things they did, but that was none of her concern.

By the end of the day, she was glad the weekend was over; at least during the week she could keep herself so busy that she didn't have time to ponder the implications of her decision to support Carrie's theory.

CHAPTER 5

GET OUT

"Good morning sweetie pie!"

Sebastian's cheeks glowed, and he beamed at Michelle, the receptionist. "Good morning."

"How was your weekend, sugar?" she said, drawling the words out as if she could taste them.

"Good," he managed lamely. "And yours?"

Michelle smiled coyly. "Oh, a little of this and a little of that. I got a new bathing suit; why don't you come over after work and I'll show you? I could use a little input, you know."

Choking on his coffee, Sebastian juggled his key card and started mumbling excuses incoherently before briskly making his way past the elevator toward the steps.

Behind him, Michelle called, "You know how to find me, darlin'!"

At the top of the stairwell, Sebastian regained his composure, straightened his bow tie, then set off toward Melanie's office.

"Knock, knock. It's me."

"Yup," Melanie responded without looking up.

"I found something over the weekend that I'd like to show you."

"Okay."

Sebastian hesitated. "I mean, if you have a sec."

"Yes, it's fine; I just have a lot on my plate, and I didn't sleep well last night."

"I can come back another time, I just thought—"

Melanie finally looked up from her computer and sighed. "It's all right, okay?" Then, in a calmer voice: "Let me hear it."

"Okay, so, I finished my research over the weekend, and I wanted to—"

"What research, Sebastian?"

"Um, just a little background profile on Dr. Jónsson and Stallson Beverage." Sebastian trailed off, chin down, shoulders slumping.

Looking him dead in the eye, Melanie asked, "And who, may I ask, put you up to this?"

"I was just doing her a favor, it was all done on nights and weekends—it's no big deal. I was interested, she was interested. Let me tell you what I found."

"It was Carrie, wasn't it?" Melanie, still sitting, put her hand on her thigh. "God damn it, Sebastian, you can't just follow her every whim."

"I know, I know, but this is different. We probably should have done it—"

Sebastian cut himself off after catching Melanie's eye.

"Fine, just give it to me."

Sebastian sat down and opened his laptop. "I just need my notes. Okay. So, Stallson Beverage company was formed a little over five years ago by Alex Stallan."

"Wait, Alex Stallan started the company? Not Dr. Jónsson?"

"Yup, typical story really: Alex ran a private equity firm in New York. He went on a weekend getaway to Iceland, found a local drink that showed promise, and thirty days later he owned it."

Melanie dragged her hand across her forehead. "You have got to be kidding me."

"Nope, Alex was kind enough to give Dr. Jónsson a small share of the company and a paycheck," Sebastian said, then looked up at the doorway, where a full-bodied woman with mousy black hair tied into a ponytail stood, her hand on her hip.

"Did you get your work done?" Carrie prodded Sebastian from the doorway.

Melanie snorted. "You're a piece of work."

"Well, someone has to do work around here," Carrie retorted.

Melanie stood up, but Sebastian beat her to it. "Carrie, that's not fair." He straightened, glaring from one woman to the other. "We're all overworked right now. The good news is, I completed the research that I *decided* to do for you." He stared pointedly at Carrie, eyebrows raised. "Now, why don't you come in and take a seat, Carrie, I was just telling Melanie what I found."

Carrie did so. Once seated, she looked at him expectantly.

"As I was saying, I found some pictures and reviews of Lifio before Stallan bought it and, well, I'm not surprised it never made it out of Iceland. It had a dark purple hue and people said it tasted like algae."

"Then why did he buy it in the first place?" Melanie said leaning in.

"It's not really clear, but I did dig up one blog post by a news outfit in Snæfellsnes, Iceland. It mentions that Alex and his wife Helen took note of the cult-like following of the drink—which, back then, was sold in mason jars with the word 'life' printed on it. They both tasted it and were repulsed."

"Who would buy something they didn't like the taste of?" Carrie said, breaking her silence.

Melanie and Sebastian exchanged glances.

"When Alex found out Stefán Jónsson was a biochemist who'd created Lifio in a research laboratory at the University of Iceland, he bought it immediately," Sebastian said.

"What?" Carrie was shaking her head.

"It's private equity, Carrie," Melanie said. "Alex found a liquid that looked bad, tasted bad, and came in a nondescript glass bottle, yet people who drank it did so habitually. Of course, he bought it."

Sebastian nodded. "Okay, so Alex's equity firm had set up Stallson Beverage. But there was a problem: Dr. Jónsson would not leave Iceland. Then, it almost fell apart because Alex refused to release the product in the US market without improving palatability, and Stefán did not have any experience in flavor chemistry. Before shutting it down, though, they did a pilot run as an energy drink, with the benefits being vague and defensible."

"Then what?" Carrie pushed.

Sebastian smirked. "As they say, the rest is history."

"Cliff notes," Melanie said, flicking her wrist.

"They put it in a sleek white can and did some pretty slick guerilla marketing. Sales started soft but exploded after three months. Stefán still would not leave Iceland, so they worked out a process to ship concentrate to bottling plants in the US. Then they built a production-scale laboratory in Iceland."

"Wait, how did the price get so damn high? Who would try a new product that was ten times the cost of an alternative?" Melanie asked.

"I'm getting there. So, they hit a supply shortage. They were building a new facility but, in the meantime, couldn't fill demand."

"What about contract production?" Carrie said.

"They refused to give up the formula, so they had to wait. In the meantime, Alex moved their price point from two dollars to three dollars per can, but demand accelerated. Then they pushed it to five dollars, which garnered national attention and had the counterintuitive effect of creating even more demand for what was dubbed 'the most expensive energy drink in the world.' But Alex didn't stop: he pushed it all the way up to twenty dollars a can before their new production facility opened up."

"It's hard not to give him credit for that move," Melanie said, staring out the window. "Sorry, go on."

"Then they went public. In a somewhat controversial move, Alex named his wife, Helen, CFO. Regardless, Stallson Beverage's IPO had a historic opening day."

"And sales didn't slow down after supply met demand?" Melanie asked.

"No, quite the contrary: they exploded. Only four quarters after going public, their revenue passed Nestlé."

"And then what?" Melanie demanded.

After a pregnant pause, Sebastian replied, voice high, "And then we pulled it off the market."

"Enough. Out," Melanie said, pointing to the door. Both Carrie and Sebastian filed out sheepishly, neither daring to say anything.

CHAPTER 6

CLEAN MEET

"Len, can you turn it down?" Michael pleaded over his shoulder from his position hunched over his laptop, a bowl of cereal at his side. A few forgotten Mini-Wheats floated, engorged with milk; he'd abruptly stopped eating and jumped frantically back into his project after a sudden epiphany.

"Len, turn it down. I can't think straight," Michael pleaded.

"Yes, yes, okay, throw Bose to me," Len replied without taking his eyes off the TV.

Michael couldn't work with gunshots and screams at ear-splitting volume, and he needed to knock out his paper on robot autonomy before noon the next day. Instead of arguing, he stood up, walked over to Len, picked up the headphones from next to him, and held them out.

"Thank you, Michael. Now turn on Bluetooth. Wait for chime. Yes, I heard it. Now come closer and slide them on my head," Len said with a straight face as he mashed buttons and steered the controller in his hands. "*Cyka blyat!* Dead. Just give them to me."

Michael handed Len the headphones and walked back to his laptop in the adjoining kitchenette. Michael and Len were both majoring in computer science, and spent most of their time in front of screens. The only downside seemed to be that they weren't very tidy, and their apartment's appearance had quickly spiraled out of Michael's control without him even noticing. The floor was littered with Red Bulls, ramen packets, cereal boxes, and dirty clothes that produced a bouquet of aromas one had to acquire a taste for. Michael had not realized the unique perfume existed until his parents came to visit. His mother had been "very disappointed in the way you are choosing to live."

"Michael, pick up controller, join us. *We could use you!*"

"I have to knock out this paper first."

"*Yes, paper! Then join!*" Len kept screaming, his headphones on.

Michael glanced up over his shoulder. "Oh. I'm not playing that crap; first-person shooters are brainless garbage," he said.

Affronted, Len put his controller down and took off his headphones. "Wrong. First-person shooter is purest form of gaming," he said.

"Ha, give me a break—all you do is roam around, mindlessly killing. RPGs? Now that take strategy. FPS games train future mass murders."

"I tell you. You join me, on my team, one match, and then I play your RPG all you want. You will see which is better," Len offered.

"Man, I got a paper. Don't tempt me."

"Yes, paper, finish paper then accept my challenge," Len said. Then he slid his headphones back on and perched on the edge of the couch they'd found on a street corner last semester.

With Len focused on his game and the apartment finally quiet enough for him to concentrate, Michael began to make substantial progress on his robotics paper. He had to make it perfect. Just as he was beginning to hit his stride, he heard a light *tap, tap, tap*. He looked around, but it had stopped. Then it came again, louder this time: *tap, tap, tap.*

"Yo, Len, check the door, would ya? I think somebody is there," Michael said, eyes still tracing lines of code.

Tap, tap, tap.

"Len, door!" He looked up and saw Len hammering buttons on his controller, completely absorbed.

Sighing, Michael stood and marched across the room. "*Move!* out of way!" Len cried as he crossed in front of the TV.

When Michael opened the door, a wave of heat flashed through him, and he almost stumbled. "Ah, it's, a …" he mumbled, all of the blood in his body flowing to his loins, causing him to press his knees together. "You are really beautiful," fell out of his mouth as a whisper. But she heard—of course she heard—because, for the first time, she looked up from the floor and made penetrating eye contact for a single fleeting moment. *Oh my God,* Michael thought, tearing his eyes from her, *what did I just do? I'm such an idiot.*

He didn't dare look directly at her, but he had to look up from the floor, and, when he did, he saw his blushing had become contagious—her face too was bright crimson.

"Hi."

"Hi."

Deep breaths, deep breaths.

"Are—are you lost?" he inquired after a long moment, not really knowing what else to say.

"I'm here to clean Mr. Lori's home," said the diminutive woman with luminous chestnut eyes after a daring second of eye contact. She wore a red blouse draped over ample breasts, with slender honey-brown arms. Dark brown hair fell onto her shoulders, and her tightly laced white tennis shoes had seen better days.

"My last name is Lori," Michael said, poking a fat finger into his chest, "but I'm sorry. Did you say you're here to clean?"

"Yes, I was hired online to clean once every other week. Today is the first scheduled date," she said in a voice just above a whisper.

Michael swallowed and glanced past her to the quiet hall outside. "Look, I don't know if this is a prank or something but, unfortunately, I didn't hire you."

The cleaning woman pulled out her phone and showed the screen to Michael. "See? Right here. Every other week starting today."

Michael went scarlet again, this time with embarrassment.

"My mom hired you," he said slowly, his hands creeping over his face in a desperate attempt to mask his shame. "God. You know how moms can be. They're impossible. I am so sorry she sent you all the way over here. Give me a minute, and I'll call her and straighten this out."

He turned to retrieve his phone, but felt a callused hand touch his arm.

"Please don't," she whispered.

"It was just a little messy the last time they came. I told her I'd clean it up myself. I can't have a cleaning service at college, it's just too embarrassing." Michael found himself still staring at the petite hand resting on his arm. Moist heat radiated through his skin.

"Please, I really need the work."

"What do you mean? The school has all sorts of jobs for students who want to work, and they're all better than cleaning our wreck of an apartment."

After a pause: "I'm not a student."

"Oh … I'm sorry, I just sort of assumed, being that you're so … young," Michael finished, trying to get things back on track.

"That's okay. I just really need the work, and you—I mean, your parents—pre-paid, so I'll have to return the money if you cancel." Her voice had a slight waver to it that had been missing before. She gazed up at him with those big brown eyes, and he felt himself disappearing into them. "Please don't cancel."

"No, no, of course not," Michael stammered, grinning lamely, "I wouldn't dream of it. Only—do you think you could give me, ah, your schedule or whatnot? You know, of the times you're going to come and clean, I mean. I want to make sure I'm here to watch you. I don't mean that I need to *watch* you, like you're going to steal or something. I trust you; I mean, I just want to know when you're coming so I can let you in and so I can talk to you, and see you, and let you in …" Michael ground unsteadily to a halt. *Oh, that was—that was bad, really bad.*

But she only smiled. "Okay."

"Great. I mean, yeah—great. Come in."

Michael ushered her inside and cringed inwardly at the state of the apartment. The front room was littered with cans and fast-food wrappers, and a pair of Len's boxers hung from a kayak propped up in the corner.

"Now, that is, how you say, piece of ass!" Len called from the sofa, bobbing and weaving over his controller.

Michael, flushing red, strode toward him and slapped the controller out of Len's hands. He tore his headphones off and tossed them on the couch.

"Hey, what wrong?!"

"Apologize," Michael commanded, pointing at the cleaning woman still standing at the door.

Len gaped. "Is it wrong to tell woman her ass nice?"

"Apologize," Michael demanded again.

"Yes, of course …" In his best English accent, Len said, "My dear woman, please excuse my brutish vulgarity. I will forever be in your service should you forgive me." He gave her a deep bow and held it, waiting for a response.

"I forgive you," she said quickly and, as if nothing had happened, Len put his headphones back on, picked up the controller, and reentered his game.

Michael mouthed his apologies and hurried to help the woman with her supplies. As he placed the last bag on the kitchen table, an awkward silence took over.

"So, um, I just have a paper I'm working on, so I'll be set up here if you need me," he said, cringing inwardly when he saw she was already surveying the apartment. "So, what else do you do if you don't go to school?"

She looked back at him, her tan face unreadable. "I clean and take care of my grandmother."

"That's nice." Not knowing what to really say beyond that, Michael tried to turn his attention away from the attractive woman preparing to clean his apartment and back to his robotics paper.

An hour later, he got to a stopping point and looked up from his screen. Len was still on the edge of the coach, yelling at his game, but something was different. Michael could see through the windows; the carpet looked new; the walls looked *brighter* somehow; and, best of all, there were no empty boxes or wrappers lying around. While he'd been focused on his paper, the cleaning woman had spun a web of cleanliness around him.

Len walked into the kitchenette. "My team is strong, but we can use you. Is paper done?" he said as he poked his head in the fridge. "Clean in here! I like new woman."

"I know. She's magic."

"Woman, woman, where are you …" Len called into the apartment, and the cleaning woman quickly scurried from the bathroom into the kitchenette.

"We will keep you; Mike here says you have magic," he said, straight-faced.

"Oh, thank you, sir."

"You stop now. Have drink. Take break. Would you like Lifio? I have."

"Oh, I couldn't."

"Why not? Take break. Have drink, you deserve," Len said, and downed a can of Lifio. Grinning, he tossed it at the garbage container, missing it by a wide margin.

The woman zipped over, picked the can up, and deposited it in the trash before Michael could stop her. Len just smiled.

"I like," he said. "Here. Come. Drink with us." He waved an unopened Lifio can he'd brought from the fridge.

"I-I ..."

"What's wrong?" asked Michael.

"I've never had it ... and, well ... it's illegal now," she said, her voice almost a whisper.

"Never try Lifio?" Len said, amazed. He glanced at Michael. "How is that even possible?"

She looked away, blushing slightly. "My grandmother, MeMa, says Lifio isn't natural and that we shouldn't drink it."

"Yes, old women always scared. What do parents say?" Len asked.

"I don't have any parents. Just MeMa."

"Nice, Len, real nice," Michael said. "Go back to your game, would ya?"

"No problem." Len tossed the can to the cleaning woman before heading back into the TV room.

"I have always wanted to try it," she said to Michael after catching the can, "but it was always so expensive, and then it went away."

"Well, why don't you try it now?" Michael suggested.

After taking a moment to consider it, she answered, "All right ... but only if you'll have some with me."

"Oh, I've had it before."

"I'd just feel better if you did it with me; would that be okay?" she said, making eye contact.

After losing himself in her stare for entirely too long, he replied with a slow nod of acceptance. He then snatched up two of his now-many clean glasses, opened the can, and poured.

"Cheers," they said in unison as they clinked glasses.

They drank and, glancing up at Michael, the woman frowned.

"What's wrong? What is it?" Michael asked.

"It's just ... disappointing is all."

"Oh yeah, I almost forgot. It doesn't taste like much, but it's not about how it tastes; it's about how it makes you feel. Give it some time and see how you feel when you wake up tomorrow."

After exchanging schedules and setting up a time for the next cleaning, Michael and his new cleaner were ready to say goodbye.

"Well, thank you for coming by," Michael said.

"My pleasure, and thank you for the refreshment," she said.

As though not knowing what to do next, she turned away and, with the click of the door, she was gone just as abruptly as she had arrived.

After a moment of reflection, Michael jumped to life as if reanimated, burst out the door, and called out to her as she entered the elevator.

"Wait, wait! What's your name?"

She caught his eye and smiled. "Ana," she said.

The doors slid closed.

CHAPTER 7
SLAP AND SOLUTIONS

Alex abruptly woke up in a cold sweat, a hot pain burning in his chest. He rolled off his side and felt a tingling sensation up and down his right arm. A moment later, he was heaving into his feather duvet, trying to catch his breath. Next to him, his wife slept on. Images of his own funeral flashed through his head, and he banged his fist against the mattress.

As he desperately pounded the blankets, Helen murmured, "What's the matter? Go back to sleep." And then she was gone, having drifted back out of consciousness.

With all of his energy, Alex held his breath, raised both of his arms above his head, and threw himself at Helen.

"I was sleeping!" she shrieked, sitting up and turning on the lights. Her frown twisted when she saw the panic in Alex's bloodshot eyes, and she jerked, slapping him across the face. Then she grabbed him. "What's wrong? Tell me. What's happening?"

"My arm tingles all over, and my chest is burning," he managed, the flame-red handprint radiating across his face.

"Calm down. Breathe with me," Helen said soothingly, taking her husband into her arms and rocking him like a child. She pulled away, rubbing his right arm gently. "Did you fall asleep with your arm under your head again?"

As she said the words, Alex knew that he had. She pulled two antacids from her nightstand, pressed them into his palm, handed him a glass of water, and gestured for him to chew and swallow. As his breath returned to normal and the pain in his

45

chest subsided, Helen explained, "Darling, you're not dying. You had a panic attack."

"Oh, thank God." He sighed.

"Panic attacks aren't good, you know!"

Alex rubbed his eyes and sank back into his pillow. It was still dark; maybe four or five in the morning. Dull yellow light from the streetlamps outside leaked through the curtains, casting eerie shadows on the ceiling. "I know," he said slowly, "but a minute ago, I thought I was dying, so you're gonna have to give me a break here, hon."

"I'll give you a break tonight, but you're going to stop drinking red wine after dinner, mister," Helen replied, already settling back into bed.

With a mutter of acceptance, Alex too closed his eyes. It had taken the couple until the wee hours of the morning to fall asleep in the first place; they'd been up for hours debating tactics for the board meeting the next day. With the company's only product, Lifio, being blocked from the US market by the FDA, they needed a plan. Even Stefán, that old recluse, was flying in from Reykjavik.

The man's unreadable face filled Alex's mind.

* * *

From Alex's vantage point, he could see most of Manhattan, its towers glittering in the low sun out beyond the Hudson River. The board of directors had gathered, and he took a moment for himself before calling the most important meeting of his life to order.

"Colleagues, friends, partners," he said finally, turning to address the room and winking at Helen, "our company, Stallson Beverage, is at a crossroads. I have the greatest admiration and trust possible for everyone in this room, and there is no one else I would prefer to have with me as we face this crisis. The FDA has pulled our one and only product from the domestic market. Without immediate and decisive action, our company will die."

He paused, letting his words sink in, and glanced from face to face.

"However, we will not fail, because I will not let us. Before today is through, we will have a detailed plan of action to resurrect our company! Now, let's get down to business. Helen, if you would be so kind, what is our cash position?"

Helen cleared her throat. "Thank you, Alex. At our current burn rate, we have enough cash on hand to give us twelve months of runway. However, if you will turn to page eight of the report in front of you, I have illustrated how we can extend that by fifteen additional months by laying off sales and marketing, refinancing short-term debt, and leasing out our US bottling plant and distribution facilities."

Don Briggs, a heavy-set man who looked perpetually tired, leaned forward. "With all due respect, Helen," he said, voice harsh from the pack of cigarettes he smoked each day, "what's the point? Why prolong the inevitable? I mean, how do we generate revenue without sales, marketing, bottling, or distribution?"

"Don does have a point," said Mike Smith, EVP of sales and non-voting board member. "If we had diversified, as I've been suggesting for the last six months, we would have had another revenue stream. We should have leveraged Lifio's demand to get shelf space for other beverage products."

Alex took a step toward the boardroom table. "Mike," he said slowly, "if we start infighting and saying I told you so, we're not going to accomplish anything today. You were right; we should have diversified. But we are where we are today, so let's stay constructive and come up with a solution we can move forward with."

"Okay," Mike said, leaning back in his chair, apparently satisfied. "So, Helen says we have at least twelve months. It's cutting it close, but shouldn't we be able to launch a new product in that time frame?"

"Unfortunately," replied Helen, "it doesn't work that way, Mike. Bringing a new product to market will accelerate our cash burn as we fund the process. Current cash on hand would only allow for about three months of operation. We just raised capital with an IPO, and with our very public standoff with the FDA, no financial institution will be willing to invest new capital. Getting the banks to refinance our short-term debt has already proven to be inordinately difficult. Don't be naïve; blood is in the water, and creditors want to be the first, not last, to collect. Alex and I have run the numbers through every conceivable scenario. Take a look at pages sixty-three to eighty-seven. There is no way to launch a new product without selling major assets or laying off most of the company."

"Alex, I thought you said we needed to stay positive here," said Mike, flashing his signature smug grin.

"I did, Mike, but we need to balance staying positive with being realistic."

"What about pressuring our political allies to put the screws to the FDA?" offered Don. "I mean, surely the American people are with us on this one. The FDA pulled Lifio without an explanation, even to us."

To this, Mike added, "I don't know anyone who's happy about this. There were even riots in the streets when they pulled Lifio. Maybe Don is right and we should go political—attack this from a marketing angle."

Alex nodded, his hands clasped behind his back. "That is definitely an option and one I don't want to shoot down, but it's far from foolproof. Last time I checked, President Williamson was a bleeding heart. She's always going to take the side of government over business, so we won't have any help from the top. And while she is up for reelection this fall, we don't have the deep pockets we need to make the necessary donations to get the Republican Party's ear, so we'd be largely hoping things go our way—and hoping, gentlemen, is not a strategy I endorse. With our cash flow issues, we can't afford to play the long game in this situation. We need to develop an initiative we can control from start to finish so as not to depend on someone else to save our ass."

"If we want to take matters into our own hands and we cannot create a new product, what can we do to get the FDA to approve Lifio officially?" asked Don.

"I'll take that one, Alex," replied Phil Kline, general counsel. "We've formally requested a written explanation from the FDA. In addition, we have filed a direct appeal of the FDA's decision with the executive branch. Once we have a formal response from the FDA, we will file a lawsuit in federal court." His all-white smile faltered. "Unfortunately, our cash will run out before we will be able to advance a case through the entire legal process."

The room fell silent. Alex, his panic mounting, glanced at the Icelandic inventor, who was staring out the window at the city below. "Stefán," he said, "you've been quiet. What are you in favor of? Any chance you have a new product you've failed to tell us about that's ready for release?"

A few chuckles rose from those gathered.

"We could sell my original formula," Stefán deadpanned.

Alex frowned, waiting for the punchline. He'd spent years with the man, but still could not read him. He was a real chameleon, a nobody, really: his short brown hair, average build, and everyman features meant he often seemed to fade from view.

Alex smiled. "So, for those of you who have not had the honor of tasting the original, let me tell you that he's joking. It tasted like water from a dirty fish tank. I'm confident in our team, Stefán, but not that confident. Any brighter ideas?"

"We could sell it in Iceland."

"Stefán, with all due respect, this is serious," said Mike, shaking his head. "We employ close to a thousand people and have a fiscal responsibility to our shareholders, and there are more of them than there are people in the entirety of Iceland."

"We have more than 360,000 shareholders?" Stefán said, and the room was silent.

"Stefán is right," Alex finally said.

"What?" Mike, Don, and Helen replied in unison.

"Not about Iceland, but about international sales." He grinned and rushed to the board table, where he crouched low, pale eyes gleaming. "The FDA only holds jurisdiction over the domestic market, right? Well, we produce concentrate in Iceland. Because we own our own bottling and distribution facilities in the US, we have always forced our international orders to flow through our US facilities. If, however, we take Helen's idea to lease out our US distribution and bottling facilities, we can inject capital while relieving ourselves of FDA jurisdiction by ceasing US operations. If we produce concentrate in Iceland and ship *directly to* other countries without touching the US, the FDA should lose control over us. I highly doubt that the EU will go against the FDA, but there are 195 countries in the world—surely we can sell to some of them."

"That's not bad," Mike said slowly, seeming to mull the plan over in his head. "I'm certain some clients will be willing to buy concentrate, bottle, and distribute themselves, especially in China and India. Those emerging markets represent enormous opportunity. If this is viable, I will have feet on the ground in markets around the world immediately."

All eyes turned to Phil, who was sitting quietly, his face unreadable.

"What do you think Phil," Alex asked, "can you defend us in court if the FDA attempts to claim jurisdiction?"

For a long moment, Phil didn't say anything. "Well," he said at last, "provided that *one hundred percent* of production takes place offshore and that we set up a satellite office to handle all administration for international sales in a friendly international country, I can defend it. At the very least, a jurisdiction battle with the FDA will take years to move through the courts."

"That's as good of an endorsement as I could expect from counsel! Does anyone have another solution?"

There was a long pause. Those gathered around the sunny boardroom glanced at one another, waiting for a comment or criticism that would send the whole plan spiraling down.

"Okay then. Right, Helen, rerun simulations with proper international freight and tariff costs and give Mike an analysis on how to price concentrate. Phil, continue pursuing legal action against the FDA to try and reopen the US. I'd like to see us have product on international shelves in sixty days. Do all members of the board agree with our plan of action?"

All members of the board raised their hands enthusiastically. All but Stefán.

"We'll be on shelves in Iceland, correct?" he said.

"Yes, Stefán."

Murmuring something to himself, Stefán raised his hand.

The board filed out, and Alex caught up with Stefán down the hall. "It's good to see you, my friend," he said, placing his hand on the smaller man's shoulder and squeezing.

Stefán stared at the hand until Alex removed it. "It's nice to see you as well," he said.

Alex gave an invincible grin. "Helen and I were planning to have dinner at Smith and Wollensky's. Care to join us?"

"Most unfortunate, but I have a flight in just a few hours. Perhaps the next time you are in Reykjavik." Stefán's brown eyes were expressionless.

"Okay, raincheck," Alex said. "Safe travels, and I'll be in touch soon."

Waving back at Stefán, Alex hurried after Helen. "Helen, I need a word," he said, and steered Helen into his office. He quickly locked the door, closed the blinds, and attacked his blonde bombshell of a wife. He slid the black skirt up her slender frame and his pants bulged as he glimpsed beneath.

"Good boy," she said, hopping on his desk and pushing him down onto his knees.

CHAPTER 8

A VOTE FOR LIFIO

President Williamson paged through the day's intelligence briefing once more as the sun began to set outside the Oval Office. The preceding months had been more difficult than she thought they should have been, but her years in politics had taught her to expect the unexpected, and she'd taken it all in her stride by forcing herself to focus purely on what she could control. While the country's commercial and political entities stood at a standstill, embroiled in a debate over Lifio, the remaining responsibilities of her office had not subsided. In the early evenings, she found respite by taking her dinner in the Oval Office and enjoying something like peace and quiet while she worked. Her staff had the courtesy to pretend that she spent her private dinner hours with her family.

Four, or possibly eight, years of never-ending stress and work had never fazed her. The president and her family had understood the sacrifice they'd been making when she'd run for office, and they stood as resolute and determined as ever. That did not take away from the pain she felt at so rarely seeing her children and husband, who lived in the White House with her but in what seemed like a different dimension. She remained acutely aware of the costs being accrued, but the gravity of those sacrifices only served to compound her resolve to do absolutely everything in her power to leave her country in a better position than when she'd assumed the presidency. She'd come to the office with bold and inspired plans, and did not intend to leave without accomplishing them.

Tucker, the president's chief of staff, burst into the Oval Office. "Madam President, you have to see this."

He guided her to the viewing room, where the ninth and final Republican primary debate raged on national television. "Go back to what we just saw: the opening remarks from Senator Givens," he barked at an assistant, who scrambled to grab a remote control and rewind.

"Tucker," Williamson said, massaging her temple. "I have precious little time to myself each evening. Must I really spend it watching a primary debate?"

"Madam President, I would not have brought you if it weren't important. Senator Givens made some statements you'll want to hear."

"So? I'll catch up during my morning briefing."

"Please, Madam President, just one moment." Tucker shifted his attention to the assistant. "There, that's it."

On screen, Senator Givens—a smiling man in his sixties, with thick gray hair—stood upon a spotlit stage, waving at an invisible crowd. "First," he said, and the applause died down, "I would like to thank the network for hosting this debate, my wife and children for putting up with my frequent travel, and the American people for supporting my run for the presidency."

Cheering erupted, but Givens waved the audience silent.

"While I remain inspired by the American dream, I cannot help but fear for our great country's future. President Williamson has stood by her political cronies and elitist friends for months while countless Americans have died due to her decisions. In only one term in office, she is single-handedly responsible for America becoming a second-tier nation. It pains me to say it, but no longer can the United States of America be counted on to lead the world's countries forward."

Deathly silence.

That's a bit dramatic, don't you think, Chuck? the president thought. She had always known Senator Charles Givens, or Chuck, to be a more of a butter knife to her saber. Tonight, however, someone had clearly spent considerable time preparing him. In his first seconds on camera, he'd called her an elitist and a killer of the American dream who'd turned the United States into a second-tier nation. Shots had certainly been fired.

"President Williamson, with her fanatical regulations, has crippled Stallson Beverage, an American company, by removing Lifio from American shelves. In that time, China and Russia have raced ahead of our once-great nation to fill the leadership void that President Williamson created. Lifio has proven, without a shadow of a doubt, to increase human lifespans and cure human ills. What kind of president would willingly withhold a life-improving and, as some would say—heck, *I* would say—life*saving* drink from her own people while other countries, our friends and enemies alike, reap the benefits of an *American product?* Why, I ask you, are Americans being made to wait?"

The crowd erupted, coarse shouts and exclamations rising above the tide of applause. Williamson swallowed. This was not good.

Givens, as if sensing his momentum, leaned over the podium and gazed out at his audience. "And all of this without *any* shred of evidence to explain why her FDA pulled Lifio off of American shelves. When my colleagues—both to my left and my right, may I add—called for greater transparency, I stayed silent. I wanted to understand; to complete my own research that I could in turn communicate to you, the American people. I have done my homework; I've met with FDA officials in confidence and read every single published study. I've spoken with foreign leaders and even consumed Lifio myself, and you know what? I'm still here. There is nothing dangerous about Lifio."

Cameras flashed; isolated cries of approval split the scene. Givens was staring now, face alive with staccato camera light, bright eyes cutting into the darkened auditorium.

"I want to say that *clearly* and on the record," he said. "There is *nothing* dangerous about Lifio."

The cheers began to rise again, but he pushed on: "The FDA pulled Lifio off the market at the order of President Williamson! Due to lack of evidence, I am forced to assume she has done so for *political gain!*"

Met with officials in confidence, my ass, thought the president. *Who does Chuck think he's kidding here? By his rationale, if he drinks it and feels fine, it's safe for public consumption.*

She spun to Tucker. "How is he doing in the polls?"

"High single digits before tonight, but after this display ... I don't know. He's been generally underwhelming until now."

Williamson sighed. "I have to say, I didn't think Chuck had it in him. He didn't strike me as shrewd enough to make a move like this."

Back on the TV, the debate moderator, looking affronted, asked, "Senator Givens, how would removing Lifio from American shelves possibly help President Williamson politically? Surely you have seen her current approval rating."

Let's see how he handles this one. Come on, Chuck.

But Givens didn't skip a beat. "Her strategy is as clear as day," he said. "Today's polls are not what matter; public opinion on election day is what matters. I believe President Williamson will officially declare Lifio safe for public consumption right before the election, and then play the hero by fixing the problem she created!"

President Williamson looked turned to her assembled staff. Everyone appeared to be studying the wallpaper and ceiling tiles intently. Finally, she asked no one in particular, "Really? Do you really think the American people are going to buy that?"

And with that, the already well-studied wallpaper got considerably more interesting.

She'd found that the closer election day got, the more her staff tended to blow situations exponentially out of proportion. While

Senator Givens's talking points were baseless and despicable, a part of her admired the calculated political gamble; he had, after all, successfully eliminated a possible route she could have taken to put this Lifio situation to bed. If Dr. Roberts at the FDA proved to be wrong and she was able to release Lifio back onto the market, she'd no longer be able to rely on the lift in her approval rating. The only positive outcome for her reelection prospects at this point involved finding and releasing evidence that Lifio caused harm, which would reinforce her decision to pull the product from the shelves.

Unfortunately, Melanie had yet to provide scientific proof that gene editing took place or that Lifio caused any negative side effects. Williamson had warned her that she could only hold off telling the American people what was happening for so long. Without proof, how could she remain silent? Worse, how could she continue to keep the product off the shelves?

There was always the option of re-releasing Lifio back onto the market, but then, if it was later found to be harmful and needed to be pulled again, it would all but kill her campaign. She kept replaying Carrie Roberts's hypothesis over and over in her head: *CRISPR technology to mutate DNA.* That did not sound good. Williamson wondered wearily whether Roberts had meant permanently or temporarily following consumption. She had an ever-growing list of questions and few answers.

If Senator Givens planned to take the stance that Lifio was one hundred percent safe, she needed to arm herself with more information. She needed to go and see Melanie in person and shake her for some real answers.

Tucker cleared his throat. "Watch this last part of Givens's diatribe. Nancy, put it on."

Nancy, a young and nervous aide, fast-forwarded to the end of Givens's introduction and pushed play.

"I pledge, if elected president of the United States of America, to immediately remove the FDA ban on the sale and production of Lifio. I will restore our great nation's health, reclaim America's leadership, and bring a great American company home. A vote for Charles Givens is a vote for Lifio!"

The raucous crowd's reaction quickly developed into a standing ovation.

Oh, that's rich. Easy to say you'd pull back the FDA ban when you don't have all the information.

The recording ended, and the room fell silent. Tucker was looking at her, brow furrowed, clearly waiting for her response.

Williamson swallowed her doubt. "Tucker," she said curtly, "call Melanie at the FDA. Tell her I need to see her and Carrie Roberts immediately. And get me everything you can on Senator Givens. I'm going to need all the ammunition I can get."

CHAPTER 9

THE GALA

On an unseasonably hot late-summer evening, the red carpet at 30 Rockefeller Plaza pulsed with excitement. Tonight, the Rainbow Room would be filled with the most powerful and influential people from Manhattan to Washington, DC. An invitation to the gala—hosted by the current darlings of Wall Street, Alex and Helen Stallan of Stallson Beverage—confirmed status and power, and the events stood as the most important on New York's social calendar. As proud guests arrived in limousines, paparazzi swarmed and jostled for photographs. Feeding off each other, the guests and crowds roiled and mingled until a great electrical current fizzed in the atmosphere. Opportunity and money scented the air like the cloud of expensive perfume rising above the warm city streets.

Alex and Helen Stallan floated around the gala, each feeling invincible and alive. Alex wore an expertly fitted Italian tuxedo, while Helen wore a slender, one-of-a-kind golden dress she had received a week earlier while backstage at a designer runway show in Paris. Stallson Beverage was the talk of Manhattan, and all of the city's socialites were in attendance, looking for a chance to rub shoulders with company executives. Supporting Senator Charles Givens's bid for the presidency was, for many, an afterthought.

Alex, striding through the fawning crowds, winked at David, an oil-slick Wall Street broker he knew from his days in private equity.

"Alex, you smug bastard!" the man exclaimed.

"David, Tom, Will—how are you, fellas? And how the hell did you get in here? Security!" Alex beckoned with his arm, grinning ear to ear.

"Alex, I have to hand it to you, when you told me about the IPO, I thought you were stark raving mad. I mean, the beverage industry? But damn, you proved me wrong!"

"Not the first, eh Tom?" Alex said, and Tom gave a hearty but not entirely convincing laugh.

"Will here was just telling us he's thinking of putting in an offer for an expansion franchise in the NFL or NBA, weren't you, Will?" Tom said.

Alex smiled inwardly. How very like Tom to wriggle away from the firing line.

"Right," Will said, watery eyes flickering in the low light, "I was telling these fellas here that the NFL wants a two-billion-dollar franchise fee, while the NBA wants one and a half." His chubby face split into a sheepish grin. "But I really like football."

"Choices, choices," Tom said.

"You know I'll buy your stock if you need to raise some cash," Alex said, raising an eyebrow.

"Who the hell are you kidding? I'm not selling this rocket ship. Our stock price has risen every day for what, thirty-four—"

"Thirty-seven days actually," David broke in, and, at once, all four of them began smirking at one another, thin lips curling.

"Well all right boys, I'm voting NFL, and I want season tickets. You hear me, Will?" Alex said. "I'll see you all later."

As Alex made his way around the room, conversations turned to the secondary and tertiary impacts of Lifio on the markets. Arguments raged over the impact of improved health and longer lifespans on the healthcare and insurance industries. Would luxury brands wax or wane as elite billionaires lived on for centuries? Would those longer lives deplete or build wealth?

How would governments around the world handle entitlements such as healthcare and social security? And, in turn, how would that impact the private sector?

Around the bar, a group of surgeons and pharmaceutical executives shared Lifio success stories with Helen. Alex overheard one female surgeon reenact how an eighty-year-old patient suffering from renal failure had used Lifio for a few months and returned to her office with completely clear scans. Convinced the scans were incorrect, the surgeon had reordered them, only to be astonished when her patient kept producing scans that looked like they'd come from a thirty-year-old. The previously scarred bladder and kinked ureter had miraculously been repaired, and there'd no longer been any signs of kidney failure. Her patient came off dialysis and never returned for a follow-up appointment.

As the story concluded, others in the group nodded their agreement, some chiming in their own unbelievable accounts of recovery and growth. Alex stood silently nearby, listening, but stepped forward when the latest speaker—an elderly pediatrician—finished his own rambling and dull story.

"Oh, Alex! Great to see you. I was just telling Helen here about my seventy-three-year-old patient who needed a knee replacement."

"Yeah?"

"You won't believe it; the lucky bastard called my office to let me know he'd walked five miles and canceled his next cortisone shot. Seventy-three; you believe that?"

"Wonderful story, Bob, really inspiring," Helen said hurriedly, "now just make sure you tell the press and our wonderful colleagues over at the FDA." She took a sip from her glass of Lifio.

Alex and Helen had pushed their attorneys hard, but had finally gotten them to agree to Lifio's presence at the gala—served, so went the compromise, in unmarked glasses so as to avoid an inappropriate photograph leak. However, everyone knew, and the blatant disregard for the FDA only added to the excitement and rebellious spirit of the night.

Alex nudged his wife and pointed with his eyes to the next group over, where Mike and his wife Meme were entertaining a large gathering with exaggerated swashbuckling tales of selling Lifio around the world. The most fantastic tale involved Mike taking raw diamonds as payment for containers of Lifio delivered to warlords in remote African ports. Alex snorted; yes, he let Mike travel, and even allowed him to bring Meme on occasion, but he would never have let him risk his life selling to warlords. And uncut diamonds? Well, that sounded like a Meme embellishment.

Alex let Mike and Meme have their fun. He enjoyed the ride in a certain way, but Helen, he knew, had far less patience; even now, she was staring at Stallson's executive vice president of sales with daggers in her eyes. She claimed she couldn't stand liars, but Alex knew jealousy ate at her because of all the attention Meme got. Helen did not like to be outdone; she was the queen, and she wanted everyone to know it. Unfortunately for both Helen and Alex, Meme refused to accept Helen's version of reality.

Helen, straightening and putting on her most winning smile, tapped her crystal glass, and the room gradually stilled.

"Good evening. Alex and I would like to welcome you to the inaugural Stallan Super PAC Gala. We've gathered here tonight to enjoy our success, but also to ensure its continuation! Today, America is in *peril!* As you all are aware, Lifio, the largest health-improvement breakthrough in recorded history, is no longer available to the American people. It is being held hostage from our country by unnecessary regulation for political gain."

The room burst into murmurs. "Hear! Hear!" someone shouted.

Helen stretched her hands out. "*Finally*, a politician has the fortitude and gumption to take a stand against our rogue president. Please give a warm round of applause for the next president of the United States, Senator Charles Givens!"

Before she'd even finished, the people gathered had turned from dignified conservatives into raucous, crazed fanatics, many of them whooping and yelling.

Senator Givens emerged from the passionate crowd and embraced Helen. He turned to the gathered guests. "Helen and Alex, you do me a great honor with your show of support. Ladies, gentlemen, supporters, and dissenters, I am afraid that what Helen has said is true. Our nation is in peril. The road President Williamson has taken us down, purely for political gain, is treasonous and has threatened to put our great country behind the rest of the world. In the coming months, I will engage the American people as the Republican nominee for president. *Now*, in this time of *peril*, is when I need your support the most. I will uphold my pledge to the American people to put an end to the farce of a regulatory body that is the current FDA and, on my first day in office, I will approve Lifio to legally reenter the US market."

Givens tried to continue, but the now frothing crowd began yelling and then chanting, *"Elect Givens! Elect Givens!"*

When the crowd finally quieted enough for Helen to be heard, she patted Senator Givens's shoulder and, with her hand resting on his back, addressed the crowd. "As you can all tell, soon-to-be President Givens needs our support! He is a friend of Stallson Beverage, Alex and me, and all of you. So dig deep tonight. Outdo one another, as I know you can, and make a donation commitment that you can be proud of."

As Helen finished, Alex stepped forward. "Ladies and gentlemen," he said, peering over the thousand gleaming eyes stretched before him, "Helen and I believe in the cause; so much so, in fact, that we are prepared to personally donate *one hundred million dollars* to the Stallan Super PAC!"

With that, gold confetti and balloons fell from the ballroom ceilings and the crowd roared. Grown men and women howled at the jeweled chandeliers and a hundred bottles of Champagne burst open at once, jets of liquid shooting skyward, music rising above the swell.

Alex, smiling to himself, turned away, his wife at his side.

CHAPTER 10

LIVING THE LIFE

Six months removed from possible ruin, Alex and Helen found themselves at a weekend retreat in the Hamptons with the Stallson executive team. As Helen affixed a jeweled bracelet around her wrist, she glanced back at her husband and winked. "Same old bracelet. How come you never buy me anything nice?"

"I just bought you this house for thirty-four million!" he retorted.

"That was *our* money, darling; it doesn't count. Why don't you buy me diamonds, like Mike always does for Meme?"

Alex scowled. Mike, he knew, had just pulled down a ten-million-dollar commission for the last quarter after record-breaking sales. "How about a Lamborghini?" he said, forcing a smile. "You buy yourself enough diamonds, and at least we can see the Lambo instead of putting it in a jewelry box."

"There you go, being cheap again. What's a Lambo, half a mil? Come on, babe. Surely I'm worth more than that?"

Before Alex could respond, Helen's smile softened. "It's really unbelievable, isn't it? Six months ago, we were dead in the water. Now we have more money than we know what to do with."

"Well, I don't know about that," Alex said with a smile. "Seems to me you have no problem figuring out what to do with our money."

The success the Lifio product had brought to Stallson Beverage company shareholders, employees, and executives ensured the coming gathering would be as lavish as any in

65

America, and Alex was sure each of his executives would be jostling to outdo one another. Alex enjoyed winning, and felt secure in the knowledge that it was *his* shooting star the attending group had latched onto—he just needed to make sure that they didn't forget it.

"Come on," Alex said, and led his wife wordlessly from their room down into the broad reception hall.

Drinks were already flowing, and a ragged cheer rose as he entered. The room reeked of bluster and bravado, and Alex grinned—things were about to get interesting. From group to group, Alex listened incredulously to stories of African safaris, private jets, space tourism, island buying, and secret chateaus.

He stayed quiet himself, reveling inwardly in the fact that Wall Street had never seen a company take a market leadership position, falter, and then regain market leadership, all while giving the federal government a black eye. With complete market dominance, unheard-of profit margins, and not a single viable competitor, Alex had the world in the palm of his hand. Share price had not dropped for a single day over the preceding quarter.

Even the meek Stefán, normally nervous in his own skin, seemed to be enjoying himself. He was floating around the room, inspecting Helen's art.

"Stefán!" Alex called, "how about that view?"

The scientist turned to appraise him. "Fascinating," he said flatly.

"It is, isn't it? The wild Atlantic in all its glory." Both men stared out the floor-to-ceiling windows at the expansive view.

"You're not still upset I hired Phillip, are you?" Alex asked.

"No, I've made that clear," Stefán said, like a father to a nervous son.

"Good, because his marketing strategy made you a very rich man."

"I'm aware. But I wonder, Alex, at what cost? Share dilution cost me money as well. Now we'll never know if it's the product or the marketing, will we?"

"Perhaps we could have gotten there without offering stock options to influencers around the world to champion our product—if we'd had ten, maybe fifteen years," Alex said, "but I got it done in less than a year. Stefán, no one pays attention to scientists writing gobbledygook in journals. Every athlete and celebrity worth a damn is a stockholder in our little enterprise, and the public pressure on the US and EU to give us access to their markets couldn't be greater. It's all because we hired Phillip to do a little marketing." With that, Alex clinked his glass into Stefán's and departed before a retort could be mustered.

He stopped mid-stride, mouth falling open. Mike had just stridden through the open door with his wife, Meme, to audible gasps. Padding beside Meme at knee height was a Siberian tiger cub, its collar and leash encrusted with shimmering diamonds.

Helen elbowed Alex in the ribs. "See, he works for us, and look at what he got his wife!"

"You don't know where they got that," Alex whispered. Forcing a grin, he strode toward his vice president of sales, raising his arms in welcome. "Mike! Meme! So good to see you. And who is this precious cat?"

His greeting finally broke the silence sparked by Mike and Meme's entrance, and the celebration resumed, though all eyes remained fixed on Meme's tiger. For her part, Meme posed and pouted, clearly reveling in the delicious attention. Alex could almost feel the heat rising from his wife's cheeks.

"Oh, this little tiger?" Meme said with a wink. "We named her Sheba. Isn't that right, Mikey?"

Mike and Meme had married after an intense and feverish courtship that had taken place while Mike had been in China, negotiating the Lifio contract with a local distributor. Meme, an Asian firecracker in her late twenties, stood more than a foot shorter than Mike, but what she lacked in stature, she made up for in panache. Her exuberant personality, coupled with her petite, tight torso framed by long jet-black hair, captivated Alex when he was in her presence. Tonight, she wore a white and gold sequined dress dripping with diamond-studded everything.

"Whatever you say, Memes," Mike replied.

"Sheba is a pure Siberian tiger," said Meme. "She was a gift from Alexander Petrovsky. He gave her to me when we were in Russia to celebrate our success. Isn't she just to die for?"

"Aren't Siberian tigers endangered?" Helen asked, wearing her disgust openly.

"Petro says there are only a few hundred of these gorgeous kitties left. That's why he gave us one. No one would treat you better than Mommy Meme, isn't that right, smuchkin?" Meme knelt next to Sheba and nuzzled the cat to her bosom.

Helen excused herself, saying, "Wonderful to see you two, but I need to tend to my guests." She promptly got as far away from Meme as she could.

"Speaking of which, Mike, did you ask Alexander about our issue with the Kremlin?" Alex said in a low voice.

"Yeah, he said no problem. They will be eager to oppose the United States' position publicly, provided we provide reports proving Lifio's efficacy and the lack of negative side effects. Needless to say, I've already done it," Mike said.

"Excellent. Wait—what are you smiling about?"

Mike winked and leaned in closer. "There's more, Alex. Israel still won't allow us to ship bulk into the country, but they've agreed to allow international shipments to go directly to consumers. And Africa is breaking wide open—I came to terms with a national distributor in Algeria after our friends in Russia put in a good word with their military contacts."

"That's why I love you," Alex said, grabbing Mike by the shoulder and pulling him in tight.

"You do realize that China and Russia are wielding the immense power of their state-controlled media outlets to promote Lifio merely to destabilize US international influence and line their politicians' pockets with stock options?" came a voice from behind Alex.

Mike jumped out of his skin. "Hey, Stefán!" He blushed, straightening. "Where did you come from?"

But Stefán had already drifted away.

"I don't know why the hell he cares when he loves Iceland so damn much," Alex said, eyeing his retreating scientist darkly. "I don't care what they get out of the deal—so long as we keep rolling."

CHAPTER 11
STEEL SPEECH

A month—only a month to go before the polls opened. President Williamson massaged her temple and let her rising panic push back her crippling fatigue. She stared down at the stump speech on the desk in front of her. While she had once hoped her reelection would be a mere formality, the sudden rise of Republican Senator Givens had required her to put herself and her campaign into overdrive. To work her magic, she knew her speeches would have to be her own. She'd done it before, she told herself—had taken the country by storm only four years prior with impassioned orations and tireless campaigning.

Now, though, was different. Instead of the young world-changer, she was the stoic face of compromise. And while cooperation and compromise had served the country well, leading to unprecedented success in her first term, it often displeased her constituency, who saw her as too soft, and failed to win over her detractors, who saw her as a "flip-flopper."

Out of all the things that could take me down, I cannot believe it's an FDA ban on a single product. Most presidents struggle with wars, recessions, pollution ...

While rumors and conjectures swirled, Williamson had offered no data or official statements clearly explaining the situation. That shortcoming lay squarely on her shoulders, and she knew it. Now, after nine months, she had to address the issue head-on or risk her reelection bid. That was how high the stakes had become—all thanks to Senator Givens.

70

Weekly updates gave her confidence that Melanie had been holding the FDA together as best she could while Carrie worked around the clock to verify and document her accusations. She knew, though, that they were short-handed—employees had been leaving the FDA in droves in protest of how the agency's leadership had been handling the situation. This, of course, had resulted in endless data leaks, some false, some legitimate, and public commentators had been quick to spin conspiracy theories and jump to conclusions. Dr. Roberts had done a good job of making sure that the scientists and researchers working directly on the Lifio project were isolated from other agency employees, but still, speculation was rife.

As the election drew closer, Elizabeth's conversations with Melanie had begun to shift in tone. One particular exchange etched itself in her memory; Melanie had sounded even more harried than usual, and before she'd been able to reach her point, the voice of Carrie Roberts had butted in: "My staff is threatening mutiny! What am I supposed to do?!"

Elizabeth knew the research team had to regularly switch sites due to media pressure; as soon as administrative FDA staff realized that Lifio research was taking place in their building, they called the tabloids and sold out the team's location for a quick payday. By the end of the day, a group of rabid freelance photographers and reporters would be camped out front, waiting for anyone in a lab coat to exit the building. Moving labs every few weeks wasted time and unsettled researchers, further delaying their work, yet it remained necessary. *If they could just work in peace and quiet without external noise,* Williamson thought, *stress levels would not be so high.*

"Melanie," Williamson had said slowly, drumming her fingers against the desk, "put me on speakerphone and have Dr. Roberts tell me what the damn hell is going on."

There'd been a pause, and Williamson heard chairs being

shuffled around. Finally, Carrie said, "My research staff fears that if the upcoming election goes the wrong way, they will lose their jobs, and Lifio will be approved without anyone seeing what we have found."

"I agree."

Pause. "What?"

"I agree with your staff, Dr. Roberts, and that is why you need to finish your work. Now, what did you mean by 'mutiny'?"

"They claim that if we do not release the current research findings before the election takes place, they will leak the documents to the press themselves."

"Carrie," Melanie had said, "please give me the name of the researcher who said that and I will have them removed immediately."

"It's all of them! As I said, it's a *mutiny*."

"God damn it, Carrie, we've talked about this," Melanie barked.

"If I may chime in," came a male voice.

"Melanie," Williamson snapped, "who is that in your office?!"

"Oh, excuse me Madam President, my name is Sebastian Dougherty—"

"Okay, yes I know who you are," Elizabeth sank back in her chair. "Please, go on."

"Well, I was going to suggest that Carrie tell her staff that she agrees with their sentiment, if not their tactics, and have them put together a comprehensive report with all of their findings to give to you, Madam President. After all, you've been on our side for this long; you deserve the right to choose how we move forward. In my humble opinion."

"If we get them focused on building a comprehensive report, they'll feel heard. Perhaps they'll put down their pitchforks," Melanie chimed in.

"Okay," Elizabeth said.

"Okay?" Carrie said.

"You heard the president, Carrie, tell your staff to put a report together detailing what we know, and keep it under thirty pages. Tell them once it's ready, I'll release it to the president, who will decide how we move forward. That's the best we can do at this point," Melanie said firmly, and with that, the call had ended.

That had been a week ago. Now, the report was open on her desk. If what it said was true, the stakes were higher than ever. Williamson picked up her phone.

Speaking with Carrie was like talking to a computer, but Elizabeth had years of experience communicating with her type and quickly got to the fundamental issue.

"Dr. Roberts, I've read your report, and I need clarity in some areas."

"Certainly, Madam President. How may I help you?"

"After more than nine months of clinical research, you are unable to prove any negative side effects."

"Correct," Carrie answered robotically.

"Please explain why this is the case, Dr. Roberts."

"Certainly, Madam President. Various studies have shown that Lifio's short-term effects are purely positive."

"If you believe in Lifio's safety and efficacy, then why do you so staunchly support a ban on the product?"

"In our tests thus far, product efficacy remains unchallenged. However, nine months of testing does not constitute a proper clinical trial for a new drug."

"I'm sorry, but did I hear you correctly, Dr. Roberts, when you said 'new drug'?"

"Certainly, Madam President. According to Merriam-Webster, a drug is 'a medicine or other substance which has a physiological effect when ingested or otherwise introduced into the body,' and Lifio clearly has a physiological effect, wouldn't you agree?" Carrie blazed forward without waiting for an answer. "A new drug typically takes twelve to fifteen years to move through our five-step process before it can be approved. Attempting to accelerate the process ten-fold is foolish at best and dangerous at worst."

"I see." *Blunt honesty is refreshing,* Elizabeth thought. "I understand that you see Lifio as a new drug and that you would like to study it for a decade before approving it." She paused, allowing this message to sink in. "However, a decision must be made now. For me to do that, I am asking that you make your argument against approval."

"Certainly, Madam President." Carrie took the deep breath of a saxophone player prior to a solo and then exhaled. "Efficacy should not be our primary concern. Dr. Jónsson has unleashed a self-propagating genetic mutation on the human race. Whether the benefits are positive or not is irrelevant. What he has done could alter the course of human existence. Just because the initial effects look good to the public, does not mean we should immortalize a man conducting a reckless experiment on us."

"I understand your—"

"You see, Madam President, the gene mutation we discovered does not suffer degradation in any of our experiments. A single dose of Lifio changes the human body fundamentally—and, potentially, irreversibly."

"Yes, Carrie, I clearly remember this was the FDA's concern months ago. What have we learned since then?"

"Everything we have learned supports the hypothesis. We do not believe the mutation will ever reverse. While we are not ready to say that publicly, we are close. We must thoroughly research this hypothesis and support it with our findings before we release it. I will not follow in Dr. Jónsson's footsteps and disregard the scientific process."

Williamson bit her tongue, fighting back her frustration. "Carrie," she said carefully, "I am not asking you to disregard your ethical concerns. I am asking you to speak hypothetically with me on our situation."

"Understood. In that theoretical reality, I'd tell you that Lifio uses an engineered bacterium that causes a somatic gene mutation in humans after it is ingested. First, the fact that Dr. Jónsson genetically engineered a bacterium and released it into the environment without anyone knowing is reprehensible. That could have ended in a far graver manner had anything gone wrong. Furthermore, once ingested, that bacterium causes a somatic gene mutation through CRISPR.

"Then things get interesting. The alteration of a person's DNA sequence takes place, but those changes are far from being understood. They are far-reaching and numerous and, at this time, we are only able to understand some of their effects. The most influential involves cell division."

"Don't human cells only divide a set number of times?" President Williamson asked, frowning.

"That is correct, Madam President. After approximately fifty divisions, human cells stop dividing, which leads to more rapid aging. This takes place because the protective layers on the ends of our chromosomes, called telomeres, get smaller and smaller with each cell division until they are non-existent, at which point cell division stops."

"Go on, please."

"We have not witnessed any shrinkage in the telomeres of chromosomes that have undergone the Lifio gene mutation. Through repeated cell division, telomeres remain unchanged, allowing for infinite cell division."

"How is that even possible?"

"It is actually more common than you might think. The calling card of cancer cells is that they divide indefinitely. They accomplish that feat by working around the typical human cell problem of ever-shortening telomeres by activating an enzyme.

The enzyme, called telomerase, adds new telomeres onto the ends of chromosomes, continually allowing for never-ending cell division. Telomerase is used by the body during early childhood development but is not present in the typical adult human body. So, my assumption would be that the Lifio mutation causes adult human cells to somehow act like cancer cells and generate telomerase in order to facilitate infinite cell division."

Carrie didn't even take a breath. "Never-ending cell division," she said, and Williamson had the sudden image of a woodpecker drilling at a tree, "coupled with various other genetic modifications, results in mutations propagating throughout the entire human body. The impacts biologically are far-reaching and significant in a number of interesting ways. For instance—"

"Carrie, you have given me more than enough to consider already," President Williamson said. "If I may, I'd like to contemplate what you have already told me. I'll be in touch in the coming days if I have any further questions. Is that all right with you?"

"Certainly, Madam President," Carrie replied quickly.

Scientific poetry to Carrie had been jackhammering to the president. Peril lay along all paths, and no true high road existed. As she contemplated the loss of human life caused by keeping Lifio off the market, she balanced it against the potential impact that a permanent gene mutation would have on the human race. How could she knowingly sign off on a product that caused DNA mutations through bacteria without understanding the ramifications completely? And, more to the point, could those ramifications ever truly be understood? Had they already taken the first step down that path? Was she merely standing in the way of change, a levy against a storm tide? More deeply, she thought, *If we change human DNA, are we still human? And how do we know there will not be further mutations?*

The fact that only one dose of Lifio was required and that the effects could not be reversed made her suddenly realize that she personally had already undergone this mutation. It was true; while she had always been slim, she'd had more energy and endurance over the past year, and she didn't seem to gain any fat when she ate like crap on the campaign trail. Lifio had clearly had a positive impact on her life—could she in good conscience withhold it from the American people? On the other hand, the product had only been available for a short period. If something *did* go wrong and the DNA mutation Lifio triggered had a darker side, the threat would be existential—if the FDA approved, the EU would surely follow suit, and the Western world would be doomed. America was waiting for her to act, and the decision would not only decide her campaign's fate, but potentially humanity's.

By 2:30 a.m. that night, President Williamson had put the final touches on her speech and gotten it to her staff for editing. Then, aboard Air Force One, she lay down for a few hours of sleep before her first campaign stop of the morning.

* * *

Wheels were down at first light, jostling President Williamson awake. She suppressed a yawn and blinked out at the blurry gray fields of the airport. She felt neither rested nor tired, but strangely detached, numb almost. She caught her reflection in the porthole glass and winced; she'd need a thorough makeover before launching into her day of smiles and handshakes—that and a strong black coffee.

Despite her more pressing concerns, Carrie's warnings continued to swirl in her head. Oddly, her body felt better than ever, though she hadn't been on a run in weeks; her stress levels, however, were as high as ever. After plucking a few white hairs, she moved through the cabin to have her hair and makeup done by the professionals.

When she stepped out of Air Force One, Chicago's signature drizzle and swirling winds wreaked havoc on her hair, which would now need to be redone before her first stop: a steel factory just outside Gary, Indiana.

From the back of the car, Williamson watched the murky smokestacks and far-reaching fields of America's Midwest flitter by in a blur. Her typical pre-appearance stomach pains were conspicuously absent. A smile spread across her face as she thought about her first campaign four years earlier: advisors reading off poll numbers and Emily, her old campaign manager, describing in great detail exactly *how* Williamson would make her event entrance. Emily, with her soft bouncy curls and green eyes … she missed Emily.

At last, Williamson's door was pulled open breaking the lonely silence and a suited man ushered her out. She was led to an impromptu stage in a cracked parking lot in front of some nameless factory well past its prime. Ahead of her, nearly a thousand union workers stared up at her silently. Williamson swallowed.

"Thank you for coming here today," she said. "I know many of you have questions—about job security, about the economy, about Lifio."

"Where's Lifio?!" someone yelled.

Williamson cleared her throat. A bad start.

"As many of you are aware," she said carefully, "the Federal Drug Administration pulled Lifio off the market nine months ago. Since that time, I have been in constant communication with Melanie Delaney, commissioner of the FDA, and Carrie Roberts, testing and analysis expert. The decision was mine and mine alone to pull Lifio in order to adequately research Lifio so as to ensure the safety of the American people. Once this research is complete—and *only* once this research is complete—I will make a declaration regarding the product's efficacy and side effects. The product was pulled because it was released without being sent to the FDA for approval; this is the fault of Stallson Beverage Company. Since removing Lifio from the market, the FDA has worked around the clock to ensure testing and analysis are completed as quickly and as thoroughly as possible, and while Lifio cannot yet be approved for public consumption, I would like to shed some light on our findings so far. At this point in time, no detrimental side effects associated with Lifio have been found. However, we have reason to believe that a substance in the product causes a mutation that can alter the body's reaction to certain stimulants. While testing continues, we still feel it is unsafe for public consumption. The product will not be approved until all research and testing have been completed."

The rain had started again, and the uninspired crowd began to turn away, muttering among themselves. There was none of the typical hooting, hollering, and catcalling she had grown to expect—just quiet disappointment. The workers begin to turn away and file back through the factory gates. There, at last: a smattering of boos, even a few degrading comments. Williamson almost smiled—even they were preferable to the drained disinterest of these men who were supposed to be her core voting demographic.

President Williamson took her cue and walked from the stage, her speech unfinished. She climbed wordlessly back into the car as the rain grew heavier. On her phone, she saw her latest poll numbers had dipped below Senator Givens's for the first time.

"Madam President, Melanie Delaney on hold for you," her aid said, offering her a phone.

"Hello, Melanie."

"Madam President, the speech did not—that is, the speech did not include the necessary details from our report—"

"Is that all, Melanie?"

"It's just that I don't—"

"If that is all then we will speak at another time." President Williamson hung up and handed the phone back to her aid.

The rain came down.

CHAPTER 12

LLAMAS

Michael jiggled the keys in the lock until he heard a click, Len at his heels. The door swung open, and he suppressed a gasp— the apartment was sparkling. Even the broken chair leg had been repaired (it had been broken for as long as he'd had it), and it had been repainted along with all the other chairs in a matching gray.

"Your woman is good woman," Len said, audibly impressed.

Michael called out, "Ana? Ana?"

Nothing. He pulled out his phone: *Where are you?*

A moment later, her reply arrived: *I went home after cleaning. Have to finish up our costume!*

He sighed. *Okay, party's at 11.*

k.

All week, he had been badgering Ana to tell him what they were dressing up as, but she'd been steadfast in her secrecy. She had taken his measurements and that was the extent of his knowledge on the subject.

"So, what do you have in your room?" Michael said, raising an eyebrow at Len.

"You will see."

"Whatever … you two suck."

"I do not suck, woman suck," Len responded, and Michael gave Len's shoulder a push. "What? Ana no suck?"

"Come on, what's your costume? You're gonna put it on in a few hours anyway."

"I will show you," Len said, and headed toward his room, "in a few hours." He grinned before shutting the door.

Michael was more concerned about what he and Ana were dressing as. *I just hope it's nothing political; I don't want to get into it with anybody tonight.* He ate dinner, showered, and watched a National Geographic special on the Himalayas—and, all the while, Len's door remained closed, the strong smell of chemical aerosol emanating from the cracks.

Finally, Ana unlocked the front door and came in, her forehead glazed with sweat and two enormous black trash bags under her arms. She set them down just as Michael reached her, kissing her cheek.

"Any more?"

"Nope, this is it," she said, beaming at him. "Go on, open them."

He pulled a black plastic away and there, so bright it hurt his eyes, was an enormous paper mâché llama covered in red, orange, green, blue, yellow, and purple streamers. Ana picked the first llama up and put it over his head—his torso passed through the central hole, while suspenders held it in place around his waist. The bulbous llama head ended just below his chin. Giggling, she put hers on. "What do you think?"

He didn't know to say. Eventually, he mouthed the word "Wow," before inspecting every angle. "You did such a good job! I can't believe you didn't buy these; they're really amazing. How long have you been working on them?"

Ana beamed at him. "I got the idea when we hiked through the canyons last week, remember?"

"The llama ranch! Of course. I can't believe you made these."

Ana gave a shy grin, her dark eyes glittering. "I was worried you might not like them. Now, hold on before you answer," she said, holding her hand out, "I haven't shown you the best part." With that, she reached out for the middle of her llama's neck and opened a small door. "Look!"

"They're pinatas! Even better!" he said, pleased with himself. "You really outdid yourself; these are freaking awesome!"

At that moment, "Get Up" by James Brown boomed from Len's room and his door swung open. Out walked Len with aluminum dryer hoses covering his arms and legs, a large cardboard box spray-painted silver over his torso, and a welding mask covering his head. As the robot danced toward the pair of llamas, Michael could not help but smile and cheer him on. Once the song ended, Len stopped his perverted dance routine and sidled up next to them.

"I love it, Len!" Ana said, "Great robot costume."

"I no robot. I machine," Len said and Ana nodded.

"Stay on the scene, like a sex machine." Ana gasped. "Oh, that's cute." Her voice was full of discovery.

"Len, check this out, we're *pinatas!*" Michael said, opening and closing his llama's neck door.

"This is good," Len said, "what we fill you with?"

"I don't know. Any ideas?" Ana asked.

"Booze. Booze and condoms," Len suggested, making Ana blush. "No other way."

After stopping at a grocery store to fill their llamas up with miniature liquor bottles and condoms (on Len's dime), they arrived at the party. It took far longer to find a parking spot than it did to drive, and by the time they pulled up on the crowded city street, they were halfway back to their apartment. The asphalt was worn and cracked, and people hung on their porches drinking forties and listen to music. After enduring more than a few catcalls from drunk townies, the trio arrived at their destination: a dilapidated mansion on the corner of a city block at the intersection of rich and poor. The hulking residence pulsed with music that grew louder as they approached, and windows poorly covered with towels or sheets showed life behind them. The three-story building looked large enough to house an entire football team.

"I find woman, see you later," Len said at the door.

Michael felt great with Ana at his side and a few minia-ture liquors in his stomach. Regardless, he wished he were taking Ana's clothes off instead of partying. He followed Ana past a handful of Senator Givens and twice as many President Williamsons, all with various fatal injuries. Vampires and hook-ers were also in vogue.

"It's a nice party!" Ana yelled above the thumping house music.

"Yeah, I don't miss them. Let's go upstairs where it's not so loud."

After heading up two sets of stairs away from the dancefloor and onto a second-floor landing, they looked out at the party-goers. Next to them were a few couches full of stoners passing a bong around. They were all wearing tie-dye.

"Anyway," Ana said, "I was saying thanks for taking me to this party. I've always wanted to go to a college party."

Michael smiled. "Well, now you have."

"Is this what they're always like?" she said, staring over her shoulder at the stoners.

"More or less. After a few, you get it out of your system. Or you don't, like these fellas." He nodded at the group of tie-dye shirts.

She smiled and grabbed his shoulder, putting her cheek against it for a moment.

"So, what's your favorite costume? Besides our llamas, of course."

"I like her," she said, pointing to a ballerina, "and them!" She grinned toward a Chinese dragon that had to have eight people stumbling around inside it. "You?"

"The dragon, hands down. I'd hate to be in it but nothing else is close." He peered down at the mass of writhing bodies below the mezzanine. "Say, you want to get another drink and maybe dance? I want to give you the whole college party experience tonight."

She turned to face him. Her cheeks had a rosy hue and her warm breath smelled of mint and vodka. Caressing her hair, he lost himself in her chestnut eyes. She pulled him close enough for their lips to touch and whispered, "And how's does the night end?"

He only started breathing again when she pulled away. Excitement and anticipation reverberated through him. All inhibitions gone, he pulled her back and their lips pressed together, his mouth open as they tasted one another. The room faded away, and there was only the flood of her. Her scent. Her taste. The feeling of her pressed against him.

With a giggle, she broke apart, and the party rushed back in a blur of noise and color. Still clutching his hand, she led him down the steps and into the music. Michael grabbed a handful of Jell-O shots from a tray on a sideboard, handing several to Ana. She grinned back at him.

By the third song, their piñatas were coming apart. The throng erupted when it saw condoms and miniature liquor bottles begin to spill out onto the floor. Michael quickly grabbed two bottles before the crowd descended upon him and hurried to the far wall, Ana at his side.

"Domo Arigato Mr. Roboto!" Michael called as the silver silhouette of Len appeared through the crowd.

"Sex machine!" Len yelled, winking and pointing at his partner, a woman dressed as a schoolgirl, com plete with pigtails and knee-highs.

"Whatever you say!" Michael said.

Sometime later, the music stopped. The next thing Michael knew, he was stumbling through alleys with Ana, Len, and the schoolgirl in search of their apartment.

As soon as his head hit the pillow, he began to lose consciousness. He watched Ana put a glass of water on his nightstand, then strip and crawl in next to him. She was the little spoon, and pulled his arm around her before turning off the light and whispering, "I love you," for the first time.

His heart now hammering in his chest, Michael could only smile vacantly. "I love you too," he said.

CHAPTER 13

HELPING HAND

Sebastian woke with a start, blinking into the gloom. Another sleepless night; another burst of short, frantic dreams. That was it; he'd leak it. He lived a comfortable life with plenty in the bank and only himself and his elderly mother to take care of. He'd be fine, no matter what. Besides, he certainly hadn't followed Melanie into public service for the money.

Everything, he decided: all the findings, all the research, everything. Let the world come to its own conclusions. After months of telling himself they were trying to protect the public, the FDA's excuses had started to feel hollow to him. Surely, more could be accomplished if all the scientists in the world were working on the problem instead of just Carrie and her team. Carrie wouldn't like it, he knew, but Melanie? He was sure she'd see that his intentions were pure. At least, he hoped so.

His Italian super-automatic espresso popped and hissed on the marble worktop. He moved through his morning routine, still before sunrise, like a conductor. A shower; silently making oatmeal with fresh berries and nuts; sipping his triple espresso. After writing a warm note for his mother and leaving it on the refrigerator, he set off for the office.

It was a gray day, and the manicured lawns and yards of Sebastian's luxury suburb were quiet. He climbed into his BMW M5 and turned on the seat warmers. Next, the radio: "With less than a week to go before the election day," a gentle-voiced NPR reported said, "all national polls have President Williamson trailing surprise frontrunner Senator Givens. Our analysts attribute this to the continuing public backlash to Williamson's ban on the Lifio soft drink, pulled by the FDA almost—"

Sebastian turned the radio off; he'd heard enough blame heaped on the president. *She simply followed sound logic in enacting our recommendation. If I can leak the information, voters will see that the president had their best interests at heart after all. Maybe then she'll get a fair shake.*

Senator Givens, Sebastian knew, had promised to approve Lifio on day one, without even seeing the classified research. He shook his head as he turned off onto the main road, early traffic skimming past him. That would be catastrophic given what they had found. If all it cost Sebastian to do the right thing was his career in the public sector, he'd gladly accept that trade. Maybe then he'd be able to sleep again.

Unfortunately, at the office, Melanie and Carrie were less enthusiastic.

"Absolutely not, Sebastian," Melanie said, incredulous. "I will not let you go down in flames for an idea that might not even work."

Sebastian could tell that Melanie *wanted* to be transparent; he even thought he could see it in Carrie's hazel eyes. For once, she was quiet, leaving most of the disagreeing to Melanie.

"Sebastian, I brought you to the FDA and I agreed with Carrie to pull it from the market. If anyone is going to take a fall for this, it's going to be me," Melanie said.

"I've had a good run," Sebastian said simply. "I'm happy, and I'm not running the FDA—you are. Let me do this."

Melanie scowled at him. "That's right, I *am* running the FDA; I gave the president enough time to notify the public and she failed to do so. It falls on my shoulders."

Carrie stood unflinching, unwilling to make eye contact.

"Besides, if you leak this without official sanction, you may face repercussions I am unable to protect you from."

The blood drained from Sebastian's face, his hand unintentionally lingering on his cheekbone.

Carrie cleared her throat. "We should all do it," she said quietly. "The last thing we can afford is for the information not to get out. If the three of us release the data in concert, we have the best chance." Looking right through Sebastian, she said, "Agreed?"

And he found himself nodding.

After a moment's hesitation, Melanie nodded too. They would face whatever fate lay in store for them together.

Carrie would upload all of the lab data to the public through cloud servers linked on the FDA's website, while Sebastian would send digital copies of everything to research organizations around the world. Melanie, meanwhile, would hold a press conference to announce what they had done and why. She'd finally get the chance to offer an explanation to the American people. The multi-pronged approach, Sebastian thought, would give them the best chance to get everything out before spin from Stallson Beverage could control the message.

It was nine in the morning by the time they agreed on their plan, and with the election in just a few days, they set out to go public by five p.m. that day. It felt good to have a plan; a plan under his control.

As soon as Sebastian began reaching out to news organizations to schedule the press conference, however, the gravity of the situation became apparent. News outlets far and wide announced that were sending reporters. By noon, news of the press conference broke, and by two p.m., nearly every television and radio station had committed to airing it live. America was poised to treat the FDA press conference like a State of the Union Address, and every time Sebastian made the mistake of turning on a news broadcast, all he saw was coverage prognosticating about what the FDA would say.

By three p.m., the pressure had clearly gotten to Melanie. She called Sebastian in to help her with her speech, but nothing he suggested appeased her. Her phone rang yet again and she gestured for Sebastian to take the call.

"President Williamson on the line for Melanie Delaney," came a quick female voice. Then, "Melanie, what is the meaning of the press conference you have scheduled? Did you find something?"

"Madam President, I'm sorry but this Sebastian Dougherty."

Melanie, her face pale green, gestured for him to keep going.

"I'm sorry, but Melanie is currently detained?" Sebastian said, looking at Melanie for direction. She gave him a quick thumbs up. "But no, Madam President, we do not have any new information."

"Then why the press conference?"

"We've—that is, we've—" Sebastian covered the receiver with his hand. "Melanie, I need a little help here! She's asking me why we called a press conference."

Melanie rose, took a deep breath, and grabbed the phone from Sebastian.

"We've decided to release everything," she said. "With the election around the corner, the stakes are too high to keep the American people in the dark. They need to know what kind of impact releasing Lifio back onto the market could have. We need to publish everything we've learned now in case we don't have another chance."

When Williamson didn't respond, she said, "I am willing to accept responsibility for whatever happens. What we can't accept are our findings being swept under the rug and not being seen by the American people. Thank you for defending us as you have, Madam President. I only wish we had been able to complete our research before this day came."

And with that, Sebastian knew the die had been cast. There was no turning back now.

After double-checking Melanie's speech one last time and confirming with Melanie and Carrie that yes, they really did want to send out all their raw data, Sebastian released seven terabytes to eighty-four research teams across the globe. Simultaneously, Carrie released the data and her summary reports live on the FDA website.

Only minutes before Melanie had to give the most important briefing of her life, she disappeared back into her office. Sebastian waited uneasily outside, imagining her climbing out a window and leaving him behind. A bead of sweat appeared at his hairline as he allowed the intimidating thought too much real estate in his mind. Then, her door opened and she walked purposefully into the hall.

"Sebastian."

"Melanie."

After exchanging nods, they started down the corridor toward the bright lights.

"Good luck," Sebastian said when they reached the press briefing room.

She didn't reply, but strode inside.

Dozens of reporters were already seated, cameras poised and ready. Sebastian shuffled through and stood at the back of the room, fingers playing nervously across his palms.

"Good evening," Melanie began. "Tonight, the FDA released all summary reports, analyses, and raw data sets generated from our study of the Lifio product. This has been done to allow the worldwide scientific community to study our raw data and help interpret it. I am not here to put the FDA stamp of approval on the Lifio product; instead, I am here to explain why Lifio was taken off the market, what the FDA has found, and how we suggest we move forward."

Sebastian scanned the audience to try to gauge reactions, but the room was so intensely focused on Melanie that he couldn't read them.

"Nine and a half months ago, Lifio was pulled from American shelves. This was at the recommendation of Carrie Roberts, our head of testing and analysis, who President Williamson and I supported after detailed reports outlining immediate threats were filed. First, let me address why we initially tested Lifio. Many if not all industries self-regulate. It is the nature of the business world. If a competitor has a distinct advantage, it is natural for companies to want to verify that the playing field is equal. Various publicly traded beverage conglomerates paid for legitimate third-party scientific testing on the Lifio product when it was initially released onto the US market, and they found irregularities they could not explain. At that point, those companies reported their findings to the FDA."

Audible gasps came from the audience, but Melanie kept her momentum.

"Carrie Roberts reviewed these submissions, prompting a review of the Lifio product. During Dr. Roberts's testing, she discovered a bacterium, one she had not seen before. This bacterium, which is inside every can of Lifio, potentially uses CRISPR technology, a simple yet powerful tool for editing genomes and altering DNA, to cause gene mutations in the cells of anyone who consumes the product. In addition, due to a chromosome enhancement potentially caused by the product, adult cells no longer appear to age and die; instead, they are able to reproduce a yet-to-be-determined number of times before they can no longer divide.

"The effects thus far have been staggeringly positive. Let me be clear: the FDA has not found any negative side effects caused by the Lifio product. The product has been withheld from the public because it has been proven to cause genetic mutations. We are not certain how this is being achieved, and we are not clear on the long-term implications. What we do know is that Lifio is far more than a soft drink. It causes a fundamental change in the human body, and nothing with that capability should be available to the public before it is fully understood."

Melanie paused, and Sebastian watched her scan the blank faces of the assembled reporters. She caught his eye for a moment, and Sebastian gave a slight nod.

"President Williamson has been the FDA's ally during this process, but she has also been our harshest critic. While she understands the need for testing and research, she has pushed us to work around the clock to understand Lifio so that access can be restored. However, with the election looming, the president and the FDA are out of time. Other potential leaders have suggested they will approve Lifio for sale the day they take office, and I am here today to tell you how grave an error that would be. Gene mutation has permanent consequences for the human race. Lifio cannot be treated like a typical food product; it must be thoroughly tested and examined before it can be re-released."

Melanie finally exhaled. "Thank you for your time. Now I will take a few questions."

The room exploded as reporters stood and jostled, their hands raised high. Sebastian strode onto the stage, pointing at a reporter in a blue suit.

"What sort of timeline can you give us regarding a possible release?"

Melanie frowned. "That largely depends on future findings. By releasing all of our data and findings today, we hope that the scientific community at large can help us dramatically reduce that period of time."

The reporter then immediately pushed his follow up: "What order of magnitude are you talking? Days, weeks, months?"

"Unfortunately, without help from the rest of the world, I am afraid we are looking at years."

A momentary hush fell over the gathered crowd and, at once, they surged forward with renewed vigor.

Pointing to a slender male reporter in the second row, Sebastian said, "You?"

"In your briefing, you said, 'Gene mutation is an advanced field with permanent consequences.' Would you please elaborate on what you mean by 'permanent consequences'?"

Sebastian had known it would come up and had tried to prepare Melanie, but he could see she still dreaded the idea of total transparency.

"Unfortunately," she said slowly, "during our research, we found that the gene mutations taking place did not reverse themselves. More importantly, we found that chromosomes had been modified in a way that led to continued cell division that did not cease over time."

The reporter gave a single curt nod, then said, "How many servings cause gene mutation, and how long after consumption until the effects wear off?"

"Perhaps I've not made myself clear. A single serving of Lifio has the potential to cause a permanent change in your body that cannot be reversed," she said. "One drink can change your DNA permanently."

A collective roar shattered the fragile quiet. Every reporter in the room was now standing, hands raised, yelling for attention. Instead of taking more questions, Melanie raised her hands. Gradually, the yelling ceased.

"Lifio has proven to have dramatic positive impacts over the short term," she said. "However, there is a price. Lifio unequivocally changes the human body through gene mutation. We have not concluded whether this mutation will transfer to our children or whether there will be late-term effects. Without research, testing, and time, we cannot know how this product will affect our bodies, our country, and our species. We live in exciting times. Lifio offers to potentially improve our entire species; however, that potential is not without risk. What we are asking is for you to be patient and allow the global scientific community time to study Lifio's effects before we make a choice we cannot reverse. This is a moment in history where we must show restraint and patience. We need leaders like President Williamson, who, over the past year, has put her political career and personal life in peril to protect the American people from possible disaster."

Dozens of hands shot up in response, but Melanie shook her head. "I'm sorry, but that will be all for today. Please look on the FDA's website for a link to our entire raw data set and all reports and findings in our Lifio product file. These are being made publicly available so that we can work together to accelerate this all-important research."

With that, Melanie stepped from the podium and quickly left the room, hounded by blood-hungry reporters. Sebastian hurried after her.

"That went well, I think," he said, closing the door to Melanie's office behind him.

Melanie's face was unreadable. "We'll see. I'm just glad it's over. Total transparency, right?"

"Total transparency. You didn't disappoint." His face split into a smile. At long last, he thought, he might be able to sleep again.

CHAPTER 14

REACTIONS

Senator Givens's office was in chaos. Campaign staff scurried from room to room, rushing to formulate an official reaction to the stunning FDA announcement. Givens knew all too well that the final hours before an election were when the gloves came off. And, while he knew he had to remain informed, he insisted that his campaign staff summarized and, more importantly, un-sensationalized the news for him. He'd fallen into the trap of riding the highs and lows of the news cycle in the past, and it took his eye off the ball.

"Sell, sell, sell!" screamed the frothing financial news host onscreen as he paced the set. "We all knew it was too good to be true, but we couldn't get off the ride, could we? Stallson Beverage just had their bloody, still-beating heart torn out of their chest on national television by the FDA! It's already too late. Stallson is cooked; the wheels are coming off."

As he ranted and raved, he pointed at the camera and hit oversized buttons that made outlandish sound effects. "When the markets open tomorrow, I'm out! You should be out too! Unless—*unless* you believe Alex and Helen Stallan can pull another rabbit out of their hat!"

On another financial news station, a more subdued host counseled his viewers to *buy* shares in Stallson Beverage. Urging them to take advantage of the negative FDA press, he argued that the premature summary results and an unfathomably large raw data set clearly pointed, at best, to overzealous government employees and, at worst, to a conspiracy quarterbacked by the government. The host reminded viewers that the FDA had found absolutely zero negative side effects after more than a year of research. With Stallson Beverage's stock poised to have its first dip in share price for over a year, now was the time to buy, and buy heavily.

Givens looked up as his campaign manager burst through the door. Seeing Givens's cigar and his well-dressed guest, he retreated sheepishly toward the doorway. "May I have a moment, Senator?"

Givens didn't acknowledge his manager, but stood, shook hands with his guest, and walked him to the door. Only once the man was gone did Givens wave his campaign manager in.

"Quite an eventful day, Senator," the manager said. "Everyone seems to have their own theory."

"Sit, sit," Givens said, gesturing toward a vacant chair.

His lips pressed together, his campaign manager obliged and waited quietly. After a sufficient pause, Givens gave him the go ahead to continue.

"The conservative spin has positioned Melanie Delaney and Carrie Roberts of the FDA as political hacks who have been weaponized by President Williamson in a last-ditch effort to win the election. They're focusing on this coming out just before the polls open as their main argument. Both of them have been torn to shreds, especially Melanie—they found a high school acquaintance who said—"

Givens had his index finger against his lip. "Just the news, if you please."

"Yes, sorry Senator. Liberal news outlets aren't holding back either; they're taking the FDA and the president to task for not releasing sooner. One particular quote I think you will enjoy was"—he shuffled through his notes—"ah: 'transparency in the waning hours of a presidency does not equate to a transparent term in office.'"

Senator Givens couldn't help but allow himself a wry smile.

"Also, the talk show scientists I've seen seem more focused on the shockingly positive effects of Lifio than worried about gene editing. After all, the data they've released on Lifio's impact shows only positive results."

Givens smirked and shook his head. *I don't know how that woman squandered the gift of a groundbreaking discovery during her first term*, he thought. *At a minimum, she could have released Lifio for clinical testing and to terminal patients.*

"Pretty good news, isn't it, Senator? Can you believe how badly she messed that up?"

"What?" Givens said, shaken from his thoughts. "Oh, well, we'd better be careful; after all, hindsight is twenty-twenty. Yes, I am happy with the direction this is headed, but we ought to remember that this issue took months to reach its boiling point. I am sure that, looking back, the president would have made different decisions. She simply allowed herself to fall out of touch with the American people. Worse, she was indecisive. That's a lethal combination for a politician."

His campaign manager's smile wavered. "Ah. Right you are, Senator."

Givens dismissed the manager and leaned back in his desk chair. The man was competent, but sometimes overly eager, puppylike almost. Still, he was right: things were going well. In an overly jubilant mood, Givens caved to his inner demons and, after making sure his door was locked, flipped on the television, catching a pearlescent news anchor mid-rant. She was firing on all cylinders, throwing nefarious explanation after nefarious explanation for the recent FDA announcement, and even called for impeachment should Williamson be reelected. Givens grinned to himself. *Fat chance of that happening.*

He flicked channels. Here too a purple-faced man was shouting: "Melanie Delaney is clearly a sycophant being used as a pawn by President Williamson to wage political warfare in order to win an election she has no right to win!"

"How would that help Mrs. Delaney?" prompted the host.

The man didn't skip a beat. "She was a political nominee appointed by the executive branch! Her future relies directly on President Williamson's success. I'm sure they cooked up this crackpot plan to save the president at the last minute. A disgusting level of self-interest on display. I'm sure Mrs. Delaney will have a cushy, high-paying job in the private sector waiting for her after that grotesque display of party politics."

Givens flicked to another channel.

"I'm not going to stop using it," a woman was saying, "I drink Lifio every morning, and I've never felt better. It's hard to get in the United States, but it's certainly not impossible, and I'm not afraid to tell all of you I drink it every day."

Another.

"How many years did the federal government take to finally tell us cigarettes were a carcinogen?" a middle-aged black man was saying, hand gesticulating wildly. "As the FDA said itself, Lifio has no negative side effects. How about President Williamson and Melanie Delaney hold off on using Lifio themselves and stop trying to tell us what we can and can't do? This is a free country, isn't it?"

Another.

"You know what I say?" a woman with her hair tied back so tight her skull seemed to bulge said. "I say that if I want to drink something that has no negative side effects and that will likely extend my life, let me drink it!"

Raucous cheers rose from the studio audience, and Givens grinned.

"I don't know about all of you," the woman went on, "but I'm not buying this idea that your body changes after one drink. I didn't feel the way I do now after I first tried Lifio. In fact,

I didn't feel this way until six months into using it. And you know what? I feel better every single day now that I drink it every day. There is no way I'd feel the same if I stopped. Any time I miss my morning Lifio, I feel off until I've had it. A lot of things don't add up here, and I mean *a lot!* I don't need to look at four million pages of data to figure out that Lifio is amazing. I can feel it every blessed day!"

So that was it then. Givens took a cigar from the box on his desk. Where the talking heads led, America would follow. It was time to celebrate.

He switched on the electric fire in the hearth and watched its flickering graphics. Almost like the real thing, he thought—though he did miss the smell. It always reminded him of Autumn, and of his childhood.

There came a frenzied knocking on his door.

"Senator," came an embarrassed voice, "I'm sorry to bother you, but you have a call."

"At this hour?" Givens stood with a sigh and unlocked his office door.

An ugly campaign staffer scuttled in apologetically, pushing a cell phone toward him.

"Give it here."

"Givens!" a voice screamed. *"Goddamn it, Givens!"*

Holding his hand over the phone, the senator glared at his ugly staffer. "What is the meaning of this, son?"

"Sorry, sir. I mean, Senator. It's Mr. Stallan. He said it was urgent. Should I—"

The senator shooed him away and lifted the phone back to his ear.

"Alex, old boy," he said in his most jovial midwestern accent, "it's wonderful to hear from you."

"Givens, damn it, don't give me that 'old boy' bullshit—"

A new voice came on the line.

"Senator Givens, this is Helen Stallan. I'm sorry for Alex's boorish berating. You see, he is quite upset."

"I understand, Helen. It's been quite the day, hasn't it? How can I help?"

"We'd like to understand what you intend to do about the blatant attack made on the Stallson Beverage Company—an American company, mind you—by the FDA this afternoon. Their unfounded, quite ludicrous accusations could do preeminent damage to our company if not handled swiftly and decisively."

Givens sighed. "What would you and Alex have me do, Helen?"

"I'd have you do what we paid you over a quarter of a billion dollars to do," Helen said, an edge to her voice. "Shut down the FDA investigation into Lifio and get the product back on American shelves. That is what I would have you do."

"You know I can't do that, Helen."

"What did you say?"

"Have you and Alex seen what is going on?"

"Of course we have. Our stock price has lost a quarter of its value in after-hours trading!" Helen almost screamed.

"Then buy as much as you can, Helen. Look—I do not mean to make light of the current dilemma, but stop watching the financial market commentators for a moment and take a look at how the press is reacting. The FDA just signed President Williamson's pink slip. No one believes a word of what the FDA put out there. We're forty-eight hours away from our goal. Can you smell it, Helen? Can you? Well, if you can't, I can."

Silence but for Helen's shallow breath.

"In forty-eight hours," Givens went on, "I'll be elected president of the United States. President Williamson, in her typical idealistic way, has agreed to follow my directives expressly and without fail during her lame-duck period. I don't think she'll agree to approve Lifio before I take office, but I will demand that she let Melanie Delaney, Sebastian Dougherty, and Carrie Roberts go immediately. Hell, if she's smart, she'll let go of them before I publicly tell her to."

"But—"

"Listen. You and Alex aren't used to politics. I am. This story will be gone in one news cycle. People love your product and will continue to love it. Look at this as a positive. Use all of the FDA reports showing the amazing health benefits of drinking Lifio in your marketing. Don't you and Alex see? This is a victory. We won today."

There was a long pause. Finally, Helen said, "I understand, Senator." Her voice was quieter now, Givens noted with satisfaction, almost deferential. "You make a fairly strong point. We need to have thicker skin when it comes to share price volatility. However, we do remain uncomfortable with the rumor that the effects of Lifio can be gained after only one dose."

"Helen, I don't want to tell you how to do your job, but, if it were me, I would hire a third-party research organization to do a few studies for you that clearly show that continued use of Lifio delivers improved results. Look, if marketing was able to convince generations of Americans that climate change isn't real, smoking doesn't kill you, and clean coal exists, you won't have any problem getting people to keep drinking Lifio—even if they don't need to." He paused, and could almost hear Helen's lip curling. He grinned to himself. "Not that I'm saying they don't need to keep drinking it; I drink it every day and will continue to do so."

"Of course, every day," Helen said tersely. "Thank you, Senator. I think we've taken enough of your time this evening. We look forward to celebrating your election victory soon. All the best."

Givens hung up and, pleased with himself, winked at the ugly staffer, who stood cowering in the doorway. The man hurried over and took the phone.

"Fetch John, will you?" Givens said.

The man nodded and hurried out. Moments later, John, Givens's campaign manager, stepped into the room.

"Get me a meeting with anyone close to us from the scientific community tomorrow morning before the day starts up for us," the senator said, barely looking up.

"That would be 5 a.m.," John said, frowning. "Are you certain you want to do this now?"

"I do. Tell them I want them to look at all the data the FDA just released on Lifio and brief me in the morning. We have hours, not days, before this election, and I need to know everything I can before the polls open."

CHAPTER 15

ELECTION NIGHT

Alex gave up on sleeping well before dawn. Beside him, Helen's light snores told him that, somehow, she was out for the count. Alex shook his head. The woman could sleep through anything, no matter how much stress she was under. But today was election day—she was outdoing even her own high standards.

He fumbled with the French press in the kitchen, trying to operate the contraption for the first time. Most mornings, the Stallan estate staff served the family breakfast in the drawing room: avocado toast with heirloom tomatoes and a medium poached egg for Helen and, for Alex, three over-easy eggs, white toast, a side of bacon, and, to drink, Lifio and fresh coffee. But not today; it was still hours before the staff would arrive.

As Alex tried to wedge the plunge back into the glass jug, Helen appeared, smiling drowsily down at him. Half an hour later, the pair were hunched over bowls of cereal and cans of Lifio, dressed, showered, and ready for the day. Alex had broken the French press and had left it in ruins in the sink, covered with ground coffee beans.

"I have to hand it to that bastard Givens, he was right," Alex said, mouth full of cereal.

"Politics sure is tiresome," Helen quipped.

He shot her a milky grin. "Not even that; the share price came right back. Nobody seems to believe the gene mutation claims. That or they don't care, and either works for me."

"The FDA proved Lifio does more than ever claimed. How it works shouldn't matter to anyone."

"Exactly!" Alex said, shaking his index finger at her.

Helen drained the rest of her coffee and slammed the cup down. "Now that Senator Givens has publicly reaffirmed his promise to us, I'm confident," she said. "He's been bought and paid for and he knows it. Now all he has to do is win the election."

But Alex was barely listening. He tapped at his phone, typing out a message to Mike to get him to send out a company-wide email making it mandatory for all employees to head out to the polls to support Senator Givens. Alex would contact every name on his contacts list if it was the last thing he did. He could not allow Givens to lose this election—not on his watch.

He felt better after pressing send, and allowed himself to tune back into his wife's chatter. Control—even the illusion of it— helped him deal with his oppressive but well-hidden anxiety.

Helen looked nervous, he realized, which was rare for her. He could tell that she needed something to take her mind off the day ahead, so he prompted her, "You think you could push yourself to wrap up October's accounting early?"

Moments later, she had her laptop open on the kitchen table. Alex watched her face relax as she dove into spreadsheets. Satisfied, Alex turned on the television to watch the morning news while scanning his phone for the latest poll results. Helen looked up from her spreadsheet and, as if sensing her husband's anxiety, glanced down at his phone. Polling data had fluctuated wildly since the FDA announcement, and the most recently published polls were no different, showing Givens ahead by impossible margins. They had seen the polls before they'd gone to bed and, after asking a few of their political strategist friends, had been told to disregard the polls showing dramatic swings in opinion immediately after news broke.

"Hey Hel, could you reach out to that staffer and see if they have any inside news?"

"Sure."

The response to Helen's message came quickly: *Nah too early, we won't have anything from the exit polls until the afternoon. Hold tight.*

"Well, that sucks," Alex said.

Alex and Helen had intended to stay out of the office on election day. They'd planned to sleep in so they could stay up late on election evening, waiting for the results to be announced. With the plan already off course, Alex figured they might as well keep themselves busy.

"Let's head in."

Helen looked up, frowning. "We told ourselves we wouldn't do that."

"We were also going to sleep late too, but that didn't work out. Plus, you're already at work," Alex said, pointing to her open laptop.

She scoffed. "That's because you asked me to get a jump on month-end figures!"

He stood and moved behind his wife, massaging her shoulders. "Come on, we'll head over to the polling station on the way in, then just stop by the office for a few hours. Knock out a few things, drain some of your nervous energy, and then we'll come back to the house for a little hanky-panky before tonight's festivities."

Helen called for their driver to bring the car—a black Escalade SUV—round the front. It was still pitch-black outside when they arrived at the address they had been given as their local polling station. Spotting a short line leading to a locked door, Alex asked Miguel, their driver, to park the car and see what was going on.

"Polls aren't open yet, boss. It's 5:35 a.m. Looks like they don't open for another twenty-five minutes." After a pause, Miguel said, "Early day for you and the missus. Would you like to wait, or should I take you into the office?"

"Office, please, Miguel," Helen said. She turned to Alex. "I'm not going to sit in this parking lot while traffic backs up. We'll vote on the way home."

* * *

A light knock on his door brought Alex's head up from his laptop. Helen stood in the doorway, face tense. "I heard from that staffer," she said.

Alex leaned back and closed his laptop. "What's happening?"

"They just said that the exit polls looked solid." Helen raised her crossed fingers and smiled.

"Well, that's as good as we could have hoped for from a staffer, I guess," Alex said. "Thanks for letting me know."

"Yup. Ready to wrap up soon?"

"Yeah, just a few more things. I'll come find you when I'm ready."

With that, Helen turned and headed into the hall. For a moment, Alex thought about following her to her office, but his eye caught an email and the thought evaporated. The next time he looked at his clock, it was almost five.

"Alex, Alex, Alex!" Mike yelled, charging into Alex's office. "We won Indiana and Kentucky!"

Alex snorted. "Like hell we did, Mike. The first polls don't even close for another hour."

"Google it! Turn on the TV, check your phone, whatever! The polls are still open, but the Associated Press called both states for Givens, my man!"

"Holy shit," Alex murmured, looking at his computer screen. "You're right. Givens took seventy-six percent of the vote in Indiana and eighty-nine in Kentucky. I gotta get out of here and get ready for tonight. Mike, you should get home too. We'll see you and Meme at the election party."

Alex jogged out of his office to find Helen, who was staring at her cell, dumbstruck, when he burst in.

"You see this shit?" he said. "Come on, we gotta get home. I called Miguel to meet us out front."

Alex's heart pounded as Miguel weaved through traffic. He opened his window and peered out at the passing streets, letting the fresh air fill his lungs. A crisp autumn breeze rushed in as they drove along Central Park, and Alex closed his eyes—only for a swirl of exhaust fumes and rotten garbage to engulf him. He pulled his head back in, coughing, but Helen only smirked at him.

Just before they arrived home, the news broke: "We are now able to call eight additional states," the man on the radio said. Alex quickly closed the windows and focused his hearing. "Delaware for Givens, Pennsylvania for Givens, New Jersey for Givens, Massachusetts for Givens, West Virginia for Givens ..."

"Miguel, can you turn it up a bit, please?" Helen interjected.

"Yes ma'am."

"Georgia for Givens," the radio anchor said. "With ten states going to Senator Givens, he has a commanding lead: 112 electoral votes to zero for President Williamson. Of course, until the polls in Ohio close in a few short hours, you never know. Ohio has of course chosen the president for the last fifty years."

With energy and excitement coursing through him, Alex burst out of the SUV before it came to a stop. He sprinted up into his bedroom, pulled out a tuxedo, and hung it on his closet door, then stripped down and jumped in the shower. Before he knew it, Helen was next to him, fighting for water in a ridiculous purple shower cap that made him laugh out loud.

"What?" she said, nudging him out of the water.

"Nothing," he said with a smile, and quickly rinsed off so he could leave her to it.

By the time they were back in the Escalade, Alex was wearing a slim tuxedo and Helen a tight white strapless dress. After an uneventful detour back through town, they approached the ballroom. Alex scrolled through his phone; reports were continuing to come in of exit polls showing Givens firmly in the lead, but still no other states had been called.

Alex hadn't anticipated arriving before 11 p.m. at the earliest, yet he found himself with Helen in an enormous lobby, invitation in hand, at 8:30 p.m. Everyone else must have felt what they did, because the lobby looked like intermission at the Metropolitan Opera. He winked at Bob and Tricia, waved at Kevin Mack, and shook hands with a tall blond German man, smiling as he whispered in Helen's ear, "What's his name?" Helen was swamped by her own gaggle of swarming dignitaries, but Alex didn't care: he could feel the win coming and, by the looks of it, so could everyone else.

The carved oak doors opened and gathering guests poured in, some ogling but some barely glancing, marching straight past the blown glass vases filled with roses centered on the dozens of clean white tables. A large, deep stage stood at the far end of the room, atop which a fourteen-person band covered Katy Perry songs. Alex grinned; evidently, you couldn't buy taste. Searching through the twinkling ballroom for table fifty-seven, Alex almost walked into Mike and Meme.

"Funny running into you here," Mike said to Alex, grasping him by the shoulders. "How long has it been?"

"Mike, Meme, wonderful to see you," Helen said, staring at Meme with a sparkle in her eye. "Meme, how is Shela doing? Why didn't you bring her tonight? I, for one, think we could use another predator in the room."

Meme's mouth dropped open. Then she looked from Mike to Helen to Alex, clenched her jaw, and said, "If you'll excuse me, Helen, I have to get a drink."

After Meme moved away, Helen asked, "What did I say?"

"It's Sheba, not Shela," Mike explained, "but that doesn't matter now. We had to put her down. She—well, she sort of bit Meme. She's really broken up about it."

"Oh, I'm so sorry, Mike," Helen said through a curdled smile, "please give Meme our condolences. Alex, shall we make the rounds?"

In a room filled with New York elites, each conversation presented its own challenges. Alex had long since grown tired of the subtle verbal sparring these events engendered, but Helen reveled in it.

"I'm gonna grab another gin and tonic. What can I get you?" Alex asked.

"Just a club soda with a lime," Helen replied before moving away to join another group. At the bar, Alex downed the first gin and caught a glimpse of Stefán out of the corner of his eye. He frowned. *Funny, how does Stefán know Givens?* It wasn't like Stefán to travel out of his beloved Iceland; Alex always had to coerce him. Then, just like that, Stefán—or, Alex thought, the man who *looked* like Stefán—was gone. Shrugging to himself, Alex headed back toward Helen.

"Here's your drink. What did I miss?" Alex said.

"Thank you, dear. Milly was just telling us about her house in the Hamptons—off Cedar Road, wasn't that right Milly?"

Milly—a gleaming brunette with laughing eyes—nodded and gave a sumptuous smile. "Exactly, darling. We have a new neighbor and they've taken to renting their home out this past season. Can you imagine?"

"What's wrong with that?" Alex asked, taking a big sip of his gin.

"They're unsavory—to put it mildly," Milly's husband put in.

"Yes, it's just not right, the Hamptons aren't for tourists. That's why you can't rent for less than two weeks," a dapper older gentleman with slicked-back hair added.

"Can they really be hoodlums if they have the money for two weeks in the Hamptons?" Alex said, taking another pull of his gin.

"That's not the point, dear," Helen said petting the back of Alex's head.

"Well, what is the point?" Alex pushed back.

The older man raised an eyebrow. "Maybe they shouldn't even allow rentals in the Hamptons."

Alex snorted, a dribble of gin coming out of his nose.

"Well, I for one think you're right. Don't you agree, honey?" Milly said, staring at her husband.

"So right," Helen said, edging slightly forward so that Alex fell just outside of the circle. "If you like, I could have a word with the mayor on your behalf."

"Oh, that would be lovely," Milly responded gleefully as Alex backed away from the circle. *Perhaps another gin*, he thought to himself, and turned back to the bar.

On the forty-foot screen behind the stage, election coverage loomed. Anchors dove into state maps, pointing out which counties had submitted votes and which had not.

Suddenly, Helen was by Alex's side, her fingers snaked around his arm. "We forgot to stop at the polls!" she whispered without moving her lips.

"Shit," Alex slurred, "should we call Miguel back?"

"No, the polls close in fifteen minutes. We couldn't get there even if we tried. If anyone asks, we voted before work."

"Deal." Without another word, Alex turned away and headed toward a group of men he recognized. Before he could reach them, though, the music cut off and the big screen's election coverage audio flicked on. After thunderous sound effects, projections came forward one after the other. Michigan, Maine, and Virginia closed for President Williamson, and Alex swallowed an ice cube as the crowd began to mutter and boo. But then, as if following a conductor poised for a crescendo, Tennessee, Florida, New York, Texas, and Ohio all fell to Senator Givens. Alex found himself pumping his fists in the air and whistling.

"What's that put us at?" He elbowed the fellow next to him.

"We're at 237. Almost there!"

"What's it take?" he yelled over the chatter, and took another swig of gin.

The man paused for a moment. "Err, 270."

Alex smiled, holding his drink aloft.

The screen flashed back on and projections came flying in. Wisconsin, Minnesota, Colorado—all for President Williamson. The crowd waited silently for the next announcement, but it didn't come. The room took a collective breath.

Exhaling heavily, Alex put his empty glass down on a nearby table and turned to his new friend. "I'm gonna go take a piss," he spat.

The man nodded. Alex pushed his way through the crowd toward the black marble bathroom. Nodding to a security guard, he headed straight for a urinal and relieved himself with one arm leaning against the wall in front. *We're gonna win,* he thought, *stock's gonna double tomorrow. Motherfuck, I'm on a fucking roll.*

A bump of bass shook the wall and Alex jumped, almost slipping. More projections were coming. He rushed to a basin lined with vases of white lilies, where he rinsed his hands before brushing them on his jacket. With that, he ran back out, fly still open.

Six more states were called for Senator Givens and, in the blink of an eye, it was President-Elect Givens—and Alex had missed it. As he made his way into the celebration, confetti and balloons still in the air, Helen caught his eye and, grinning, hurried toward him. They collided and she kissed him passionately; dimly, he even felt her hand rub up against his manhood. Then she pulled away, whispering in his ear, "Your fly was down."

Alex just snorted and rubbed his face. "Thank you, dear."

By the time President-Elect Givens took the stage an hour later, Alex and Mike could hardly walk. They stood shoulder to shoulder, each trying to keep balance and a straight face. He made the briefest moment of eye contact with Givens before the president-elect looked away. Alex couldn't quite make out what Givens was saying during his acceptance speech, but he could tell Helen was not pleased by her tightly pursed lips and cold eyes. Alex just hoped that whatever had pissed her off didn't stop him from getting her clothes off soon.

Speech apparently done, Givens made the rounds, shaking hands with the big donors—but, before he reached Alex and Helen, an aide leaned in to whisper something in his ear and he abruptly left the room.

"I've called Miguel," Helen said, "he'll be up front in five. Why don't you head out there with Mike and get some fresh air."

"What? Well, why don't you come too?"

"I'll be right behind you," Helen said, "I'd just like to say congratulations to Givens—if I can find him."

"All right, but don't take too long," Alex slurred, leaning into Mike.

Riding home after the big win, his head gently resting on Helen's lap, Alex felt the rush of the evening's emotions overcome him. He had to keep telling himself that Givens had won. That meant no more FDA problems and full, unfettered access to the largest economy in the world. Helen's hand gently caressing his cheek, Alex finally let go and allowed himself to drift off to sleep.

CHAPTER 16
SHAREHOLDER CALL

Alex woke far too early the next morning. He winced at the strands of light leaking through the blinds and wobbled slightly on his way to the bathroom. After scrolling through election news on his phone long enough for his left leg to fall asleep on the toilet, he stood, then limped over the heated tile to the vanity. Shaking his legs and rubbing his eyes, he looked in the mirror and worked his cheekbones. *Still as handsome as ever, you devil,* he thought to himself. After a shave, hot shower, and a few ibuprofen, Alex banged out a few push-ups and sit-ups, then dressed for the day before heading downstairs.

He braced himself before heading into the kitchen. He had the well-worn feeling of not wanting to look Helen in the eye after yet another night of excess. With coffee and some food in his stomach, though, he felt recovered enough to open his mouth.

"How about last night, eh?" he said carefully, taking a swig of coffee.

"How about last night," Helen said slowly with a sly smile. She kept her eyes on her avocado toast.

"Givens pulled it off. I still can't believe it."

When Helen didn't answer, he tried to keep his cool, but felt sweat glisten on his forehead. "What happened?" he said finally. "Did I do something?"

"I knew it. What's the last thing you remember?"

"Leaning against a wall and taking a piss. Shit."

"You didn't miss much," she said, looking more relaxed. "You and Mike were on rare form though." Then, after finishing her last mouthful of toast and wiping her mouth with a napkin, she said, "I did notice that the president-elect did not have time to see his largest donators, however."

Alex shrugged. "Busy night—he was elected president after all. I'm sure he'll reach out today when the dust settles." He shoveled another mouthful of fried eggs into his mouth.

Helen said nothing, but stared out the sliding glass doors into their vibrant garden.

Alex had been surprised by how good he'd felt after breakfast, but the ride to the office proved too much.

"Pull over, Miguel!" he shouted, clutching his stomach.

The SUV swirled to the shoulder and came to a halt. "Yeah, boss?" Miguel said, putting his arm on the passenger-side seat and peering back. Alex flung the door open and retched his breakfast onto the blacktop. After a few minutes sat still, squinting against the swirling lights, Alex gestured for Miguel to go. "Slowly if you can," he said, groaning. "Try to avoid potholes."

"You got it, boss," Miguel said as the SUV veered. "Sorry boss, won't happen again." Alex lay his head back and closed his eyes.

It was after lunch by the time Alex felt well enough to work, and he decided to call an emergency shareholder meeting for the next day. He knew that the election represented a monumental win for Stallson Beverage, and he wanted to capitalize on it. He'd had Mike working on a relaunch plan since the day the FDA had put the domestic sale of Lifio on hold. Alex did not want to just enter the US market; he wanted to dominate it from day one. He'd have Mike fill shareholders in on his plan, and then Alex would throw the knockout punch with the findings of his latest pricing elasticity study. He was hellbent on getting his stock price moving back in the right direction and on putting the fiasco that was the last ten months behind him for good.

Helen swung by his office toward the end of the day. She'd been working on preparing bottling and production contracts for domestic firms eager to partner with Stallson Beverage.

"I've been taking calls all day from early birds," Helen informed him, smiling.

Alex looked up. "Early bird gets the worm."

"So it seems. I could lock in pricing right now at nine percent below our lowest international contract rate, but I think I can push it to eleven."

"Hell, why not get crazy and push for twelve?" Alex chortled.

"I very well may, but I can guarantee at least nine, so you can mention we're going to improve margins as well as diversify risk by adding more partners."

"Excellent. I have to make one more call before I close out; let's meet in the lobby in ten."

His wife nodded and turned away, sashaying from his office.

* * *

By the time the 10 a.m. shareholder call started the next morning, Alex had the confidence of a prize bull. He gave a fifteen-minute preamble, reviewing year-to-date metrics, before handing the spotlight over to Mike Smith.

"We have standing contracts with the top ten grocers, all publicly traded convenience stores, and all nationally recognized alcohol retailers," Mike began, grinning, as cocky as he'd even been. "The development of point-of-sale displays for each sales channel will be our top priority to aid launch impact. We have proposed endorsement contracts to ninety-five public figures in sports, television, film, politics, health, and fitness, with plans to double that count before the domestic relaunch. We will use a shock-and-awe campaign to blanket US consumers with knowledge of domestic access to the Lifio product. Our network of influencers will drive grassroots awareness, and then we will accelerate our marketing efforts with a full-press advertising blitz segmented by age and region so that we hit the widest swathe of the population possible."

Mike paused to let his words stew.

"We expect to hit domestic shelves the day of President Givens's inauguration, so we've already begun leaking product to influencers so they can use the holiday season to build anticipation. In addition, we're in discussions to release limited-edition glass bottles of Lifio for each of our top influencers. They will collect a healthy license fee, but the additional cost of those bottles will more than offset those fees. This will align our influencers' interests with our own and increase profit margins at the same time. With the Super Bowl closely following inauguration and Lifio's re-release, we've already started discussions with the NFL to be the title sponsor in addition to heavily investing in unique commercials during all four quarters of the big game.

"I think it is fair to say that, under Alex Stallan's leadership, Lifio's launch back into the US domestic market after ten months will be an explosive event—at least from a sales perspective."

Mike wrapped up to chuckles from the giddy shareholders on the call.

"Mike, thank you for the vote of confidence," said Alex. "Our next topic for this call revolves around the price-elasticity studies we have been conducting over the past quarter. As most of you are aware, Lifio began life with a two-dollar retail price tag. Once seen as the ceiling for a twelve-ounce can in a convenience store, we upended that false reality when we moved to five dollars per can and sales grew. After quarterly increases, we reached twenty dollars a can and stopped retail price escalation—that was nearly twelve months ago. That decision has continued to bother the leadership team at Stallson Beverage, as we did not test the full extent of our price elasticity. Increasing retail pricing had a dramatic positive impact on sales as escalations pushed user adoption while prices were low and, although consumers commented negatively on price escalation, it also drove curiosity to try Lifio and resulted in more press for the company and its products."

"Yes, Mike," Alex said, "tell us something we don't know."

Mike winked. "I'm getting there; just a little scene-setting. Over the past three months, we have undertaken small pricing model tests in international markets and are confident that Lifio has a much higher ceiling than the current retail price of twenty dollars per can. We feel the price could escalate in established markets to as high as forty-nine dollars per can before we see curbed demand."

Excited murmuring from executives and shareholders alike.

"To this end, our domestic US launch will market at twenty-nine dollars per can, up from the current retail price point. Discounts to retail partners will not change, so this will positively impact both parties. We project strong growth regardless of price due to the opening of the US domestic market, so now represents the best time to increase retail pricing. Following this adjustment, it is Stallson Beverage's plan to increase retail pricing by five dollars per can each quarter until it reaches forty-nine dollars or until we see demand diminish. This pricing escalation will drive consumer adoption and exponentially improve profits for you, our shareholders."

Mike took a breath. "The limited-edition glass-bottled products, endorsed by influencers, will retail immediately for fifty-nine dollars per bottle. This will represent an early price-elasticity test and will be a signal to the public of the value of the Lifio product."

"Thanks, Mike," Alex said, trying to contain his rising feeling of triumph, "now, let's open this call up to questions. Please submit them in writing via the conference portal if you have not done so already."

"Okay," Alex said after a moment, "one question I am seeing posed in various ways is in regard to the Thaifio Trash Man video."

Recently, a YouTube video of a homeless man in Chiang Mai, Thailand, had gone viral when a tourist had captured him boisterously singing about Lifio. In the video, the filthy man, dressed in tattered rags and a hat he had fashioned from Lifio cans, sang something in Thai that roughly translated to, "I drink Lifio. I live forever."

The video had quickly passed twenty million views, prompting an international reporter to bring the Thaifio Trash Man in for an interview. That was when the world heard how the Thaifio Trash Man had lost everything and started living on the streets because he'd spent all his money on Lifio. By his own account, he consumed a can per day, spending his entire earnings on Lifio and leaving nothing to take care of his wife and seven children. He pedaled a pedicab to earn enough to support his habit. He claimed that he felt so good after drinking Lifio that he would never stop, no matter how much it cost, and, after taking a battery of tests imposed by doctors, he proved to be in excellent physical shape—despite how he looked and, Alex imagined, how he smelled. The weird story had generated a tremendous volume of memes and late-night fodder, and stood as a potential black eye for Lifio; indeed, Alex knew investor distress could turn into share liquidation if he did not provide a strong response. Thankfully, he'd come prepared.

"First, let me start by putting this situation into context," he said, careful but confident. "Working in New York City, I am in contact with homeless people daily, and this affliction is both serious and pressing. Studies show that approximately one quarter of the homeless population suffers from extreme metal illness. The situation we see with the gentleman in Thailand should be addressed head-on, and in a serious way, by the government, not a private company. We believe it would set an unfortunate precedent if Stallson Beverage were to directly help or otherwise intervene in this individual's life.

"However, a response is indeed necessary. Therefore, Stallson Beverage has plans to donate generously to foundations for homelessness and mental health in the coming months. By staying above the tabloid-level reporting and reframing and refocusing on the root cause of the kinds of mental illness that led to this video, we can control the message and remind consumers that Lifio did not cause this man's suffering—his illness did."

There were murmurs and nods of agreement.

"Anecdotally," Alex went on, "I have seen homeless people wearing gold chains they refused to sell for shelter or food, and I've also seen them rebuff charity, such as shelter during winter, when it was offered to them. Homelessness is a serious epidemic that governments around the world must focus on. Fortunately, Lifio guaranteed this man good health during a hard time in his life. That should be the lasting message taken from this situation by the public, and I am confident that our team will be able to deliver this message in the coming days through a concerted communications effort."

Alex waited for responses and, when none came, glanced over the list of remaining questions. He'd need something to bring up the mood, he knew, something to show off their company's position. "I see one analyst asking about flavored products and assortments," he said. "Mike, could you fill our shareholders in on this subject?"

"Certainly, Alex. Flavored product has been a focus for our research and development teams of late. Due to our health-oriented product, we want to stay away from the soft drink, soda, and juice box categories; we'd prefer to push our competitors further into those segments, as we see them declining over the long term. When Stallson Beverage releases new products, the focus areas will be coffee, tea, smoothies, and sports drinks."

Damn right, Alex thought to himself. Dimly, he imagined himself walking onto the mound, then tossing a perfect strike as the first pitch of a World Series game.

"I'll briefly discuss some of the opportunities we see in each segment," Mike was saying. "With the sheer size of the coffee and tea markets, it's clearly a segment we need to address as we continue to grow. A diverse array of unique providers comprises the coffee bean and tea leaf markets. We do not feel Stallson can provide a strong enough value proposition sourcing ingredients and creating blends, so we will take a different approach: we will sell a coating that can be applied by any and all coffee bean and tea leaf producers that will provide the same benefits to products brewed using their ingredients as you get from a can of Lifio. This will allow Stallson to sell to all market players, both big and small, as providers scramble to be associated with Lifio."

"Mike, if I might cut in," Alex said with a smile, "I received a good question through our portal that you should perhaps comment on before you continue."

"It would be my pleasure."

"Everyone seems to be asking if we've begun negotiations with any of the major coffee retailers yet, namely Starbucks and Dunkin' Donuts."

"I'm not at liberty to announce any agreements," Mike said with a wink, "but I can verify that we have spoken with both names, as well as half a dozen others."

"Wonderful," Alex said, scanning the faces of his shareholders, "please continue."

"In the smoothie market, we plan to adopt a similar tactic, the main difference being that our product will be turned into a fortified, nutrient-rich powder. This powder will provide all the benefits of drinking Lifio once it's mixed with a liquid. By utilizing powder as a vehicle for adoption, we will benefit from the years of legwork the protein powder segment has put into training gym-goers to put expensive powder into their drinks. Once released, boutique smoothie bars will have a significant upsell opportunity and, before you ask, we have already opened dialogs with the most notable market participants.

"Finally, the sports drink space. This industry is currently dominated by giants such as Gatorade. We've decided to sell today's liquid Lifio product wholesale to segment leaders; in turn, they'll sell versions of their current assortment with a Lifio badge on the label. A key tactic employed here is one hundred percent crossover. In order to come to terms with Stallson Beverage, providers must be willing to make all of their current products available with Lifio. This has already been agreed to by the team at Gatorade, and will be standard in all of our contracts moving forward."

Again, excited chatter from the shareholders. Alex suppressed a grin; they were eating out of their palms.

"This brings me to an important point," Mike said, not even trying to conceal his grin. "All products containing Lifio's proprietary formula will bear a Lifio badge. The badge, currently in design, will be a clear indication to consumers that they are buying an authentic product that uses Lifio as an ingredient."

"Thank you, Mike," said Alex. "Very exciting indeed, but those developments have not yet taken place, so let's put any new questions on this topic on hold for another video call. Today's call, after all, is focused on the monumental news that Givens won the election, meaning Lifio will be back on American shelves after his inauguration. I see a question on this very topic just came through: a shareholder asked if we plan to use some of the FDA findings in advertising campaigns and how we plan to combat the FDA claim that Lifio only needs to be used once in order to be effective."

"Excellent question," Mike said. "We have indeed considered using the FDA findings in our advertising materials, but have not yet determined if we will do so. We did something similar in Russia when we first launched, using government approval testing to generate the interest of the public.

"However, it's different in the US. The 'only once' lie, as we are calling the FDA's claim that Lifio need only be used once, clearly has no basis in reality. Most, if not all, of the people on this call drink Lifio regularly, so I do not need to explain to you how much better you feel the more you drink it. When I first started drinking Lifio, I was fifty pounds overweight and had high blood pressure and cholesterol. Now I'm fit and trim, with no heart or cholesterol problems whatsoever—but that didn't happen overnight. It was a gradual process that took a year of drinking Lifio to take place. To attack this false claim, we plan to work with our vast team of influencers inside and outside of the United States. During this holiday season, you will see each of them tell their story, just as I have told you mine, of their Lifio transformation. We feel these will be powerful stories, and they will thoroughly debunk the 'only once' lie."

Alex cleared his throat. "It looks like we've run out of scheduled time on this call. As always, I thank you, our shareholders, for your support. We have great things ahead. Have a wonderful day."

As soon as the call ended, Mike's head popped around Alex's office door. He strode in, fist-pumping the air.

"You killed it!" Mike yelled.

"No, you killed it!" Alex yelled back, getting up from his desk, full of nervous energy. He felt elated; they'd knocked it out of the park, and he couldn't wait to see how the stock price reacted.

"You hungry?" Mike asked, looking bullish.

"You bet," Alex responded, immediately picking up his coat.

"Let's get big bloody steaks," Mike said with a wide grin, and Alex nodded as he strode out the door, Mike on his heels. After months of living under the shadow of the FDA, Alex finally felt like they were back on track.

CHAPTER 17
INAUGURATION DAY

Meme strode free of the hotel's revolving door, only for a sharp, cold blast to threaten to carry her away from Mike, who followed close behind her.

Alex buttoned his coat as he watched Meme right herself and rush into the waiting limousine. Helen leaned toward him and murmured, "We have to share a limo," then pulled down her hat and exited the hotel. Alex hurried after her, climbing into the toasty limo.

"I'm just used to better accommodation is all," Meme was saying. "I'm sure Alex will back me up here." Alex glanced up to find Meme's brow furrowed, the palms of her hands turned toward him.

"DC's not New York, what can I say?" Alex deflected, shrugging. But he could see Helen's expression and he could read her mind. She was a numbers person and, considering the amount of money they had donated to the cause, Alex felt was certain his wife was unimpressed by the accommodations Givens had arranged for them thus far.

"We're here, aren't we?" Mike said, playing peacemaker, "we might as well make the best of it. I mean, how often do you get invited to an inauguration ceremony, right?"

Mike was right. Alex wanted to stay positive, but he couldn't quiet the itch in his belly that told him something was wrong. The communication had felt scripted and lacking exclusivity; he'd grown used to overindulging his access to Givens during the campaign, and finding that access reduced now felt … off.

"Honestly, Alex," pouted Meme, "I would have thought Givens would have called you directly to invite us to the inauguration."

"Meme, let it go," said Mike, his voice strained. "I'm sure the man's busy getting ready to take over the country and all."

Meme turned away from her husband, arms crossed, and stared out the window. Alex managed to suppress a grin; Meme's tantrums always amused him. He turned to his wife, hoping to share a raised eyebrow, but found Helen's eyes hard and cold. Even Mike avoided his eyes.

Alex swallowed, trying to reassure himself. Limited access wouldn't matter if the day went as promised. President Givens had told the American people countless times throughout his campaign that he would restore their access to Lifio on inauguration day. If he broke his promise to Stallson Beverage, Alex knew he would also be breaking his promise to the entire nation.

* * *

Michael sighed as he flicked from one channel to the next. Ana, snuggled next to him under a blanket, said, "Go back—what about that? *House Hunters?*"

Michael shrugged in response and did as he was told. Len, in briefs and a t-shirt, as always, sat down on the other side of the couch, eating from an open can of tuna with a fork.

"Is disgusting," Len said, dropping the can on the coffee table. Before Michael could stop her, Ana was in the kitchenette with his tuna.

Len looked at him. "What? Covers? You share?" he said, pawing at the blank spot only recently vacated by Ana.

Michael shooed him away as Ana came back and handed Len a tuna salad sandwich on a plate with carrots on the side.

"Woman good," Len said, making Ana smile as she snuggled back into Michael.

"Is it on yet?"

"Is what on yet?" Michael asked.

"The power transitions today."

"What power?"

"Your president. The power."

"Oh, the inauguration. We're not watching that—what, are you crazy?" Michael said, almost laughing.

"Is very rare thing for power to change," Len said softly. "You should watch."

"I'll tell you what: you watch and let me know what happens," Michael said, flipping the remote control to Len. "Come on, let's go for a hike down the Blue Ribbon Trail," he said to Ana.

* * *

After a three-month lame-duck period, Melanie knew her time at the FDA—as well as Carrie's and Sebastian's—was coming to an end. Melanie had watched Carrie work herself to the bone, trying to do the impossible and finish ten years of research work in only a few months. In the meantime, Melanie, with Sebastian's help, had attacked the task of preparing for the transition of power at the agency, documenting all plans and strategies still in action.

Melanie felt nauseous reminiscing on her time at the FDA. *I can't name one good thing I did,* she thought to herself as she took her first bite of a bagel in the lobby atrium. Carrie emerged from the elevator with Sebastian at her side.

"Good Morning," Sebastian said to Melanie as they approached, and Melanie did her best to choke down her mouthful.

"Morning," she managed, covering her mouth.

"Well, here we are," Carrie said, in her beige trench coat.

"You know, Carrie, we haven't always got along—" Melanie started.

"You don't say."

"But," she continued, brow furrowed, "I have to tell you that what I enjoyed most about my time at the FDA was that most of the people I worked with were truly focused on doing good. And you were one of those people. I just wanted you to know that."

Sebastian looked the other way, pretending not to hear.

"Thank you," Carrie said, her cheeks a little rosier than normal.

"Well, it looks like our car's here," Sebastian said, saving Carrie from having to say anything more. He hurried to the doors and held them open. "After you."

While the sun was shining, the wind had an arctic bite to it, causing them to hurry into the SUV for the long ride through traffic to the Capitol Building. Melanie felt that the inauguration would at least give her a sense of closure and something concrete to commiserate over with Sebastian and Carrie—something to mark the end of their long road.

"I love your coat, Carrie," Sebastian said, beaming.

"It was my father's," Carrie said simply.

After a few moments of silence, Sebastian turned to Melanie and asked, "Have you ever been to an inauguration before?"

"No."

More silence. Minutes later, Sebastian said, "Why don't we go to some of the museums on the Mall tomorrow? We could make a day of it."

"No," Melanie and Carrie said in unison, and the ensuing silence carried for the rest of their ride.

* * *

Only when the figure of President Givens appeared behind the podium and a voice announced that the inaugural address would commence did the crowd still. Mike reached across Helen and tugged Alex's jacket to get his attention.

126

"How the hell did Stefán get better seats than us?" he said, pointing to the area just behind and to the left of the president. There, on the landing where the president stood for the inaugural address, was Stefán Jónsson.

"What the fuck?" Alex breathed, frowning. "I didn't think Stefán even knew Givens."

Never one to miss an opening, Meme piped up: "Well, judging by his seats, he must know him better than we do."

"Maybe they put him up there on stage because he's the inventor of Lifio. It's a publicity stunt," Alex said, as much to convince himself as the others.

Helen pulled him close and whispered in his ear, "You made this company, Alex. Stefán was just a failed nerd before you took an interest in his little drink and turned it into something. Givens is a real piece of work, not having us up there. As soon as this is over, I'm going to give him a piece of my mind. If he ever wants another penny from us, he'd better get in line and remember who got him elected in the first place. It certainly wasn't *Stefán*." Helen said the inventor's name too loud, causing Meme to smirk.

After a further moment of silence, President Givens raised his arms to the crowd.

"My fellow citizens!" he began. "Today we celebrate a new era in human history. Our nation and our world are changing faster than ever and, as the world's oldest democracy, we must change with it in order to endure. Our founders understood that change was timeless and never-ending, and today, we must change to preserve our ideals of life, liberty, and the pursuit of happiness. I stand before you now as an agent of that change.

"But before we can usher in a new America, we must take a moment to honor my predecessor, President Williamson, for her service to the American people."

President Givens extended his arm toward President Williamson, who, Alex saw, was stood behind to the side of the stage. She took a step forward and, face strained, waved out at the audience, to light applause. Before the boos could get too loud, Givens moved on.

"And I thank the millions of men and women who have served and who continue to serve in our armed forces. Without your resolve and sacrifice, our nation would not be what it is today. We are forever in your debt for the service you have done our great country."

With that, the large contingent of armed forces personnel in attendance stood and applauded, with shouts of "Hoo-rah!" ringing out.

"Our country is no longer that of our mothers and fathers," Givens said, his tone softening. "Change is ever-present and immediate. Improvements in technology, communications, and medicine have taken us to new heights, and we are only constrained by our ambition to climb that ladder. Breakthroughs that would have been considered miracles a generation ago are happening daily, and it is our generation's challenge to harness these developments so that they may not be wasted or squandered.

"Our country's first president, George Washington, famously embraced the modern science of his day by wearing some of the first dentures ever produced. He did this because he inherently knew that those who embraced change would always overcome those who worked to oppress it. Powerful forces threaten to stifle innovation and slow progress in the name of caution. Yet the urgent question of our day is whether there will be a greater price to pay for caution than for advancement."

Alex scowled. He could feel the crowd leaning into Givens's words, drinking them in as if they were water in a desert.

"Scientific achievements have created a changed world, a world we cannot deny. This new world has improved the lives of billions around the globe, who are now free of disease and are poised to live far longer lives than they ever dreamed possible. But political dysfunction and bureaucratic red tape held back our rights and freedoms; the benefits of our discoveries were enjoyed by the rest of the world but withheld from hard-working Americans."

A rowdy member of the crowd screamed out, "Freedom!"

"We have hard choices to make and difficult first steps to take. Yet we have not done so. We have meandered and pondered, studied and deliberated, but at what cost? At the cost of the ill, at the cost of the poor, at the cost of the elderly. Too high has the cost of our inaction been."

Givens paused and peered theatrically out at the crowd. A charged silence rang out, and Alex caught a small smile appearing on the president's lips.

"The greatest modern discovery of our age," Givens began again, his voice swelling, "has been made not by a company but by a man. A man named Stefán Jónsson. Born in a small town in Iceland, he studied science from a very early age. Throughout his illustrious career, he focused on breakthroughs that could improve the human condition, and he has been successful—wildly successful. While many may know products containing his proprietary additives, I am here to introduce you to the man."

Chants of "Stefán, Stefán, Stefán!" broke out among the crowd. Alex could hardly believe it; even now, President Givens was turning to gesture toward the man whose name hundreds of Americans were chanting. Alex saw the appreciation, the *admiration* in the president's eyes. Helen's fingers tightened around his arm, and Alex felt his body go cold.

"Far too often, our dysfunctional bureaucracies have withheld groundbreaking discoveries from our people. Now I stand before you as your agent for change, and with all the authority of my office, I ask the Congress to join with me. But no government can undertake this mission alone, so I ask my fellow Americans to support this necessary change by embracing it fully."

Alex swallowed, his ears ringing.

"As my first act of office, I will create a new agency: the US Department of Human Evolution and Development. This agency will be separate from the US Department of Health and Human Services, and will focus solely on the continued evolution and development of our species. And, as my second act of office, I proudly appoint Dr. Stefán Jónsson as the first commissioner of the US Department of Human Evolution and Development."

The crowd erupted with applause. Alex watched as if through water the scientist he had plucked from Iceland stand, smile, and raise his hand to the crowd, who cheered their adoration. Adoration, Alex thought, that should by right be *his*.

When the applause quietened, Givens leaned once more over the podium. "In the 1920s, widespread deficiency of an essential nutrient, iodine, became evident. Change was necessary, so change we did, and by 1924, most salt in the United States contained iodine. This ingenious delivery mechanism led to a complete reversal of a nutrient deficiency epidemic and has been credited with improving the average American's IQ by more than three points.

"In the 1950s, again we answered the call to action. After decades of research on tooth decay, it was discovered that trace amounts of fluoride, to be added to our nation's water supply, would prevent it. By 1951, the US Public Health Service released a policy mandating that all publicly supplied water must include fluoride, eradicating a problem overnight.

"Our rich history is filled with scientific and technological developments creating powerful positive change. Today, one such change is upon us. Dr. Stefán Jónsson, appointed but not yet confirmed commissioner of the US Department of Human Evolution and Development, will inject our nation's water supply with the same chemical compounds found in the product he is famous for inventing: Lifio."

It was as if Alex's stomach had fallen from his body. His knees began to shake, and the crowd seemed to close around him. He wanted more than anything to be gone—anywhere would do, anywhere but here. Helen was shouting something, fingernails digging into his arm, but he couldn't make out her words.

"Today," Givens said, eyes scanning the crowd, "I put the American people first, and cut through our nation's red tape. No longer will Americans be made to wait because of their government's indecision. Today, the politicians stop telling you what you can or cannot drink; today, you, the people, get a win."

Applause. Bodies jostled against Alex's back and he swayed like a reed, just barely managing to stay standing.

"In order to make this change a reality, I need you, the people. We need each other. There will be dissenters and naysayers who will try to take this away from you. But, with your help, with your support and backing, we can win this battle. We can do more than celebrate America; we can rewrite the idea of what it means to be American—an idea born in crisis and soon to be challenged. An idea tempered by our united resolve and strengthened by our sense of equality.

"And now, with no secrets left between us, I ask you to unite with me, my fellow Americans. Unite against the bureaucracy that may challenge us. Unite against those who threaten your freedom. Unite and follow me into our new world.

"Thank you, and God bless you all."

Before President Givens could finish his last word, the crowd erupted with the force of a hurricane, surging forward and backward as the body of people became one in their jubilation. Alex, caught in the tide, finally allowed himself to fall.

CHAPTER 18
DON'T LET THE DOOR HIT YOU

The Oval Office smelled of freshly cut flowers. Down the long, broad corridors and hallways, men and women buzzed in a flurry of activity. When his fifteen-minute time slot finally arrived, Stefán stood. The president's chief of staff, an angry little man with a razor-sharp tongue, ushered him into the office and into a plaid blue and yellow chair across from President Givens, who looked utterly at ease.

"Mr. President," Stefán said.

"Dr. Jónsson. We must stop meeting like this." Givens grinned. "Do you remember when we first met?"

"I do. It was at the fundraiser at Alex's home in the Hamptons."

"That is correct. Do you remember what we spoke of?" he continued gently.

"Yes, Mr. President—I just don't understand why I am here exactly, sir."

The president took an audible breath as he rose from his chair and walked to the window. "We both want to change the world."

"Yes."

"And we both want man to be the architect of the next stage of human evolution. That was our shared ambition. Do you not want to restore the greatness of man?" The president said, the cadence of his voice rising.

"Well?" Stefán said, unsure how the president expected him to answer. He remembered Givens telling him that Alex was holding him back, that he needed to be pushed out of his nest: that

132

it was time to fly. But he certainly did not remember promising to restore man to some form of past greatness. That sounded biblical and, Stefán thought, more than a little sexist.

"Ah … I do remember agreeing to treat the water supply so we could liberate your country from the ills of corporate greed." *Alex and I made our money—enough money for several lifetimes.*

Givens turned back to face him and shook his head. "Our goal had nothing to do with greed; the free market takes care of greed in time. The goal has always been to dictate our own evolution so that we may realize our God-given potential."

God-given potential? This is the first time I've heard the word "God" come out of your mouth.

The president stared back out the window. "Matthew 5:48: 'You therefore must be perfect, as your heavenly Father is perfect.' This is why you are here."

Scripture? Stefán swallowed. "I'm sorry, Mr. President, but I am woefully lost."

The president picked up the phone on his desk and said something into it. Moments later, Givens's chief of staff was back in the room, shouting a torrent of questions at Stefán.

"We supplied a twenty-four-page department overview memo, detailed interim steps, case examples of how the department will serve our country, full organizational flow charts, a year-one sample budget, not to mention countless other peripheral details, and you have done nothing!" the little man said, now blue in the face.

"Now do you see the problem?" the president asked.

Stefán had been working himself to the bone trying to set up a laboratory in the archaic building that had been bestowed upon him. The enormous building on the Mall did not have a fiber connection, or even proper light or ventilation. *What had they expected him to achieve in a few months? Contractors would need the better part of a year to get the building up to his standards.*

"No, I'm afraid I don't," Stefán replied.

"I-I-I can't," the little man stuttered, "Mr. President, Dr. Jónsson has not filled a single high-level position in the Department of Human Evolution and Development. He is too focused on setting up the laboratory."

Now facing Stefán, the angry little man said, "I've begun to fill administrative positions to the best of my ability in order to keep up appearances, but you're not even giving those people any direction or guidance. What did you expect when you accepted this political appointment?"

Not knowing what to say, he told the truth: "I expected to have the financial backing of the United States to continue my research."

The man gaped at him. "But surely you understand that we are close to the end of the president's first one hundred days in office and yet the newly minted Department of Human Evolution and Development is not yet functioning, nor has it made any positive impact on the American people."

One hundred days? Stefán thought. *You expect me to rebuild my lab from scratch and provide tangible results that an American could understand in one hundred days?*

"Look," Stefán said slowly, glancing at Givens, "I need to be in my lab in order to make an impact, not building a new one or filling in organizational charts."

The president, who had so far remained a spectator to their exchange, said, "Stefán, I want you to remember our common goal: to be in a position of power, you must make sacrifices. I've told the American people that we will pursue God's work by transforming our lowly bodies to be like his. And, regardless of the work you are doing in your lab at this moment in time, we need you to focus on building a government agency. Fill out your department's organizational chart, set up some initiatives, give them goals—and then you can return to the laboratory."

"Yes, Mr. President," Stefán said quietly, not sure what else to say. He turned and made his way out of the Oval Office and into the hall, where the vice president's chief of staff ambushed him: "The vice president would like a word. If you could please follow me."

Sighing, Stefán followed closely, only to be deposited on the vice president's couch to wait. *How do I get out of this place?* he thought. Absentmindedly, he stood and moved around the room, examining the bookcases. The door remained open and, as he moved closer, eyeing a painting of a Civil War naval battle raging on the open sea, he couldn't help but overhear the president's voice. He leaned more closely to the painting in order to hear every word.

"He won't make it much longer," the president said.

"He better not," came the chief of staff's voice. "He might be a genius, but he doesn't know a lick about running an organization."

"Just have someone ready, someone like—" and the president's voice cut off as the door finally closed.

Flustered, Stefán stood to leave just as the hulking vice president entered the room.

"Mr. Vice President," he said, offering his hand.

"Dr. Jónsson." After pleasantries, the vice president—a slumped-over man with colorless eyes—meandered between pointless topics until he mustered the courage to ask about the progress, or lack thereof, at the Department of Human Evolution and Development. From the VP's line of questioning, Stefán could tell that the entire cabinet must have read a similar briefing. Mentally exhausted, Stefán nodded through the meeting, then exited the West Wing and headed for the laboratory he had spent the last few months of his life creating. *Alex always handled the organization—why couldn't they? That's what they do, isn't it?*

Anxious and depressed, Stefán decided he'd head back to Iceland for a few days—or, he thought, for as long as he could before the Americans started making a fuss.

Right off the plane, Stefán's mood softened as the clean, fresh Icelandic air filled his lungs. It was getting dark already, though it was only midday, and he could taste salt from the nearby shore. He took a cab to the home his parents had left him—the home he'd grown up in. It was a low-rise whitewashed two-story with burgundy trim and shutters, and stood overlooking the gray sea stretched out below.

Once he finished settling in, he bundled up and took a stroll along the harbor. Seals played in the waves and gathered on the rocky shoreline, hoping for a few hours of midday sun before going out to feed. The ocean churned with white caps brought in by a heavy arctic wind. He did not run into anyone on his walk, and all the better—the solitude suited him. *This is my home,* he thought to himself as he lay in bed that night, staring out at the sea. And he knew then what he had to do.

CHAPTER 19

A DREAM COME TRUE

After careful deliberation, Ana selected a strapless dress with a pink and white floral pattern—one of her favorites. It was Michael's graduation, after all, a big day. Len and Michael had left the apartment earlier for the ceremony, leaving Ana to wait for Michael's father to arrive and escort her. Her palms clammy, she buzzed around the apartment straightening things. Finally, the doorbell chimed, and she jumped.

Lewis Lori, a short, brown-eyed man with slumped shoulders, stood in the doorway wearing a melancholy smile. "Hello, Ana. It was wonderful to finally meet you last night. Shall we go?"

After rushing to grab her purse, Ana looked in the mirror one last time and then followed Mr. Lori to his red convertible mustang.

"I love your car," Ana said quietly, trying to make conversation.

"I do too," he said with a sigh, "I'll miss it."

"I'm sure you'll be able to find a new one," Ana said with an apologetic smile. Michael's mother had lost her life only months prior during a burglary gone wrong, and positivity was running in short supply. "Speaking of new things, Michael told me your house sold. Congratulations."

"It's true," he replied, voice a monotone.

"I think it's wonderful you've chosen Hawaii as your new home; I hear it's beautiful."

"It is."

"Park just up here on the left," she said, pointing to an approaching parking lot sign.

They hurried through crowds of photo-taking parents decked out in suits and dresses into the main hall, where they took their seats. The graduating student body was front and center, and Ana waved at Michael, who shot her a quick smile. Several unmemorable speeches from various academics and officials followed, and time wore on. Mr. Lori did not speak to Ana unless prompted, and even then, she received only one-word answers. When the students finally threw their hats and filed out to find their families, it was a great relief. She hurried toward Michael, who was making a beeline for them, Len behind him, and hugged him.

"Congratulations!" she said, kissing him on the cheek.

"Well done, Magnum Cum Laude," Mr. Lori said, coming up behind Ana, "Your"—he looked down, choking something back, then righted, swallowing—"I'm proud of you." He leaned forward and whispered something in Michael's ear. "And you too," he said to Len, straightening and forcing a smile. "Congratulations." He extended his hand, and Len shook it.

"Thank you, sir."

"Shall we go to lunch?"

Ana rode with Len and Michael. Michael was silent as Len watched the road, his car weaving after Michael's father's.

"Did your parents watch the graduation?" Ana asked at last.

"Yes, online," Len said, not taking his eyes from the road.

"That's nice."

"*Da*. How long you and Michael stay in apartment?"

"Until the end of the month," she answered.

"I go then too."

"We'll miss you," Ana said, glancing at Michael. With Len heading back to Ukraine and she and Michael off to Texas, she wondered if they'd ever see each other again.

"We will see each other, just on screen, like parents," Len said, shooting her a quick smile.

Ana just nodded. *Does he believe that?* she wondered, *or is he just trying to avoid feeling something? The three of us have been so close this last year.*

Ahead, Mr. Lori pulled into a parking lot. Len frowned as he reversed in alongside. When the car was finally still, the three climbed out and headed toward a bright building surrounded by well-manicured flowers. Soft island music and the scent of hibiscus greeted them as they entered the Lagoon Grille. Mr. Lori stood waiting for them. A smiling hostess led them to a table, where Michael pulled out Ana's chair for her before taking a seat opposite. Michael tended not to talk much when he was nervous, and Ana noticed that Len carried most of the conversation through lunch. As the waiting staff cleared their plates, Michael got up and stood behind his father, clutching his chair. His father turned to look up at him and said, "What is it?"

Michael took Ana's hand and lowered himself to one knee.

Ana felt her face flush, and sweat rolled down the back of her neck as she turned to stare at Michael, unblinking. They had talked about it a few times, but she'd not thought it would happen any time soon. Her hands were shaking, and she clutched them together to still them. Len had a silly smile on his face, while Michael's father looked puzzled.

"Ana, ever since the day we met, I've known we were meant to spend our lives together. You have been with me through the worst. This year has been a challenge and a triumph and I could not have done it without you. I never want to go through another year without you. Ana, will you marry me?"

She fell into his embrace while he knelt and kissed his cheeks. "Yes, yes, yes!"

Eventually, they stood, and a wide grin spread across Michael's face. Mr. Lori had begun to sob and held his face in his hands.

"Mr. Lori? Lewis, are you okay?" she asked.

"I'm happy for you," he said through his tears, "I just … miss her."

Michael's smile faded. "I miss her too, Dad. Come on. Let's get out of here," Michael said, helping his distraught father stand, eyes on the floor.

"What? No Champagne?" Len asked with a frown.

"Let's do that later," Ana whispered as she put her hand on Len's. "Come on, let's go."

* * *

Michael's parents had put him through college but, since his mother's death, Michael had refused all help from his father. It wasn't a problem for Ana, who had been earning her living from an early age, but instability was new to Michael. They were married by a judge, with only Ana's grandmother, Michael's father (after Ana insisted), and Len as witnesses. Before they knew it, the end of the month came and they were moving out.

"Mama, stop crying," Ana said—her grandmother, a small plump woman who smelled of tamales, had fallen to pieces when she heard of their plan to move. "I will still see you; I promise!"

"But Texas is so far," the old woman said through her tears.

"I know, Mama, but California is too expensive to start a family. You know this; you're always saying how expensive everything is here. Come on, help me pack these dishes."

"But why so far," Mama said, taping and shifting another box, "why not Arizona?"

"I can work anywhere, but Michael wants a career in software development and Austin is known for that."

"So is San Francisco!"

"Mama, it's too expensive," Ana said, frowning.

"Where are you going again?"

"Mama, you know this: New Austin, in Texas."

Mama took a seat at the kitchen table and started crying again.

"Mama, you have to stop."

Ana spotted Michael poking his head around the corner and waved him into the room as her grandmother tried but failed to wrap her small arms all the way around her.

"I'll take care of her," Michael said, entering with a concerned smile.

With the station wagon fully loaded, Ana kissed her Mama goodbye, giving her a final squeeze before climbing into the car. "Drive," she told Michael, waving to her sobbing grandmother through the window. She'd not thought it would be this hard; if they didn't leave Mama now, she never would.

She wouldn't let Michael waste any of their savings on hotel rooms, so they took turns driving while the other slept. Their first night driving through the desert, they pulled off the highway onto a dirt access road. After hiking a few miles up a small hill, they gazed out over the valley, washed raw with pale moonlight. They stood together for a long while, neither of them saying anything.

By the time they returned, the air was crisp. Ana rubbed her neck, wincing at the tightness there. Michael covered the roof of their station wagon with blankets and, holding one another, they felt fast asleep, the stars glittering above them.

The next morning, pink blended into purple and dark blue on the horizon. Ana rubbed sleep from her eyes, a soft smile on her face. She turned and watched Michael's chest rise and fall, then rubbed her cheek against his scratchy beard. She pulled her leg over his hips, straddling him and nuzzling his neck. She ran her fingers through his short brown hair, pawing at him. As his eyes began to open, she kissed him, sucking on his lower lips and biting it softly, then harder, until she could feel him. His face cracked into a smile.

* * *

After several days of roving over miles of desert by road and foot, they finally arrived. It was a sunny Thursday afternoon, and the Texas air was thick and hot. The cheap month-to-month rental they'd settled months ago was nicer than Ana had been expecting: it was an old ranch house, and though the seventies décor made it feel like someone's grandparent's retirement home (complete with ramps), it was light and spacious. Ana loved the rocky trails and the view of the valley below, but the low cost was explained the first time they tried to drive into New Austin; it took almost two hours. On their next trip, Ana's first stop was a real estate agency located on an alabaster avenue in downtown New Austin.

"Hello," a gleaming woman in a red jacket said, "welcome to Smith and Smith realtors."

"Hello," Ana said, smiling. "My husband and I are new to the area and we would like some help finding an apartment."

"Wonderful," the woman said, "take a seat. Perhaps you could tell me a little about what you're looking for."

Ana did as she was told. She couldn't help but notice the high ceiling and the vast oak-finish desks scattered around the glass-fronted office. She wondered if they could find an apartment with similar features. "We're from Pasadena, California, and we'd like a two-bedroom two-bathroom apartment in New Austin—ideally close to the city center."

"Okay, that should be doable. Is this a company-sponsored relocation?"

"No," Ana said, frowning. "I clean and my husband just graduated from Caltech as a software developer. He'd really like to walk or bike to work."

The woman paused, appearing to choose her next words carefully. "I understand … perhaps I could give you a rundown of the area so you can, err, *fine-tune* the neighborhoods we'll be considering."

Ana smiled, relieved. "Yes, that's exactly what I need."

"New Austin has been called the next Dubai because it's purpose-built and it sprung up almost overnight. New Austin has all of the swanky technology jobs and many corporations are relocating here from New York, Silicon Valley, Los Angeles, you name it. There are only next-generation malls, restaurants, houses, offices, and parks. Everything built in New Austin has to follow strict building standards, which results in gigantic properties. It is quite possible the fastest-growing city in the world; everyone is flocking to it, but few can afford it."

"Oh, I see, so it's Texas's Beverly Hills?" Ana said slowly.

"In some respects, yes, or Silicon Valley," the woman said, smiling apologetically. "Particularly in terms of price."

"Oh." Ana suddenly wondered why'd they'd bothered leaving California; if New Austin was as expensive as San Francisco, why'd they come all this way? "Okay," she said, "that doesn't sound like somewhere we can afford right now. Where else might you recommend that would give my husband access to the technology job market?"

"Austin, sometimes called Old Austin, would be the place. It has high rises, low rents, and is filled with eager up-and-comers."

"That sounds nice," Ana said, her voice flat, "and how far is it to New Austin from Austin city center?"

"Half an hour without traffic. If you want to look outside the city, there are always smaller homes and housing developments that will be less expensive, but the commute will be longer."

"It sounds like an Austin high-rise would be better; I don't want him in the car all day long. I'd prefer it if we didn't even have a car."

"That might be possible in the city," the agent suggested.

"Walking paths and parks are important too; we like to be out in nature as much as we can."

"That all depends on what your idea of nature is," the woman said with a knowing smile. "There are plenty of parks and places to walk, but it's still a city."

"Okay." Ana knew they weren't going to get everything they wanted, and earning a living had to take precedence. "Tell me a little bit about the neighborhoods, please."

"Well, the smaller homes outside the city absorb the working-class population, so it's a more down-to-earth feel, with people doing their best to keep food on the table."

"And how about Austin city, where you were suggesting?"

"Old Austin was the hippest city in Texas a decade ago; now it plays second fiddle to New Austin. But where doesn't?" The woman's teeth gleamed, her shoulder lifting as Ana nodded. "During the week, Old Austin is quiet, but that's only because it's filled with younger people. The city still has that urban funk to it. Still, whenever someone makes it big, they tend to head to New Austin."

"I see. And New Austin?"

The woman's face lit up. "Well, as I was saying, it's a real sight to behold. Wow—I mean, wider streets and houses of increasing size have swallowed up square miles at a blistering speed. Massive urban sprawl, led by a demand for bigger buildings, led to New Austin in the first place."

"Okay."

She reached out and patted Ana gently on the arm. "I know it's a lot, but rest assured there are vibrant and distinct districts in both New and Old Austin. Working this market for the last few years, I've seen two worlds diverge and grow separate and unique characteristics."

Like the evolution of secluded island species, Ana thought to herself.

"Don't give up on Austin; it's filled with nostalgic barbecues, music venues, and even a natural swimming pool at Barton Springs. It's like New Orleans: people have a little grit and dirt underneath their fingernails because they work hard."

Finally, Ana felt herself relax. *I work hard*, she thought. *That sounds good.*

"Is it possible for you to take us on a tour before we pick an area to focus our search on?"

The woman nodded and glanced back at her laptop screen. "It would be my pleasure."

It was true: after spending the day walking down the huge, empty streets, Ana knew that New Austin was not for them. Old Austin, on the other hand, had a worn, rugged appearance and a distinctly competitive edge that Ana found both endearing and compelling. She'd never expected to live a pampered life; hell, she didn't *want* to. In Austin, half the city took their lives one day at a time, and the other half spent every moment looking for a way up. It would suit them both.

That first night in their new apartment, Ana and Michael slept on the floor. The view from the ninth floor had sealed the deal for Ana; from their living room, they could see an old marble fountain across the street and, on a clear day, even the orange peaks of a few mountains on the horizon. The rooms were small and they only had a single bathroom, but the price was right and the distance to the city center would allow them to sell the station wagon if Michael managed to find a job within walking distance. It was everything Ana had dreamed of and more.

CHAPTER 20

THE FOUNDATION

It was a cool late spring morning when Melanie met Sebastian and Carrie for an early lunch at *Boragó*, a Chilean restaurant she knew Carrie loved.

"Hey Mel, how was Aruba?" Sebastian asked as she entered, standing to hug her.

"It was great, but I'm ready to get back at it. Any luck with the job search?" Melanie prompted, pulling out a chair.

"A few opportunities have come up. Ted Evans, you remember him? Anyway, he wants me to help him with a lifestyle apparel brand he's running. It's nothing groundbreaking, but the money is good, so I'm considering it."

"How about you, Carrie? You have anything new lined up yet?"

Carrie stayed seated, peering up at Melanie, her face unreadable. "I'm considering an opening at Columbia," she said.

Melanie smirked involuntarily. "Well, I'm going to cut right to the chase."

Sebastian immediately put in, "I'd expect nothing less."

"I have an opportunity, but it's not something I'm willing to consider unless the two of you come on board as well. So here we are."

"Intriguing," replied Carrie.

"Well, are you going to just keep us hanging in suspense, or are you going to tell us about it?" asked Sebastian.

"I'm waiting for another guest, actually. Let's order some food and give her a minute to get here."

When the waitress came over to take their order, Melanie deferred to Sebastian, who gleefully launched into a lively back-and-forth in Spanish with the waitress. After an intense round of bantering, the waitress trotted off, seemingly satisfied. Ten minutes later, the table resembled a mosaic, brightly colored tapas dishes strewn across it. Melanie's mouth began to water as wafts of saffron and charred meat rose from the food.

Just as they were about to dig in, a group of five well-dressed men with inconspicuous earpieces came through the door and began scanning the restaurant. After the obvious inspection concluded, a black SUV pulled up outside and a woman got out, escorted by three more men with earpieces. After the woman entered the tiny Chilean restaurant, her escorts blocked the door, positioning themselves as guards.

"Madam President," Melanie said, standing to shake the former president's hand. She caught a glimpse of Sebastian sat frozen in place, his mouth agape. Carrie, meanwhile, continued to eat as if nothing had happened.

"Please, call me Elizabeth. Madam President is a formality that is no longer necessary, given the circumstances."

Finally able to close his mouth and regain a semblance of composure, Sebastian said, "Madam President, ah, I mean, Elizabeth? It's a pleasure to make your acquaintance. If I might ask, to what do we owe this honor?"

"Straight to the point—I appreciate that. Hasn't Melanie told you?"

"Actually," Melanie said, ushing Elizabeth into a seat, "I haven't. I wanted to wait for you."

"In that case, you seem to have a wonderful table of food here, and I am famished. Why don't we break bread together, and then we can discuss the opportunity. Is that chorizo?"

Carrie finally looked up from her plate and responded with a simple, "Yes," then returned to her *chancho en piedra*.

"Carrie, please pass the chorizo and the *polbo á feira*," Elizabeth said.

The room had been quiet since the former president had entered, but now the buzz began to return. Gradually, the atmosphere relaxed.

"You like octopus?" Carrie asked as she passed the dish. The smell of grilled lemons washed over Melanie.

"I do. Charred is my favorite."

"I see." Carrie looked as if she'd carefully processed this information and filed it away for later reference.

With the delicious food and superficial conversation dwindling, Elizabeth finally approached the subject that had brought them together: "So. I'd like you to continue your work."

"Excuse me?" said Carrie.

"After taking the time to look back over my time in office, I have my regrets, but I do not regret any of the actions we took at the FDA. I regret that my sound judgment was weaponized for political gain, but I continue to stand by that judgment. This makes completing your research all the more important. The American public needs to understand the implications of the decisions that are being made on their behalf. We need to know if there will be negative side effects or unintended consequences to Lifio so that we can properly prepare, and there is no way to do that without proper research."

"That's a noble cause, but how do you intend to pay for continued research without the federal government?" asked Sebastian.

"I've asked Melanie to be the chief operations officer of my new foundation, the Williamson Foundation. Its focus will include researching the effects of the Lifio gene mutation, and I have committed four hundred million dollars of my own personal wealth toward this endeavor."

"And I've told Elizabeth," Melanie said, eyeing the former president, "that I will only take the position if you, Carrie, accept the position of chief science officer and you, Sebastian, accept the role of chief communications officer."

"Well, that depends," Sebastian said. "How much are you paying?" After a swift kick in the leg from Melanie, he hastily added, "I jest. It would be my pleasure, Madam ... sorry, I mean Elizabeth."

"Will I have the authority to hire my own staff?" asked Carrie, looking like a bulldog ready to pounce.

"Yes, of course," replied Elizabeth.

"Forty-five people. I need to hire forty-five."

"That's a very specific number, but yes, you can hire forty-five staff members."

"Forty-five of my colleagues, career FDA scientists, lost their positions at the hand of President Givens because of their diligent research on the Lifio gene mutation," she explained in response to Melanie's quizzical look. "If you'll hire them, I'll take the job."

"Done," Melanie said, and then she looked to Elizabeth for reassurance.

"Done," Elizabeth said with a nod.

"When do we get started?" asked Sebastian.

Elizabeth gave a rare smile. "Well, that depends on how quickly you can get to San Francisco."

* * *

Melanie spent the entire afternoon moving into her new office at the Williamson Foundation Research Center, just outside of San Francisco. Floor-to-ceiling glass walls poured light into her office, while the meeting area in the adjoining room featured a full wall screen for teleconferencing. Her office furniture reminded her of her former life in the private sector: open collaborative spaces had been very fashionable in the business world, and every desk, chair, and table had been geared toward teamwork. Everything she needed was at her fingertips, including a private fitness room decked out with the latest and greatest every-exercise machine she promised herself she would use occasionally. As she adjusted the monitor on her desk, Carrie appeared above her.

"I sent a purchase authorization request," she said brusquely, "have you approved it yet?"

Melanie frowned—she was leaning against the spotless yellow accent wall.

"I didn't see it. When did you send it?" Inwardly, she thought, *What more could you possibly want? Every outlandish piece of equipment you've requested we've supplied.* "Never mind, I'll just pull it up."

After pulling the email up on her screen, she noted the request had been sent six minutes prior. She resisted rolling her eyes. "Here you," she said, refusing Carrie the satisfaction of a challenge, "approved."

Ready for a fight she wasn't going to get, bewilderment flashed across Carrie's face. Deflated, she turned to leave.

"While you're spending the foundation's money so frivolously, I could use a personal refrigerator in my office," Melanie called after her.

For a second, she thought Carrie was going to turn, but she just kept walking.

Melanie allowed herself a grin.

Sebastian sauntered in looking happy. "How about these offices, huh? First-class through and through. I almost don't want to get down to work; I'm scared I'll solve all the world's problems and not get to come here anymore."

Melanie nodded. "You're right to be worried—gone are the days of broken-down equipment and faulty test results due to outdated tools. Carrie should be able to move at warp speed with this amount of funding. You don't want to know how much that laboratory of hers cost."

"You know who I just ran into? Denise. I didn't know she came on board; it feels like we have the old team back together."

"To be honest, I can't believe so many of them were willing to move. Only six declined."

"They must really want to work with Carrie," Sebastian said, winking at Melanie.

Melanie laughed. "I'm sure Carrie had plenty to do with it—that and all the money, of course."

By late fall, the foundation felt lived in. With the honeymoon quickly ending, Melanie found herself working more closely with Carrie to break old habits she had picked up after decades in public service.

"Carrie, I don't need these reports," she said, leaning against her desk.

"Which reports are you referring to?"

Melanie sighed; she could smell Carrie from across the room. She'd clearly spent another night in the lab. "All of them: weekly lab comment logs, monthly study comment and feedback forms, monthly public posting summaries, weekly web feedback notes, all these wasteful FDA-style reports."

"I see," Carrie said, "but we need records of our work."

"Carrie, these are reports required for a federal agency. We are a private research foundation. We need to work as efficiently as possible to achieve breakthroughs in science and then explain them clearly through well-documented research. We don't need bureaucratic reports like these."

Carrie frowned, apparently not understanding. "But what should I do with Stephanie and Mariel? Would you like me to let them go? They write these reports for us. In fact, they have been writing these reports for the FDA for the last thirty years."

"Carrie, I'm not telling you to get rid of them, but we are private now," she said, massaging her temple. "That means there is not a set of rules you must follow. You can do your work as you see fit—within reason, of course. Repurpose Stephanie and Mariel; I'd have them write reports you would find more useful to your research. Do you ever use the weekly web feedback notes? Did you ever even use them at the FDA?"

After a brief period of introspection, Carrie replied, "I think I fundamentally understand your feedback, however flawed the delivery. I did not realize until now that I'd replicated the FDA research framework when I did not have to. After many years in public service, I yielded my free will toward organizational design and roles. I will take this feedback to heart and make sufficient changes in the near future to become more efficient."

"That's all I can ask. Thank you."

Days later, Sebastian asked Melanie what had gotten into Carrie. She had completely rearranged her team's organizational structure and dictated an entirely new reporting and record-keeping system, and the team seemed to be moving at a far greater speed. Not wanting to steal Carrie's thunder, Melanie shrugged. It was only after Sebastian had gone that she mentally patted herself on the back, knowing she'd helped the cause in her own way by coaching Carrie.

With limited communications work going Sebastian's way, Melanie endeavored to find another way to fill his time and help the foundation as research restarted. After brainstorming with Elizabeth, she decided to focus his efforts on studying the non-biological effects of the Lifio gene mutation, including sociological and economic impacts. Although he didn't have an academic background in the social sciences, he'd read enough research papers to know the basic structure. Documenting the changes taking place for posterity felt as important as understanding the mutation itself. After putting together a small team of two assistants to do some of the more academic background research, Sebastian seemed to have finally found his calling.

Only months into their new endeavor, the highly focused team finally had the necessary time and funding to do their research the way it needed to be done. The lack of public pressure allowed for a more positive and focused research environment. San Francisco's high cost of living had some of the team on edge until the luxuries of California life began to convert them into West Coast believers. After the first six months, no one mentioned Washington, DC ever again.

CHAPTER 21

REGEN

After a few hectic months in Snæfellsnes, the fanfare of Dr. Jónsson's return home faded away, and his life returned to the way it had been years ago. It had taken a while to shake the dozens of universities and corporate suitors offering him professorships, honorary degrees, and well-paying jobs—he'd lost track of the number of times he'd explained emphatically that all he wanted was privacy—but they'd finally left him to it. He built himself a robust (yet small by recent standards) laboratory on the vacant lot next to his residence. The lab looked the part of a typical Icelandic building, blending into its surroundings with subdued, muted tones and low stature. Stefán had been able to accomplish that feat by excavating down into the earth, allowing for a full subterranean level. The exterior featured a solid burgundy façade, which matched his home's wind-worn shutters. In a final flourish, he'd turfed the entire gently sloping roof—now, it looked as if a giant had laid a grass blanket overhead. The end result was a modern laboratory that looked like a typical Icelandic home, only it was built into the side of a small hill. The rear of the laboratory, meanwhile, boasted huge windows, allowing for an unfettered view of the sea.

Arriving for his first day of work in his new lab, Stefán hung his coat, placed his packed lunch in the break room refrigerator, and then turned on the coffee maker.

"No music. Let's get straight to work. Big things today," he said. He had always worked in private, and it felt entirely natural to speak to himself out loud, as if he were with a partner. Often, he caught himself having both sides of a conversation. It helped him see different perspectives and make better decisions, or so he told himself.

"Breakthrough day, is it?"

"Exciting stuff. Let's check our samples from yesterday, shall we?"

Since his return to Snæfellsnes, Stefán had breathed new life into his research by focusing on regeneration. While the Lifio mutation had proven successful, it did not represent a completed project. Alex Stallan had pushed Stefán to introduce his product to the world before he'd consider it ready—the mutation had been stable, but the effects not nearly as dramatic as Stefán had envisioned. Simply prolonging life felt like a pitstop on the road to his real goal: optimizing humankind. For his next stop, Stefán had the accelerated regeneration of full body parts in his sights. For years, he had been performing the necessary research. His latest mutation had proven successful in Pan troglodytes—indeed, Stefán himself was surprised by how quickly his chimps' limbs had regrown.

"Hey, Wilson, how's the hand?" Stefán said, feeding the chimp a medicated treat.

"And you, Peggy, foot's looking good. Joshy, you have ears again!"

Once the treats had administered their desired effects, Stefán took the chimps out of their enclosures one at a time to take their vitals and blood and to inspect their regrown limbs.

"Amazing, wouldn't you say?"

"Inspiring, if I do say so myself. Look: full bone growth, skin, vascular, even hair. I think we found it; this time, I think we have the right sequence." Wilson's hand, while smaller in comparison to the original, appeared to be growing in real time. The almost translucent skin showed blue veins and taut muscle fibers. Hair had started to appear in random tufts upon the back of the hand. The ears, too, were nearly perfect replicas of those that had been cut off. *Clearly the regenerative duration is a corollary to extremity complexity.* Scratching the side of his head, he contemplated the implications.

After his inspection, he added to his log file on the laptop at his desk and wondered what he would make for dinner. Cooking had been his only passion beyond science for a long time now; he fondly remembered cooking what his father brought in from the sea alongside his French mother. By the age of eight, he could make a perfect hollandaise and, by fourteen, he was all but classically trained at his mother's hand. *This is not a time for food; back to work,* he scolded himself. *I may have finally unlocked the keys to regrowth, and all I can think about is food.*

But it was no good. He hurried through his notes, his stomach moaning. Finally, he looked up at the wall clock. Well, he thought, that made sense: lunchtime had come and gone. He packed up and headed into the break room, poured himself another cup of coffee (extra cream and sugar), and pulled his brown bag from the refrigerator.

"Anybody want to trade? I got tuna salad again," he said, chuckling to himself. *Nobody wants tuna salad. It turns the bread to mush by lunch, but I sure do love it.*

After working until 6 p.m. on the dot, he packed up for the day, said goodbye to his lab and chimps, and walked the few feet to his home. He unpacked a splendid meal of lamb shank in pomegranate sauce with chickpeas, roasted carrots, and potatoes dauphinoise that he had prepared the night before and reheated it in the oven while setting the table. Finally, he sat and reviewed the day's progress.

"I think it's time."

"You may be right."

"Tomorrow, then?"

"Tomorrow."

156

He spent the remainder of his evening preparing tomorrow night's duck confit. The fresh pine smell of rosemary tickled his nose as he submerged duck breasts in fat and herbs. His six-burner Wolf range, complete with French top, allowed him to revel in the freedom of self-expression. Fresh baguette dough now rising on his counter, he felt his energy wane and resolved to head shortly to bed.

The next morning, he rose at 4:14 a.m. After bundling up in his father's old sheepskin jacket and pulling on a hat and gloves, he headed out into the crisp, salty air. He strolled past his turf lab and up the hill, walking in the middle of the road. When he crested the verge, he could see the entire town. He strode past a grocery store stocking up for the day, and a delivery man unloading his truck turned to frown at him.

"Stefán?" the man said, "is that you?"

Stefán stopped in his tracks, peering through the darkness. "Magnús! I haven't seen you since my mother passed."

"I see you are world-famous now," Magnús said, still unload-ing crates, and Stefán smiled in reply, trying to think of some-thing to say.

"Where have you been? I've not seen you in years."

"I moved to Vik with Kristín. It did not go well, so I came back home. Just like you."

"Well," Stefán said. "Have a good day." He waved and turned, his walk cut short, to head back up the hill.

"Wait!" Magnús called after him. "What are you doing out at this hour?"

Stefán turned back to see Magnús had stopped lifting boxes. Now, he was staring at Stefán, frowning. "I enjoy walks to start my day," Stefán said.

"But this early?"

I walk early so I do not have to explain myself to everyone in town.

"Just getting an early start today." Stefán turned back around and started back up the hill. He could feel Magnús's eyes boring into his back.

The walk back home and then to his lab passed without other interruptions, and Stefán found himself at work earlier than normal. Excitement had taken hold of him—years of testing and research had brought him to this day. After flipping on the coffee maker and depositing his lunch in the break room, he quickly made his way over to Wilson, Peggy, and Joshy.

"Hey, guys ... and girl. Sorry, Pegs. How we feeling?"

The chimps jumped and hollered as they usually did, but they looked none the worse for wear; their regrown limbs were more fully developed today, in fact, and there were no apparent negative side effects. Stefán's final precursory check went off without a hitch, and he could feel himself sweating with excitement. He hurried into the break room, pulled open the door, flipped the top off a beaker, and downed the clear liquid in one gulp. *Here we go.*

"Woo," he said, before rushing back over to the chimps.

"We did it!" he told them. "We're officially on human trials!"

The chimps jumped and banged their cages.

"You know what that means, right? That means I won't have to cut anything else off you guys! Isn't that great?" Smiling, he headed back into the break room, grabbed his coat and a large beaker from the fridge, and bolted out the door, his excitement building.

After a short drive to the end of town, he pulled into a small dairy farm. An old farmer heard his silver Land Rover and popped his head out of the barely standing red barn.

"Hey, Stefán. It's finally ready?"

"It is," Stefán said, grinning as he handed the old farmer the beaker.

"How do you want it bottled? Same as we used to do?" the man asked, wiping his hands on his filthy overalls.

Stefán nodded excitedly. Jon ran the only bottling operation for miles; he used it to bottle the milk from his dairy cows and, every so often, locals would bring their home brews. More than a decade ago, he'd bottled Lifio for Stefán—long before Alex had stumbled upon it.

"Yeah, same as before."

"All right, this will take me a few hours, but I have to finish the cows first. It'll be ready first thing tomorrow morning," the old farmer said, and with that, Stefán headed back home to wait.

After tossing and turning most of the night, he woke well before dawn and made his morning loop three times before the sun finally rose. *I'll have to figure out which days Magnús delivers so I can take another route*, he thought. Finally, it was time: he got in his Land Rover and headed to the dairy farm. As he pulled in, he spotted a neatly stacked pallet of cases in the driveway, and he smiled.

"Morning!" The smell of manure assaulted him the moment he opened his mouth.

"Morning," Jon called. "Got you twenty-four cases all bottled up. Only thing is, you didn't tell me what you wanted on the labels, so I left them there for you. You'll have to print them up yourself. What are you naming this one, anyway?"

"Regen. What do you think?"

"Hell, I don't know, but I didn't think too much about the last one, either. Shows you how much I know," Jon said, his dry, wrinkled face scrunched up into a wry grin.

"What do I owe you?"

"Oh, that's on the house." He turned his head and spat through his front teeth.

"No, I couldn't," Stefán protested.

"If you think I'm taking money from a national hero, you're crazier than I thought."

Stefán gave an embarrassed smile. "If you insist, but next time,

I'm paying you. This is just a test run, anyhow. Will you at least take a bottle for you and the wife as a small token of gratitude?"

"That'll be just fine." The old farmer nodded and then helped Stefán load the cases into his car, bar two bottles.

Stefán drove out of the driveway, headlights cutting through the blue-gray dark, and headed down the road toward town, careful not to hit any potholes that might damage his precious cargo. He parked outside Gunnar's market and headed in.

Gunnar looked up as he came in, his broad face widening into a smile. "Hey, Stefán. You got that new product you've been promising me?"

"Sure do, but it's not labeled yet. Think you could help me with that?"

"Certainly. What are we calling it?"

"Regen."

"I like it. Did Sigurður give you the stick-on labels?"

"I have them in the back of my car."

"Great. I'll have Helga put together a nice-looking label, just like the old days. What are we charging for this one?"

"Ah, whatever you want, Gunnar," Stefán explained. "I'm giving them to you. Charge whatever you think is fair."

"Stefán, you're a saint, you know that? Can't wait to taste it myself," Gunnar said, winking at Stefán. Then, he turned to the back and yelled, "Aron, come up here and unload Dr. Jónsson's car."

"I do have one favor to ask," said Stefán, eager to be done with this part of his day. "Please record the name and contact information of everyone who buys it, if you don't mind."

"Sure, Stefán, anything. But why? I mean, I don't need to know or anything, but people are bound to ask me why I need their contact information."

"I'd like to follow up with some of them for feedback—you know, just trying to dial in the flavor and everything."

"Right, makes sense. I'll take note of everyone who buys it; I'm sure you'll know most of them."

"Thanks, Gunnar. See you later." And with that, Stefán took his leave and drove back to his lab, relieved.

He could not stop wondering what it was going to feel like. He knew deep down the science was right, but the thought of something going wrong still troubled him. *We must take risks to achieve greatness*, he told himself.

Time continued to tick away and, in a short week, he'd resolved to conclude his experiment. He had a fitful night of dreams and, to calm his nerves, he overate at breakfast, a truth his scale told him.

By lunchtime, the anxiety was eating away at him. He felt bloated and uncomfortable, and he endlessly imagined the conclusion of his experiment. *I hate pain; I don't want to feel pain.* His phone rang, breaking his chain of thought.

"Hey, Stefán," came Gunnar's voice.

"Hey, Gunnar."

"Stefán, we sold out! Helga and I can't thank you enough. We sold out in a few hours, and we were charging three thousand króna—high prices like you used with Lifio. So, I got that list of names for you if you want to pick it up."

Stefán hung his head back in frustration and let out a sigh. No matter what he did, everything revolved around money. But he didn't want to ruin Gunnar's merry mood. Next time, he'd just set the price himself. It had been a test, anyways. Who knew? Maybe there wouldn't be a next time.

"Yeah, I'll come right over and grab it from you."

"Hey, Stefán, think you could bring more? I got lots of folks asking about it and all. You know, once word gets out, everyone in town has to try it."

"I don't have any more right now, but I'll let you know as soon as I do. See you in a minute," Stefán said, and hung up the phone.

Five minutes later, Gunnar was passing Stefán the list.

Murmuring his thanks, he endured a few minutes of Gunnar and Helga begging him for more before escaping back to the lab.

That afternoon was spent cataloging the list of names, most of which he recognized. Before he knew it, dinnertime arrived. After a pork schnitzel and a warm potato salad, he went to bed early to try to catch up on his sleep—but another restless night spent tossing and turning lay in store.

In the morning, his anxiety, now worse than ever before, led him to overeat again. On the third day, the scale jumped by twenty pounds, and he could feel lumps just under his skin all over his body. He skipped his walk through town due to an uncomfortable chafing feeling between his legs, and instead made his way slowly and painfully to his laboratory.

After turning on the coffee maker and placing his lunch in the refrigerator, he heard a car skid to a halt out front. Then he heard the loud *crack* of wood splintering and a man yelling his name.

Stefán stared dumbfounded out the lab window, as if what was happening was in fact happening to someone else entirely. The man, louder now, wilder, shrieked his name, his voice raw. Stefán could hear his furniture being hurled aside, his windows being smashed. Then, from the second floor, the bull of a man made eye contact with Stefán through the laboratory window. An instant later, far faster than Stefán could process, the door of the lab flew inward and the giant of a man stormed through, a woman holding what looked like a newborn behind him. He grabbed Stefán by the shoulders, lifted him into the air, and hurled him across the room. Stefán landed in a sitting position and his head whipped backward, smashing against the tiled floor with a horrible crunch. Everything went dark.

* * *

Stefán opened his eyes. Dark, and spots of bright light. He sucked in a ragged breath, but regretted it almost instantly—he felt sick, and his head was shrieking at him. Something was very wrong. His back felt like ice, and his vision was blurred. *Where am I? Am I on ice? Did I fall in the sea?*

"You bag of shit, wake the fuck up," the giant said, stepping into focus. Before Stefán could say anything, the man swung something into his shin.

Blinding pain, of the sort Stefán had never imagined, exploded through his nervous system, and he convulsed. Vomit bubbled out of his mouth, threatening to choke him. He could smell the iron in his own blood as he felt it ooze out of his leg.

He tried to move, but found he was buckled to a metal table. Struggling, choking, gurgling, he tried to speak as the giant—and the woman too, Stefán saw, the woman with the child—gazed at him through glazed, dead eyes. Then the giant grabbed the metal table and flipped it on its side, violently jolting Stefán and spattering the white tile with a putrid cocktail of urine, blood, and bile.

With one enormous arm, the giant pulled the table upright, Stefán still glued to its surface, stammering, trying to put words together. Stefán could tell it was a man now—a man wearing green plaid and light blue jeans, everything splattered with blood and dust. *Why are you doing this!* he screamed, but no sound came out.

The man cocked his head, the hammer held ready.

Please don't, please don't.

Then the room reverberated as the shattering of bone catapulted blood and bits of flesh into the air. Stefán howled, vomit exploding out of him—and, mercifully, his brain overloaded. He shut down.

Seconds later, he regained consciousness, opened his eyes, and gasped. He tried to inhale but could not; his body felt frozen in time. His brain commanded his lungs to inflate again, but they refused. *I'm going to die,* he realized. The giant was slapping him across the face, but he could no longer feel. And then, like hitting ice-cold water, one hard slap jolted him back into the moment. Stefán's face had betrayed him. Lungs rushing with air, he felt an exhilarating moment of relief. *I'm alive.*

"Look at her!" the giant frothed, his blood-streaked face a grimace of rage. "Look at her!"

Aloft, he held the body of a baby, swollen, tumors protruding from every inch of her tiny form. Cold and stiff, the giant held her as if she might wake at any moment. The woman stood behind him, a ghost as white as snow stark against the spatters of deep red blood.

"She drank my milk," the woman said slowly, her voice a tremulous whisper, "and *look what you've done!*" She was shrieking now. *"Look at my baby!"*

She gently took the tumor-ridden corpse from the giant and pressed its swollen, blood-blistered lips to her bare, lumpy breast. Rocking back and forth, she began humming a lullaby. In one sudden twist, she looked at him, cold rage in her eyes. "She won't feed anymore. *Why won't she feed?*"

Without a word, the giant moved to the counter, grabbed something, and worked it with his hands. Then he pressed down on Stefán's head with such force it felt as though it would burst.

He screamed until his voice broke. At last, darkness swallowed him.

CHAPTER 22
SYMPOSIUM

Carrie preferred her lab coat to the too-tight tweed pantsuit she now wore, which was unfortunately necessary if she were to present herself appropriately at the International Research Symposium in Copenhagen, Denmark. Her two years at the Williamson Foundation had proved fruitful, yet the reward for her achievements felt more like a punishment. As she ascended the stone steps of the pristine building, she could not help but appreciate its architectural grace: the glass structure cantilevered out over the harbor like an oddly shaped iceberg. As Carrie crested the steps, a grand atrium filled with scientists from around the world greeted her.

"Good morning, Dr. Roberts," a young man smiled, and handed over her credentials as well as a leaflet listing scheduled seminars. Her own talk, she saw, would take place in two hours.

"Here," she yelled, waving Sebastian over after spotting him ahead of her. Sebastian sauntered over, by the looks of it enjoying himself, bringing a guest in tow. Carrie forced a smile.

"Dr. Schneider, may I introduce you to Dr. Roberts," Sebastian said, gesturing to Carrie.

"How do you do?"

"Fine," Carrie responded.

"I was just telling Dr. Schneider here about your breakthrough on germinal mutations," Sebastian led.

"Yes, fascinating," Schneider said, nodding. "When Dr. Jónsson stepped down from his role in the US government, he assured the world that his work had focused exclusively on somatic mutations."

"Dr. Jónsson clearly took liberties no scientist should take," Carrie jabbed.

"Surely you recognize the value his work has provided to society," Dr. Schneider said with mild indignation.

Carrie glanced at Sebastian, whose eyes had widened. But she had come here to share her views with the scientific community, not to coddle old fools.

"Your beloved Dr. Jónsson used CRISPR, hijacking bacteria to trigger gene mutations in humans. He planned for them to be somatic in nature so they would not be transmitted to progeny. He was not a god. And, although he may not have intended it," she said, pronouncing those last few words as if speaking to a child, "he opened a path to germinal mutations."

Carrie's voice had started to harden, and Sebastian cut her off with a desperate smile. "Shall we grab a coffee before we head in?"

"No, thank you," Carrie responded before Dr. Schneider could get a word in. "We've proved that rapid bacteria evolution *in our water supply* caused the mutation to affect male sperm cells, crossing the germinal line and allowing transmission through sexual intercourse."

When she finished, they stared at her for a moment and, coldly, Dr. Schneider excused himself.

"Might be good to cool down that temper before you give a talk," Sebastian suggested with a sigh.

"Noted, thank you," Carrie responded. *Where is Melanie when you need her? At least she doesn't wilt when challenged.* "On second thought, perhaps I should appear irritated."

"Oh?" Sebastian responded with an expectant look.

"I continue to see President Givens and the late Dr. Jónsson hailed as miracle workers or disciples from the heavens, when they should be seen as—"

"I think I get the point," Sebastian cut in.

Carrie stared at him. "Sebastian, Dr. Jónsson was killed in a murder-suicide and, over the following two weeks, an unexplained sickness killed five hundred people in the same town—a sickness that causes rapid uncontrollable tumor growth that didn't spread. It was just another experiment gone wrong," she said, poking Sebastian's chest with her pointer finger.

"I'm here to support you, Carrie. You're right, I know you're right. But Dr. Jónsson is gone. We need to open the world's eyes to the implications of his mutation; if you focus on the man, it will be seen as petty. If you focus on the effects we are now seeing, however, we can inspire investments that will accelerate our work. We need to focus on that."

"Fine," Carrie said, unwilling to give him any more than her begrudging acceptance. They strolled around the atrium and Carrie's stomach growled; jet lag was not helping her mood. She took a back seat while Sebastian worked the room. He had spent the better part of the last two years combining Carrie's research findings with socioeconomic data to create cause-and-effect relationships, so she tried to push down her anger and let him talk about his contributions.

Sebastian's easy nature lent itself to this type of free-flowing networking. He paid his audience compliments and looked for places in the conversation to insert himself and inform his listeners. Carrie, on the other hand, felt like a bull at a tea party.

"Much of my socioeconomic study revolves around the unsustainability of the world's escalating death-to-birth ratio," Sebastian was telling a group of nodding scientists. "Did you know that, according to the World Bank, before the introduction of Dr. Jónsson's mutation, there were two and a half births for every death, a ratio already well known to be unsustainable? After the introduction of the mutation, that ratio steadily increased, and now it's topped eight births for every death, accelerating nearly every global problem we have."

He turned to Carrie, smiling. "Carrie, perhaps you'd like to tell these gentlemen a little about your most recent research."

"Have you told them about the piece you wrote about economic expansion?" Carrie said, parrying his attempt to engage her.

Sebastian's smile wavered only for a moment. "The great economic expansion has not, actually, been so great when taking into account the rapidly growing consumer population," he explained, eyes darting at her. "Gross domestic product has declined when viewed per person, and leaders continue to parlay false growth into reelection campaigns instead of focusing on the long-term impacts and their costs. I wrote the paper Carrie is referring to as a counterbalance to the often-oversimplified political spin of the changes taking place in our world."

Carrie took her chance to pull away from the group for a much-needed breath of fresh air. Outside, she noticed a café across the street and, with her stomach now controlling her body, she headed for it. With two pastries down and another in hand, she finally felt satiated. By the time she returned, Sebastian was outside, searching for her.

"Come on, we have to head backstage," he shouted. "Your presentation starts in ten minutes."

Carrie attempted to hustle, but her suit wouldn't permit her to run and she ended up doing more of a hopping jaunt toward the door as she inhaled her last Danish.

On stage, in front of nearly a thousand colleagues, she began going through the intricate details of her most recent research. Her research had produced some chilling data, and she lingered on particularly pressing points before ending on what she considered an impassioned call to action. However, when she scanned the audience after the applause had died down, she did not see the abject horror, frustration, or amazement she had anticipated. In fact, she didn't see much of anything—it was as if she had just recited a short story rather than the details of groundbreaking research.

Sebastian was speaking now, his hands held aloft, but Carrie had heard him practice his speech so many times that his words had washed over her. Now, though, she saw it: the enraptured faces of the audience members. They were totally captive.

"After the mutation, however, the number of deaths from non-communicable diseases shrank rapidly, while those caused by communicable diseases remained steady, and injuries began to rise," Sebastian was saying. "We found that birth rates did not take a dramatic upswing; on the contrary, as a percentage of the population, they continued to decline worldwide. The birth-to-death ratio was the key."

Carrie watched, slack-jawed, as members of the audience jostled for their pens and scribbled down notes, some murmuring to their neighbors.

"Sixty-four million people died worldwide the year Lifio appeared on the market. This year, only twenty-eight million people perished. The only causes of death that have increased this year are malnutrition and starvation."

The room fell silent as Sebastian paused, and Carrie detected genuine widespread concern.

"When comparing food prices to wages, the amount of food a standard hour of labor can earn has increased rapidly over the past hundred years, yet after Lifio's introduction it is in decline. In the United States, food expenditures per person have risen steeply. When faced with food price escalation, first-world inhabitants offset those added costs by eating at home more often. But, in developing countries, food price escalation often translates to food scarcity."

Hanging on Sebastian's every word, the room collectively held its breath as Sebastian reached his speech's crescendo.

"Our research, along with the highlighted data, show that malnutrition and starvation have already doubled around the world and will multiply by a factor of eight over the next ten years if nothing is done. By next year, we forecast malnutrition and starvation will be the leading cause of death worldwide."

Gasps rose from the audience, and Carrie leaned back in her chair, shaking her head and allowing herself a wry smile. *Typical Sebastian!*

CHAPTER 23

SHANGHAI

Elizabeth, having utilized her political connections to gain access to international government agencies, had finally begun cataloging impacts by country in order to add depth to the foundation's findings. The work satisfied her thirst for travel and coalition building; from her failed reelection bid, she was acutely aware that doing the right thing alone was not enough. So, she focused her and the entire foundation's efforts on disseminating research and encouraging international cooperation.

After stepping off her private plane at Shanghai Pudong International Airport, Williamson was quickly ushered into a black SUV. At the Four Seasons Hotel, she intended to meet with other foundation leaders from across Asia and Europe, as well as researchers in pursuit of funding. Her well-appointed suite, covered in muted beige, brown, and gold tones, offered her respite for a few hours before the delegation's first meeting that afternoon.

Dressed in a sleek white suit, simple diamond earrings, and subdued makeup, Elizabeth entered the ballroom on the third floor. The room held a dozen blue tables appointed with fresh fruit, bottled water, and packets of information. Her bodyguard directed her to an assigned table but, before she reached it, a short woman with silky black hair past her shoulders took position at the front of the room and cleared her throat.

"Good afternoon, Madam President, I am Shu Lee from the XAVO Foundation. We focus on equality and civil rights issues in China. I am very excited to meet you." The woman bowed low and held it until Elizabeth spoke.

"It's very good to meet you, Shu Lee," Elizabeth said, returning the woman's bow. "Why don't we take a seat at my table and you can share some of your work with me?"

"Of course," the woman said, and glided toward Williamson. "We follow the Williamson Foundation's research quite closely," she said, her hands folded neatly on the table in front of her. "We feel the changes in our world will affect China acutely due to our existing population problems." Elizabeth could sense that Shu was testing the waters. In her experience, Chinese researchers kept their observations closely guarded to avoid the intervention of the central government.

"Over the past two years, China has touted the success of its strict regulations on childbirth in curbing population growth. Could you shed more light on those policies from a real-world perspective?" Elizabeth asked, pouring herself a glass of sparkling water.

"Much has been made of that policy's success," Shu said, nodding. "However, I am afraid our findings do not support our government's claims."

That's not shocking, Elizabeth thought.

Taking the American's calculated pause as a prompt, Shu continued: "Couples are required to file official requests to obtain birth licenses, and those requests require justifications based on the family's prior successes."

"And what constitutes a success to the authorities?"

"No one knows," Shu said with a rueful smile, leaning across the table, "but the results are clear. Upper-class families legally reproduce at will, while procreation has been criminalized for low-income and rural families. Government-controlled orphanages have sprung up in every city because, by law, children born without a birth license are to be separated from their families. China's office census data shows the world dramatically reduced birth rates because they only report the number of birth licenses issued."

"That is distressing," Williamson said. "Have you tabulated actual birth records to bring light to this situation? Perhaps international pressure could be applied with proper coverage."

"Actual birth records mimic birth licenses because only families with a license go to the hospital for recorded childbirth. This leaves China with a large and growing population of undocumented people with no official records of citizenship."

Shu stood abruptly, and a young black man from an institute she'd not heard of in Algeria introduced himself. After a brief conversation, she discovered that Egypt had yielded military aid in order to gain access to international food subsidies on corn and soybean crops. Meanwhile, Ethiopia and Tanzania had lobbied the European Union for aid packages to help fight food storages.

As the man spoke, Elizabeth spotted Melanie enter the room, and she quickly excused herself and made a beeline toward her.

"How was your flight?" she said, smiling at Melanie.

"Exhausting," Melanie said through a worn smile. It was true: she looked exhausted, and Elizabeth decided it was probably time to slow down the foundation's hectic travel schedule.

"I've been eyeing that group in the corner by the window since I arrived," Elizabeth said, nodding toward them. "Shall we go and see who they represent?"

Melanie nodded, and they proceeded.

"Hello," Elizabeth said to the gray-haired woman closest, "I am Elizabeth and this is Melanie. We are from the Williamson Foundation. What brought you to this gathering?"

"Madam President, it is an honor to meet you—you as well, Melanie," the woman stammered, seemingly awe-struck.

Her associate, a straight-faced younger woman, stepped forward. "We're seeking funding for our research on aging populations."

"I see."

"It's really a fascinating area of study; my name is Dr. Angelica Scarabello. This is Dr. Maria Ricci."

The older woman, apparently recovered, nodded. "We plan to focus our study on Italy and Japan's aging populations, which have traditionally slowed economic growth—but, due to the improved health of the elderly, the talent pool has been injected with a large number of highly experienced workers."

Taking her cue, Angelica continued: "In the past, generations would age out of the work force. Now, however, entire generations are coming out of retirement. Our main focus of study will revolve around growing generational conflict, unemployment escalations, and wage depression as workforce supply outstrips demand."

Melanie perked up. "Didn't Japan just debate forced-retirement laws?"

Angelica nodded vigorously. "Yes, they debated it, but could not push through legislation."

"Italy has been focused on entitlement programs, which are quickly becoming unsustainable due to unknown life expectancies," Dr. Ricci added.

"Madam President, has the Williamson foundation considered any age-related research?" Dr. Scarabello asked.

"While I do find the idea of studying the new human lifespan fascinating, we do not plan to make that a focal point for the foundation. We remain committed to understanding all facets of the mutation so that when—or rather, if—negative impacts are uncovered, we are able to counteract them," Elizabeth explained with an apologetic smile.

Disappointment overtook her listeners' faces, and they quickly excused themselves.

Returning to their table, Melanie plucked an apple from the tray and took a bite.

"So," Elizabeth began, "how was Moscow?"

"Bizarre," Melanie answered, scowling between bites. "I was given a tour of Moscow by our contact at the Ministry of Agriculture. He claimed that the country has 'extremely strong food stores' and, on the tour, everyone I encountered genuinely appeared happy and well fed."

Elizabeth gave a knowing grin. *The Russian propaganda machine at work.*

"So, I extended my trip by a day, that's why I arrived so late. I hired a private outfit to take me on a tour of a few towns and rural communities a hundred miles from Moscow. As you might have guessed, there were devastating food shortages as soon as you got outside of Moscow."

"And Germany?"

"The Germans that are left in the country are generally very happy with their country's emigration initiative."

"Is that so?" Out the corner of her eye, Elizabeth saw a group watching them, clearly looking for a way to introduce themselves. She turned abruptly away, focusing all her attention on Melanie.

"Incentives were set up to encourage people to move out of the country and thereby reduce the burden of extreme population growth. But, because the policy offered a flat amount per person emigrating, it created a reward inverse to wealth, meaning only lower-income families have left the country. The policy effectively pushed lower-class Germans into member EU countries, which, as you might have guessed, has led to a great deal of animosity, mainly from the French and Italians. There is mounting international pressure on Germany to discontinue the program, but it's working so well to depress population problems that the Christian Democratic Union is so far refusing to back down."

"That sounds like a precarious situation. I'm happy I don't have to deal with it!" Elizabeth took a calming deep breath, a moment to enjoy her pleasant circumstances. Researchers would come to her to share their exciting research and she would decide if she wanted to fund them, and that was all. The freedom of mind created by her reduction in responsibility soothed her soul.

"The Scandinavians, as ever, have come up with a refreshing approach to the Lifio mutation. While the rest of the world adopted universal water treatment, Sweden, Norway, and Finland declined. They offered treated bottled water instead, allowing citizens a choice in their exposure to the mutation. They also made research available to the public and held town hall meetings and national debates on scientific developments. I attended one of those national debates before I left Sweden; it was inspiring to see that level of democratic process and transparency. It felt almost utopian."

"I wish I could have joined you on that trip," Elizabeth said with a sigh, as a group of three older men approached their table. Overweight and shabby, they looked out of place among the otherwise elegant attendees. One dressed in an ill-fitting brown suit, the other had a navy-blue sweater over a white shirt and apple-red tie, and the third wore jeans and a black blazer. They smelled like they had come from a farm, and Elizabeth struggled to keep her expression gentle and even.

"Hello, Madam President," the man in a brown suit said with a heavy accent.

"We're up from New Zealand."

"We're Kiwis."

"As you may know," the first man continued, "New Zealand has held a national referendum annually for the last two years regarding the treatment of our water supply."

"Yup," the navy man said, "and each year, we decide against it!"

"The Aussies tried to do it, bless 'em," added the man in jeans, "but they failed. Too much international trade and exposure and all."

The suited man grinned. "But we Kiwis remain pure. It's our badge of honor!"

"And we study it!"

Elizabeth's head was spinning as she looked from one scientist to the next, following as they finished each other's thoughts. *They spend entirely too much time together.*

"You see," navy man said, "New Zealand's population is a large control group for tests being run on the mutation."

"That's right!"

"And we hear the Williamson Foundation wants to figure out the mutation so they can fix any problems with it."

"So," said the jeans-wearer, "we're here to help."

Elizabeth held her response to see if they were done but, before she could formulate a response, Melanie said, "Excellent. You should get in touch with our chief scientific officer, Doctor Carrie Roberts. I'm sure she would love to hear from you. Here is her information."

"Excellent."

"Wonderful."

"Thank you, Madam President."

Speechless, Elizabeth watched the three men retreat, and found herself suddenly regretful that she had not taken a different approach to Lifio during her time in office. She had proven to be too protective as president, standing in the way of inevitable progress instead of working with it. Given what limited information she'd received during her campaign, it was hard to blame herself for her decisions, but, with hindsight, she saw all her poor choices with blinding clarity. The moment she'd learned of the possible effects of the Lifio mutation, she should have met with Dr. Jónsson. While she did not like President Givens, she respected that he had gone directly to the source, gotten answers, and acted on them. She should have done that, she now saw. As a result of her uncertainty, President Givens had treated the water supply—an unmitigated disaster that haunted her to this day.

Elizabeth absently poured herself another sparkling water. Melanie handled most of the talking as she let her mind wander.

How could social security be restructured to provide a benefit to the elderly while we seek to rediscover when old age now begins? How will explosive population growth be avoided without taking away the right to reproduce? What state-funded research is taking place now in the Department of Human Evolution and Development? Is that department working on future human mutations? If so, will the public be given a choice?

For the first time since her loss, she found herself wondering whether she should pursue reelection. She almost laughed. *Am I nuts? If I lost a second time to Givens, it would forever tarnish my legacy. My presidency will go down in history as an exemplary one. I resided over the country during a period of immense prosperity and only lost reelection because I did what was best for the country. In time, my legacy will shine, and Givens's will fade. No—it would look downright awful if I lost. We're doing the work we need to at the foundation without having to worry about running the country. I started the foundation to create a legacy, not to close it after a few years and go chasing a grudge match.*

Elizabeth looked up in time to see several more scientists approach her table, faces nervous. "Hello," she said, standing and holding out her hand. "Welcome."

CHAPTER 24

THE MARKET

"Hey, Mel, you playing the stock market these days?" Sebastian asked. It felt good to be engaging in friendly banter back in the office, he thought—he'd spent too much of the last year on a plane. Elizabeth, perhaps sensing burnout, had grounded the foundation's leadership team for a few months, and it had done wonders for Sebastian's mental health. Now more than ever, the Williamson Foundation felt like a dream: bright colors, high-end finishing, and kind of excitement usually found only in Silicon Valley or New Austin.

"You know full well I'm not in the market," Melanie said, crossing her arms and glaring at him.

"Just checking." He had a new suit on, a three-piece in a loud but not too loud sky blue.

"Oh!" she said, a mocking smile spreading over her face, "you want to see if I read your op-ed in the *Wall Street Journal*. That's why you're asking me about the market. Of course I read it. You emailed it to me."

Sebastian grinned. "So, what did you think?" He caught his reflection in a picture frame and straightened his bow tie.

She paused for a moment. "I think it was spot on."

"But?" He tilted his head and raised an eyebrow.

"But it's not going to do any good. Everyone who reads the *Wall Street Journal* is focused on making more money. They're not reading it to be told we need to be more long-term oriented and responsible. Most of their readers are day traders, for God's sake."

"Well," Sebastian said, "I'm glad you liked it. So, do you want to go check in with Carrie?"

"Do we have to?" she said, smirking.

"I'm afraid so," he said with a wink.

They made their way down a suspended glass corridor to Elizabeth's office, and the three of them headed down the steps to Carrie's first-floor lab. They found her bent over a desk, rifling through papers, and Sebastian could immediately tell they'd be dealing with Angry Carrie today.

"How's your work going?" Elizabeth asked carefully as they approached.

"I am sorry to report that it is not going well," Carrie replied curtly.

"You always say that, Carrie," said Melanie.

Sebastian winced inwardly. *Oh, not a good start.*

"Care to elaborate? Have you made any progress since our meeting last week?"

Don't ask that!

Carrie bristled, her eyes darting toward Melanie. "No, we have not made any progress since last week, and no, I do not care to elaborate. However, I will if I must …" She glanced at Elizabeth.

"That's all right, Carrie," said Elizabeth. "You look stressed. Why don't we take a little break? We don't want you to update us right now. Let me treat you all to lunch, and then you can perhaps tell us more."

After a deep breath, Carrie agreed, and the group scattered. Sebastian ran up to his office and grabbed his wallet, sunglasses, and car keys, then returned to wait in the lobby. Minutes later, they headed out together en route to El Limon.

"Prices went up again," Melanie said as they were seated in a booth by a polished waiter.

"The prices go up so fast they don't even laminate the menus anymore," Carrie said, scowling and turning her menu over in her hands.

"Food price inflation has to get more attention," Melanie said.

"As long as the negative effects remained quarantined to developing countries, Americans won't listen," Sebastian responded, eyes scanning the menu.

"That's unfortunately true," Elizabeth interjected. "To make matters worse for the world's poorest, most first-world countries, such as ours, are starting to withhold international aid for food and redirect it to their own populations. This, of course, only exacerbates the problem by insulating the populations of wealthier countries from the crisis while rapidly accelerating the loss of life in struggling countries."

Then, out of the blue, Carrie looked up and said, "That bastard Jónsson was so focused on documenting how to how to breed and keep alive his precious bacteria that he failed to document how to reverse what he had created. Now I have to spend years of my life trying to reverse an engineered mutation by indexing millions of people's DNA. Things would go faster if it weren't for the enormity of the data sets we're dealing with."

There was a moment of awkward silence before Elizabeth turned to Sebastian and said, "I read your article in the *Wall Street Journal*, Sebastian. Excellent work."

Sebastian blushed, smiling wide.

"I am not sure if you saw it, but there was another op-ed next to yours that was very interesting."

"I'm ashamed to admit it, but I only read my article," he replied, unable to stifle his grin.

Elizabeth returned his smile. "It was about how Fortune Five Hundred companies exist in an alternate reality. With unprecedented demand due to population growth and an oversupply of highly skilled labor, companies no longer need to invest to create growth.

"Effectively, sales demand is causing inflation, while labor oversupply is causing wage deflation. It's a perfect environment for company profits to soar while everyone else struggles."

Melanie sighed. "On that miserable note, here's to four more years of President Givens!" She stood, raising her water glass for a toast. When no one got up, she sat back down. "If I can't laugh about it, I'll cry."

"This conversation is making me want to cry," Carrie said.

The waiter returned, placing chips and guacamole on the table, and Sebastian watched, mildly awed, as Carrie cleared three quarters of the bowl immediately. *She sure can eat!*

When she looked up again, she seemed to be in a better mood already—food always helped with Carrie. Sebastian had learned that long ago.

"Is now a good time for that update Carrie?" Elizabeth asked.

Sebastian looked down at the table, cursing inwardly. *Just a little too soon.*

"It is not pleasant," Carrie said. "We're finding the indexing process to be cumbersome. I am concerned."

"Surely, there are some positives to report?" Sebastian suggested.

Carrie thought about it for a moment, her burrito held aloft, and finally said, "The mutation does not alter the same DNA in all subjects. It modifies various DNA sections, but which section is dependent on the subject. It's maddening that I cannot speak with the man that created this."

"I shouldn't torture yourself over that," Melanie said. "It's not as if he would tell any of us anything even if he were still alive. During our time at the FDA we asked him for information hundreds of times, and he never once responded."

"Do you feel like we are making progress toward being able to reverse or augment the mutation?" Sebastian asked carefully.

Carrie stared at him, her expression impossible to read. Finally, her face relaxed, and Sebastian breathed a sigh of relief. "We've been transparent with all of our findings since we set up the repository online so. Everyone in the world can now work with our data. That's a positive," Carrie said.

"But if you had to guess how much longer we'll need?" Sebastian said, knowing he was pushing his luck. "Is it a month, six months, a year?"

"Years," Carrie said, avoiding eye contact. "Many, many years."

CHAPTER 25
SIX YEARS LATER

Ana watched Michael robotically scoop cereal from the bowl and into his mouth, his eyes glued to an angler struggling to reel something in on the distant TV screen. Sipping her coffee, she heard *tik, tik, tik* and looked across the counter for her phone. But no—not hers. She put her hand on Michael's shoulder.

"Are you going to get that?"

As if from a dream, Michael jerked awake, snatched up his cell phone, and saw his calendar app's appointment alarm was going off.

"Shit!" he said, leaping up. "Honey, I'm gonna be late. I forgot I have a meeting in fifteen minutes." He lunged toward the door, only to trip on a stray cushion.

"Well, don't just leave that there," replied Ana, pointing to his abandoned breakfast. "I know you're late, but that's good food. You can't just leave it."

"I gotta go, really!"

"At least take it with you. I'll put it in Tupperware for you. Give me just a sec."

"I can't be late to this meeting. Love you."

"I'm not letting this go to waste, Michael. I'm putting it in the fridge for you, and you can eat it tomorrow," she said, but he was already out the door.

Ana shook her head, muttering to herself about him wasting food. He knew they were on a tight budget, yet he always made himself giant servings and then left before finishing. She loved him but, at times, his disregard for money really frustrated her.

Instead of making her own breakfast, she finished his. Then, she tidied the kitchen after her husband. *Nothing like cleaning before heading out for a day of cleaning*, she thought grimly, knowing full well she was happier than most. She couldn't resist complaining, though, even if it was only to herself. She loved and truly believed in Michael; sooner or later, they'd save enough to raise a family of their own together.

After her second-hand breakfast, Ana grabbed her cleaning basket and vacuum and took the elevator to the eighth floor. "Hi, Mrs. Harris," she said to the nearly blind old woman who answered the door. The apartment smelled of mothballs and lightly soiled linens.

"Oh, hi, dear. Is it Wednesday already? So lovely to see you. Come have a seat. Can I get you a cup of coffee?" little old Mrs. Harris said as she ushered Ana into the apartment.

"I'll just get started if it's no problem, I have a busy day. However, I would love a cup of coffee, thank you. You're sure it's not a bother?"

"Oh, of course not, dear. Coming right up."

Mrs. Harris didn't pay Ana for her weekly cleaning, but she always made her coffee and fixed her lunch before she left, which was close enough. Ana enjoyed helping Mrs. Harris and keeping her company; the old lady hadn't had a visitor since her son had stopped coming last year. Regardless, she always talked fondly of her son, making excuses for his absence, and Ana, too polite to ask, never pushed the issue. Mrs. Harris needed someone to help her keep her small apartment clean, and Ana appreciated the food and the opportunity to help someone in need.

"Ana dear, would you teach me to make tamales some time so I could make them in time for your visits?"

Ana remembered the last time she'd hugged her Mama. She'd told her they'd still see each other; now, it seemed more and more likely that she'd never see her again. Suddenly she was a child again, the aroma of chilis and corn enveloping her as she sped around the kitchen, masa flour in her hair, her laughing Mama chasing behind.

"Ana?"

Ana looked at Mrs. Harris and rubbed her cheek. "Sorry. I'd love that, Mrs. Harris," she said. Wordlessly accepting the cup of coffee Mrs. Harris held out to her, Ana carried her supplies into the living room, lost in memories.

After lunch with Mrs. Harris, Ana headed to another apartment on the same floor. As she scrubbed the kitchen tile, she noticed dust building up on the underside of a ceiling fan in the living room, so she borrowed a step ladder from Mrs. Harris to clean it off. Even with the extreme heat in Texas, the apartment didn't have air conditioning—fans were all anyone in this block could afford. Content that she'd cleaned everything to her standards, Ana moved up two more floors to another apartment.

"Louisa, hi!" Ana said when a middle-aged blonde woman opened the door.

"Ana! come in, good to see you—the boys made a real mess before they went to school today and I didn't get a chance to clean it up. Please see to that; I'll just be in the bedroom. I have my afternoon shows to watch."

Ana forced a smile. "Sure. Err, Louisa?"

"Yes, Ana? My show's just about to start," she said, pointing over her shoulder.

"Well, you're behind on payments and I wanted to see if you could pay me."

Louisa's smile wavered. "Oh, okay," she said, "how far back am I?"

"It's been two months, so that would be eight visits. I know Havier is having a tough time at work—"

"Ana, I would love to help you, but that's a lot of money," Louisa said, smiling. "I don't think I can do that, but I can pay you half for this visit. How does that sound?"

"If that's all you can do, I would appreciate it."

"Good. Okay, I'll head back and watch my show and get it to you after you're done," she said as she marched off and closed the door.

Ana picked up all the toys, then started to work out the new stains in the carpet. Three hours later, she finally finished sweeping up the curly black hairs around the toilet. *What a morning*, she thought, wiping sweat from her brow.

Returning to the hallway, she knocked on Louisa's bedroom door. There was no answer but, with the volume on the TV so high, perhaps Louisa hadn't heard. She knocked again, louder this time, and yelled out, "Louisa!"

Maybe she fell asleep.

"Louisa? *¿Puedes escucharme?*" She tried once more, banging on the door. When no answer came, she packed up her cleaning supplies and headed across the hall. Next was Mr. Little's apartment.

Mr. Little was not home—he never was when she cleaned, but she had a key. Her stomach rumbled as she eyed the fresh apples on the kitchen counter, but she didn't consider taking one. As a trusted cleaner, she did not want to do anything to betray her clients' trust. After cleaning the already neat apartment and finishing early, she decided to pull everything out of his cabinets so she could wipe down the insides. Finally, she packed up her supplies and looked for the envelope on the kitchen table that would hold her payment. After looking high and low for it, she decided to write Mr. Little a note to let him know that he had forgotten to leave her payment again.

* * *

Michael only had ten minutes to make a fifteen-minute walk from his apartment building to the office building where he worked. As his brisk walk turned into an all-out run, he began to sweat in the Texas morning heat. When he finally arrived in the ice-cold lobby, he had a sheen of perspiration that quickly began to dissipate as he slowed back down to a trot. By the time he got on the elevator, he was already late, and was sure he smelled ripe.

The meeting had been called by one of the vice presidents of Frost Technologies, the proprietary software development company Michael worked for. Vice presidents ran development projects, and some even wrote code, but they also maintained relationships with business partners. This particular VP worked the Toyota account. Their firm had designed the proprietary automated assembly-line software for Toyota's US-based plants. The meeting request had come after a request had been issued to the team of thirty eighth-floor developers to come up with outside-the-box efficiency improvement suggestions. With Toyota planning to bring a new plant online in twenty-four to thirty-six months, the VP clearly needed some ammo to ensure they kept their contract. Whoever provided the answer would take a giant leap forward in their careers. Michael thought he had an idea but, after spending all night and half the morning trying to put it all together, he'd still come up short. He needed more time—time he clearly didn't have.

Just before the elevator doors closed, a delicate hand poked through and the doors reopened. Kai Lee hopped into the elevator, clutching a broken heel in one hand. Michael felt flushed, as he always did when he saw Kai. He found her exceedingly beautiful, so much so that it made him uncomfortable. She was a tall, fit Japanese-American with silky black hair.

Smiling, she turned toward him, but landed funny on her good heel and toppled forward, directly into his arms. As he stood frozen, she quickly regained her composure and then kneeled down to start gathering what she had dropped.

"Oh, I'm so sorry," she said from her knees. "I'm late. I'm sorry. Did I hurt you?"

Still speechless, Michael failed to reply. *How could a gorgeous Japanese woman with perfect porcelain skin and scarlet red lips possibly hurt me by fall-hugging me?*

"Michael, are you okay?" she said again, now staring directly into his eyes for just a moment before breaking eye contact.

"Yeah, Kai, sorry. I'm trying to work something out is all," Michael finally replied, dragging his mind out of the gutter.

"Are you supposed to be at the meeting that started like five minutes ago too?"

"Unfortunately."

"Well, at least we're both late."

At last, the doors opened, and Michael hurried out, relief flooding him. They made their way together to the large glass conference room at the center of the floor. Most of the cubicles they passed were empty, and Michael winced—the meeting had definitely started already. He didn't even have an excuse. He couldn't say, "I just zoned out over breakfast," or "I got stuck in traffic."

The office they walked through looked like it had been state of the art about fifteen years ago, when this had been the company's main office. Now, most of their offices were located in New Austin, where there was more space, which meant higher ceilings, bigger offices, larger parking spaces—all the perks expected by those who'd made it in the modern world. The office that Michael and Kai were making their way through had been relegated to a waypoint, a stop on the way up the corporate ladder. In here, the ceiling was only eight feet high and the doors three feet wide. Simply put, it wasn't made for today's upper class.

Still at a loss for an excuse, Michael opened the conference room door and walked in with Kai behind him. Better to pull the Band-Aid off quickly, he thought. The VP, who looked to be giving a presentation, stopped and stared at them as they walked in and took their seats. With everyone's eyes upon them and the silence building, Kai broke the ice.

"Sorry we're late. I broke my heel and twisted my ankle on the walk in, and Michael here was kind enough to give me a hand," she said, holding up the point of her broken heel.

"We're glad to have you, Ms. Lee. I'm sorry about your ankle, and thank you, Michael, for being decent and helping Ms. Lee," the VP said.

Michael had seen the effect of Kai's beauty in the past; hell, he had just fallen victim to it on the elevator. She enveloped anyone she gave attention to—and apparently, it even worked on the higher-ups.

The VP restarted his presentation from the top so that Kai and Michael could hear what they had missed. After half an hour, the VP asked for any suggestions the gathered developers might have to improve the efficiency of their automation coding. After a pause, one pitched the idea of using a virtual reality simulator to improve training for the maintenance staff that would maintain the new automated Toyota plant, but the VP quickly squashed the idea as not bold enough and with limited upside. Another developer pitched an idea that could potentially reduce error rates, but the possible benefits weren't great enough compared to the implementation costs. Even Kai Lee presented an idea but, regardless of her ability to turn men into mush, she too was shot down by the VP.

Then, without knowing why he did it, Michael put his hand up.

"Okay, Michael, what have you got?" the VP asked.

"I'm not sure yet, but I think I've got an idea. I think we need to leave our current Toyota automation software alone."

"Okay, Michael, if Toyota will sign on for that, so will I. Now, does anyone have another idea?"

Michael pushed on. "If we divert our efforts from updating our machine code and instead pour our time into developing an artificial intelligence system that we can layer over top of the current software we've been using for the last decade, we could potentially save them the cost of implementing a new system, and the improvements our AI system develops would be backward-compatible. When we launch a new system, we go through hundreds, if not thousands, of hours testing and tuning our automation and, over time, part wear and mainte-nance diminishes quality. If we develop an AI that can test and tune continuously by way of code, we can use it to constantly dial in our current automation implementations."

"Now that's an idea!" the VP said. "Any idea how to do any of that?"

"Not exactly, sir."

"I didn't think so. All right, everybody, I've heard enough for today. Meeting adjourned."

Michael knew he'd not been ready to present. Nevertheless, he tried to focus on the fact that he'd tried, not that he'd failed. As he made his way from the conference room to his cubicle, Kai caught up with him.

"Hey, I liked your idea, Michael," she said.

"Thanks. It clearly needs a little work still." He gave an awk-ward smile. "So, er, see ya."

As they parted ways, Michael couldn't stop imagining an animated Kai with voluptuous proportions bending over to grab her broken heel with an extremely short skirt on. In his imagination, a helpless, submissive Kai asked what she could ever do to repay him for catching her. And, just as his daydream started to get good, a hand clasped onto his shoulder.

"Michael, I liked where you were going in there. Grab your things, I'm taking you to lunch. We can chat more about your idea."

Michael looked over his shoulder and realized it wasn't Kai's soft, supple hand on his shoulder; it was the VP's enormous paw.

"Michael, you in there? Let's go!" said the VP.

Michael got to his feet, grabbed his stuff, and followed the VP through the office to the elevator.

"Sir, sir? It's only 9:30," Michael said after catching up.

"Well, I'm famished. We're heading across town for a lunch meeting. They usually go on a few hours. I want to flesh out your idea and see if we can turn it into something."

Michael had to keep running; the VP was gigantic, and covered twice the distance Michael did with each stride. He felt like a toddler trying to keep up with a parent.

They emerged into the parking lot, and Michael noticed that the VP had parked in the middle of two parking spaces and that his car was sticking out the back of the space. Michael didn't know cars very well, but the VP's car certainly looked impressive: low to the ground, with two long doors and a lava orange paint job, it didn't look like any other car Michael had seen before. It almost looked too wide for the street.

After he got in, the VP told Michael to stop calling him sir and to call him Dave. Then, with a grin, he told him to buckle up. Michael did as he was told.

CHAPTER 26

LUNCH FOR KINGS

The first thing Michael noticed about the building when they pulled up outside was its sheer size. The whole street was colossal; even the lot opposite looked more like a dump truck depot than a parking lot. Cars he had never seen before were parked next to one another in different rows, towering in size. Suddenly Dave's car no longer impressed him—it looked like a toy compared to some in the lot.

The brick building, adorned with ivy and large gold lanterns every few feet, loomed over them as they approached. Well-dressed doormen, one on each side, quickly pushed the two-story doors open, beckoning for Michael and Dave to enter. Michael suddenly felt underdressed as they approach the maître d', who greeted them as a showman would address an audience participant.

"Welcome, welcome, gentlemen, and how may I help you today?" the maître d' boomed, his arms open wide. A large man in his own right, he stood like a deity casting judgment, looking down on them from an elevated platform behind a grandiose podium.

"Reservation for lunch," said Dave. "Should be under Frank Graham. We're a bit early."

"It's never too early to eat, my fine gentlemen!" The maître d' snapped his fingers and pointed directly at them, cueing a man behind them, who Michael had not noticed, to relieve them of their coats. Another man in a tux arrived swiftly from the dining room to led them to their table.

"Take good care of them, Bobby," the maître d' called out.

Along the walls of the dining room, oversized high-back booths on raised platforms isolated select guests, while the main floor held tables and chairs of varying sizes. Michael noticed that the farther they went back into the dining room, the larger the furniture appeared to be. The marble floors, deep wood tones, and gold embellishments imparted a nostalgic atmosphere, more old-time Manhattan than new-world Austin.

After leading them to a mildly oversized booth less than a third of the way into the immense dining room, Bobby gestured for them to take their seats. "Here are some menus, gentlemen, while you wait for the rest of your party to arrive," he said before hurrying back to the front of the house.

Almost immediately, a flurry of attendants arrived and set down dishes in front of Michael and Dave.

"Courtesy of the house; something to satiate you while you wait. Charred octopus over gruyere polenta with pickled onion," the server said before disappearing. The scent of a charcoal grill and the ocean breeze mingled, inviting them to taste.

"Ah, I love this place. I'm famished," Dave said as he plucked up his fork to dig in.

He was a well-built Irishman, close to seven feet tall and about three hundred pounds, if Michael had to guess, and clearly he had an appetite: before Michael could take a bite, Dave's plate was empty.

Toward the back of the room, Michael noticed a group at one of the larger tables, and he glanced over, trying to avoid calling attention to himself. The sheer size of the men clearly marked them as professional athletes, yet he couldn't place any of their faces. He followed all the Texas pro teams—but then, maybe they were college. No, he thought, surely not—this place was far too expensive for college kids.

A black man, even taller than Dave, approached the table. "Dave, I see you waited for us," he boomed in a southern drawl, "thanks, old buddy."

194

The largest man Michael had ever seen followed closely behind him.

"I'm Frank," the gigantic man said as he took a seat next to Dave, making him feel like a toddler.

"Hey, guys," Dave said. "This is Michael. Michael, this is Frank. Frank here is an executive vice president. And this is Mola. We do all the work, and Frank gets all the credit. Isn't that right, Mola?"

"Seems that way to me," Mola said, raising an eyebrow.

"Cut the bullshit," said Frank. "We all do pretty well. How else would we be eating at Olivia's?"

"Your expenses account, Frank," chirped Dave, "that's how we're eating here."

"I'm certainly not paying for this," Mola said quickly.

"Ah … Dave, your little guy's freakin' out," Frank said, making everyone pause and turn to stare at Michael.

Michael was processing the banter, but his face must have projected concern; he didn't know what the hell was going on, and it clearly showed.

"Hey, Michael, we've all known each other for almost a decade," said Dave.

"Yeah, we're just bustin' balls," Frank put in.

"We came up together in the company, that's all," Mola added.

Michael gave a shy smile, and the conversation shifted to the reason why he was there in the first place. Dave recapped the earlier pitch meeting to Frank and Mola, going over each of the ideas that had come up and shooting them down until he got to Michael's.

"I think Michael's got the right approach for the new Toyota contract. He suggested we work up an AI program that can overlay on top of our current automation programming and fine-tune it continually in real time. The idea has merit, and Toyota will love the culture fit of a system that continuously improves since, well, that's what they are known for: continuous process improvement."

Just then, a waiter arrived at the table. "Hello, gentlemen. Can I offer you a beverage while you get settled in?"

"I'm good with water for now," said Frank. "We'll take the executive tasting meal for the table, thank you."

"Excellent choice. May I ask if there are any food allergies or dietary restrictions?"

Everyone at the table shook their heads in unison.

Before they knew it, several servers were placing new plates in front of them: croissants with truffle butter and house-made raspberry jam.

"I like the AI angle," said Frank. "You're right, Dave—that will play well with the execs over at Toyota. Trouble is, we don't have any experience developing AI."

"My senior-year dissertation dealt with AI and its implementation as a tool to extend the life of legacy technologies," said Michael.

"I think this little guy just called our Toyota automation code 'legacy technology,'" Mola said with a big grin on his face.

Over courses of salad, cheese, and soup, Michael downloaded everything he could think to tell them about AI. Dave, Mola, and Frank picked it up quickly; they'd obviously risen through the company's ranks for a reason. Michael liked the camaraderie and banter; it quickly made him feel like he belonged, even if he didn't.

Over a seafood tower large enough to feed a small army, the conversation drifted back to personal matters, with Frank gushing over his two girls and how well they were doing. His youngest, Grace, was captain of her soccer team, and the oldest, Lilly, had made the honor roll. Dave went on and on about his car and his plans to upgrade his turbo and fuel system. Mola seemed content to listen, while it was all Michael could do to take it all in.

Given his Italian ancestry, Michael had thought he could eat with the best of them—but this? This was something entirely different. Even without enjoying much of the seafood, he felt stuffed and, when the server tried to place a ribeye steak in front of him, he cried uncle.

"No, thank you. I'll have to pass. I'm done," he said to the waiter.

The group gave him questioning looks.

"Not much of an appetite, I can see," Frank said with a grin. "We'll see what we can do about that."

After the ribeye came roasted chicken, then braised lamb, then stuffed pasta, then more cheese, and, finally, three decadent dessert courses. Michael watched, flabbergasted, as Dave, Mola, and Frank cleaned their plates without hesitation.

Conversation ebbed and flowed through the long meal. Michael learned about the office Frost Technologies had just built in New Austin, outside of the downtown Old Austin scene. According to Frank, all the executives had flocked to the new office space, buying spacious homes in New Austin. Listening to the gigantic Frank talk about huge suburban houses and expensive cars, Michael felt like he was finally seeing what success looked like—and he was enjoying it. His father never made it this far, he thought with a grim sense of satisfaction. Then the old resentment flooded in. He swallowed hard as he pictured his smiling mother. Not now, he thought, not here. He forced a smile and glanced at each of the large men, all of them tearing into the last of their desserts. Midday gourmet meals on the company dime, larger-than-life houses, spacious next-generation cities—he imagined these things for himself, pushing the image of his mother out of his head.

"Dave, how's your family getting on back in Connecticut?" asked Frank. "I can't imagine how the East Coast plans to cope with rescaling their infrastructure. It's not like there's space in Manhattan to build bigger."

"Family's fine. They're not too big, and they live a modest life, remember? But they did say Manhattan and Boston have turned into ghost towns. All the bigwigs that used to run the financial centers moved their offices because they couldn't get the scale they needed; the infrastructure no longer works. Think about how tiny their roads are and everything. My brother Tim, the real estate broker, thinks the old downtown centers will get bought up and redeveloped over the next decade. The prices need to fall, and then someone will swoop in and rebuild it right. That or new cities will take over—like New Austin did."

"New cities are taking over, if you ask me," said Mola. "Everyone loves new stuff."

"I don't know," said Michael. "I think you guys might be underestimating the value of history to people. Those cities are some of America's first; they're not going to just tear all that history down to build bigger buildings and roads."

Frank and Mola shared a knowing glance. "Money runs the world, Michael," Frank said, looking down at him, "history won't pay the bills."

Michael gave a shy smile and looked away.

After Frank paid the bill, the waiter placed two large bags of leftovers in front of Michael. Not wanting to offend anyone, he took the bags and thanked the waiter for wrapping everything up for him. Then it was back to reality and the office in Old Austin.

After carrying his leftovers home that night, Michael's arms were tired; the long day had taken a lot out of him. But, as he opened the door to his apartment, adrenaline flooded through him—he couldn't wait to tell Ana everything.

She greeted him in the kitchen and asked where the leftovers had come from. Unpacking them, she said, "These should last us a week! Did they give you everyone's leftovers?"

"Nope, that was all for me!" Michael said, grinning. "Ana, you should have seen these guys. They ate everything—everyone else at the table cleaned their plates."

"What? All this? I can't believe they ate it in one sitting," she said, shaking her head.

"It wasn't as good as your enchiladas, but it was close," he said with a grin. "I'll get us some plates."

As she and Michael settled in at the kitchen table, they sampled leftovers while Michael recounted his day. Full of enthusiasm and excitement, they sat for hours at their tiny kitchen table.

"Wow, that food was amazing. I can't believe we ate that much," she said, looking content. She kissed Michael on the cheek and started cleaning up the empty containers.

"We keep eating like this and we'll have to move!" Michael quipped.

"All right, *signor*, let's just hope they still like your idea after sleeping on it," Ana said, perching on his lap.

CHAPTER 27

MOVIN' ON UP

Michael exploded from his bed the next day, full of energy. After a quick shower and shave, he sidled up to the kitchen countertop with Ana and gobbled up eggs and crispy bacon before she could even butter his toast.

"Sorry, hon, I gotta run," he said after giving her a quick kiss on the cheek. He grabbed the toast and hurried out the door as he heard her say, "hey, I thought we got up early so we could hike Turkey Creek Trail?"

He spun around and shot her an apologetic smile. "Another time, promise."

With some pep in his step, he made his way to the office on foot, moving in and around people walking without purpose. *Come on*, he thought, sidling around a gawking intern, *let's go!* He had a meeting with Dave. After his memorable meal with the VPs at Olivia's the week before, he'd been working closely with Dave on the details of how they could use AI to attack the Toyota project. The loose plan certainly needed work, but it remained the most inspired idea to come out of the office.

After getting to his desk and settling in, Michael fidgeted, his stomach twisting and turning in anticipation of his meeting. He avoided opening his email, not wanting his mind to go off on a tangent, and he stopped himself from working on any of his current projects because, by the time he got his mind into his work, it would be time for the meeting.

In an attempt to get out of his own head, he got up and headed over to the break room to get a coffee and pass the time through mindless chatter with his coworkers. As soon as he sauntered in, he noticed Kai pouring herself a cup of coffee. Her presence always made him feel uneasy; it felt as if he were cheating on his wife merely by experiencing a physical attraction to another woman. The fact that Kai was a coworker, and a very kind and considerate one at that, only made the feeling worse. Before Michael could turn around, she looked up and caught his eye.

"Morning, Michael," she said with a smile and a wave.

Michael smiled and tried to reply, but only a combination of cough, deep breath, and mumble came out, making Kai smile wider as she sipped her coffee. After getting a grip on himself, Michael said, "I think I'm late for a meeting. Have a good one," and he promptly turned around and marched back to his desk.

Fifteen minutes later, he gathered his notes and headed over to Dave's office.

"Michael, good morning. Please take a seat," Dave said, gesturing toward the small meeting table in the corner of his office.

Michael nodded and turned, only to find Kai, her hair in a tight bun and her suit blouse hugging her bosom, already sitting there, sipping her coffee. When she made eye contact with Michael and smiled, he froze.

Dave made his way over from the other side of the office and sat down as well. "Michael, sit. What's the matter? Did you forget something?"

Michael sat down without a word.

"I have exciting news. Frank likes what we've come up with. He likes the AI direction and wants us to form a team that can turn your idea into a reality. Now, before you get too excited, I've been through this before. On a big pitch like this one, two or three teams will work up ideas and they'll be pitted against each other internally before the winner gets to give it a real go with the client. Got it?"

Michael remained mute.

"Not real talkative today, huh," said Dave. "Okay, well, today we're going to pick our team to work on this project for the next twelve to thirty-six months, so we'd better like each other. Michael, Kai happens to be the only person besides you with any background in AI, so she will be on the team. Kai, why don't you tell Michael about your experience in AI?"

"I graduated from MIT last spring with a focus in computer science and artificial intelligence," Kai said, blushing. "I basically lived in the CSAIL. Oh, sorry, I always forget that not everyone knows the acronyms we used at school. CSAIL is the research institute for computer science and artificial intelligence at MIT. I really loved your idea to layer AI on top of already-in-use automation software, and would really enjoy being a part of this team if you will have me."

"Certainly, certainly," Michael found himself saying. "We would love to have you on our team."

"Wonderful," said Dave. "Now we just need to find a few more soldiers. Any ideas?"

Needing a minute to think and process what he had just done, Michael grabbed a donut from the center of the table and stuffed it in his mouth. Once he was done chewing, he said, "I think we ought to keep the team small, at least until we come up with our AI project theory and have some semblance of how we'll tackle the problem. The last thing we need is a room full of antsy developers who want to start coding before we've decided on strategy." Michael couldn't help but notice Kai batting her eyes at him.

"I like it, small and streamlined," said Dave. "Okay, Michael, you're in the driver's seat here. You and Kai get started on that AI project theory and outline the strategy you'd like to implement to knock this out. After you have a working rough draft, bring it to me so I can finish it up with you, and then we'll add to our team. What sort of timeline do you need for something like that?"

"Three months, maybe four?" Michael guessed.

"You got two weeks, maximum. All right, get out of here. You two can set up in the conference room down the hall so you have some privacy while this project remains active." Dave got up from the meeting table and, before hearing a reply, he ushered them out of his office and closed the door.

"Well, I'm just going to swing by my desk and get a few things. I'll see you in the conference room in a few," Michael said, and Kai nodded.

After grabbing his laptop, phone, and a notepad, he headed into the conference room and plugged in. Kai came in and set up across from him. The large empty table and pregnant silence made it hard to know where to start. Thankfully, she suggested an idea board and, when Michael nodded, got up, and wrote the word *ideas* on the dry erase wall behind her. With the ice broken, ideas started to flow.

"I'm going get a coffee," Michael said during a break in the conversation.

Kai murmured something but didn't look up.

When he returned, Michael found Kai deep in thought, so he went to his computer and sat, trying to calm his mind and think about the problem abstractly. Projects like these were always a challenge, and knowing that the fate of his career lay in the balance did not help his nerves. Kai's intoxicating aroma— lavender, he thought, and juniper—didn't help either. Before Michael knew it, a porter knocked on the door and pushed a cart holding a buffet of lunch items in.

"Is that all for us?" Kai asked.

"Looks like it," Michael said, standing up and rounding the table to take a closer look.

As they worked through lunch, their ideas began to coalesce. With a semblance of a starting point as a foundation, they made difficult but early progress and, by late afternoon, excitement had begun to build.

Michael could see the sun setting and the office emptying out when the porter returned with a dinner cart. Clearly the company was sparing no expense to keep them full, happy, and, most importantly, working. The food came with such frequency and in such variety that Michael and Kai both took extra bags home, Michael to the wife he never spoke of and Kai to—well, Michael didn't really know who, if anyone, Kai went home to.

After the first three days together, Michael came to two conclusions: one, Kai's knowledge and understanding of artificial intelligence rivaled his own, and two, she had no idea how beautiful she was.

"Kai," Michael said at the end of day four. "We have to update Dave. Let's go."

"Just one second," she said, covering her mouth as she ate a chocolate chip cookie. "I have no self-control when it comes to these cookies."

"Those are good!" Michael grinned.

Kai rose and followed him out, walking a half step behind him, and, upon entering, she spoke when spoken to. She acted differently with others and, after spending the last few weeks alone with her, Michael was only just now beginning to notice.

"So, how's progress?" Dave said, looking at Kai, who nodded and gestured toward Michael.

"Good, I think we have something here," Michael said. "We make an excellent team; Kai deserves a lot of the credit."

"No, sir, Michael deserves the credit," Kai put in.

"You can both have credit, that's not an issue," Dave said, rolling his eyes, "but can you give me a little more detail on what we have and how we can accelerate our progress?"

With so much exposure to Kai over the last few days, Michael found that her siren qualities had diminished, allowing his guilt over imagined adultery to wane. "Kai, can you take Dave through our proposed framework?" he said.

Michael thought he saw Kai flush, but she launched into their plan after only a moment's hesitation. Predictably, Dave agreed with their premise, and the team of three ballooned to fifteen, with Kai remaining the only woman.

After months of working together, the team hit its stride, and progress continued. Once the steep AI learning curve had finally passed, contributions came from everyone. Michael was proud of the team they'd assembled, and Dave increased his involvement, seeing a potential positive outcome on the horizon.

Over time, the raging lust that Michael had once felt for Kai faded, replaced with admiration and respect. Not only did Kai have to contend with being a minority in a male-dominated field, but she also had to deal with the awkwardness of colleagues unable to look beyond her beauty. Michael often witnessed her offer brilliant input, only to see it wasted on a team member stuck fantasizing in his own head. Michael felt ashamed of how he'd objectified Kai when he'd first met her and, as time passed, he did all he could to break down walls for her.

Things got even better when Dave came through with new office space on a different floor where they could set up. The team continued to get free meals, snacks, and drinks delivered preemptively, allowing them to stay on task and, with no repercussions to indulging any more, Michael and the rest of the team took full advantage of the company's generosity. Because no one else in the company had meals supplied for them, moving the team to a separate floor, away from jealous eyes, proved beneficial.

Michael twisted slightly as he squeezed through Kai's office door. As he entered, it suddenly struck him that Kai looked larger than before. She was in terrific shape; that wasn't it. She just seemed proportionally larger than she had a few months ago. She'd been wearing what appeared to be a new wardrobe these last few weeks, so maybe that was the reason she looked bigger, Michael thought.

"Kai, you should come and see this simulation I'm running," he said.

"K, I'll be right over."

After coming over to his desk a few minutes later and looking over his shoulder, she said, "Michael, you finished training the neural network, and these prediction tests look great!"

At this, Michael beamed with pride. It felt good to finally have some functioning code after all the planning and strategizing.

"We should take this over to Dave," Kai said. "Great work, Michael."

Dave looked relieved after Kai and Michael shared the new progress with him. Toyota had pushed up the deadline, he said, and he had just received the news. Preliminary pitches to Toyota's team were being scheduled, and the team only had another month to put together a presentation. Dave calmed Michael and Kai down, explaining that the presentation did not mean they needed a functioning idea now; they just needed to sell Toyota on the direction they would take.

When the day finally came, Michael and Kai ended up not uttering a word for the entire pitching session. That day, they learned how valuable a role Dave played. He knew every Toyota executive at the table, and he wielded Japanese decorum expertly, from bow height and duration to his presentation of a gift before the meeting. Dave had a far deeper understanding of what they were doing than Michael realized, and he summarized their proposed application of AI eloquently. By the end of the meeting, Michael would have bought anything Dave was selling.

"Frank said we crushed it in there," Dave said to Michael and Kai after the meeting. "Great job, guys, really awesome!"

"Thanks, Dave, but that was your show in there. Very impressive," said Michael.

Dave gave a gruff grin. "I'm just the pitchman. You made it happen. So, anyway, Frank said the big bosses are going to promote me if we get this Toyota contract."

"That's wonderful, Dave," said Kai.

"That's not all—you didn't let me finish. A rising tide raises all boats, am I right, Michael?" At the confused looks on Michael's and Kai's faces, Dave shook his head. "Guys, for being as smart as you are, you're pretty dumb. If I get a promotion, you're getting promotions too! So let's get back at it and lock this Toyota contract up!"

CHAPTER 28

TO NEW AUSTIN

Deep red clay caked Ana's tanned hands, the earthy aroma bringing her back to childhood with her mother in Mazamitla, just south of Guadalajara, before she sent her across the border to live with Mama. She'd loved pottery since her mother taught her to mold clay from the riverbeds, and had spent her teenage years making pots, vases, mugs—everything, really. After Michael had reignited her passion with a gifted pottery wheel, she'd slowly put together a small studio in a corner of their apartment. She'd peer out of the window for inspiration, then get to work.

Humming to herself, Ana dipped her hands in and out of the tub of water before throttling the pedal and shaping a vase. A smile glued to her tan face, she didn't notice when Michael came in until his strong arms snaked around her, his skin catching the afternoon sun streaming through the window.

By the time she finished her vase, Ana could smell a heavenly aroma from the kitchen.

"Smells glorious," she said as she made her way through, still wearing her clay-spattered denim overalls, a tight black shirt underneath.

Michael shook his head.

"What is it?"

"Chicken parmesan, *capelli d'angelo* pasta, and caprese salad," he said as she hugged him from behind. "I didn't want to interrupt you, but that vase looks amazing."

"Thank you," she said, pleased that he had noticed.

"Why don't you get cleaned up and I'll finish up dinner?"

Ana jumped in the shower, unable to stop herself from smiling. Things were going as well as she'd ever dared hope. Michael had just been promoted. Catherine, Frank's wife, was helping her fit in with the other wives. They had food on the table and money in the bank.

She glided out of the bedroom, relaxed after her warm shower, and sat down to a waiting dinner.

"You look like you're in a good mood," Michael said.

She smiled at him. "I have a lot to be thankful for."

"I think we should look for a new place," he said, passing the caprese salad.

"What?" Disbelief crept into her voice. "I mean, I realize your commute to the new office is longer, but do you really want to move?"

"I just thought we could use a few more bedrooms," Michael said, looking at his food.

Her heart aflutter, she said, "That sounds wonderful," and they ate in silence for a while. Ana's mind ran wild. *With home closer to the executive office in New Austin, our children would go to the best schools. Mama would have been so proud. I have to call Denise and Catherine.*

"Michael," she said breaking the silence. "Do you remember Dave and Denise's? How tall were those ceilings?"

Michael looked up. "Dave said they were something like fourteen feet with four-foot doors. I think that's the minimum in New Austin by code."

"It felt really big. What do we have here in the apartment?"

"Ah, standard from back in the day—nine-foot ceilings and three-foot doors."

"Oh, wow."

"That's not the half of it," Michael said, a grin building on his lips, "the office is much bigger than all that—but, after a while, you get used to it. I promise."

Getting up and taking their dishes into the kitchen, Ana tried to imagine living in a scaled-up house. Three days later, she found out: she and Michael headed out early, met an agent, and were led around several homes on the market in New Austin. As the broker took them through various neighborhoods, he asked her whether she wanted her guests to feel comfortable coming to their new home, and used her affirmative answer as the basis for his argument that they needed a house with large proportions, even if they were not yet big enough to warrant the need.

After what felt like a hundred showings, Ana finally decided on a home only a stone's throw away from Dave and Denise's house and just a mile from Garfield Falls State Park. Excited by the prospect of knowing their neighbors and having hundreds of hiking trails at their fingertips, Michael agreed with her choice, and they closed sixty days later.

The hardest part of the transition came when Ana had to say goodbye to all her former customers in their apartment complex. She had stopped cleaning for them only recently, and now she was leaving their lives for good. Michael came with her for moral support, and the couple quickly found themselves inviting many of their old neighbors to a housewarming party they had not yet decided to have.

By the time Ana got to Mrs. Harris on the eighth floor, she was a wreck. When the old woman opened the door and presented her with homemade tamales, Ana broke down, tears streaming down her face.

"Dear, what's wrong?" asked Mrs. Harris, handing the tamales hurriedly to Michael and crouching down to rub Ana's back.

"I'm leaving, and I won't be able to see you anymore," said Ana, leaning into Mrs. Harris's embrace.

"Where are you going, dear?"

"We're moving to New Austin," Michael said from behind his wife.

Mrs. Harris gave a small smile. "Oh, that's wonderful, dear. Why are you upset? You can finally start a family."

"She's right, Ana," Michael said, putting a hand on his wife's shoulder, "and we'll only be a half an hour away. You can come see Mrs. Harris any time you like. Isn't that right, Mrs. Harris?"

"Of course. You know you're always welcome here, and I'll want to meet your little ones as soon as you start filling up that new house of yours."

Ana pulled herself together and finally released the old woman.

It had taken the better part of an entire Sunday, but she and Michael had finally said goodbye to their apartment complex. With a final glance, they left the old world behind.

It only took a few hours to move all their belongings into their new garage and, over dinner on the floor, they scribbled down how they'd lay the house out once they bought some new furniture.

"We need everything, *mi alma*. Can we really afford all of this?" Ana asked Michael, looking at the cavernous, empty home they'd just moved into.

"Of course," Michael said. "We can, and you know it. You've seen my paycheck now. I know it's a big jump from that old apartment to this place, but we got this."

"It is exciting," she admitted, pushing the last scraps of her pasta across her plate.

The next morning, they woke up early and headed out to the furniture stores of New Austin. Everything felt oversized, as if made for giants. Ana thought the oversized look was in vogue, but Michael didn't see any other style options. Regardless, they liked what they saw, and they did have a huge new home to fill up, so Michael didn't complain when they settled on furniture with gargantuan proportions. Once Ana saw the bill, Michael again needed to convince her they could afford everything—though he had to admit, he was a little concerned himself. He pushed these thoughts back, convinced Ana they were all set, and pulled the trigger.

Settling into bed on an air mattress that night, Ana asked, "Do you think we're moving too fast here? I mean, even if we can afford it, everything is happening really fast, don't you think?"

"I think we have to just take life as it comes," said Michael, looking into his wife's eyes. "Let me put it this way. A year ago, I didn't know that we'd have this much money, that I'd be a vice president, that you'd be a burgeoning artist, or that we'd be living in a huge house in New Austin. But I did know I loved you and I wanted to have children with you. So, yeah, a lot has changed, but it's all peripheral stuff. I mean, as long as we have each other, right?"

A smile spread over Ana's face and she glanced down at the carpet. "I love you," she said softly, then turned off the light and climbed on top of him.

* * *

With their home freshly furnished and littered with vases of roses, Michael and Ana welcomed guests to the housewarming party they'd hastily organized. After a morning spent vacuuming and straightening their home, it looked like a model—lived in, yes, but perfect. Dave and Denise were the first to arrive, living only next door. Denise and Ana puttered around the kitchen chatting while Dave and Michael grabbed beers and headed out to the backyard. Shortly, Mola, Frank, and their families arrived, with the kids swiftly relegated to the front yard. Guests from their old life began to arrive too, and Ana quickly greeted her old cleaning clients before giving them the grand tour. The house smelled of cookies and roses in bloom.

Teresa, one of their old neighbors, was gazing around, her mouth hanging open. "Ana, we had no idea! This place is a palace. Did you hit the lottery or something?" She swept her long black hair out of her hungry eyes. "How high are these ceilings? My lord, this place is crazy."

"Hey, can we move in?" Miguel, Teresa's silver-tongued husband, quipped with a snort.

Ana forced a smile. She'd never liked Miguel; what Teresa saw in him was anyone's guess. She'd never experienced envy before, and suddenly found herself trying to downplay their new home—hopelessly, because its size spoke for itself.

On the next tour, Ana skipped their master bedroom, but still felt a cold guilt settle in her gut when her guests gaped, so she decided to stop. Showing off—even unintentionally—felt wrong. Thankfully, Dave and Mola, both extroverts, took well to hosting, and before she knew it, they were guiding everyone who wanted a tour around their home, doing their best to make everyone feel comfortable. The fact that Dave and Mola stood several feet taller than Ana's old neighbors made it look like they were elementary school teachers leading their pupils.

Ana took Michael aside and asked, "Were they always small people, or do they look like they shrunk to you too?"

"You remember how it is, Ana, when you're on a budget," Michael reminded her.

On the other side of the room, a group of their old neighbors were clustered together. Ana couldn't help herself. "What do you think they are talking about?"

"Don't worry about anyone else, Ana, just try to enjoy yourself. The party is excellent."

She nodded uncertainly and headed into the kitchen, through the mudroom, out the garage, and around the front of the house. "Hey kids," she said, waving, then scurried over up the front steps before pausing to inspect the siding of her new house. Her old neighbors were in her hallway, only a wall and a few feet away. If she stood still, she could just about make out what they were saying.

"I'm not blaming them, but I mean, this is quite a leap. Did you see Michael's work friends? They are enormous. I felt intimidated just standing next to them," Mr. Little was saying.

"I know what you mean, and did you see the spread of tapas Ana put out?"

"It's a veritable smorgasbord. I've never seen so much food in my life."

"That would cost me a week's paycheck, no joke," Havier said.

"And that guy, Frank?" came Louisa's voice, "the freakishly big one? He just piled his plate higher and higher. It was absurd."

"While we're here, we might as well eat, but then I want to get out of here. All these giants give me the creeps."

And with that, Ana crept back the way she'd come and reemerged into the house.

Michael seems to think the party is going well. And a lot of our new neighbors have turned up—at least they're mingling and having a good time.

Quashing her unease, she plastered a grin on her face and carried a plate of churros just out of the air fryer over to her old neighbors.

"Can I interest you in a churro?" she said, smiling.

"Oh, I couldn't possibly," Louisa said, and everyone followed suit, shaking their heads.

"Clifton?" Ana said, her smile growing desperate, "how about you? You always loved my churros."

"Well, if you insist," Clifton said with a shy grin, grabbing one and taking a bite. His face instantly lit up. "Oh yes, these are delicious."

"Thank you. You know, Hameda, doesn't your son love basketball? I think Frank's kids are playing in front of Dave's house next door. Maybe they'd like to play."

"That's nice—thanks, Ana, I'll go down and see if they want to."

"Great." With a final smile, Ana hurried back to the kitchen. *Well, that went well,* she thought, *they just needed a little help feeling comfortable.*

A hand closed around her arm, and Ana spun to find Denise beaming down at her. "Ana!" the large woman boomed, "your cooking is to die for!"

Ana felt herself blush. "Oh, thank you. Are you enjoying the party?"

"Oh yes," Denise said, "it's been great. You'll have to give me the recipe for your corn salad, I've never tasted anything so heavenly."

When Ana finally returned to the kitchen, she noticed her old neighbors had left the hall. She poked her head out back— no one. Hitching her bright orange skirt around her knees, she hurried outside to Dave's front yard and saw only Dave and Frank's kids playing basketball. *They must have gone.*

Later that night, as she and Michael cleaned up, Ana thought about her old friends' unease. She wondered if she'd let them down, or if they'd simply changed. Perhaps, she thought with a feeling of disquiet, they weren't the people she remembered at all. Sighing, she threw a beer can into the trash and looked up at Michael.

"I still can't get over how no one from the old apartment made any effort. I mean, I threw this party for them, and they all left early!"

Michael chuckled. "Don't worry about it, sweetie," he said, peeling a paper plate from the tablecloth, "it's a lot, coming across town and seeing this place. I'm sure they were pretty surprised when they saw the house."

"I know it's big, but we're still the same people. I just wanted them to feel welcome, and they clearly didn't. I couldn't even get them to eat anything—all that food and they didn't eat. Did you see them eat?"

"I saw Doug and Elain eating your tamales, but not very much, really. Before you go worrying about it too much, do you remember when you used to save my cereal for later if I didn't finish it? Food's expensive. They've probably never seen this much food in their lives, and they just freaked out a little bit. Give 'em a pass."

"You're right," Ana said softly, sinking into an armchair. "Hey, did you hear Tom talking about the neighbor two houses over?"

"I didn't hear what Tom was saying, no, but Dave and Frank were going on and on about how delipidated it is."

"They're right, you know. I would never say anything, but I wish that house looked better. Maybe I could offer to help them."

Michael shot her a wry smile. "Ana, let's try to avoid you working for free," he said. "Anyway, Frank seemed pretty frustrated about it, so hopefully he'll come up with something—some way to help them out For now, let's leave it to him."

Ana sighed and stood. "Okay, *mi alma*. Can we go to bed? I can finish cleaning up in the morning."

CHAPTER 29

AN OPEN DOOR

Mike bopped his head and shimmied to his own beat as he made his way down Fifth Avenue toward the financial district. He had always reveled in the Manhattan daybreak, as the lives of night owls and early risers comingled for a fleeting moment. Well-dressed suits steered clear of strung-out partygoers as drunks and promiscuous twentysomethings took their walks of shame—or, as Mike preferred to think of them, strides of pride. He grinned. Mike had played professional and walked the wild side himself, and he enjoyed watching how people handled when the sun broke.

"Watch where you're going, *asshole,*" a dapper young man in a suit yelled after Mike sashayed directly into his path, clipping his shoulder with his own.

"My bad!" Mike yelled in response, a wicked smile painted across his face. He had braced himself for the impact, turning his shoulder into a rock to knock the young buck down a peg or two. *Oh well,* Mike thought as he started to skip down the cluttered sidewalk. The motion was so shockingly unexpected that the seas of pedestrians parted for him—everyone wanted to stay clear of a man with a screw loose. He accepted the role of morning madman with glee and pushed the limits, singing *Blurred Lines* in his head loudly and swinging his arms as he cantered.

After a block or two, the allure of shocking the masses wore off, and Mike blended back in, slowing to a normal pace to catch his breath. His mind could run for days, but his body didn't have that same power. *Coffee*, he thought and, before long, he saw a grungy neon sign advertising the world's best cup of coffee for a buck. He pushed his way into the packed deli.

The queue stretched back to the door, but Mike excused himself, pushing through the crowd and heading to the restroom in the back. Door open, door shut, locked, a few sprinkles shaped into a line on the top of the urinal, a quick dab on the gums, and he was back out the door, alive again. He moseyed up to the pick-up counter and took the Styrofoam cup of black coffee that the gum-snapping waitress had just set down, yelling, "Fred! Black coffee!"

After pushing his way back out the door, he clicked his heels together, happy as a lark, and continued his daybreak stroll through Manhattan.

"Why, hello, young lady," he said as he spun round and round, dancing with an invisible partner in front of his old apartment building. "You look extraordinary this evening, if I may say so. May I have this dance?" He bowed low, his arms outstretched to ground and sky.

The little old lady eyed Mike suspiciously, not the least bit amused, and squeezed the railing. "Barty! *Barty!*" she tried to yell in her addled voice.

The doorman popped out the front door immediately, a concerned look on his face. "Mrs. Shankweiler, what's the matter?"

She pointed at Mike, who was still in a pose, with a look of utter disgust.

"Oh, Mrs. Shankweiler, that there's just Mr. Smith," said Barty. "He came back to see us, ya see. He used to live in this building with you, Mrs. Shankweiler. Do you remember? Must a been, what, ten years ago? Isn't that right, Mr. Smith?" He held her arm and walked her down the steps to a waiting car. After he put Mrs. Shankweiler in the car and tapped the hood, the car sped off.

Mike finally broke his pose, tossed the Styrofoam cup away, and gave the doorman a bear hug, lifting him off the ground.

"Mikey, my man, where have you been? We've missed you!"

"I'm up in Hell's Kitchen now. How you been, brother?" Mikey said, smiling like a million bucks. But his teeth were stained and his breath was sour, making Barty cringe.

"Good man, good. What's up with you? Got anything good cooking? Anything new I should be investing in? You know, me and the missus own our place in Harlem now because of you. Just glad we sold when …" Barty caught himself. "Ah, never mind all that. Come on in. Let me show you around the place. Bossman has been fixing this place up. You gotta look around inside."

"Nah, I don't want to kill my vibe, man. I just wanted to see you, see how you were doing," Mike said.

"All right, all right, that's cool. To be honest, Mikey, I'm good, real good. I run the building during the third shift nowadays, so I guess you could say I'm the boss this time of day. At least for another twenty minutes," Barty said with a wide grin.

"Aw, man, that's awesome. You deserve it, Barty. I always told Meme you were going places." Mikey stepped in closer. "So, I've been taking it easy for a while, ya know, lookin' around, weighing my options, and, well, I get bored having so much time and money on my hands. You know how it is."

Barty eyed him curiously. "Sure, Mikey, yeah. I mean, I don't really have money like that, but I can imagine."

"Good, good. Anyway, Barty, what do you think about hookin' me up?"

"What, now? Hell, it's five somethin' in the morning. I didn't know you were still partyin' like that and all. Thing is, I stopped dealin' when bossman gave me responsibility for the building and all. Wanda told me, Barty, you got to keep it straight now and, well, I caved."

"Nah, nah, nah, I mean hook me up with a job," Mike said.

Barty stared at him, dumbstruck. "Now, why in the hell would you want a job at your old building?"

"I don't want just any job, Barty. I wanna work with you. I always admired how you guys look, all dressed up in your suits and hats and everything. Plus, you get to meet new people every day. I get lonely is all, and I just figured, why not get paid and hang out with my main man Barty?" Mike said with a twinkle and his selling smile.

Barty gestured for Mike to follow, and he walked into the building. Mike noticed Barty didn't hold the door for him as he strode across the foyer and yelled at someone to watch the door a minute. After passing through a brass-trimmed, employees-only door, Barty stood in the middle of a tiny break room that doubled as a security office, one wall covered in surveillance screens.

"Now, look here, Mike. What kind of shit you trying to pull?" Barty said, a stone-cold look on his face.

"Barty, I just wanna—"

"I said, cut the shit, Mike. You turn up here after ten years, high, scare Mrs. Shankweiler shitless, and then ask your old dealer for a fucking job?"

"Man, it's cool—"

"No, it's not fucking cool, Mikey. Your ass owned a motherfucking penthouse in this building. What the hell happened to you?"

"Bad idea. I get it. My bad, Barty. I'll get lost," Mike said as he turned to leave.

"Fuck you will," Barty said with the face of a concerned friend. "Come on, brother, after all the shit we've been through, you know I'll always help you. You just can't lace your webs of bullshit with me. You gotta bring it real with me, Mikey."

Mike looked at the ground. "Look, I need it, Barty," he said quietly, "I need the work." It was the first real thing he remembered saying in quite a long time.

"My man, that's all you had to say. You know I got you," Barty said with a grin. "Now, let's see if I got something that fits you. It'll be you at the door with me tonight. Shift starts at ten and ends at six."

After rifling through a rack of dry-cleaned suits, he picked one that looked like it would fit and passed it over.

"Here's a suit. We'll get you a proper doorman's outfit next week, but you'll need a fitting for that, so, for now, you use the loaner. Now, go home and sleep that shit off. Don't you fucking come in high or wasted tonight, or I'll smack the shit outta you."

Mikey smiled and made his way to the door. "Thanks, Barty."

"And don't lose that fucking suit, Mikey!" he heard Barty yell as he left the security closet.

* * *

As much to his surprise as Barty's, Mike showed up clean-cut and fresh at 10 p.m. on the button. Mike looked good, and it felt good to do something that helped people, even if that was only opening doors and hailing cabs.

As he stood with Barty, he got caught up on all the goings-on at the building over the past decade—but, before he could build up the courage to ask about the Stallans, a knockout in a shimmering gold dress and stilettos stepped from the elevator. Trying not to ogle a resident on the first night, Mike put his head down and pushed the door open just as Barty made his way across the foyer, en route to the restroom.

"Evening, Mr. and Mrs. Avery," Barty said, and he nodded as he moved past the couple.

As they approached the door Mike was holding open, he raised his head again and made eye contact with the golden goddess. He froze.

"Mike," she said, mouth falling open.

"Helen!"

"It's been ages," Helen said, recovering quickly. "Mike, meet my husband, David."

"It's a pleasure to meet you, David," Mike said, easily falling back into superficiality.

"What, what are you doing here?" Helen asked.

"Oh, just, ah, picking someone up," he said as Helen's disinterested husband continued to walk down the steps to a waiting town car.

"Helen, I'm so sorry about what happened to Alex," Mike murmured.

"Water under the bridge," she said in her laissez-faire way.

Mike peered into her ice-blue eyes. "No, I'm really sorry. I just disappeared on you and everyone."

"Look, Alex drove that Porsche off a bridge, not you," she said coldly. "Or did you?"

Mike stood, speechless. No one had been with Alex when he'd flown off a bridge at two hundred miles an hour and disintegrated, only a few days after Stallson Beverage had been taken from them.

"Honey, we're going to be late," David said, and he waved at Mike. "Very nice to meet you, Matt, but we have to be going. Honey, come on now."

"He's right. Well, Mike, take care of yourself," she said as she pulled Mike into an embrace and kissed his cheek, "or don't." She held him at arm's length for a moment and then scurried off down the steps and into the car.

The building door swung open, and Barty stood there, pulling at his belt and straightening himself. "What did I miss?"

* * *

In the black town car, Helen and David exchanged disgusted glances.

"Who was that gentleman on the steps?" he asked as she

powdered her nose, her eyes fixed on her pocket mirror while the car jostled around.

"Just one of Alex's flunkies. That idiot owned the apartment below ours ten years ago and squandered it all away," Helen explained.

"Well, that makes me think even less of him. You know he was wearing a Timex?" David said, and Helen let out a cackle. "So, how did he lose it? I mean, you have to be quite accomplished to lose that much money."

"Oh, he had help from his slimly little bitch of a wife, Meme," Helen said as she finished her lipstick. "She was a dumpster fire who helped him burn his money. When Stallson went belly-up, she spent everything and then left that idiot for another, a Russian slimeball who bought her a tiger. You can't even make this stuff up, it's so ridiculous."

"You know he was working as a doorman and trying to hide it?" David said. "Barty told me earlier he had a new guy starting this evening. I'm certain that was him. Did you see the ridiculous suit he was wearing?"

"*No,*" Helen said in disbelief, her mouth hanging open. "David, darling, that's not going to work. I don't want to see him again—not ever."

"Oh, I know. I've already taken care of it," David said, and at that, Helen mounted him and, her arms around his head, kissed him wildly.

The car slid on through the yellowing night.

CHAPTER 30
LIFE IN THE BIG LEAGUES

By the second week at the new office complex in New Austin, Michael had started to get his bearings. At first, it had felt like a hospital or Vegas casino with oversized everything, but now that he'd settled in, he couldn't imagine going back to the cramped cubicles and tiny chairs of his last office. His new office space had a floor-to-ceiling glass window through which he could just make out the peak of Mount Ranger on the horizon. Kai's office, across from his, didn't have the glass or the view, but it made up for it in sheer size. The executive offices made Michael feel like he'd finally made it.

After grabbing a few muffins from the complimentary bakery basket in the executive lunchroom, he ran into a few colleagues chatting about the news.

"On my way in, they were talking about food shortages in China again," one of them—Steve, a balding manager from down the hall—said.

"Yeah, I heard about that last night," a woman Michael didn't recognize said. "The Chinese have put martial law into effect in a few rural regions to start rationing. Terrible!"

Michael jumped into the conversation. "You mean like the old Soviet Union bread line from back in the day?"

She glanced at him distastefully. "Yeah, something like that."

"I keep hearing about it. Sounds miserable. Apparently, each household gets coupons for grain or flour, rice, oil, milk, eggs, staples like that, and that's all they get. They can't buy more than they are allotted," Michael said.

"I guess that's communism for ya. Glad to be in the good ol' US of A," Steve said.

"Hey, how are you doing in the market lately?" Michael asked. "You still day trading on the down-low in your office?"

Steve leaned in conspiratorially. "I tell you, the place to be right now is in commodity futures." He gave a quick wink. "I was day trading for a while and I made out okay, but it took too much time, so I moved over to index funds. Then my broker told me to check out futures, and that's the ticket. Did you know that corn futures have beaten returns on S&P 500 index funds for the last seven quarters? Soybeans, wheat, and rice are on a tear as well. Any agricultural products that are high in calories … oh yeah, and sugar, that's done really well."

Michael nodded. "That makes a lot of sense with the price of food nowadays. Man, you wouldn't believe my bill at Olivia's last week. I don't want to know how much the company spends on all the food they have around all the time."

Having gotten his quota of investment advice for the day, Michael excused himself, grabbed a hot chocolate, and walked over to Dave's office to shoot the breeze. Finding the office empty, he headed to Mola's and then back to Kai's, desperate to tell someone about the Canyon he'd explored over the weekend with Ana—but Kai was focused on her computer screen. Disappointed, he headed back to his own computer and forced himself to stop procrastinating and get to work.

That night, Michael arrived home to the smell of something sweet baking in the oven.

Ana appeared, grinning, and ran toward him, leaping into his arms. "*¡Mi alma!* We're pregnant!" She gave him a sloppy kiss on the mouth while squeezing his cheeks before turning and running back to the kitchen.

Michael dropped his things and quickly followed her,

grabbing her from behind before she could open the oven. "That's amazing news!"

Ana squirmed free and turned to face him, a glowing grin enveloping her whole face. "I know, isn't it so exciting? Ahh. I'm baking a chocolate chili cake to celebrate; we're having a baby!"

The dinner Ana had cooked told Michael she'd known all day, because course after course of delicious dishes came out. By the time they got to the decadent cake, they both felt full to bursting, but still managed somehow to find room. Then, leaning into one another over the dimly lit table, they talked about how their lives would change. They discussed names; Ana liked Heather for a girl and Ronald for a boy, and Michael liked Lewis for a boy and Sarah for a girl. Neither of them would admit if they wanted a boy or a girl, but they both agreed they'd like at least one of each one day.

"Okay, so not Ronald, but how about Carlos if we have boy?" Ana said softly, sinking her fork into another slice of chili chocolate cake.

"I don't like it," Michael found himself saying.

She stared at him with raised eyebrows and he stood up with a wink, carrying his plate toward the sink.

"Say, I know we just moved in here, but do you think it will be big enough?" he asked over his shoulder. "I mean, the proportions are awesome and everything; we don't need to turn or duck through doorways, but it's only four bedrooms, and I want to have at least four kids."

Ana almost spat a mouthful of cake across the kitchen. "Let's have the one first!" she managed, laughing. "Then we can talk about a new house!"

"Okay," Michael said, grinning, "I'm just excited." He dried his hands. "I can't wait to take him camping, show him the constellations—I'll teach him how to kayak and build a fire!"

Ana gave him a stern look.

"Or her! Him or her. You know I'll love whatever we have, just like I love you," he said quickly, moving closer to peer into her mahogany eyes.

The next morning, Michael headed out to the mailbox before work. As he was opening it, he noticed someone in a hooded sweatshirt walking briskly down the driveway to the dilapidated house two doors down. He decided to walk over and introduce himself, maybe see what was up, but the person was walking quickly, hurrying away from him.

Michael called out, "Hey—hello!"

The person slowed and turned their head back to glance at him; as they did, their hood slipped off, and Michael caught a glimpse of a bald scalp pockmarked with patches of thin brown hair. Then they turned back around and picked up their pace until they disappeared behind a corner.

Michael, pace slowing and raised arm falling uncertainly, finally gave up, and found himself standing in front of the broken-down home. The yard immediately called attention to itself, with knee-high grass and patches of brown that had once been flowerbeds breeding supersized weeds. All of the lights in the house were off, the windows were all shut, and the curtains looked to be drawn. Michael had half-expected the house to be abandoned; no cars were in the driveway, and he hadn't seen anyone enter or exit since moving in—at least, not until today.

"Hey, beautiful, you won't believe who I just met outside," Michael called when he walked back into the house.

"Who's that?" Ana yelled from the kitchen.

"You know the house with the overgrown lawn?"

"No, you mean someone actually lives there? I thought it was deserted—a foreclosure or something."

"I didn't get to talk to them, but I did see someone leave the house and head down the street. They looked kind of sickly if you ask me. It looked like their hair was falling out, actually."

Ana frowned. "Do you think it was a burglar? Did they break in and run away when they saw you?"

"They had a key. I saw them lock up the door before they bolted, so I don't think that's it. But something weird is going on over there. I'll ask Dave at work if he's noticed anything. You should keep a lookout too, see if you notice anything. Anyone coming or going."

"Aye aye, *capitán*," Ana quipped.

As Michael pulled into his office's parking lot that day, he noticed work crews taking up a number of spaces. Walking into the lobby, he saw that the left side of the building had been cleared of furniture. He asked the girl at the front desk, Tammy, what was going on. In his short time at the new office, he had found Tammy knew everything first.

"Oh, you didn't hear?" she said nonchalantly, "they're knocking out the second floor in that wing and turning it into just one floor. All the big kahunas want bigger offices and whatnot," she said, blowing and popping her gum as she spoke. Then, glancing left and right, she whispered, "They're having a private kitchen put in as well for the c-suite chef. I met him. His name is Marco." This was followed by a wink and another bubble gum pop.

The office couldn't help but chatter about the renovation news. Most of the team took it as a badge of honor that the company was doing so well that it needed to renovate. Michael caught up with Dave and Mola chatting with Frank, and sat for a while, listening to the details of Frank's new office. It sure sounded spectacular, and he couldn't help his mind drifting to the questions of what he could do to keep moving up the ladder and get one of the big new offices in the new wing. He was sure that if he stayed focused on the Toyota project, good things would continue to come.

Michael couldn't wait to get home and tell Ana about his day.

Sure enough, he found her as excited as he was and, when the topic of his company's leaders' homes came up, Michael remembered he'd gotten Frank's home address at the housewarming party. They rushed to look it up online.

"Holy shit, Ana, you have to look at this." Michael handed her his phone. Frank's house was absurdly enormous. The front door had to have been fifteen feet tall, and the windows reached almost as high, meaning the ceilings must have been twenty feet tall on both levels. The doors were wide, and the pool resembled a small lake. Through the windows, they caught a glimpse of the furniture—huge, gilded couches and tables looked fit for royalty. Michael and Ana had thought their home and furnishings were a bit oversized, but what Frank had was more like double-sized. Frank was a big boy, Michael supposed; he had to have been one of the largest men Michael had ever seen, likely nine feet tall and four feet wide, so he had to turn sideways when he went through standard doorways. Still, though—this house looked like it had been built for a man one and a half times Frank's size. Michael wondered how Frank found the time to eat so much.

The next morning, over coffee, the subject of their personal budget came up.

"I did the budget for last month, if you want to take a look," Ana said proudly, pointing to her laptop on the table. "You can see how everything looks now that all the new home expenses are in."

Michael spun around the laptop and smiled—he'd taught her the basics of putting together an Excel budget after she'd insisted on understanding their finances, and she'd really gotten the hang of it.

"Looks good to me," he said. "We're still saving ten percent of our earnings after getting into this new place. I'm happy."

Ana frowned at him. "I've been reading, Michael, and I think we should try to get that up to twenty-five percent. Really look and see if there is anywhere you think we can save." Ana gestured back toward the screen.

After examining the spreadsheet more carefully, Michael chuckled. "Damn, we spend more on food than we do on the mortgage. Is that right?"

"Exactly. Back in the old apartment, we spent a quarter of what we spend now on food."

"That's not really fair, Ana, but I get where you're coming from. If you want to try cutting back, let's cut back. That's why we did the budget in the first place, right? We can always drop it if it's too hard."

"I hoped you'd say that," she said, kissing his head. "Because I've already started." With a smile, Ana passed him a box of cereal.

Michael chuckled. Figuring he may as well take it in stride, he poured himself a bowl. Since they had moved into the new house, Ana had been treating him to mouthwatering breakfasts: huevos rancheros, pumpkin pancakes with cinnamon whipped butter, *tres leches* oatmeal, and breakfast burritos filled with chorizo, eggs, and cheese. Now it looked like cold cereal and a glass of water would be all that was on the menu for the foreseeable future.

After Ana stopped him from filling up his cereal bowl a third time, he gave her a kiss on the forehead and headed into the office.

Over the next few days, Michael did his best to keep his food expenses in check. With plenty of treats and snacks served at the office, he didn't have a problem reeling it in until his coworkers invited him to lunch and he was forced to watch them enjoy copious amounts of food at the fine restaurants clustered around the high-end office parks of New Austin.

Michael knew Ana was struggling to reduce the time and money she spent on food. Food had become an important part of their new lives, and she liked cooking big, delicious meals—which, of course, he loved enjoying with her. It gave them time to talk at the table, and something to talk about—after all, they had both grown up with food at the center of their homes. But, once they imposed their budget, desserts stopped; then, steak was replaced with canned meat, fresh vegetables with frozen, and fresh bread with prepackaged. It was tough.

A week into their effort to cut back their food budget and, in turn, the amount they ate, Michael and Ana sat down to eat a nice meal she had cooked.

"Hey, *mi alma*. How was your day?" asked Ana.

"Not bad. It's exciting, watching the office renovation come together," Michael replied as he dug into his plate of spaghetti and meatballs. "They're working around the clock, so it's moving really fast. What about you? How was your day?"

"It was good. I felt the baby kick a few times in the morning."

"What does that feel like, exactly?"

"It's just kind of a little flutter in your stomach."

They finished their servings, and Michael asked, "What's for dessert?"

After a brief pause, Ana's eyes started to well up.

"Ana? Ana, what's that matter?" Michael asked, jumping out of his seat and holding her.

Through shaking sobs, she said, "Nothing."

"Oh, come on, now. You can tell me, whatever it is," Michael said in a soothing voice.

Through her tears, Ana said, "There is nothing for dessert." She sobbed harder, unable to speak. "And I want dessert, Michael. I want dessert, and we don't have anything," She fell into him, her tears seeping through the thin fabric of his shirt.

"Ana, is that all this is? Please don't cry."

She murmured something unintelligible into his shoulder.

"You're pregnant, honey. Maybe now isn't the right time to go on a diet to save money."

"Okay."

"Why don't you get your coat, and I'll take you out for ice cream?"

"Okay, that would be nice." Ana sniffed, wiping at the tears from her cheeks. "But are you sure I'm not being too weak? Shouldn't we be able to eat less if we decide to, without me breaking down?"

"Ana, listen. I'm at work all day, and there are snacks and treats everywhere. I've been eating a ton at work for free these past few days. Meanwhile, you've been at home, starving yourself just so we can save a few bucks. Let's try this experiment another day, when you're not pregnant, maybe. Please, we're lucky we can afford to eat the way we do. Not everyone can. Let's enjoy it."

"I am eating for two …"

"That's right—it's only fair that we hold off attacking the food budget for now, don't you think?"

"As long as we promise each other we'll cut back in other areas," she said making eye contact with him until he nodded.

"I'm sorry I've been so snappy lately. Not eating has really made me emotional."

"I know what you mean. I've been a real dick at work the past couple of days, even with all the junk I've been eating. Without your delicious breakfasts in the morning, I start the day off in a foul mood. I'll be glad to enjoy your cooking again instead of cereal."

"Deal—but first, take me out for that ice cream you promised."

After banana splits with all the fixings at an ice cream parlor down the street, the now-content couple went to bed early, looking forward to a long, leisurely weekend.

The next morning, a Saturday, they headed over to Dave and Denise's house in the afternoon to hang out by the pool and enjoy a barbeque. As Dave's kids splashed around, the wives poked around Denise's flowerbeds while Dave and Michael had a couple of beers.

"Reno's looking good isn't it?"

"Yeah, I can't believe how fast it's coming together."

"This a stout or a porter?" Michael asked, examining the unlabeled brown bottle.

"It's a porter. What do you think?"

"Your best yet!"

"Yeah, I like this one. Stouts use unmalted barley, which creates that classic coffee flavor. Porters use malted."

"Huh, I didn't know that," Michael said, following Dave along the property line of his house. Kicking at the tall grass, he said, "You know, the other day I saw someone leaving that house." He pointed at the dilapidated house next door.

Dave raised an eyebrow. "Oh yeah? Did you talk to them?"

"Nah, I tried, but they didn't seem too interested in getting to know me," Michael said with a smirk.

"I wouldn't feel too bad about it, Michael. We've never met them either, and we've lived here longer than you." He passed Michael another beer. "Ain't that right, D?"

"What's that?"

"Our delightful neighbors who take such good care of their yard. I was just telling Michael here not to feel bad. They avoid us too."

"Oh, *mi alma*, did you tell Dave you saw somebody?" Ana chimed in.

"Yeah, I was just telling him. So, I went out to get the mail the other day, and someone in a hoodie came out of the front door, locked up, and then bolted down the block. I tried calling after them, but they were having none of it. They hightailed it out of there. Weirdest thing was, their hood fell down for just a minute, and it wasn't pretty."

"Ooh, gossip. Tell me, tell me," Denise said, bouncing with glee in her white shorts and yellow blouse.

"It looked like a guy, but, well, it looked like he was molting or something—just these patches of thin brown hair smattering an otherwise bald head, and ..."

"Yes, and?" Denise said, then turned to Dave. "Can you get me another drink?"

"Yeah, yeah, just let me hear this first."

"Well, he made eye contact for just an instant, but his eyes looked so ..."

"Yes, come on, Michael, out with it." Denise was now frothing with anticipation.

"Sad. His eyes were hollow and sad. It's why I stopped chasing and calling after him. It was like he shot me with the opposite of Cupid's arrow, and after that I didn't really want to introduce myself at all."

No one spoke until Dave broke the rapidly forming ice. "Well, shit, Michael, that's a real heartwarming gem of a story. Now I really feel like a horse's ass for never trudging over there and saying hi myself."

"I see them every morning before Dave gets up," Denise said quietly, "walking past the house. I know it's not right, but once, I followed them."

"You did not," Dave said, turning to stare at his wife.

"Oh yes I did."

"Are you nuts, woman?"

"I took care. I was safe. You know I'm curious. How could I leave a mystery like that alone? I mean, who leaves the house on foot every day and doesn't return until I've gone to bed? And believe me, they don't return while I'm awake because I've watched like a hawk out my window."

"Do you see what you've done here?" Dave said, rounding on Michael, "Do you see what you started, Michael?"

Michael only grinned.

"So, where did they go, Denise?" Ana asked, concern in her voice.

"It's not very exciting, actually. That's why I never really mentioned it. They just walked through the neighborhood, down

Kelly Drive, and to the bus stop at the corner of Washington. City bus picked them up, and I came home."

"Well, that was anticlimactic," Michael said.

"They're probably just tight on cash. They used to have a car—I remember it, a navy-blue Suburban. Haven't seen it in a few months, but they did have one. More than likely, they got themselves into a cash crunch and sold it, and now he takes the bus to work every day. Hey, now I'm happy I never went over; he'd probably ask me for a loan." Dave clinked his beer against Michael's and chuckled.

"That's not nice, Dave," said Denise. "Michael said they were losing their hair. You never know, maybe they have cancer or something."

"Cancer, D? Who are you kidding? No one's died of cancer in a decade. Could be drugs though. That would make a lot of sense: selling the car, low on cash, yard looks like crap."

"Either way, we are neighbors," said Ana. "I feel bad. What if they just need some help to get back on their feet? Can't we help them, Michael?"

"How? They won't even talk to me—they ran away when I tried."

"Let's go knock on their door right now and invite them over," Ana suggested. "If that's all right with you and Dave, of course," she quickly added, looking at Denise.

"No use," said Denise. "They're not home. They left around five this morning, and no one will be home until after eleven tonight."

"D, what the hell?" asked Dave.

"I'm just keeping tabs on them. You mind your own business."

"Never make my wife your enemy, Michael. She's resourceful." Dave chugged the rest of his beer.

"I wouldn't dream of it," Michael said.

"Isn't there anything else we can do to help them?" Ana pleaded. "Anything, Michael?"

"Dave and I could go over there and cut their lawn," Michael suggested.

"Oh, that would be wonderful. They'd come home after a hard day's work and see their yard all tidied up and taken care of."

"Plus, the neighborhood would look a lot nicer," Denise said, giving Dave a look.

"Ahh goddamn it, Michael, you had to open your big mouth," said Dave. "Well, it was your big idea, so get your mower and meet me over there in ten. I'll get my clippers and edger."

"Ana and I will go down to Wanamaker's and pick up a few flats of flowers and some mulch," Denise announced. "If we're going to do it, we might as well do it right and add a pop of color."

A few hours later, they were finished and, just like that, the neighborhood's sore thumb was tucked in. Michael had knocked out the lawn on his riding mower, Dave had edged and clipped, and the ladies had weeded the flowerbeds and planted flowers here and there to add some color. Drenched in a mixture of sweat, dirt, and grass, they hopped in the pool to cool off before dinner. The four of them felt content and warm after doing a good deed for their troubled neighbors, and Denise kept going on about how she could hardly wait to watch their reactions through her window when they arrived home and saw their well-manicured yard.

Dave loved to barbeque, and the meal did not disappoint. He had been marinating porterhouse steaks, chicken, and a whole salmon all day. When he stacked the meat on his dinner-table-size charcoal grill, the mouthwatering scent of rendered fat drifted on the air.

By the time dinner was served, Michael could have eaten a horse. After gorging themselves on steaks, chicken, salmon, corn, mashed potatoes, macaroni salad, green beans, beet salad, and baked beans, they enjoyed warm rhubarb pie with ice cream for dessert. Then, a little while later, everyone had to try Denise's warm, double-chunk chocolate chip cookies she had whipped up specially.

"Denise, those cookies were over the top," said Michael.

"Delicious," added Ana.

"You know what's delicious?" asked Dave. "Have you ever seen those red vans driving around that say 'Roadies'?"

"Oh, Dave, we just had a nice meal with the Loris," said Denise. "Don't go ruining it with your disgusting rumors."

"They're not rumors. You heard my cousin. Anyway, guess what those vans are doing. You'll never guess."

"Sorry, Denise, but now he's got to tell us," said Ana. "You can't leave us with a cliffhanger like that."

"Okay, Ana," Denise said, rolling her eyes at her husband, "but don't say I didn't warn you. It's gross."

"They pick up roadkill," said Dave, "process it on the spot in the van, and then smoke it or flash-freeze it right there. My cousin says they make a killing."

"That is revolting," said Michael.

Ana shuddered. "Oh my, I feel so horrible for those people."

"Don't feel bad for them, Ana. Meat is meat," said Dave.

"I'll divorce you if you ever bring home roadkill. You hear me, bub?" Denise wagged her finger at her husband.

At that moment, they heard the distant wail of a siren. As the seconds passed, the sound grew louder and louder. Drawn by the sound, the group headed through the house and out into the front yard, where they saw an ambulance in the driveway of the house next door, flanked by the glittering lawn.

Just as quickly as it had arrived, the ambulance doors closed, and it raced off again, sirens blaring.

"I wonder what happened," Ana said to break the silence.

"I don't know," said Dave, "and I doubt we'll be able to figure it out tonight. Maybe we can try going over tomorrow to see if everything is all right. We did just cut their lawn. The least we can do is go and beg forgiveness."

"Well, besides that downer to end the night, thanks for having us over," Michael said with a smile. "Your cooking was as marvelous as ever, Denise, and Dave, your food was passable."

Dave laughed. "Yeah, yeah, funny guy. See you both soon."

And with a final wave, Ana and Michael headed back home.

On Sunday morning, they woke up late and enjoyed coffee on the porch.

"I wonder if Dave and Denise found out what happened with that ambulance," Michael said thoughtfully.

"So do I, it's really concerning," Ana said. "I think I had a dream about it, but I can't quite remember it."

"Let's head over."

"I can't go over looking like this," she said, her hand gesturing to her hair.

"Oh, come on, you're beautiful."

"I'll be right back," she said, hurrying back into the house.

When Ana reemerged manicured and groomed, they headed over to Dave and Denise's, finding them already heading out.

"Oh, hi! Heading over too? Let's go together," Denise said, walking past Dave and Michael and locking arms with Ana. Michael and Dave fell in behind them and, together, the group crossed the still-dazzling lawn of the house next door.

At the door, none of the jests about the rundown house seemed funny anymore.

Michael was thinking about suggesting they head back when Dave took the plunge and knocked heavily on the front door. To their great surprise, the door swung open.

"Hello? Anybody home?" Dave yelled as he stepped across the threshold. The group followed him slowly, nervous eyes darting from room to room. The grand space was largely empty. Sections of drywall had been removed where it looked like piping had been dismantled and taken out. The entire first floor was completely devoid of furniture. A small stack of wood stood next the former home of an electric fire. It had been ripped out, and the blackened walls suggested the space had recently been used to burn wood, with half of the smoke going out a hole punched in the wall and the rest pouring into the house, leaving a cloud of black soot caked onto the ceiling. Next to the makeshift fireplace sat a large cast-iron pot with a mismatched lid and a large, empty red bucket. Trash and wrappings were scattered over the floor, and huge blue burlap sacks lay all around the fireplace.

As Ana and Michael, nearly paralyzed, stood surveying the first floor, Dave was already up the stairs to the second.

He yelled down, "Nobody's home. I checked all the rooms."

A small-framed police officer appeared in the open front doorway. "Are you the homeowners?"

"Sorry, sir. No, we are not," replied Michael. "We're the neighbors."

"Then what are you doing in these people's home?"

Dave nonchalantly glided down the steps. "We wanted to check on them after the ambulance last night and, when we knocked, the door swung open, so we checked to make sure no one was in distress."

The officer's frown didn't budge. "Well, the force appreciates good Samaritans like you fine people, but I am going to have to ask you to leave."

"Our apologies, officer. We'll be on our way," said Denise. "Is there anything you can tell us about what happened to our neighbors? Our neighborhood is a close one, and everyone will want to hear if the … if our neighbors are okay."

The officer gave a bitter laugh. "Look around, lady. Does it look to you like the neighbors, whose names you don't know, are okay? You people are all the same. Go check the Williamson

Foundation if you want someone to tell you what the hell happened here." The officer shifted his focus from Denise to Dave. "Now, if you don't mind, please exit the property, so I can finish my job, big guy."

"All right, that's our cue," Michael said, cutting through the tension.

One by one, they filed out of the house in silence. The officer kept his eye on them until they reached Dave's front door.

CHAPTER 31
PARTY TIME

It was several weeks later when Ana received an invitation from Frank and Catherine to attend their daughter Grace's birthday party. Ana had wanted to see their home in person since the day she and Michael had looked it up online, and this presented the perfect opportunity. By the time Michael arrived home from work, Ana already had a present for Grace picked out: a teal purse from a boutique downtown.

As the weekend party edged closer, Ana fretted over her decision. When she was fifteen, she'd been worried about her next meal and little else; she had no idea what rich girls wanted. So, with no common experience to fall back on, she decided to treat Grace like a woman, thinking that was what all teenage girls wanted. But would that look bad in front of Catherine and Frank? Michael talked her off the ledge by suggesting they bring a bottle of Scotch for Frank and yellow roses for Catherine to make sure they made the right impression.

Finally, the party date arrived, and Michael forced Ana, who had started to show, into the car with the flowers, Scotch, and the teal bag, which was wrapped in a flamboyant multicolored designer box.

As they approached the Grahams' enormous home on what Michael would have taken for a four-lane road were it not for the single strip down the middle, they noticed a short man waving them into the circular driveway. After pulling up to the mansion, two mild-mannered valets opened their doors and handed Michael a ticket. *They must frown on parking on the street around here*, Ana thought to herself.

As they approached the front door, Ana's jaw dropped. It was one thing to see the scale online, but it was quite another to experience it in person. She pushed the front door open and a glamorous-looking woman just a bit taller than Ana embraced her. The sequined dress the woman wore chafed Ana through her thin floral dress and, as they embraced, the woman's ankle twisted, and Ana caught her weight, helping her regain her balance.

"Thank you, Aunt Ana," the woman said with a smile, and only then did Ana realize the woman was the birthday girl.

"Grace, you look gorgeous! Wow, look at that dress. And those heels. You're really a stunner." Still holding Grace's fingertips, Ana gently pushed her away to get a better look at her. "When did you get so tall? I think you're as tall as me now without those heels."

"Really? Oh my God, Aunt Ana ... you just made my day," said Grace. "It's really hard keeping up at school. I have to eat, like, all the time just so I don't look stupid. Dad tells me to eat whatever I want to, but I don't want to eat all the time. Well, at least I'm not a football player. Ugg. Those boys do nothing but eat. High school is, like, the hardest thing in the world."

Grace's cell phone vibrated, and she held it up and stared at the screen. "Sorry, Aunt, I have to take this. Daddy's in the back. Go through there." She pointed down a hallway the width of a stadium concourse.

Michael held up the enticingly wrapped present Ana had worked so hard on. "Hi, Grace. Where should we put gifts?"

"Just put it over there. I'll open it later," Grace said before walking off while jabbering to someone on the other end of the phone.

"Well, that was interesting," Ana said to Michael as they walked over to a table covered in presents. Surveying the present table, she once again wondered whether she'd made the right choice. Michael convinced her to put the present down, assuring her that the thoughtful gift would be well received.

Still carrying the roses and Scotch, the couple retreated from the foyer, heading deeper into the sprawling home. Large walls lined with gold-framed works of art passed them by and, after crossing from the more formal front of the estate into the more casual side toward the back, they made a wrong turn and found themselves in an industrial-sized kitchen in full concert. A woman in a white apron and hat quickly but gently ushered them back out the way they'd come and, after a number of twists and turns, left them at the doorway of a great room filled with party guests.

Around them stretched the estate's sweeping grounds. Ahead, an enormous yet elegant square pool was built into a low rise, marble fountains glittering at its two farthest corners, framing the cascading hot tubs beyond. There was a wide slate stairway, from which water flowed down into the pool, leading up to the elevated tubs.

Swallowing her awe, Ana followed Michael through the throng. Up ahead, a sliding wall of glass, floor to ceiling, disappeared into a wall around a corner, transforming a great room into an impressive open-air space.

"I don't know anybody here, Michael," she whispered, "do you?"

"Ah, look, that's Catherine right there. Let's go give these to her," Michael said, pushing his way through the extra-large crowd on his way to Catherine. Equal parts regal and motherly, Catherine stood a solid three feet taller than both Ana and Michael. Dressed in an elegant black silk blouse draped with an oversized gold necklace, she *glittered*: dangling gold and diamond earrings hung from her ears, while burnished bangles and bracelets bedazzled her arms. She gave a tight smile as they approached.

"These are for you," Ana said, handing Catherine the yellow roses.

"Oh, dear, you shouldn't have. They are lovely. Thank you."

"Grace welcomed us at the door. She's really growing up fast," Ana said, trying to break the ice.

Catherine gave a heavy sigh, her smile wavering. "I know, I know. My babies are all gone—turned into these *creatures*."

"Kids aren't that bad, are they?" Ana asked, feeling queasy.

"Kids? Kids are wonderful, Ana. Don't listen to me," Catherine replied, finally making eye contact with Ana and bending down to pat her jewel-encrusted hand on Ana's stomach. "Teenagers are another story. All they do is eat, complain, and stare at their phones. Oh, how I miss my little babies." Catherine turned away, staring out into the crowd.

Sensing his cue to leave, Michael asked, "Where's Frank? I brought him something I'd like to give him."

"He's probably out back with the boys."

* * *

Michael, relieved to be away from Catherine, hurried away from the crowd, eyes peeled for Frank. He passed through lovingly tended flower gardens, past marble statues, and around lake-sized ponds, but still no luck. He was about to give up the search when he noticed a wisp of cigar smoke coming from behind the back of the pool house. Sure enough, he found Frank and three other enormous men camped out on lawn chairs, smoking big, fat cigars.

"Hey, Frank. Hey, fellas," Michael said as he approached the gathering.

"Sorry, Michael. Tommy here took my last one," Frank said.

"Oh, that's all right. I'm not a big smoker. I was just looking for you to give you this." Michael handed Frank the bottle of Scotch he'd spent an hour picking out.

"Ah, Michael, you shouldn't have," Frank said, taking the bottle. "Look, guys, Michael here got us some of the good stuff." He waved the bottle in front of them. In his hands, the fifth of Scotch Michael had spent a fortune on looked tiny and insignificant.

Then, in one motion, Frank slid his thumb up the neck of the bottle, popping the cork and pouring a healthy amount down his throat. Wiping his mouth, he held out the bottle to Michael.

"Come on, Michael, you have to partake. You're the one that brought this little treat."

Michael grabbed the bottle and took a small swig, and then Frank grabbed it back and passed it on to the next man.

"Michael, you hear anything about those new factories the American car manufacturers are touting? 'By hand is back' is the slogan they're using. They're planning to build big cars for us by hand. You believe that?" Frank took the last swig from the bottle as it came back around to him.

"No, I haven't heard anything about that, Frank," Michael said, finding his voice and tearing his eyes away from the empty bottle.

"Well, it's a real threat to all of us," Frank said. Then, getting up, he said, "All right, I gotta get back into battle, boys, or Cat will have my head."

Maybe this is why you should never mix work and pleasure, Michael thought as he excused himself from the secret gathering and headed back in to find Ana. She looked like she had enjoyed her time alone about as much as Michael had, so when he suggested they head home, she accepted without complaint.

* * *

After the stressful weekend, Michael was ready to get back into work mode. With chocolate chip pancakes drowned in butter and syrup deposited in his belly, he made the short commute to the office, content and reinvigorated. He even lucked out and scored a parking spot close to the entrance. Executives at the company set their own hours, and most, if not all, had children, so for the most part, the office ran on school hours. Because Michael enjoyed sleeping in and coming home to dinner on the table, he usually had to park at the back of the parking lot.

With a smile smeared across his face, Michael got out of his car and headed in. He waved to Tammy, whistling a jingle he couldn't get out of his head, before picking up a coffee and a donut from the break room and sitting down at his desk. Opening his laptop, he typed in his password and got the error that popped up every sixty days, forcing him to reset his passwords. Stuck on the error, he held the power button down and, while the computer was rebooting, he decided to check in with Kai and see how her weekend had gone. On the way, he thought, smirking, he could grab a few more donuts.

"Hey, Kai," he said, walking into her office and stopping abruptly—she wasn't in yet. He took a quick detour back to the lunchroom, where someone from IT whose name he couldn't remember gave him a funny look before scurrying back out the door.

Two chocolate donuts with sprinkles later, Michael was back on the move, stopping at Dave's empty office first and then down the hall at Mola's. *What the hell is going on?* he thought. *Did I miss a holiday or something?* He checked his phone, but there was nothing on his calendar; it was just a normal Monday. *Huh.*

He rounded the corner back to his office and spotted Tammy peeking into the room.

"Hey, I'm right here," he said, waving at her. "Mail or something?"

She nodded, her normal smile conspicuously absent.

"Do you know why this place is so empty? Is anybody else in yet?"

"Ah, just a few," she said meekly, avoiding eye contact.

"Well, how can I help ya, young lady?" Michael asked, glowing.

"Mr. Graham would like to see you in his office in the west wing."

"You got it. I'll head right over."

"Um, Mr. Lori … Mr. Graham asked me to walk over with you."

"Okay, Tammy," Michael said, a little surprised, "but let's make a pit stop in the break room. I'm gonna grab a hot chocolate and a snack, if you don't mind." Without waiting for an answer, he strode toward the break room. "I was actually at Frank's house this past weekend," he said over his shoulder as Tammy trailed behind him. "Oh, Mr. Graham's first name is Frank; he had a birthday party for his youngest, and his wife, Catherine, invited my wife. His house is to die for, let me tell you. If you think this place is big, wait until you see Frank's place."

Michael plucked a donut from the box and held it between his teeth as he emptied and stirred a hot chocolate powder packet into a cup of whole milk he'd pulled from the refrigerator. After putting the mixture into the microwave and transitioning the donut from his mouth to his hand, he glanced at Tammy. "You like hot chocolate? No, don't answer that if you haven't had hot chocolate the way I make it. First, you need whole milk—you can't use water—then a packet of Swiss Miss combined when cold. That's the first secret. Then you microwave it for two minutes, no more, no less. Finally, you put two large marshmallows in a cup and pour the hot chocolate over, top it with whipped cream, and you're set. Just like this." He waved his perfectly made cup of hot chocolate in front of her. "Can I fix you a cup?"

She gave him a tight smile. "No, Mr. Lori. Thank you, sir."

"Oh, right, we're going to see Frank. Let's go. Follow me. I know where his office is. Have you heard my wife, Ana, is pregnant? Second trimester. We don't know what we're having yet. Man, I can't wait to meet him or her." He smiled vacantly, passing back through the lobby toward the west wing. Tammy, he realized, was trailing behind him, and stopped at the end of

Frank's hallway, watching him. Michael shrugged before poking his head into the spacious room Frank called an office.

"Michael," Frank said, the back of his gargantuan black leather chair facing the door. "Have a seat."

Michael sat down in a chair opposite Frank's desk, taking up only half the seat. He heard a click behind him. He turned to see the door was now shut.

Frank swiveled around to face Michael. Looking him directly in the eye, he said, "You're out, Michael. Last week, Toyota pulled the plug. They're going with a Japanese AI company out of Osaka."

Michael felt the blood drain from his head. He felt himself rise free of his body, and saw himself suddenly, small, pathetic, cowering on the oversized throne opposite the giant.

With no response coming, Frank said, "Since the AI division only had one customer and that customer is now gone, some tough decisions had to be made. It's been difficult for me here, I'm sure you can see that, but the decision has been made to shut down the entire AI department."

Then, as if in slow motion, Frank reached across his desk, pushed a button on his phone, and said, "We're finished."

Two hulking security guards strutted into the office and gestured for Michael to get up. As if in an otherworldly dream, he heard only muffled words, the guards' voices seeming to come through water. Roughly, they led back to the lobby, and Tammy handed him a box of his things, a carton of donuts from the break room sitting on top. She tried to smile at him, but looked away as soon as their eyes met.

After being placed in his car, the box on his lap, Michael stared out at the frozen world. Finally, one of the guards banged on his hood and waved him away. He drifted out of the parking lot, his hand mechanically raising donuts to his limp mouth.

Michael floated into his home, put down his box of things

on the kitchen counter, and then headed to his bedroom. He crawled under the covers.

Hours later, Ana arrived home and saw the box in the kitchen under the empty carton of donuts. A folder filled with exit paperwork told her everything she needed to know. After reading it thoroughly, she set off to find Michael. When she discovered him in bed, she curled up next to him and whispered, "Oh, Michael, I'm so sorry."

A few hours later, Michael started to rouse himself, and Ana asked, "Do you want to talk about it?"

"Not really, but we'd better," Michael said, and recounted his morning in painful detail. "I just didn't see it coming, ya know? I thought we were doing well. I don't know what happened."

"Well, at least you got a package."

"A what?"

"Didn't you read the paperwork they gave you?"

"To be honest, I didn't even see it."

"They are giving you twelve weeks' severance, but it's contingent on you going to weekly counseling seminars—there was all this paperwork on food and nutrition. Probably just stuff they have to include." Ana handed him the paperwork. "Here, read these, and I'll go fix us lunch."

A half an hour later, Michael headed down to the kitchen, finding Ana standing over a plate of cheeseburgers. "Are you feeling any better after reading about the severance?"

"Yeah. Well, at least I'll have some time to find something before the baby gets here. Thanks for the burgers." He gave her a weak smile.

"I was thinking," Ana said meekly, "we have a little saved, and this is the first time you've had any real time off in a few years. Plus, we have a baby coming. What do you think about taking a little vacation, just the two of us? You know, before you start looking for another job and before I pop?"

Michael leaned back, softly chewing on a mouthful of burger. "That depends on where you want to go ..."

Six weeks and one vacation to the Florida Keys later, Ana and Michael were sitting back in their kitchen, opening the mail, when she saw a letter from his old company. After reading it, she gave Michael the CliffsNotes version. If he didn't show up to the remaining counseling seminars, his severance would be cut short. This got their attention, because Michael had yet to even get an interview with another firm.

The very next Saturday, Michael found himself in a high school gymnasium filled with fired executives and employees. Not in the mood to see anyone from his old company, he signed his name on the attendance sheet, headed to the bathroom and, from there, to his car.

This went on for a while but, eventually, still unable to even get an interview in his field, he decided to sit through a seminar—the last before the end of his severance.

He flopped down on a flimsy folding chair that could barely hold his weight and looked around, taken aback by the number of people in the gymnasium and miffed that they were not serving any snacks or drinks. Every time he saw a support group on television or in movies, the alcoholics were always eating donuts and drinking coffee while they spilled their guts. He could really go for some donuts right now.

Then, none other than Kai sat down right next to him.

Michael swallowed. A long moment of silence stretched on before Michael finally glanced at her. "Hey, Kai," he said, "long time no see. Sorry for not answering your calls. I just needed to take a break. How are ..." Michael stopped talking. His eyes settled on her sunken eyes, her gaunt cheeks.

"Michael, it's good to see you," she said, barely turning.

The flower Michael had worked with and once lusted over sat wilted in front of him. He found he didn't have any words, so when the speaker asked for everyone's attention, he sat up and focused forward, not knowing what else to do.

"Good afternoon," said the speaker. "My name is Mary Hastings, and I am a representative at the local Williamson Foundation food bank. If you are here, you've lost a job recently, and you've been identified as being at risk due to your body mass. Many of you did not ask to be here, don't want to be here, or don't think you need to be here, but there is nothing further from the truth. We are going to start with a brief video. Please be warned, it may be disturbing, but it is important that you know the consequences of inaction."

The lights flicked off, and a video started up on the screen behind Mary.

Former President Elizabeth Williamson appeared and began explaining that, for the past six years, her foundation had endeavored to understand the Lifio gene mutation and one day reverse its negative consequences. Charts popped up on the screen, conveying the exponential increase in population over the years; death rates had fallen precipitously as world health had steadily improved. Companies were growing unnaturally due to this population explosion.

The video cut to a medical doctor, who explained what the foundation had learned about the gene mutation. It was hard for Michael to understand, but he thought the doctor was saying that the mutation allowed for indefinite cell division, resulting in uninhibited growth. Caloric intake resulted in energy production and body growth but not fat storage. This caused people to keep growing while staying lean.

Clips showing food lines in third-world countries came on, whole towns of giant shriveled corpses in Senegal, people who'd died from starvation due to the poor crop yields of a single harvest—even outlandish foreign news reports of possible cannibalism in Poland and Ukraine. Michael swallowed, remembering Len, his old roommate. Surely *he* was okay. One clip showed an investigative reporter interviewing a village leader somewhere in Africa. The leader described in excruciating detail how, if hunting parties did not return with game, one of the hunters would be sacrificed to feed the village.

"It is natural for what we are telling you to scare you," Mary said as the video ended and the lights came back on. "If you're not scared, you are not taking this as seriously as you must. Without taking the necessary precautions and making serious lifestyle and eating habit changes, you risk paying with your life."

Mary paused, surveying her audience, then sighed. "From the looks on your faces, I can tell that half of you in this room do not believe me. I understand your skepticism. You have been living the lives of kings and queens for years. That is how you have ended up here. But do not let those years of excess blind you from the facts we are presenting. The road you are taking is fraught with peril. The Lifio gene mutation can be a blessing—it has all but cured hundreds of diseases and illnesses that used to kill millions per year—yet it can also be a curse, and that is what we are here today to show you.

"Many of you in this room have lost high-profile, high-paying jobs. Can any of you tell me the cost of a gallon of milk?"

After no one raised their hand, Mary said, "A loaf of bread? A fifty-pound bag of rice? Anyone? Surely someone can wager a guess?"

After another moment of silence, Mary answered herself: "A gallon of milk averages nineteen dollars sixty-two cents. A loaf of bread averages thirteen dollars twenty-one cents, and a fifty-pound bag of rice averages one hundred and thirteen dollars ninety-four cents. I know because I buy a lot of them. Rice is the highest calories per dollar carbohydrate money can buy, something you would be wise to remember."

A snort from a giant man in the back row, who wore a smirk on his face.

Mary ignored him. "Now, you've seen the horrific possibil-ities in our video, but you're probably thinking that it couldn't possibly happen to you. So, let me be the first to tell you that it absolutely can. Every one of you in this room has grown steadily, year after year. I know this because that is simply the only way you could be as large as you are today. Unfortunately, our bodies are only built to go one direction, and with added lean body mass comes a strict requirement for more calories.

"Thankfully, body mass growth can be controlled through diet. You will only grow larger if you eat excess calories. However, you must not allow your caloric intake to get too low, even for a short period. Because the mutated human body now carries such low levels of fat stores, we no longer have the capacity to cope with calorie deficiency. When you become calorie deficient, even for a short period, your body will rapidly shift to consuming muscle mass and then organs, resulting in accelerated death by starvation or organ failure."

Michael glanced back and saw the smug man's smile had faded.

"Another question for my lovely group of giants," Mary said. "What do you believe is the leading cause of death worldwide?"

After a pregnant pause, she answered herself: "No one? I'll tell you: it's starvation. And it's twenty times more deadly than the second leading cause."

Her face hardened. "I implore you to watch your caloric intake and make use of our body-mass-to-caloric-intake cal-culators online in order to determine the exact amount of food you require each day to stay well-nourished without causing further body mass growth. Overeating and indulging must be avoided at all costs; there is only one way that story ends."

Apparently finished, Mary's face relaxed. "Now, please allow me to welcome a special guest from the Williamson Foundation: Dr. Carrie Roberts. Dr. Roberts was head of research and testing at the FDA during the Williamson presidency. While at the FDA, she advocated strongly for a cautious approach to the Lifio product. Over the past six years with the Williamson Foundation, she has led the field in the study of the now-famous mutation."

Carrie stood and took Mary's place at the front of the seated group. She was small and stout, with a hard, humorless face—but not unattractive, Michael thought. "Thank you, Mary, for that auspicious introduction," she said, her voice matching her features. "This is my first time speaking at one of these seminars. I requested to come along while visiting the foundation's food bank in Austin, so unfortunately I do not have a prepared speech. But I can tell you what the foundation is doing and what you can do to help us and yourselves. At the foundation, we continue to study the human gene mutation originally actuated by Dr. Jónsson and found in Stallson Beverage's Lifio product. We have a far greater understanding of what he has done today than we had in the past, but it is not yet a *full* understanding—and, until it is, we will not be able to successfully reverse the mutation, which is the foundation's current focus. However, any mutation we discover to reverse Lifio's effects will not likely reduce body mass. In all likelihood, it will only stop indefinite growth. Therefore, I counsel all of you to recognize this new reality. Do not, under any circumstances, consume any more calories than required to sustain life, and demand action from your government. You have a voice, but to use it, you must vote. Vote for representatives focused on the dire circumstances we find ourselves in today. Thank you for your time."

On that unclimactic end, Dr. Roberts marched from the stage and disappeared through a door at the back of the gymnasium.

With that, the seminar ended, and those assembled—most of whom looked like Kai, Michael noticed—got up and started to file out the doors. The line of hulking, morose giants ducking from the room struck a chord within Michael. He remembered how, as a teenager, he'd watched drunk driving videos in health class intended to scare high school students into being responsible. Over-the-top videos hadn't worked on Michael then, just as the starvation video somehow hadn't convinced him now. But, when he saw what had become of his colleagues, particularly Kai, ducking as she passed through the exit, he knew something really *was* terribly wrong. Then, all of a sudden, thoughts of his soon-to-be-born child flooded through him, and he ran up to Mary. He had to talk to her.

"Hi, Mary," he said, catching her as she headed out. "My name is Michael Lori."

"Hi, Michael," she said, glancing at him. "It's nice to meet you. How can I help?"

"I loved your seminar. Well, love might be too strong a word. I appreciated your seminar a great deal."

"Thank you, Michael. I'm glad to hear that. Do you think the seminar will inspire you to make a change?"

"I do, I really do—if not for myself, then for my child."

"Oh, how many kids do you have?"

"This will be our first. Bun's still in the oven."

The woman smiled. "Congratulations, Michael."

"Thank you. Actually, that's why I came to talk with you."

"How can I help?"

"Well, with a baby on the way and neither of us working, I'm concerned. I mean, what if we run out of food?"

"Michael, you look rather healthy at the moment. Do you still have money in the bank? Have you sold any of your belongings?"

"Oh, no, we're not in that much trouble. I mean, we still have a nest egg in the bank."

"Well, that's great to hear, Michael, but I really don't think you need our help—at least, not at this time."

"Really? What? I thought the company wanted me to come here in order to get help from you?"

Mary gave a wan grin. "I might have scared you too much. You're not going to starve if you don't eat one meal. I mean, most of the people who come to us have already used up all their other options. They've sold their cars, houses, and assets, and have run through all their money. If they do work, they spend all their money on food, and it still isn't enough."

"I see," Michael said soberly.

Mary reached out to pat him on the arm apologetically. "Look, I just don't think now is the time for you to seek our assistance. It is imperative that you look up that calorie-to-body-mass calculator that we have online and to make sure you don't overeat. That's the most important step for you to take right now."

"Okay, I will do that, but is there any assistance available now?"

"We offer all new sufferers five hundred thousand calories."

"Great. How can I get that? Do you have it here?" Michael asked, lightening up.

"No, it's not here. Let me explain. We only offer new sufferers five hundred thousand calories, and it comes in the form of bulk rice bags."

"Ah, that explains the rice comment. So then, where can I pick it up?"

"The five hundred thousand calories is a one-year allotment."

"You mean that's all you get for an entire year? Bags of dried rice?"

"Unfortunately, yes. There are more sufferers than you know, and that is all we can afford to offer. To be honest, our supply is under intense strain as prices continue to climb. That is why we highly suggest you use your allotment wisely and only when the need is dire."

"I understand. Is there any additional allotment for families? Or, at least, for children?" Michael asked as his relief slowly turned to concern.

"Children receive the same annual five hundred thousand-calorie allotment. I truly am sorry, but look on the bright side: You still have time. Like you said yourself, you still have your nest egg. Just watch what you eat. There is nothing more important for you now that you have a child on the way."

Michael stared at Mary, trying to take it all in, but his roller-coaster ride had taken one too many turns. His teeth rattled, his head pounded, and stomach turned, and he abruptly lurched away and staggered for the door, his mind racing.

Children in middle America with distended stomachs; blue bags, blue bags all over the house, surrounding a charred fire-pit; lines of thousands of people, tall and short, all dressed in rags like walking skeletons, standing in never-ending lines. Kai's face, shrunken, bones jutting out. The whole parking lot empty, no one left, everyone gone. Hulking gang warlords with shaved heads, eating human legs like drumsticks. Tiny children crowded around a shriveled, decomposing corpse. Ana, her huge stomach protruding from skin and bones. A hooded figure with a patched, pockmarked scalp, running away from him.

And then there was President Givens—feasting, mountains of mouthwatering food piled high in front of him. Ana, meanwhile, neatly covering his half-eaten cereal with cellophane and placing it in the fridge. Enormous teenage football players pigging out on greasy bags of fast food. Graphs of the population exploding while food supply declined. Millions of dead bodies strewn over famine-torn countrysides. Frank, ginormous Frank, emptying a bottle of Scotch down his throat like it were a shot. Blue rice bags all over his house. Dr. Jónsson grinning, a can of Lifio in his hand. Their budget, all food; they'd spent everything on food. Dark houses all over his neighborhood, not foreclosed on, but dead, all dead.

Michael, now catatonic, moved in slow motion through doorways, up the stairs, past Ana, and into bed.

CHAPTER 32

MICHAEL HAS A PLAN

The next morning, Michael woke before Ana. Skipping break-fast, he proceeded to quietly shower, shave off his beard, dress, and jump into his car. After taking the highway across town, he pulled up to a beaten-up warehouse on the outskirts of Old Austin. The sign on the front gate read *Williamson Foundation Food Bank*. The building was surrounded by a twenty-foot chain-link fence topped with razor wire.

As he arrived at the gate, a night watchman came out to greet him. He was a frail man, with a dark chocolate complexion and graying hair under his cap. "Mornin', sir. How can I help ya?"

"I'd like to speak with Mary Hastings," Michael said.

"Well, sir, ya see, the food bank doesn't open until 8 a.m., sir, and, well, being that it's only six in the mornin', it's gonna be quite a while 'til we see Mrs. Mary, sir," the guard explained in a slow and steady voice, like he was calming a wild horse.

"I understand. I'll wait just over there," Michael said, point-ing at his car in the lot beside the gate. "Please let her know I'm here as soon as she arrives."

His stomach continued to growl while he waited, churning and twisting as it searched for something to digest, and he could taste the acid bubbling up his esophagus. After what felt like hours, a car pulled into the lot, and a lady who looked like she might be Mary got out. She hurried over to the guardhouse. Then, after a brief moment, she passed the guard and entered the warehouse. As soon as the door swung shut, the guard gingerly waved Michael over.

"Now, you have to understand here, sir," the guard said slowly, "we see some real nasty types at the food bank, sir. People are not always happy when Mrs. Mary can't give 'em no more rice, ya see. You gave Mrs. Mary an awful fright, you did, sittin' in your car over there. She's had a whole lotta them nasty types follow her home, ya see, sir. But I told, I told her, you, you was as harmless as a fly, sir. You harmless, ain't you, sir? You ain't gonna turn me into no liar, are ya, sir?"

Taken aback by the ever-present threat the food bank apparently operated under, Michael quickly worked to put the guard's concerns to rest and found himself unconsciously mimicking the old man's mannerisms and steady voice. "No, sir. I met Mrs. Hastings and Dr. Roberts at a seminar given at North Hills High School yesterday, and I'd like to offer my help."

"Well, that there is good to hear, sir. We need more volunteers around this place. Mrs. Mary does everything round here all by herself. And o' course, I try to help as best I can."

After realizing Michael was unlikely to respond, the guard picked up a beaten-up old phone handset and said something that Michael couldn't quite make out. Turning around to face him again, the guard told him to go on through and that Mary would be waiting for him.

Michael passed through the gate at the sound of a buzzer. He heard a click when he arrived at a rusty metal door and, when he pulled it, it opened.

The only part of the place that looked as if it came from this century was the surveillance system. Cameras stared down at him from all angles. With no one to guide him, Michael walked across the drab brown carpet and down a poorly lit wood-paneled hallway until he reached two doors. One, straight ahead of him, was made of metal, with a keypad above the knob. To his right, an open door invited him into an office with a single window pouring morning light onto a scraggly, pathetic houseplant.

Michael stepped into the office and immediately made eye contact with Mary, who sat behind her metal desk. She seemed to recognize him, and restrained fear melted into concern and then into mild frustration.

"Nice plant you have," he said, doing his best to break the ice.

"Thank you. As you can see, I don't have much of a green thumb," Mary said. "But I don't think you came here to talk about botany. How can I help you, Mr. ..."

"Oh, yes, sorry. Mr. Lori—Michael Lori. Ah, we spoke just yesterday."

"Yes, yes, you're having a child. I remember. But how can I help you today? I was led to believe you wanted to volunteer. Unfortunately, we cannot pay you. All of our funding—"

"I'm a developer specializing in artificial intelligence," Michael said, then came to an abrupt halt. "Do you mind if I take a seat?" He grabbed his stomach and hunched over.

"Certainly, please."

Michael grimaced as he sat down in the metal folding chair opposite Mary.

"When was the last time you ate?" she said, frowning at him.

"I'll be fine." Michael tried to smile while bile turned his mouth sour with the thought of food.

"Have the rest of this. You clearly need it." Mary pushed the last few bites of her blueberry muffin across the desk. Michael didn't want to take it. His mind told him no, but every fiber of his body wanted sustenance. Before he could regain control of himself, he snatched the remaining bits off her desk and swallowed them whole.

"You were telling me you are a developer. Unfortunately, we are only a food bank. We do not offer any type of career services."

"I'm sorry. I didn't sleep much last night, so I'm a bit out of sorts."

"I understand. It's a lot to take in," she said. "I am pleased that our seminar had the desired effect on you, however painful your realizations may be. But look"—she was shaking her head now—"it seems you did not listen to everything I was saying. You cannot solve your problems by abstaining from eating. At your body mass, you require a high caloric intake just to maintain yourself. If you do not eat enough, the effects will be dire."

"Malnutrition results in alterations to your brain's underlying chemistry, which will cause heightened anxiety and depression. In extreme cases, you will experience a warped sense of reality. You'll lose time. So do me a favor, Michael, and use our calorie calculator to find out your required caloric intake—and then stick to it. Actually, why don't we do it together right now?"

Mary turned her attention to her computer screen and, in a few clicks, was navigating the Williamson Foundation's website.

"After listening to Dr. Roberts yesterday, I feel confident that artificial intelligence can dramatically improve her research work if it is not already being utilized," Michael spat out.

"Oh, I see. I'm sorry to tell you this, but Carrie—I mean, Dr. Roberts—left for San Francisco last night. I dropped her off at the airport myself."

For a long time, neither of them said anything. Then Michael noticed Mary's comfort level dwindling, and he shifted gears.

"That is unfortunate. May I ask what is in San Francisco?"

"Oh, that's the Williamson Foundation's headquarters, where they do all the research," Mary said, looking far more comfortable now that they were talking again.

"When we lived in California, my wife and I spent a summer backpacking from Sequoia National Park through Sierra Forest, Yosemite, and Stanislaus Forest. Then we made our way over to San Francisco and climbed the Golden Gate Bridge before returning to school," Michael said softly, staring up at the ceiling.

He shook his head suddenly. "I'm sorry, I hadn't thought about that in years; I guess I lost my train of thought. So, is it safe to assume that contact information for Dr. Roberts is available on the same website as the calculator?"

"Well, yes and no. Dr. Roberts is very busy, so naturally her contact information is not shared publicly, but if you want to give me a message, I will make sure it is received. Or, of course, you are welcome to call the main number at the foundation. That is available online."

"Oh, I don't think passing her a message is necessary. I'll reach out on my own," Michael said, trying his best to appear nonchalant. Mary was clearly a dead end on the research front, but he still had one more task to complete.

"Now, about the foodstuffs, how can I claim my allotment?"

"I don't really think it's time for that," Mary replied, face falling.

But Michael didn't care if he'd disappointed her. "Mary," he said, turning on his charm, "I completely understand your concern, and if I were in your shoes, I would be doing the very same thing as you. But you must admit, this place does not feel exactly, well, *safe*, now does it?"

Mary stared at him for a moment, uncertainty behind her eyes. "Well, no," she said slowly, "it doesn't, but it's the best we can do given the circumstances."

"Oh yes," Michael said, nodding, "it's clear you're doing your best. I just feel that my family's allotment of food would be safer in my own care. I mean, you never know what tomorrow will bring, right? What if the foundation halts funding or something equally bad happens? Without having control of my allotment, I feel very anxious, to be quite honest."

Mary sighed. "So many people squander their allotment. I'm just trying to protect people from themselves."

"And you are. You're doing great work here," Michael said, pleading with his eyes.

After further prodding, he learned that OSHA had recently passed a regulation requiring employers to track employee body mass and fund last-resort food banks. Mary explained that, once Michael had used his family's calorie quota in full, no other foundation-funded food bank would allow him to receive more for one year. Michael remained staunch in his demand for his entire quota to be filled at once, and Mary, unable to stop him because of his former employer's funding, allowed him to claim three allotments after a lengthy verification process. Hours after his arrival at the Williamson Food Bank, Michael piled eighteen heavy bags of rice into his car and set off for home.

A white van caught Michael's eye a few too many times and, out of an abundance of caution, he decided to take a round-about way home. The eerie food bank security scene had set him on edge, and all he wanted now was to be home, where he could eat something and share his burgeoning plan with Ana. As he sped through his neighborhood, a woman push-ing a stroller eyed him and waved disapprovingly for him to slow down.

Pulling into his garage, Michael quickly turned off his car and shut the garage door. Then, in the sudden quiet, he sat, staring out the windshield, and took a deep, ragged breath. Finally, feeling a little more composed, he began methodically unloading the eighteen bags of rice into his bedroom closet. When he was done, he collapsed on the bed next to Ana, who had been watching him as he worked.

"I could've helped, you know," she said.

"You're pregnant, Ana. Let it go," Michael replied, spent after carrying all that weight upstairs.

"So, are you going to tell me what all this is about, Michael?"

With Ana lying next to him, listening raptly, Michael recounted the seminar that had set everything in motion and his morning with the guard and Mary. Then, he continued into the future, detailing his plan as it had come to him. At some point, he became aware that Ana was weeping. She pulled Michael closer just as he had gathered the strength to rise.

"I'm scared, Michael," she whispered.

"I know. I am too. Keep the rice secret. Don't tell anyone about it, and only use it if you have to. I'm taking a taxi to the airport. Sell both of the cars and any of the furniture you can immediately. We have to start liquidating and hoarding the cash until we have another income."

And with that, Michael was gone, leaving Ana alone with her thoughts and their unborn baby kicking inside her.

Twelve hours later, Michael was on the ground in San Francisco. He took a taxi to the Williamson Foundation Research Facility and, as the cab pulled away, he realized how he must look: not a good way to make a first impression. He made his way across the street to a Starbucks and did his best to get himself presentable in the public restroom. Then he grabbed a power bar to settle his stomach and a coffee in a to-go cup, trying to look the part of a concerned citizen rather than a strung-out bum, which was what he felt like.

A few smiles and lies later and he was standing in a conference room at the Williamson Foundation Research Facility, waiting for none other than Carrie Roberts. Moments later, a gentleman of short stature wearing large glasses entered the room and introduced himself as Sebastian Dougherty.

"Unfortunately, Dr. Roberts is detained at the moment, but I understand you believe you can help with the foundation's research. I am here to learn more."

"I would really like to speak with Dr. Roberts. I saw her at a seminar recently, and I am certain I can accelerate her research."

"I understand you are passionate, and we need that sort of passion to solve big problems, but, as I said, Dr. Roberts is detained. If you are willing to review your ... your *ideas* with me, I will make certain they are delivered to her."

Michael closed his eyes and rubbed his throbbing temple. "What sort of machine learning or AI schemes have you employed in your research?" he said.

"Unfortunately, we do not share how we carry out our research with the public. Perhaps you can tell me your ideas ... Michael, is it?"

Ignoring his question, Michael said, "I was on a team that designed and implemented an advanced artificial intelligence program designed to overlay on top of a legacy automated system and improve that automation. We won three international awards for breakthrough AI technology advancements over an eighteen-month period and spearheaded the design of the latest Toyota automated assembly plant."

If he was impressed, Sebastian didn't show it. Instead, he kindly replied, "You are clearly an expert in artificial intelligence, but how does that have any significance with regards to the foundation's research?"

"The human genome has billions of base pairs. From my limited interaction with Carrie Roberts, I understand that the foundation is not utilizing the most advanced methods for data analysis. With a pool of hundreds of millions of Americans and billions of genomes in each human, you have an enormous data set. Artificial intelligence excels at mining large data sets. By allowing AI to process whole sets of raw genomic sequence data, you could arrive at conclusions it would take humans hundreds of years to find. Of course, artificial intelligence is only as good as its underlying artificial neural network. I've spent the past year of my life developing the world's most cutting-edge deep learning system by utilizing nearly every known class of artificial neural network and combining them into a unique network architecture. Convolutional neural networks, recurrent neural networks, autoencoders, deep belief networks—"

"Okay, okay, stop, stop," Sebastian said abruptly, standing up. "Wait here."

Fifteen agonizing minutes later, Michael's heart dropped as two thick bodyguard types dressed in suits entered the room. They stood Michael up and patted him down. Then, to his relief, they took up positions at separate ends of the room, each staring straight ahead with one hand resting on the opposing wrist. Sebastian reentered and introduced Melanie Delaney, Carrie Roberts, and former President Elizabeth Williamson.

Everyone took a seat, and Sebastian said, "All right, Michael, this is the foundation's entire leadership team. Tell them what you've told me. From the beginning, please."

Michael, still trying to get over being in the presence of a former president, gathered himself. "Carrie, I believe—"

"You mean Doctor Roberts," Carrie injected.

"I'm sorry: Doctor Roberts, I believe you could utilize artificial intelligence to accelerate your research by developing a more robust artificial neural network. I understand—"

"Very little of my years of research on this topic; you are yet another overconfident—what, what are you," she stammered, looking up. "Regardless, you can't come in here and hijack my research. If you want to save the world with your big idea, do it your—"

"Now, wait just a minute," Michael said, frowning. "I am certain that I can overlay AI on top of your research framework. I'm not trying to hijack anything; I'm trying to help you. Can't you see that?"

Carrie's eyes bored into him.

"Okay, Michael," Sebastian said, getting to his feet, "I think we need to have a word internally. Why don't you go grab a bite to eat and we'll see you in, let's say, two hours."

Even though Michael didn't have anywhere to go or a car to get there, he agreed, mainly to keep up appearances. He didn't want to let on how desperate his personal circumstances were; he was certain they'd take him for just another desperate giant staring death in the face.

* * *

Once Michael had left, Sebastian, Melanie, Carrie, and Elizabeth regrouped in Sebastian's office.

"I don't see why I was pulled from my research to entertain a developer who walked in off the street with a pipe dream of using a computer to replace research," Carrie blurted out as soon as the door closed.

"Carrie, I don't think you're being fair here," Sebastian said. "He flew in from Texas to see us, and a quick search says he's not lying about his background."

"Martin, did he check out?" Williamson said to the Secret Service agent stationed at the door. They had all been around them for so long that it was easy to forget they heard and saw everything.

"Madam President, yes. Mr. Michael Lori graduated from the California Institute of Technology Magna Cum Laude and then started a career in software development, where he rose quickly through the ranks to become vice president of artificial intelligence development at Frost Technologies. He did win various awards in the field of AI and currently lives in New Austin with his pregnant wife, Ana. He checks out."

"Thank you, Martin."

"So, if he checks out—is a leader in the field, even—then we owe it to ourselves to at least hear him out. I mean, how can we not?" Melanie chimed in, and Sebastian nodded.

Carrie shook her head in exaggerated disbelief. "Hundreds of people contact me every week to try and assist in our research," she said. "Why don't we hear all of them out?"

Melanie rolled her eyes, but Carrie plowed on: "We don't because we know what we are doing. We are the leaders in our field. If AI could be applied to my research, don't you think I would have done it by now? I am connected to every institution of higher learning with a research laboratory around the world, and not one of those colleagues—colleagues who *lead our field*—utilize AI. This is just some arrogant corporate VP thinking he can solve all of our problems with an ounce of effort."

"Carrie, Mel and I were VPs in a former life," said Sebastian. "Heck, we were probably arrogant too. That doesn't mean we can rule out everything he's saying."

"Maybe you can't rule it out, but I will. This is a waste of my precious time. Instead of making progress, I am somehow here defending my own research."

"Carrie, no one is attacking your research," said President Williamson, rounding on Carrie. "Sebastian and Melanie are just doing their due diligence. You must agree that artificial intelligence as a tool for our research should be considered."

"With all due respect, Madam President, no, no, I do not think we should be wasting our time chasing down new technology when we have a sound, proven research protocol we've been reliably executing for years. No one likes how long this process is taking—I certainly don't—but if we give credence to every new technology or research method brought to us by an outsider, it will take us twice as long."

"Carrie, the man is a leader in his field. He's not just a guy off the street," Melanie said.

"A poor choice of words. Nevertheless, he is a leader in a field that is not relevant to our research. If any of my research colleagues brought this to me, I would listen, but Mr. Lori freely admits he has no expertise in biology, chemistry, or medicine. If you determine we should consider the implementation of

AI in our research, fine, but what I am not willing to do is let an outsider come in here and turn us into the laughing stock of the medical research community when he has no idea what he is doing. We cannot allow our research to be turned into a guinea pig for Mr. Lori."

"Carrie, I understand your concerns, but aren't you being a little hasty?" asked Sebastian. "Michael is clearly qualified and has offered to help us. Why would he do that if he was not sincere?"

"If the technology was where Michael said it was, why haven't any studies or papers been released?" Carrie said.

"Companies hoard technological advantages," said Melanie. "That's how they make money and keep a competitive edge. If I had a VP on my staff who could do what Michael says he can do with big data, I'd kill him if he wrote a paper or published a study on it."

"Melanie is correct, Carrie," said President Williamson. "You spent your career in service of your country as a scientist. In those walks of life, transparency is required. In business, the opposite is often the case."

Carrie snorted. "I respectfully disagree. If developments such as the ones Michael claims took place, they would emerge on the open market. Breakthroughs are not kept secret for the sole sake of profits. Ego and the need for approval push inventors to announce their discoveries. If nothing is available to prove Michael can do what he says he can with AI, I do not believe he can do it."

With both sides still dug in by the time Michael returned to the lobby, the team had yet to eat anything themselves, and it fell to Elizabeth to break the stalemate.

* * *

Michael swallowed his nerves and stood as the conference room door finally opened. Elizabeth Williamson entered first, trailed by Dr. Roberts, Sebastian, and Melanie—Michael dimly remembered her as the FDA's head honcho who'd come under fire during the Lifio crisis. It felt like a lifetime ago now.

"Michael," Williamson said, and Michael snapped from his thoughts. "You're clearly an expert in artificial intelligence; your background checks out, and I believe you truly mean to help our cause. The advancements in AI you have claimed and your capability to apply them to genomic research, a field entirely new to you, remain unclear. Your theories sound plausible, but none of us have the necessary understanding of AI to challenge anything you've said. You've come halfway across the country to share your expertise with us, and we appreciate that a great deal, but you've also told us we would need to invest half a million dollars' worth of computing power in order to even begin implementing your ideas. While I appreciate your enthusiasm, it's not plausible to ask us to invest anything, let alone half a million dollars, before we do some of our own research.

"First and foremost, we need to be assured by your current employer that you are not violating any agreements or utilizing technology that does not belong to you. After that's cleared and we've executed our due diligence, we would be willing to consider working together in some capacity."

Michael cut her off. "That will take too much time. Listen, I know what I'm telling you is a lot to take in, but I know I can do this."

"Mr. Lori, you can't legitimately expect us to hand over the keys to our research," Carrie said with contempt, "research, I'll remind you, I have been doing for close to seven years, just because you say you can do it. Oh, not to mention, you also want us to give you a half-a-million-dollar computer."

"Let me prove it to you," Michael begged. "I just need access. Give me access to your data and I'll show you what AI can do here. Please—it costs you nothing. Just let me show you."

"We could just connect him to the National Center for Biotechnology Information. He'll be able to access the data and we'll be able to see what he can do," Melanie said to Elizabeth.

Elizabeth looked at Carrie for her opinion.

"Fine by me," Carrie replied. "That's why we connected to the NCBI in the first place—so everyone could access the data and do with it as they see fit. As long as he's not taking up any more of my time, I don't care what access level you give him." She got up and walked out.

Elizabeth paused, clearly mulling something over in her head, before standing and following Carrie out. Before leaving, she said, "Michael, it was a pleasure to meet you. I truly hope you are able to do what you believe you can. Mel, give him research-level 1RO access."

Of the four levels of access, Michael learned, he had been given the highest, meaning he would access raw result sets from all data source facilities. His access level, however, granted him read-only privileges; he could see everything, but could not edit or add to it as other researchers could.

Once Michael had scanned the NCBI servers and understood how to access their data, he quickly said his goodbyes and departed, taking a taxi from the Starbucks across the street to the airport. On the plane home, he began to calculate how many servers and how much computing power he would need to run AI on a data set that large. Once he got an artificial neural network up, it could start optimizing, and he'd potentially need less horsepower—but he knew that line of thinking was fool's gold. He needed as much processing power as he could possibly get his hands on.

Arriving home close to midnight, Michael found his familiar position in bed next to Ana, and for the first time in the last few days, he fell asleep content.

CHAPTER 33
HOME OFFICE

The next morning, Michael was in high spirits, on a mission. Ana seemed relieved that some sense of direction had been restored—they had money in the bank and bulk food in the closet, and Michael looked like he was ready to take on the world. After a small but tasty breakfast of oatmeal with brown sugar, butter, and apples, Michael set up one of their spare bedrooms as a home office.

When he had a full understanding of what he wanted to do and all that was left was the actual coding, he moved into a functional yet tranquil state. As the days passed in rapid succession, he undertook the dynamic challenge of harnessing everything he'd learned working on Toyota's AI architecture and repurposing it for scientific research. Every alteration he made changed another facet of the AI system he had built, often forcing him to abandon tactics he'd previously relied upon and retrace his steps. Progress came in fits and starts.

He reached out to Kai's cell to try to bring her into the fold, but there was no response to his first few texts. Frustrated, he tried to call her.

"Hello," came a husky voice on the end of the line.

"Kai?" Michael said. "Sorry, is Kai available?"

"Sorry," the voice said quickly, "wrong number."

"Wait don't hang—"

The line cut off. He didn't want to believe it, so he called again.

"Listen fucko, stop calling this number. I'm blocking you now, bye-bye."

Michael let his phone drop into his lap. Trying to avoid thinking about what Kai's repurposed number might mean, he drove himself harder.

After several hours, Ana swept into the room, grabbed him under the armpits, and pulled him up from his desk so she could make eye contact with him.

"You have to take care of yourself; you can't work this hard. Take a break, come on." She dragged him to the kitchen table, where she forced him to drink some water and eat a small snack. After placating her with reassurances, he kissed her goodnight and promised he wouldn't be too late, then headed back to work.

Eventually, Michael found a way to track the data accessed by researchers through the NCBI portal. He was certain his AI overlay could use data points like access requests by researchers to narrow the field and make deductions. At the same time, this would highlight the data points potentially being neglected.

Michael spent large swathes of time answering his own questions about data quality and structure. For his AI to work, data quality had to be at a very high level and, to ensure this, he focused on data sources, building algorithms to predict their quality based on a variety of the factors he had access to. The data structure proved challenging, forcing him to build entire new systems to restructure large data sets.

A month passed in a blink, and Michael thought it best to call Sebastian from the Williamson Foundation to update him on his progress. Sebastian remembered Michael and sounded genuinely happy to hear from him. After updating Sebastian, Michael decided to see if Dave or Mola would help, but neither of them returned his calls or texts.

One day, Michael decided to take a short walk over to Dave's house. He found the curtains drawn and the lights off—had Dave moved out of town? Why hadn't he told him? Remembering the seminar, he decided he owed it to Dave to ring the bell, just in case.

After no one answered, he tried a few more times before shrugging to himself and turning to head back home. From the corner of his eye, he thought he saw a blind on the second floor flutter, but he couldn't be sure.

When he got home, he went to find Ana—he needed to settle his nerves. He'd gone as far as he could go without processing power, and now that Kai and Dave's help was off the table, he needed to find another way forward. While sitting down with Ana, he looked up the cost of leasing the servers he needed, and discovered that it would cost them everything they had in savings if he pulled the trigger. So, after hemming and hawing for a few hours together, he and Ana decided he should call Frank to ask for help with the work. Kai and Dave had been laid off too and evidently had their own problems; Frank, meanwhile, was living large. He represented their only chance. Trying to psych himself up, Michael reasoned that he didn't need any money from Frank, he just needed access to the server cluster the company had used to test the Toyota AI project. It was leased off-site, and he knew the contract hadn't ended, meaning the site was up and available with no business purposes. It would cost Frank nothing.

After working up the courage with Ana for the greater part of the evening, Michael called Frank and, to his surprise, Frank picked up.

"Michael, my man, what's happening?" Frank bellowed.

"Ah, not much, not much. How are you, Frank?"

"Me? I'm doing great."

"Good, good. Have you heard from Kai or Dave at all? I was trying to reach them, but I can't seem to get them." Michael regretted saying it as soon as the words left his lips.

"Michael, what's up? What can I do for ya? I'm hosting a dinner party here at the house."

"Oh, sorry. Well, I called to ask if …" Michael felt his mouth go dry. This wasn't exactly going how he'd envisioned it.

"Yeah, yeah, I'll be right there. I just have to finish up with this guy we fired," Michael heard Frank telling someone.

"Maybe this was a bad idea," said Michael, feeling ashamed. "I'm sorry I bothered you."

"Now, Michael, don't be like that. You called me for a reason. How can I help you out?"

"Okay, well, I'm working on a research project for the Williamson Foundation on gene mutation, and it's imperative that I solve a problem they're having. Well, I need processing power, power I don't have at home. When we had the AI division, I set up a cloud-based server cluster for testing AI. I lost access to it when I was let go, but we had a year-long contract, so it should still be up for a few more months. If you could just reinstate my access, I could use it, no cost to you or the company."

Frank cut him off before he could continue.

"Michael, are you crazy? You want access to a company server cluster to do a research project for someone else? I thought you were going to ask me for a recommendation letter or something. You know I can't give you access to our network. What were you thinking, calling me with this bullshit?"

It took Michael a moment to realize that Frank had hung up immediately after the curse.

He told Ana what had happened. Together, they resolved to sleep on it and look at the problem again the next morning when they were fresh.

Michael knew what he had to do, and the terrible night's sleep he went through—tossing and turning at the leap he was about to take—didn't help matters. If Michael wanted to complete his project, he was going to have to spend their safety net. They'd only have enough for eight months left, but he felt confident he'd need only half that much time to get a working AI overlay to the Williamson Foundation. If he proved to them that it worked, they'd fund the project—he was certain of it.

Michael pulled the server contract and, after running the numbers again and again, he called Marlon, his contact at the server-hosting company.

"That's going to be a pricey rig, Michael—quote's coming around four-forty."

"That's impossible—the last contract with you had clusters at half that price."

"Come on, Mike, this is apples and oranges: you can't expect me to match prices from a year ago."

"And that's the best you can do? Marlon, I can't make that work. What can I get for two hundred?" Michael said, knowing that would be everything they had in the bank.

"Michael, a year for four-forty is a good deal. Call around—the other guys aren't going to get close to my price."

"A year? I don't need a year. How about access for six months for one-fifty?" Michael offered.

"You know I can't do anything for less than a year. Come on, it's not even worth our time to set up a cluster for less than that."

"Marlon, is four-forty the best you can do, really?" Michael asked, panicked. "After years of working together?"

"Michael, my hands are tied—you're a retail customer now. I'll get my ass handed to me for giving you your old company's price; you know they spend eight figures a year with us. I'm already doing you a solid here."

"Shit, I can't do it, I just don't have it," Michael said.

"All right, well you know where to reach me," Marlon finished.

For the rest of the week, Michael emailed every last server host he knew or could find online. The lowest negotiated price for the specs he was looking for came to $595,000. By the end of the week, he felt like he'd lost all hope. Ana had been selling odds and ends around the house to raise as much as she could, but nothing would get him close to where he needed to be. Lying in bed with Ana, his mind flying, he blinked—darkness—and then Ana gently tickling his forehead.

The next morning, he turned to stare at his wife sleeping peacefully next to him and thought about how he'd used to wake up next to her in college. He remembered making their way to Texas in their old station wagon, then snuggling up in a sleeping bag that first night in their old apartment and falling asleep together. He wanted to take a picture of it—it would do his heart good.

Lazily drinking a cup of coffee, he checked his email and saw a note from Marlon.

Subject: Project Cheeta Server Cluster 1 Year Contract

Michael,

I can't get the price below $440,000 or reduce the term down from a year, but I was able to secure you some better payment terms: $360,000 upfront and $80,000 after 3 months. Let me know, buddy.

"Shit," Michael cursed under his breath. A creak behind him made him almost jump out of his skin.

"What?" Ana said.

Michael exhaled slowly. "You scared me, that's all."

"So, what are you going to do?"

"What do you mean?"

"About Marlon's offer. It's a start, isn't it?"

"It's hopeless."

"He came back to you—that means he wants to deal. At least see how far you can get him to come down," Ana said, and Michal smirked.

When his wife headed from the room, Michael drafted a response. He figured he'd offer half now and half in six months and see what happened. Then, after clicking send, he played a game of chess online.

It was an hour later when he burst into the kitchen and grabbed Ana by the shoulder, shouting, *"He took it!"*

Now it was Ana's turn to jump. "Jesus … he took what?"

"My offer! I offered him half upfront and half in six months, and he took it!"

"That's wonderful, but do we have that?" Ana said, looking slightly concerned.

"We're short five thousand, but if we can scrape that together, we'll have six months of access," Michael said, looking exhilarated as Ana sat down, hand on her stomach.

Michael's smile faded. "What is it? Is it the baby? Are you all right?"

She was breathing deeply, her eyes closed.

"It's just a lot; I mean, it's everything."

Michael's heart had slowed now, and he kneeled down next to his wife. "Look, I know I can do this—we still have the house and the food reserves. But I won't do this without you on my side. If you think the risk is too great, I'll stop."

She looked at him with sad, loving eyes, and put her hand on his cheek.

With Ana's approval, Michael signed a one-year contract for access to the server clusters he needed and transferred the entirety of their safety net. He had six months; now he needed to put his new servers to work.

Just like the old days, when Ana would watch TV after dinner and Michael would code all hours of the night, they fell back into a familiar routine. Michael allowed himself to be enveloped by his work, making less and less contact with Sebastian at the Williamson Foundation. Updating him did not seem essential.

Now that he had processing power he required, he just needed to learn how to wield its enormous power.

As he worked to retrofit his AI onto the scaffolding of the foundation's immense data sets, he began to see opportunities to connect AI-determined outcomes, and worked to develop an input/output system that would allow a scientist without an understanding of AI to make use of its power. As the days drifted by, he sat down for fewer and fewer meals with Ana, and ate in front of his computer more frequently. He'd heard Ana talking to him about selling some of their stuff, but he didn't notice as the house started to empty.

With Ana's due date rapidly approaching, he forced himself to pull away from his work and give her the attention she needed. He would hold her and put her to bed, stroking her brow as she lay in the Texas heat. Then, once she'd fallen asleep, he would sneak back to code until morning. He offered countless times to turn the air conditioning back on—he knew it was excruciating for her to be pregnant in Austin's intense summer heat—but she always declined, refusing to waste a cent when they were in such dire circumstances.

Early one morning, before the sun began to rise, Michael heard Ana moaning in their room, and he ran in to find her sitting up, eyes wide. "Michael," she said, voice breaking, "it's time."

Twenty-six hours later, they welcomed baby Vanessa into their lives, and for the first time in a long time, all was right with the world. After months of coding, the pleasant days spent in the hospital felt like a dream. Nurses doted on Ana and Vanessa around the clock, and the first time Michael held Vanessa he felt alive like never before. She cried but he soothed her—it came naturally, without thought, and before he knew it, she was asleep in his arms. She stayed there, dozing in and out of dreams, cradled against his chest.

When she awoke, Ana waved him over and took Vanessa

from his arms. Michael reeled, shocked by the sudden sense of absence—it felt like a piece had been taken out of him. She smelled like farts and dryer sheets, but he couldn't get enough. He picked up the yellow bowel movement journal and carefully noted each one that had taken place over the preceding hours.

Their third and last morning in the hospital came far too soon for Michael. They had spent days without saying words, not needing to, able to feel each other's wants and needs as if linked by an invisible connection. Michael woke early in the recliner next to Ana's bed and watched the center of his universe snuggle skin to skin with Ana, her tiny fists and eyes squeezed tight. As soon as they woke, they were released, and the three came home as a family.

Vanessa slept through most days in Ana's arms and Michael held her and hugged her as much as he could, but the magic of their first three days in the hospital was slowly fading. With Ana feeding Vanessa and sleeping with her around the clock, mother and daughter bonded so tightly that every day it became easier for Michael to code for hours on end. Before Michael knew what had happened, Vanessa could push herself up during tummy time. The days were getting shorter and colder.

His work continued to progress, propelling him to spend more and more of his waking hours in front of his computer. Ana again began delivering him his meals in his office, but baby Vanessa's crying often tugged at his attention, and slowly he began closing his door more often to allow his mind to focus on his work. He didn't notice at first when his meals consisted solely of rice and butter; but when the bowls at his door were rice alone, with not much in the bowl, he realized he needed to speak with Ana. But he didn't—if he asked, she would tell him, and then he would know, and he did not want to know. He tried to put it out of his mind, but it kept rushing back in.

She'd begun using the rice in the blue bags. How long had she been serving him rice? Vanessa still looked healthy, and Ana's breasts felt firm and full. Blue bags meant his time would run out soon. He had to make a breakthrough or stop, regroup, and find a way to provide for his family again—but he was so close.

Michael closed the door to the crying and pounded his fingers into his keyboard, trying not to think of the blue bags. Drifting in and out, he vaguely remembered Ana checking in on him and bringing Vanessa in to lie on the floor behind him. But he focused on his work: he was making progress, but not enough. If only he could …

"Michael? Michael …"

Ana's voice pulling at the edge of his mind. *There's a loop here, why can't I see it? Maybe if I close and go back—*

"Michael!"

He looked over his shoulder, still typing.

"There's no way you're going to save the world without food or sleep."

His mouth slightly open, he turned back to his screen.

"Michael, are you listening to me?" Ana shouted into his back. "Look at me! Please, *Michael!*"

Michael could hear Ana's voice, but the words were strange, formless. He tried his best to respond. "Yeah, I hear you. What's up?"

"Stop typing and look at me!"

Michael pulled himself out of autopilot and looked at her.

"Come with me." Ana grabbed his arm and yanked his bag of skin and bones from the chair.

After forcing him to eat a larger-than-normal bowl of rice, she took him by the arm, put him in the shower, and handed him a razor and a toothbrush. After he was done, she dried him off like a baby after bath time and helped him into bed.

Nearly twenty hours later, Michael woke up, yawned, and headed into the bathroom.

In the mirror, a gaunt man with hollow cheeks and biceps

so thin he could put his fingers around them peered back at him from behind sunken eyes. He stared at himself for a long time, a dull horror settling in his gut.

"Ana," he called finally, his voice hollow, "are you okay? Where's Vanessa?"

To his relief, Ana did not look half as bad as he did. Vanessa smiled and giggled, without a care in the world, which immediately made Michael's chest feel lighter.

"Ana, how much is left? How many blue bags are left?"

"Two," said Ana.

Two bags. That was one hundred pounds. There were 1,655 calories in each pound of uncooked rice, which meant 165,500 calories in all. He thought they could get away with three thousand calories a day each for him and Ana, which meant he had a month left, give or take.

"Ana, I'm close. I'm so close."

"I know," Ana said with understanding, a look of melancholy on her face.

Modestly rejuvenated, Michael worked as fast as he could, taking shortcuts wherever possible, and started testing his AI overlay live. He had to take chances if he wanted to make it. As he sorted through the bugs in his code, he fell back into reclusion. Frustrated, he wasted hour after hour fixing mistakes he should never have made. Finally, he turned around to answer Ana.

"What?"

She did not respond, so he tore his eyes off his screen. It was darker than before. Ana was not in the room. He looked to his left and saw a glass of water with condensation on it and no ice. Next to that sat a warm bowl of rice. His mouth began to water, and he couldn't get it into his mouth fast enough.

"Motherfucker! Ana, what the hell? This shit is cold!" The bowl of rice in front of him was room temperature, so he looked back at his screen, found what he had been searching through his code for, and began playing his keys again.

After a while, he looked up again, stretched his neck, and saw another bowl of rice and a glass of water to his left. The glass had no ice and no condensation. He wasn't going to drink water without ice. He liked it cold—ice cold.

"Goddamn it, Ana! Ice! I need *ice* in my water!" he yelled from his chair. "And why in the hell did you give me another bowl of rice? You know that if I eat that much, we'll run out! What are you doing?"

Then he grabbed the bowl of rice and shoveled a forkful into his crusty mouth. The rice immediately came back out and into the bowl. It was cold, and now a mound lay coated in saliva.

"Ana, *what the fuck?!* If I have to eat rice every day for every meal, you had better heat it the fuck up!" he screamed over his shoulder. He peeled his eyes off of his code and quickly glanced around the room. It was pitch black, and he couldn't see anything. His eyes began to water.

He placed both hands on the table, pushing himself up, turned his torso to the right—and collapsed into a heap. His legs were completely numb. He lay there, his eyes watering, his neck and back burning, and massaged his legs until the blood returned.

"Ana, come help me up!" he screamed.

With his feet working again and the wobbly feeling subsiding, he gingerly got to his feet and grabbed the bowl of rice in one hand and the glass of water in the other. As he stumbled out, something smashed him in the face, and he stopped abruptly. The water and rice both covered his chest, and he stared at the dark wood inches from his face. He had run straight into the closed door.

Wasted food. Goddamn it, what was Ana doing closing this door? He fumbled to open it. After searching the kitchen, family room, and dining room, he made his way to the master bedroom.

"Ana, I need *ice* in my water! Ana, *ice!*"

"*¿Que, mi alma?*" Ana said, rolling over in bed.

"Ana, you served me too much rice! I need to maximize my time, not shorten it, damn it!"

"What's going on? Is something wrong?" Ana said, finally opening her eyes and sitting up.

"Ana, I want ice in my water, and I want my rice hot. Why are you serving me cold rice? What the hell is going on?"

Ana just stared at him.

"And why did you serve me dinner twice? Are you trying to kill me? I mean, what the fuck, Ana!"

Ana got up, walked around the bed, and held Michael. Then she sat down on the side of the bed with him. "Michael, I didn't serve you dinner twice."

Michael frowned, trying to focus on her face, his vision swimming. "You didn't? Then how did I get served twice? You didn't give me yours, did you? Ana, don't do that—"

She put her finger to his lips.

"After I put Vanessa down, I brought you your dinner in your office. One hot bowl of rice and one tall glass of water filled with ice, just as you like it. I put it right down next to you and ate mine right there, but you were so engrossed, and you kept saying just another second, so I decided to let you work. Then I came up and went to bed."

Ana looked over at Michael, who had fallen asleep as soon as they'd settled on the bed. She got up, picked his feet up, and placed them on the bed, shifting him so she could get back under the covers on her side, and then she drifted into a fitful, worried sleep.

* * *

The next morning, Michael woke to an empty bed. All he could remember about the night before was that Ana had been over-serving him and that he needed to finish his debugging. From now on, he'd stop himself from finishing the servings she gave him. After all, she wouldn't let it go to waste, and he was certain he could survive on less than she gave him. Then, as he fell deeper into his work, becoming more obsessed, he moved from three meals a day to two, then just one, and did not allow himself to accept any other offerings from Ana. He'd ration for himself if she would not do it for him.

Ana, more fussy than usual, began bringing Vanessa into his office more frequently, and he was forced to explain to her that seeing his child only prolonged his work as it broke his concentration. He was, he explained, so close. So very close. Each time she interrupted him with Vanessa, it took him more than an hour to get back into the right frame of mind to work, and then she'd interrupt him again under the guise of checking up on him.

Then, on Tuesday, he locked his door. It was his most productive day of work in months. He finally had the long, uninterrupted period he'd needed, free from food, from Ana, from Vanessa, from sleep, from anything that might slow his progress.

To: Carrie Roberts
BCC: Sebastian Dougherty; Melanie Delaney
From: Michael Lori
Date: Sunday 4:08 a.m.

Subject: AI Overlay Framework

Ran out of processing power, but this AI overlay should be self-explanatory. Please run as soon as possible, Carrie. I think I found it.

https://www.dropbox.com/mlori/dJ78Kli89ReTT509

Thanks,
Michael

CHAPTER 34

DECEMBER IN SAN FRANCISCO

Carrie bundled up as she headed out the door and into the blustery Mission District. The Muni, San Francisco's bus and metro system, had a line that ran from the front of her building to the Starbucks across the street from the Williamson Foundation's headquarters.

Though the locals enjoyed complaining about December's cold, Carrie didn't mind it as long as it didn't rain too much. December in San Francisco reminded her of fall in DC, her favorite time of year. The crisp, cool air made her feel alive; it felt healthy, natural somehow. She didn't miss the snowstorms, and happily put up with the extra rain to avoid them.

When her stop came, she got off the bus, but instead of heading right into the office, she decided on a detour. A toasted white chocolate mocha was calling her name, and after she'd been healthy all weekend, it only seemed fair that she treat herself. Besides, what better way to start off the week than with something to warm her bones on this lovely winter day?

With drink in hand, she walked through the door of the foundation building. Smiling, the receptionist greeted her and then shyly touched her lip with a giggle. Carrie wiped a touch of whipped cream off her lip and nodded her thanks as she scanned her ID card and headed up toward her office. She set down her purse, put her cellphone face-up on her desk, and then flipped open her laptop. As she savored the warmth of her mocha, she scanned through the hundred or so emails she'd

286

received over the weekend. One caught her attention, but before she could open it, Melanie was standing at her office door.

"Hey, Carrie. Have a good weekend?"

"I did, it was relaxing. How was yours?"

"Ah, same old, same old. Looking forward to the holidays?"

"I'm heading back to DC, so yes, I am."

"Well, I'm working out the office Secret Santa this year, so pick one." Melanie held out a bowl filled with folded-up slips of paper.

"Ah, I don't have time for this. Have the receptionist take mine."

"Carrie, you're not getting out of this. How would you feel if your Secret Santa didn't get you a present?"

"I'd feel like they were being efficient with their time," Carrie said, taking another sip of her mocha.

Melanie scowled.

"All right," Carrie said, rolling her eyes, "give me the bowl. I'll take one, but they're getting a Starbucks gift card no matter who they are." She unfolded the slip of paper and read the name: *Elizabeth Williamson.*

"Nope. Give me another one. No way …"

Melanie headed for the door. "Sorry, no double pulls. You got who you got."

Damn it, Carrie thought. *What can I possibly get a president that she doesn't already have?* With a sigh, she turned back to her computer.

The email she had been patiently waiting for from a Harvard Medical School scholar didn't contain the news she'd hoped for. Their findings from their study on genomic sequencing would not be released in this month's journal. *Oh, well. It's only another month. That will give me something to look forward to after the holidays.* The mocha had done its job, keeping her optimistic even after the unlucky Secret Santa name pull.

Moments later, Carrie was standing in the doorway to Sebastian's office.

"Hey, Sebastian. Have a good weekend?"

He turned, evidently surprised to see her, and smiled. "Yes, I'd say so. The Forty-Niners won, so I'm happy."

"Perfect. I don't know if you checked your email yet, but Harvard delayed releasing their findings another month."

"Well, that's too bad."

"So," Carrie said smoothly, "did you get a visit from Melanie yet?"

"I did, I did. Who'd you get?"

"I'm not sure how it's supposed to work, but I don't think we're supposed to tell each other. Any chance you want to trade?"

Sebastian studied her closely, but Carrie's poker face was the best around. "Hmm, that's an interesting offer. Sounds exciting. Let's do it."

"All right. Swap at the same time, okay?" Carrie held out her hands, one with the folded slip of paper in it and the other with the empty palm face up.

"Deal," Sebastian said as he dropped his folded-up slip into her palm and deftly nabbed hers.

Carrie unfolded the tiny paper ball Sebastian had dropped in her palm, but by the time she'd straightened it out enough to read and process the name—Courtney Frame, their ditsy receptionist—Sebastian had already swiped it back and deposited the slip with Elizabeth's name back in her hand.

Before she knew what was happening, he was ushering her out of his office. As he closed the door, he said, "Oh, no, you don't."

God damn it. After trying similar tricks on several of her lab techs and coworkers over the course of the morning, Carrie finally resigned herself to finding a present for the former most powerful person in the world.

On her commute home, Carrie got off close to the Neiman Marcus in hopes of findings some inspiration for her impossible

Secret Santa gift. Elizabeth didn't get to walk around in public often, so maybe something new this season would be appropriate, something she would not have seen online.

After an hour of wandering, Carrie decided to give up; it wasn't going to be that easy, apparently. The next few days followed the same trajectory as she scoured high-end department and specialty stores on her way home each night.

On Thursday morning, Carrie woke up with the perfect idea, but she would have to wait until after work to look for it in Chinatown. When she arrived at the office, she procrastinated, starting her day by dropping in on Sebastian on her way to her lab.

"So, did you get a gift for Tammy yet?" she asked.

Sebastian looked puzzled.

"Secret Santa, remember?"

"Oh, yeah. Nah, didn't try and tackle that yet. Why, you got any ideas?"

"I was having a hell of a time with *el Presidente*, but I know what I'm getting now. I just need to find it," Carrie said with a smug smile.

"Nice," Sebastian said, scanning something on his laptop, distracted. "What did you come up with?"

"You'll just have to wait and see." Switching gears, Carrie said, "If you haven't noticed, Tammy does talk about aromatherapy all the time, so that's a clue."

"Ah, thanks for that!" Sebastian replied, finally looking up at her. "Hey, whatever came of that email from that guy Michael?"

"What email? Michael who?"

"Michael Lori, the AI guy. Remember him?"

"Oh, yeah, I remember him. He wanted to take over my research. How could I forget," Carrie said dryly.

"Well, he emailed you last weekend."

"I don't recall any email from him. Maybe he never sent it."

"I know he sent it because he bcc'd me. He sent it last Sunday.

It was short and had a Dropbox link. I believe he said he'd 'found it,' whatever 'it' is. So, I was interested. I'll resend it to you, and maybe you can have a look at it today—pretty please with a cherry on top." Sebastian winked at her.

"I'll give it a look, but I'm not making any promises as to when. All right," she said, her mood soured, "I'm going to get a coffee and get to work."

* * *

Melanie was sitting at her desk, comfortably sipping a cup of tea and staring at her computer screen, when Sebastian sauntered in, smiling down at her.

She looked up. "Morning, Sebastian."

"Morning, Melanie. You remember Michael Lori?"

"The AI guy. What's up? Did he find something?"

"That's the thing. I haven't spoken to him for months, and then, out of the blue, he emailed Carrie, of all people, this past weekend with a Dropbox link and a cryptic message. Only reason I know about it is because he bcc'd me. I mentioned it to Carrie, and she acted like it had never happened."

"It's funny you mention it, because he bcc'd me too. Sent it last Sunday, early in the morning. I remember because I saw it come through."

Sebastian looked disturbed. "You saw it come through? Melanie, you've got to get a life. There's no reason to be checking your work email that early in the morning on a weekend."

"Putting aside your disgust for the way I decide to spend my weekends, it must have been something for him to bcc both of us. Did Carrie download the link?"

"I tried to coax her into taking it more seriously, but I don't think I got the message across. Think you can give it a try? Just wait a little bit. I don't want it to seem like we're ganging up on her. She'll just get defensive."

Melanie nodded. "Okay, I'll check in with her before I go to lunch."

"Thanks, Mel. Right, back to work for me. See you at lunch." And with that, Sebastian turned and hurried out.

Melanie dove back into her emails and, by the time she looked up again, it was close to eleven: time for her first meeting of the day. She got up and headed down the hall to the bathroom and, on the way back, poked her head into Carrie's office.

"Hey, Carrie, how's your day going?"

"I can't complain. Busy but productive. New staff are always a challenge, but I think we got a good one."

"Yeah, I know what you mean. Hey, Sebastian and I were just chatting"—as the words left Melanie's mouth, she watched Carrie's smile evaporate—"and he mentioned …"

As if watching a time-lapse video, Melanie could see the fortress walls climbing ever higher around Carrie, and her advance slowed. "Well, he mentioned an email from this weekend."

"Yes, by all means, continue," Carrie said. In mere moments, battle lines had been drawn, walls erected, troops placed at the ready, and the drawbridge slowly lowered, inviting Melanie into an ambush.

"As I was saying, Sebastian said he—I mean you—received an email from …"

Carrie stared through her, eyes black and unflinching.

Melanie swallowed the lump in her throat. "That AI guy. You know the one?"

"I get a lot of email, Melanie, most of it spam. Sebastian asked me to look through my junk box." Before Melanie could put in a word, Carrie shot her a penetrating look. She closed her mouth.

"Now," Carrie said brusquely, "if that is all you came to say, I have important work to do. Please close the door behind you." She took a seat at her desk and turned her attention to her computer.

Melanie knew better than to argue; after years of working

with Carrie, she knew how to handle her. Direct conflict never ended well, so she decided to retreat and regroup with Sebastian. *So much for easy*, she thought.

At around two that afternoon, she knocked on Sebastian's open office door.

"I heard it didn't go well," he said, glancing up at her.

"You got that right. I guess that's why you asked me to do it."

"I hoped you would have better luck, but apparently not."

Melanie paused, weighing up their options. "Why don't we—you know—just download the link and check it out ourselves?"

Sebastian nodded slowly. "I don't know. I don't want to get blamed for pulling down a virus or something that takes down our whole network."

"If that's our only concern, let's get IT to take a look at it before we pull—"

But Sebastian already had the phone to his ear. "Thanks," he said, "see you soon." He hung up and turned back to Melanie. "They're coming over now."

As soon as Melanie and Sebastian had been assured that the linked file didn't contain a trojan horse or a worm, they sent IT away and opened the Word file labeled *Program Documentation*. Approximately half of the seventy-eight-page document was dedicated to connecting the application to various data sources for inputs. The second half started with a section stating the premise of the program:

> *After all input sources and all processing resources have been connected, the configuration panel will direct the system. Once configuration has been completed, the user should select Analyze and Report. Duration will be directly impacted by processing resources: more resources equates to less time. After completion, a report will be logged in the log file.*

This application connects to input sources, which act as the AI engine's knowledge base, connecting DNA to specific attributes. The configuration tables allow the user to modify attribute likelihood by percentage. The Analyze and Report tool will use the AI to process the requested modification and provide a prediction on what DNA must be changed in order to achieve the desired outcome. AI learning reduces processing times by an enormous amount, but this is still an extremely resource-intense tool.

In the configuration tables, pay close attention to the settings for maximum- and minimum-allowed DNA markers. The window this tool analyzes directly corresponds to processing time.

Sebastian then opened a filed named *Carrie READ ME.*

I'm close. In order to process the Lifio mutation reversal, start with the configuration default that I've set and continue to fine-tune the calibration. Then, Analyze and Report and rerun after each tweak until you get it where you want it. As you can see, the attributes at 0% in configuration were clearly augmented by Dr. Jónsson. Each time the AI runs a report and analyzes it, it will add to the configuration tables as it develops new understandings and connections. The AI has not been automated to run continuously, so you will retain complete control and can adapt its learning. Due to my limited processing power, I had to run the analysis with very small DNA marker windows. With huge processing power, I am certain this engine will get you where you want to go faster than your test tubes. The answers are all in the data already. This will help you tease it out. Please call me as soon as you believe. I'm out of time, and my family needs your help.

"Shit," Melanie said when she got to the bottom of the page. "That was Sunday. Check the log files."

Sebastian did as he was told and saw that the last result set had reported thirty-two gene markers based on the latest configuration. It had taken nine hours to run.

"All right," said Melanie, "we have to get Carrie to look at these markers and the configuration settings to see if she can make sense of it. Meanwhile, I need you to get in contact with Mr. Lori immediately and make sure he and his family are okay. Then bring them back here. I'm going to let Elizabeth know what's going on."

She marched from the office with purpose, hoping they weren't too late. She found Elizabeth in her office, and immediately started talking. For a moment, it felt like the Oval Office all over again, with the fate of the world held in the balance.

"Elizabeth, Michael Lori, the AI specialist from Texas who asked for funding to apply his AI system to our research—well, he delivered something."

After getting Elizabeth up to speed, the two women strode toward Carrie's office.

They walked into her lab to find her dancing in place and singing under her breath as she methodically went about her work. With smirks on their faces, the pair waited for her to notice them.

It took Carrie only a few seconds to catch a glimpse of the two women behind her. She came to a sudden halt and, blushing, looked slowly up, cringing. She pulled out her earbuds and started apologizing, but Melanie and Elizabeth were already laughing. Despite herself, Carrie's face creased up, too.

"I must have looked ridiculous," she said through her hand as she doubled over.

"Whoo, I needed that," Melanie said, her hand on her chest.

"Okay, okay," Elizabeth said, smiling. "Carrie: Melanie and Sebastian pulled down the file from Michael."

Carrie's smile vanished, and she turned to glare at Melanie.

"And he discovered thirty-two markers on his AI's first analysis. We could have known about these months ago if you'd not so stubbornly refused to consider new technologies."

Carrie staggered beneath her employer's daggers before regaining her composure. "Possibly," she muttered, her eyes filled with rage.

"Wrong. You were wrong, Carrie," Elizabeth said, the stinging words hanging in the air until Carrie's defiant stare finally wilted.

She mumbled something that sounded like an apology.

Elizabeth gave a sideways smile. "You made a mistake, Carrie," she said, "but all that matters now is how you recover from it. Sebastian is going to bring Michael here. In the meantime, we need you to look at his work and make sense of his tool. Melanie here will get you started."

Carrie wordlessly did as she was told, looking to Melanie for direction.

Melanie pulled the files down on Carrie's computer and went over everything she knew. Carrie kept sulking until she opened the log file. Then her demeanor changed dramatically.

Melanie glanced at her. "What are you thinking?"

"I can't believe he found these markers; it's taken us years to identify twenty-four gene markers in the Lifio mutation, and all of them are listed in this log file."

"Well, what about the other ones? He found thirty-two, didn't he?"

"I-I-I just don't know. I have to look at research on those," Carrie said. After a long pause, she said, "I have to see him. Michael. I must see how he did this. I can't believe it."

"They're getting him, and you can apologize later. Before all of that, you have to look at the configuration screen and get another analysis running. He said in his letter that each time it runs, the AI learns more, adding to accuracy and configurability."

Melanie directed the cursor to the configuration menu. Carrie began scrolling through settings, murmuring to herself—and suddenly grabbed Melanie's arm.

"Get IT now."

As Melanie ran off, Carrie texted her entire research team, something she never did: *Come to the lab immediately.*

CHAPTER 35
DEAR MICHAEL

Sebastian sat in the airport terminal, waiting for his flight to Houston. After emailing Michael, Sebastian had decided to call him, but the number had been disconnected. Knowing full well that Melanie would not be happy if he stood around waiting for an email from a man with a disconnected phone, Sebastian had booked the next flight available to anywhere close to Austin. It left in just a few hours and, from Houston, he could drive a rental car over to Austin and find Michael. At least he had his address, which he'd pulled from the foundation's food bank registry.

Carrie, meanwhile, felt like she'd won the lottery. Her team, which had by now completely assembled, crouched over the configuration table in the lab, putting the finishing touches on the changes to variables. The time to press the *Analyze and Report* button for the first time had arrived, and Carrie eagerly clicked it.

Michael, during his initial run, had only used one input: the Williamson Foundation's official human genome database. He had not known that countless foundations and governments around the world had devoted themselves to the same pursuit and had their own sets of raw data. Unsurprisingly, the foundation had access to far more data than Michael could have ever dreamed of, and Carrie delighted in having her team plug in all of the additional data sets.

The processing prediction tool built into the software let them know it would take roughly seventy years for the calculations to complete if executed on Carrie's laptop. That changed after Elizabeth made a phone call to a cloud computing behemoth; within the hour, the foundation had access to far more processing power than Michael had requested during his visit months before. The presidential treatment meant that access to the immense cloud computing repository was free, but only temporarily. If they needed access to continue in perpetuity, the foundation would need to pay. Still, it amazed Carrie how much Elizabeth could accomplish with a mere phone call.

With additional raw data sets, vastly increased processing muscle, and dialed-in configuration settings, Carrie stared eagerly at the screen. The new estimated time before the report would be complete was eight hours and fifty-five minutes. Carrie told everyone to go home and get a good night's sleep, but it came as no surprise when no one left.

* * *

By the time Sebastian got into Houston and found his rental car, the clock display read 11:15 p.m. With a three-hour drive still in front of him, he settled on stopping at a hotel halfway there to catch some shut-eye. Showing up at two in the morning would be inappropriate; besides, a good night's sleep and a shower would help him look more presentable when he did finally see Michael, his tail firmly between his legs. The comment about running out of time had spooked him, but he didn't know how he could avoid waiting for the morning.

Unfortunately, he did not sleep well and, the next morning, he needed two cups of coffee just to get out of the hotel lobby. At 8 a.m., he reached the Loris' neighborhood. Driving slowly in order to read the mailbox numbers, he noticed an inordinate number of the vast, alabaster homes had overgrown lawns. Some even looked abandoned, which struck Sebastian as odd—odd, and more than a little worrying.

After driving past three dark and dilapidated houses in a row, he found the Loris' home. He pulled into the driveway, watching for signs of life—lights, movement behind the curtains—but saw nothing. After gathering himself for a moment in the car, he got out into the knee-high grass of the front yard. Unsure whether he was at the right address, he leaned against his car and looked through the notes on his phone to confirm. He walked to the end of the driveway and checked the mailbox and street sign, confirming that he had indeed come to the location on file.

Still spooked by the condition of the homes in the neighborhood, he walked up to the garage at the top of the driveway and, on the balls of his feet, peeked through the window. The barren garage did not bode well, and Sebastian felt sure that, somehow, this was not the right address. Still, he had traveled this far—he couldn't leave without knocking, could he? Gathering up his courage, he ambled up to the enormous front door and rapped hard; the doorbell did not seem to work.

Minutes passed—nothing. His fist throbbing, Sebastian decided to change tactics and tap on the windows surrounding the front door. After a few raps, he heard the wailing of a child, and his heart sank as he imagined Michael and his wife trying to put their newborn down for a nap just as a stranger started beating at the door.

Despite the crying baby, no one came to the door, putting him in the awkward position of not knowing what he should do next. He finally settled on checking the first-floor windows to see if he could peer through the blinds.

He made his way around the house, but the blinds were drawn tightly over every window. Then, as he rounded the third corner and walked back to the driveway, he noticed a side door to the garage was wide open.

He tentatively called out, "Anyone home?" before entering. Then, as the child's screams sounded closer and closer, he opened the door between the garage and the main home. After passing through a mudroom, still calling out but receiving no reply, he arrived at an opening between the kitchen and hall.

He froze as an intermittent buzzing hit his ears, on and off, on and off, followed by vibrations in his hand. Looking down, he saw the name *Melanie* across the front of his cell. He let it ring.

* * *

A festive mood had swept through the Williamson Foundation building after the first analysis report log came through. Michael's program had found two additional markers and, more importantly, it predicted a 98.7 percent accuracy rate, up from 78.9 percent following the changes Carrie and her team had made to Michael's configuration file.

"Michael may be a computer genius, but his scientific knowledge leaves a lot to be desired," Carrie said to Elizabeth, giving her an evil grin.

"Where is our hero, anyway?" Elizabeth asked Melanie. "Has Sebastian found him yet?"

"I spoke with him on his way over to Michael's house," Melanie replied. "But he didn't answer my last call; more than likely they're talking now."

"You do realize you'll need to apologize when he gets here, Carrie," said Elizabeth. "I mean, if the two of you are going to be working together."

"I'm liable to hug him if he doesn't watch out," said Carrie, beaming. "Let bygones be bygones. I'm big enough to admit when I'm wrong. I just can't wait to pick his brain and see how far we can take this."

Elizabeth and Melanie exchanged expressions of exaggerated shock.

Carrie's team was poring over new variables and setting them carefully in preparation for another run of the analysis tool, which, to their great satisfaction, would conclude in just seven hours and fifty-three minutes. The reduction in processing time, coupled with several new configuration variables, meant that the platform had indeed learned from its last analysis.

"Still not picking up," Melanie said, hanging up.

"Ah, it's early still," Carrie said with a grin. "I'm sure he has a lot to talk to Michael about. Give him some time. I'm sure he'll call once he's got him."

Melanie nodded, frowning. "Yeah."

Carrie was oblivious to her doubt: "You know, after a few weeks of analyses, we should have a completely viable Lifio mutation reversal therapy. However, once we stop the continuous cell division, propagation throughout an organism's body will be more of a challenge."

"Do you have a solution?" asked Melanie.

"I do, but it, um … how shall I put this? It will have its detractors."

"Go on," said Elizabeth.

Carrie smiled mischievously. "Well, we could use a CRISPR gene drive to replace the DNA sequence on one chromosome with a drive and altered allele."

"Layman's terms, please," said Melanie.

"We use CRISPR to cut out a DNA sequence, and we replace it with the DNA we want plus CRISPR, allowing it to cut and paste itself throughout the organism. That's why they call it 'gene drive.' It has detractors because it will be a self-propagating mechanism, allowing the genetic variation we develop to spread through the population through breeding. Basically, we can eradicate the Lifio mutation, if we so choose."

Melanie and Elizabeth raised their eyebrows.

"Interesting, indeed," said Elizabeth. "Hypothetically, we could do this with any gene sequence, correct? Meaning, we could work to rein in some of the suboptimal results of the Lifio mutation and perhaps enhance the more beneficial effects?"

"That's a slippery slope," said Melanie.

"Indeed it is, but I don't know how well America would respond if we took away the Lifio mutation and put everything back the way it was. If, however, we could somehow show we are taking a step *forward* and not backward, we could save the world *and* improve it at the same time." Elizabeth was grinning now, not looking at either Melanie or Carrie, lost in her own fantasy. "With Michael's AI tool, we now have the predictability that's always been missing from serious gene editing projects. Obviously, we'd need to test the concept, but if I understand correctly, AI can tell us what the effects of changes will be, thereby making it far more feasible to improve the human condition rather than just stabbing in the dark."

Melanie shot Elizabeth a concerned look. "I don't think that aligns with our stated mission."

"Oh, Mel, don't look at me like that. I, of all people, understand we need to be exceedingly careful. Our number-one priority remains reversing the Lifio gene mutation. I'm simply stating that if we are able to partially reverse it instead of completely eradicate it, we may be able to maintain some of the progress we've made and not return to square one. I, for one, like the way I feel and don't relish the idea of bringing back cancer, obesity, and traditional aging."

"Traditional aging? That's a new one," Melanie said incredulously. "Carrie, are you going to say anything here?"

Carrie gave a shy smile. "Ah, I abstain."

"For once you've nothing to say. Thanks," Melanie said, rolling her eyes as her phone began to ring. She looked down. It was Sebastian.

* * *

Sebastian stared through the barren room into what must have been the family room, trying to understand what he was seeing. With all of the blinds closed and the power seemingly shut off, he was having trouble interpreting what exactly the mound of blankets in the center of the floor was. A curdling cry broke the silence again, and he could see a lump in the middle of the pile writhing around.

When it stopped, he edged closer, and his eyes started to water as the stench of decay filled his nostrils. He staggered back, clutching his mouth, and the writhing and screaming began again.

Pushing past the nauseating smell, which he now realized was feces and urine, Sebastian crept over to the far reaches of the pile and clutched a sodden corner. He pulled back the blanket, and the wailing came loud and sudden. He yanked the cover free, a putrid perfume of odors hitting him like a freight train, assaulting his senses overloading his system. He spun around, his shoulders tight, and doubled over, dry heaving until his breakfast came pouring out of his mouth to splatter all over the wooden floor.

He wiped his face with the back of his hand, still heaving, and tried to ease the enraged baby from his mother's stiff grasp—but, with a sigh like wind through dead leaves, the woman pulled the child back into her cloying embrace. Then, without registering Sebastian's presence, the woman sat up, climbed to her feet, and walked over to the staircase. She lifted a deflated breast from under her shirt and offered it to the angry child. The baby desperately bit and tore at her swollen nipple, but it failed to produce a single drop of milk.

Able to take no more, Sebastian retreated into the garage. Trembling, he immediately called 911.

After ten excruciating minutes, he heard the EMT at the front door and went back through the house to let them in. Child services followed the EMTs, and the home quickly filled with emergency service staff. Once the blinds had been opened and the woman and her child ushered into the kitchen by soft-voiced paramedics, Sebastian finally allowed himself to process what he had seen.

The man he had once known as Michael Lori lay atop a pile of blankets in the corner. Shirtless, Michael's collarbone and ribs protruded, and his skin had flaked off near his joints. His arms looked like long bones with slack skin draped over them. From head to foot, he looked almost ten feet tall, with large hands and feet devoid of any muscle. His head, full of thin hair, looked out of proportion, and his eyes were sunken in his skull, the lids stretched over.

Sebastian wondered how long Michael's wife—Ana, was it?—had lain by Michael's side with their child. Had she been lying there when he'd passed or had she laid his body down there to get close to him after he'd gone? When had he died? Sebastian had so many questions and no one to answer them.

When a police officer finally took him aside for questioning, he blurted out the question he wasn't sure he wanted an answer to: "How long ago did he die, do you think?" He tried to keep his voice as flat and calm as possible.

"Oh, not too long ago," replied the officer. "He's not bloated yet, so it had to be within the last forty-eight hours. Poor fella must have saved all his food for his girls. Starvation's a nasty way to go, but when they get this big, you know, they need a lot of calories else something like this happens. How did you know the family?"

Sebastian couldn't stop replaying the past two days in his mind, wondering what he'd been doing when Michael took his last breath.

After the officer thanked him and sent him on his way, Sebastian walked out to his rental car and called Melanie.

"Put Elizabeth on the phone, please. We have a problem in Texas."

ACKNOWLEDGEMENTS

Many thanks to my editors Fred Johnson and Jefferson for working through countless drafts and to my family Samantha, Sandra, Keira, Gwen, and Sadie Pulli who supported me through this endeavor.

ABOUT THE AUTHOR

Jonathan Pulli is a successful entrepreneur currently serving as the Chief Executive Officer of Turn 14 Distribution, which he co-founded in 2007. Jon has built a career promoting sustainability, work-life balance, communication, and symbiotic partnerships and has been recognized with several industry awards. Outside the office, Jon is an avid cook, fisherman, traveler, and father to three daughters.